SEVEN SEALS

SECOND EDITION

DARK SAVIOR SERIES
BOOK 2

JIM CLOUGHERTY

Published by Jim Clougherty

Copyright © 2020-2024 Jim Clougherty

Book cover, spine, and back copyright © Jim Clougherty 2024

All rights reserved.

2nd Edition

For more information and updates on the Dark Savior Series, visit https://www.jimclougherty.com/

Amazon Author Page: https://www.amazon.com/Jim-Clougherty/e/B07TXCK9XZ/

Book cover, spine, and back by Jeff Brown

Maps by Adriano Bezerra

Illustrations by Jonathan Leyton Vera

Copy and line edit by Carol Tietsworth

Book formatting by Lisa Hannan Fox

No part of this publication may be reproduced, distributed or transmitted in any form or by any means, including photocopying, recording, or other electronic or mechanical methods, without the prior written permission of the publisher, except in the case of brief quotations embodied in critical reviews and certain other noncommercial uses permitted by copyright law.

Note: This is fiction. Names, characters, places, and incidents are strictly from the author's imagination. Any resemblance to actual people, names, or places is coincidental.

NOTE TO READER

If you enjoy *Seven Seals*, join the newsletter and receive free side stories set in the Dark Savior Series world! You'll get all side stories released up to this point, including *Slaying the Beast, Ground Into Dust,* and *The Seer's Game*. As more are released, you will receive those for free as well!

https://www.jimclougherty.com/subscribe-fantasy

CAERULE

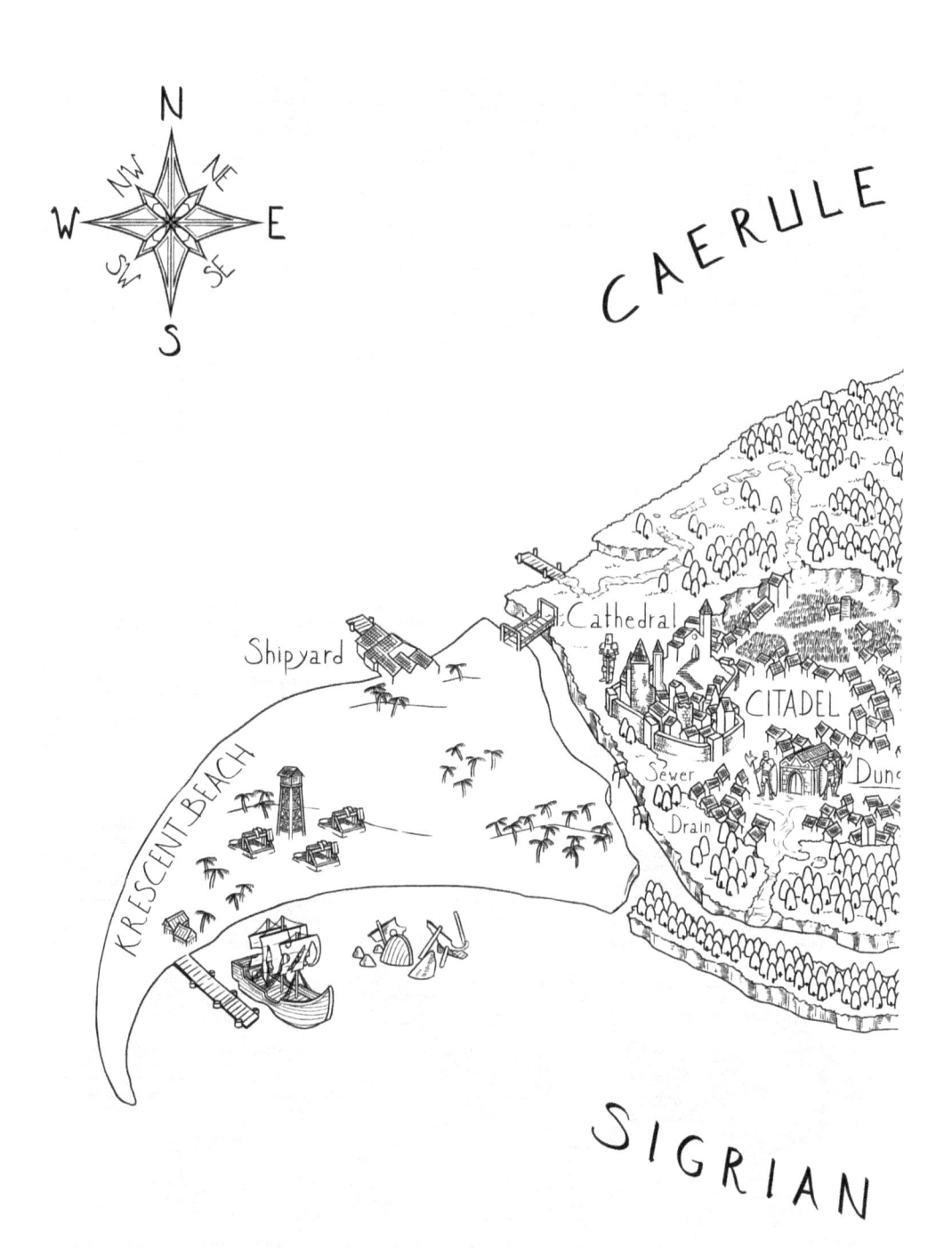

BOSFUERAS

SIGRIAN

- Shipyard
- Krescent Beach
- Cathedral
- Citadel
- Sewer Drain
- Dun(geon)

OCEAN

SWIFT RIVER

CHANNEL

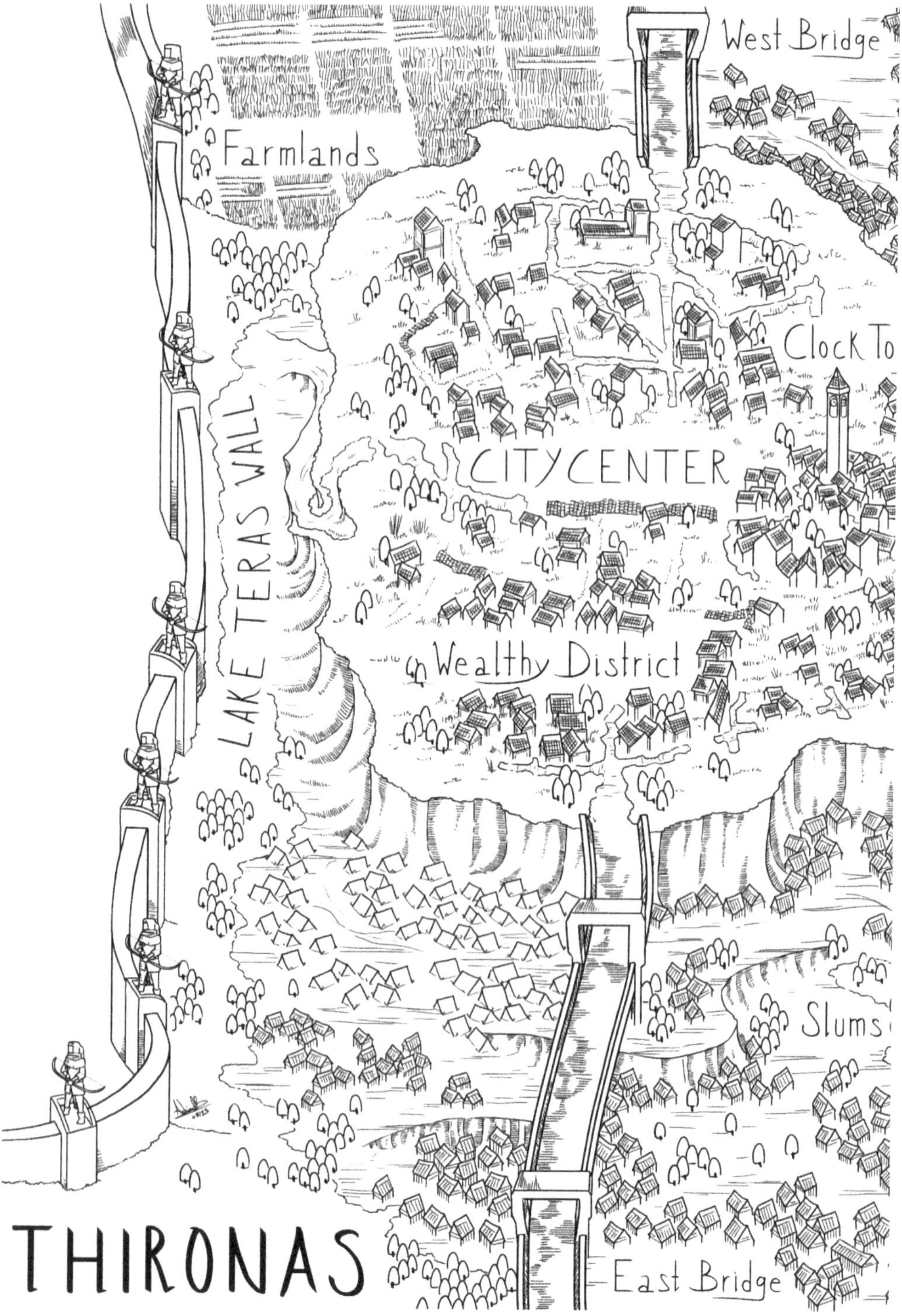
West Bridge
Farmlands
Clock To
CITYCENTER
LAKE TERAS WALL
Wealthy District
Slums
East Bridge

THIRONAS

wer

SYNOPSIS

This is the second story of the Dark Savior Series.

In the first story, *Gold Fever*, the mining village of Faiwell had come up short on previous expeditions, causing a precious metal shortage. Without materials to trade, a famine loomed, and so they looked to a long-abandoned site, Mt. Couture, hoping to turn their fortunes around. Knowing that the mountain was one of the most dangerous places in the world, Aldous the Wizard and his mute cohort Joel set out to prevent catastrophe by joining up with the two mining teams on their respective expeditions.

Joel found himself on the second team, where he met some new friends: Alistair, the loudmouth with a soft heart; Conrad, a cunning, curious man who'd only ever known a financial setting prior; Lucia, a mercenary with a chip on her shoulder of similar size to her unwieldy claymore; and Henic, the formerly estranged neighbor of Joel. On the journey to the mountain, Joel met some new enemies, as well: Edith, the beautiful, scheming daughter of the Mining Guild president; Wolfgang, the brute with a short temper and penchant for violence; Angus, the powerful yet even-tempered giant of a man; and Bronrar, the nervous friend of Angus who wanted nothing more than to live a worry-free life.

Upon entering the mines of Mt. Couture, the second team encountered a beautiful, sparkling ore called black gold, which Joel warned would poison their minds. However, he refused to elaborate fully on its dangers, and so his pleas eventually fell on deaf ears. The miners became enamored with the precious metal and even began to turn on Joel until the attacks began: First, a beast with an otherworldly howl called the Nightcrawler chased them out of the tunnels at night, and then, the mischievous little devils known as knockers killed several men and stole their treasures.

Faramond, leader of the second team, decided to split up, with one group led by him that would search for the missing first team of miners. The other group, led by Conrad, was to guard the stash of black gold at the base camp outside of the mountain. Conrad and Henic had their hands full with Brice and the hooligans, five vitriolic men with a distaste for authority; and upon some strange happenings with the weather, worries grew that there was a Dark Wizard in disguise amongst the group. Meanwhile, Joel, Alistair, and Lucia faced the wrath of Wolfgang and Angus until their group was attacked by the vicious dratagons. Many miners died in the attack, but only Joel and the others realized that the two ruffians had killed more than the creatures.

On the perilous journey to find the first team of miners, many more of Joel's group perished at the hands of the deadly riggits, the invincible Nightcrawler, and a crazed Wolfgang, who succumbed to what became known as 'Gold Fever'. He killed Faramond as he made love to Edith: a part of her and Angus' devilish plans to take control of the group and get them all addicted to the black gold. Joel's friends came to understand the dangers of the beautiful ore, and Bronrar allied himself with them upon realizing that his best friend Angus had become a murderer.

After many trials and brushes with death, Joel and his group finally found the first mining team, led by renowned warrior Dalton, on the other side of the mountain. With the two groups' combined efforts, they pushed through the deadly sand pit, but Edith's treachery continued, and she turned the Gold Fever-infected miners against their leader. Ultimately, Joel, Dalton, Alistair, and Lucia left the group.

Conrad and Henic ran into the tunnels to help a miner who was being attacked by the knockers, but they came to find that it was Wolfgang. He mortally wounded Henic with his pickaxe, and in the resulting chaos, there was a tunnel collapse that separated Conrad from his team and the black gold he was supposed to be guarding. However, in a fateful meeting, Aldous the Wizard appeared in the wreckage and temporarily kept Henic alive with a potion. The trio made their way up to the higher points of Mt. Couture, where the Wizard attempted to escape by building an icy path down the mountainside. However, a storm conjured up by the mighty Mountain King halted their progression, and they found themselves stranded.

Joel's group eventually met up with Aldous and the others, and the Wizard revealed that Mt. Couture was home to a sealed-away spawn of the *Dark Savior*, named Greed. The monster had created black gold to lure unsuspecting people into freeing him from his prison. Aldous and Joel had been protectors of the area for some time, but due to restrictions, were not supposed to help humans who dared enter the mines. The combined group sought out the Mountain King for help, but to their horror, the black gold had corrupted him, and a battle erupted between the Gold Fever-infected, the soul slaves of the Mountain King, and the miners of sound mind. Wolfgang went on to slay Henic, Bronrar, and several other miners in battle, but he was killed by Conrad after an intense duel.

In the chaos, Edith, who had been tasked by her corrupt father Drake and a mysterious Dark Wizard to unleash Greed, succeeded: The monster roamed free once again. However, she had been misled, and when she attempted to control the beast, he took over her body; a process that left her paralyzed. Joel was then left with a choice: to repair the seal that had locked away Greed or save his new friends, who had been captured by the monster. He ultimately chose his friends and lost the only key that could repair Greed's seal.

The group narrowly escaped from the clutches of Mt. Couture, but with that, many questions arose: What had happened to the black gold and the miners guarding it? Could the vile creature Greed be stopped without the ability to lock him away? What were the true plans of the Dark Wizard and Drake? And where had Angus and Edith disappeared to?

Devilry is afoot…

CHAPTER 1
THE IMPOSSIBLE DECISION

Thousands of years ago, a great war raged on. The combatants were the advanced luxians, flight-oriented avian, and sea-based marinian against the scrappy humans and battle-hungry melior. The long and bloody series of battle came to be known as *the Trial of Lux*: an attempted extermination of the luxian species. The mastermind behind the carnage was a shadowy, powerful being who had appeared out of nowhere, Stalmoz. He was also known as *the Dark Savior* to his followers. With the humans' great numbers and the mighty melior's battle prowess, the Dark Savior forced the luxians to retreat across the sea; to their last refuge in the west. Soon after, Stalmoz began an invasion, aiming to wipe out the last of their species. The luxians had been pushed into a corner and became desperate.

With the combined might of the Wizards and knowledge of the luxians, a destructive beam of light powered by the sacrifice of a million souls struck a critical blow to Stalmoz. He survived the blast, which wiped out his entire country, but the accompanying poison had done its damage, and he was weakened. It was then that the humans turned on their master. As a show of peace and an attempt to end the bloody war that had lasted 14 long years, the humans offered to turn over a battered Stalmoz to the luxians. Celebrations broke out on all sides, as they believed the war to be finished. As they were soon to discover, however, it was too early to celebrate…

THE IMPOSSIBLE DECISION

~

On a quiet afternoon, two luxian boys, Joel and Pierce, traveled to their hometown of Stellinam down a long dirt road surrounded by acres of farmland. Joel's light brown hair fluttered in the wind, and his boyish cheeks were rosy from the air smacking against them. He was short compared to most human men, but average by luxian standards.

Joel had gone through vigorous training since age 10 to be a warrior for the luxian army. By age 14, he and Pierce had reached the top of their class, and rumors floated around that they would soon join up with the luxian forces despite an age requirement of 16. A top general had taken interest in them for their great potential.

Pierce was Joel's adoptive brother and best friend. Since Joel's parents had died in the war, Pierce's family had taken care of him like one of their own. One day, Pierce received word that his father had returned home from the war with many spoils. Both he and Joel had been granted permission to leave their training to visit and celebrate with their family for the day.

The two boys walked in through the archway of Stellinam with smiles on their faces. It was filled to the brim with white, two-story tall buildings that were beautifully crafted. Each home had many bright blue lines of light going in and out of them along the walls and ground. The path through town was crafted out of fine marble with small pebbles carved in for traction, and great fountains of water filled the empty streets.

Joel's eyes wandered over to Pierce. He was tall by luxian standards; about the average height of a human, and had black hair with bronzed skin from training outdoors all day, every day. He looked back with dark, striking eyes. There was something about his look that always had Joel on guard. Pierce had always been good to him, but his eyes reminded him of daggers.

"Odd that no one's outside, isn't it?" Pierce asked.

"I had the same thought," Joel said.

"Well, there doesn't need to be a big celebration for the war heroes. A quiet night with my parents would be better."

"I don't mind it. But it's uncommon for the town to be this quiet when the soldiers return home."

Pierce narrowed his eyes and smiled. "You were looking for an excuse to see *Riza*, weren't you?"

Joel shrugged. "I just want to work on my maps while I have some free time."

"What is the point of working on maps when so many already exist?" Pierce asked with a snort. "If I had someone like Riza looking at me like *that*, I'd ditch the maps and spend my free time with her."

"Maybe she's using me to get to you," Joel replied.

"Or maybe you should get your nose out of those maps and appreciate that someone actually *likes* you," Pierce said.

"She knows where I live," Joel said.

"Stubborn, as always…"

The boys made their way up a hill on a winding path with houses on each side of them. They both wore traditional luxian tunics, which were light blue and decorated with several engraved markings designed by their ancestors. They also sported impact-resistant pants and new brown boots. The getup was what officers in the army would wear when off-duty, and today they wore them with great pride. For it was meant to signify that they would be taking positions with the army at an earlier-than-expected age. On the trip home, Pierce had talked up a storm about how excited he was to impress his father.

Pierce's father, Jed, was considered a war hero and beloved throughout Stellinam. His status showed in the size of his home and its desirable location: It was three stories tall unlike the others, and stood at the top of a hill overlooking the town.

When the boys arrived at the house, it seemed as quiet as the rest of town. As Joel entered, the wind howled, and his neck hairs stood on end. He could have sworn that under the veil of the wind, he had heard a scream from off in the distance. However, Pierce hadn't reacted to the noise, so he figured it was his imagination. Truthfully, he'd been on edge for the past six months. Their training at the academy had become more intense than ever, and such screams were not uncommon from other recruits. Sometimes, he had nightmares about the things they had trained them to do.

"Hello? Is anyone home?" Pierce asked aloud. There was no response. The pair searched around the first floor. Everything seemed to be in order. There was meat with a knife sticking out of it on the spotless countertop in the kitchen. It smelled fresh, but different than any aroma that Joel was used to.

"They left us dinner, at least," Joel quipped.

"But where are they? I wrote to them. They should have known we were coming…" Pierce trailed off before grimacing. "Unless that good-for-nothing avian failed to deliver the letter."

"Let's not jump to conclusions," Joel said, bobbing his hand. He knew his friend all too well: Sharp and cool at first, but easily riled up. "I'm sure they went out to get some food or drink. They already made dinner for us." He pointed to the cooked meat.

Pierce sighed. "I suppose you're right." He then looked down the hall, at the basement door. A smile crept onto his face. "What do you say we go downstairs and have a few practice matches?"

"I don't know…"

"What's wrong? Afraid your winning streak will come to an end?" Pierce asked with a smirk.

Joel sharpened his eyes. "You've been doing so well, lately. I wouldn't want to harm your confidence."

With a scoff, Pierce said, "You may have passed me on the academy's depth charts this past year, but don't forget who led the pack in years prior. Besides, I've learned a few new moves since our last duel."

"Well, now you've got me curious," he replied with raised eyebrows. "One match couldn't hurt, I suppose."

The pair walked down the hallway, but before they could reach the door, it opened in front of them. Before the boys stood a man with black hair and dark brown eyes. He looked similar to Pierce, but he seemed to lack those intense eyes that kept Joel on guard.

"Ah, you're finally home!" Jed said as he walked up and gave them both a hug.

The pair didn't respond and instead smiled back as if waiting for something. Jed stood back and looked them over. After a few moments, his eyes lit up and he gasped.

"Those tunics… they're letting you join the army? At such a young age?" Joel and Pierce looked at each other with proud smiles. "Wait until your mother hears about this. She'll be so happy!"

"Don't you mean she'll be worried?" Pierce asked with a raised eyebrow.

"Oh… err, right. I suppose you are a little young. But it matters little. Everything is about to change. The army will soon have different priorities," Jed said.

"A fine point. The war is coming to an end soon, isn't it?" Joel asked.

"I wouldn't say that," Jed replied, holding up a finger. "But I can at least say that history will smile upon us fondly."

Joel tilted his head. He had been told by nearly everyone at the academy that victory was at hand after the humans had captured the Dark Savior. They planned on turning him over in exchange for peace. Without him, the melior, their primary enemy, would surely be defeated or perhaps even surrender.

Jed cupped his hands and shouted, "Osanna! The boys are home!"

"I called out to both of you when we came in. How did you not hear us?" Pierce asked.

"Ah, I was busy storing my war spoils. Just wait until you see what I plundered! It'll take your attention entirely, just as it did mine," Jed replied with a sly smile.

Pierce's face lit up as his mother entered the kitchen behind them. She had the same black hair as the others, but it was long and straight. She was obviously where Pierce had inherited his dagger-like eyes from, although she too had always been good to Joel. He had no problem calling her 'mother'. She wore a long, green dress with an apron over it. Red meat stains covered the apron, and that same thick, mysterious scent came from her as he had smelled earlier. Joel wondered once again what that meat was. Perhaps something that Jed had brought home from the war?

"There you are, boys! It's good to have you home," she said in a pleasant tone. "Are you three hungry? I cooked a specialty meat to celebrate your return."

"Sounds good to me," Pierce said.

"What kind of meat is it?" Joel asked.

Pierce scoffed. "You *would* care."

"What? I'm only curious," Joel said with a shrug.

Osanna paused for a moment and then shot a warm smile Joel's way. "It's a surprise."

"Good enough for me! Let's eat," Pierce said, as he walked toward the kitchen. He was stopped by his father, who grabbed his shoulder.

"Hold on. Before we eat, there's something that I wanted to give you," Jed said.

"Sure, what is it?" Pierce asked.

"It's in the basement. Come with me. You're going to love it," he said, his voice cracking with excitement.

Joel started to follow the pair toward the entrance, but he was stopped by Osanna.

"Sorry Joel, dear. This is something special for Pierce."

Joel's heart sank. The Thaeon family had always gone out of their way to include him, but it made sense that their blood-related son would get the best treatment. Even still, it was another oddity. Had he really been gone so long that their attitudes toward him had changed?

"But don't worry, I got you a little something," Osanna said with a smile. Joel smiled back at her. She always knew how to raise his spirits when he was down. "How about you come in here and cut up the meat while I go upstairs and grab your gift?"

Joel nodded and walked into to the kitchen to cut up the meat as he was told. He decided to eat a small piece to see what it tasted like. As he chewed, he noted how different it was from anything he'd ever eaten before. The thickness and chewy quality reminded him of pig's meat, but the taste was different; sweeter.

～

MEANWHILE, Pierce followed his father down the stairs.

"By the way, did you receive the letter I sent? Or did that useless avian foul it up?" he asked.

Without turning back, Jed said, "Don't say such foolish things. It is not the avian who are useless. It is *we* who are useless... but it doesn't have to be that way."

"What is that supposed to mean?" Pierce asked as they reached the bottom of the stairs. The basement was a flat area that was normally empty, making it perfect for combat. Today, however, various chests and treasures lined the walls, enough for a king. Pierce's jaw hung open.

Jed smiled so hard that it made the corners of his eyes twitch. "I want to give you something. Something precious to me."

"If it's something from this collection, I'm sure it will be a kingly gift! What is it?"

"Let me show you…"

Jed walked to the corner of the room and knelt before one of the chests.

～

OSANNA RETURNED DOWNSTAIRS WITH ELEGANT, smooth strides as Joel finished slicing up the meat. He looked down and his cheeks reddened in guilt, but her pleasant demeanor didn't waver. She was holding a small wooden box.

"Did you sneak a piece of the meat, Joel?" she asked.

"Fine, I admit that I tried it, but only because I couldn't figure it out… what is it?" Joel replied.

"I told you it was a surprise, didn't I?"

"Can't you surprise me now?"

"Well, alright…" Osanna said as she passed him the wooden box. Joel opened it slowly to be greeted by beautiful sparkles. He gazed upon the marvel with distracted eyes, not fully recognizing what it was, yet. *"That meat was peeled from the skin of the non-believers who plagued this town."*

As the words bounced around like pins and needles in his brain, Joel finally comprehended the full contents of the box: A black ore that sparkled like only the night sky could. Goosebumps overcame his whole body.

"Mom, I-" Joel paused, his jaw now slack. What did she say? 'Non-believers'? 'Skin'? "Are you trying to tell me I've *eaten someone*?" He closed the wooden box and stared a hole through her.

Osanna smiled back at him as if everything were normal.

"Why yes, you have. But don't worry, Joel dear, they were non-believers. Nothing but sacks of meat. Not *pure*, like us," she said with narrowed eyes. Her smile no longer felt warm.

"And this! What is *this*?" Joel said with growing anger as he held the box out in front of her. "Why do you have black gold? It single-handedly started the civil war!"

"Don't be silly Joel, dear," Osanna said as she pushed the box slowly back toward him. "It's only a gift, and it's one you should be honored to have. You've been chosen. Chosen by our Dark Savior to rid the filth that plagues our society!"

"'Dark Savior'? Listen to yourself!" Joel shouted with panic in his voice.

Just then, he heard several *thuds* in succession, coming from the basement. It sounded like a struggle was happening.

"I'm going to check on them," Joel said as he turned to walk away. Osanna jumped in front of him with shocking speed and blocked the hallway.

"Not until you've accepted your gift."

Joel glared back at her. Her breaths were becoming heavier as if she were excited. He looked down at the wooden box for a moment and then threw it back toward the house entrance. The box shattered on contact with the floor, and the black gold skidded across until it stopped at the door.

"That's what I think of your gift," he said.

Osanna flashed a callous, demonic frown that sent chills down Joel's spine and left him frozen. He could have sworn her eyes had turned yellow for a moment. She hissed and narrowed her eyes like a snake about to lash out. He'd never seen her behave like this before. It was as if some ghoul had possessed her.

"So… you are a non-believer, then?" she asked, tilting her head almost completely sideways. Joel thought he was imagining things, but he could have sworn that her skin was turning gray.

"No, I-"

"After all I've done for you… taken care of you, loved you… this is how you react to my generous gift? Do you not realize that it was my most prized possession? It was painful to give it up, yet it is even more painful to know that I chose to bestow it upon someone so ungrateful!"

Then, there was a tense silence about the air, occasionally interrupted by the odd commotion from the basement. She stared at him with those daggers for eyes: a scornful look that she had never dared to show before. *That's it*, he thought. The glare that Pierce had inherited, in action. It felt like a stab in the gut.

"So, you are like the others, then. As evil and disgusting as they are…" Osanna said, her brow twitching with rage. *"Trash."*

Taking a few steps back, Joel prepared himself. She was hunched over now, and her hands were balled up into shaking fists. None of it made sense. It had to be a nightmare, he thought.

"I always loved you like a son, but…" she said, baring her teeth like a feral dog. "You're no son of mine!"

Osanna lunged out while shrieking like a banshee, and in that moment, Joel's instincts and reflexes took over. He sidestepped the attack while simultaneously grabbing her shoulder, and in one smooth motion, he threw her into the counter. She collided with it face-first with a nasty *thud*. Blood shot into the air as she flailed across the counter and knocked the meat and knife to the ground. She too fell and swiftly collapsed into a sad heap. Osanna covered her face with both hands and began shivering and sobbing.

Joel eyed the basement door and then looked back at Osanna. Blood from her collision with the counter seeped through her fingers, and it made him shudder. He remembered all that she had done for him. How she had treated him as one of her own, and helped him through a traumatic childhood. He couldn't just *leave her*. Even if the black gold had taken her, he had to make sure she was alright. Just as she had loved him like a son, he loved her like his own mother.

"Mom, are you alright?" He knelt over and put a hand on her shoulder. She was curled into a ball, shivering. "I'm sorry… it's just… you attacked me…"

She continued to sob.

"Is there anything I can do?" Joel asked.

Osanna slowly sat up, face still covered, and finally stopped shivering.

"Joel, dear…" she murmured. He raised an eyebrow at her sudden change in tone. "*Die.*"

She uncovered her face, and Joel was horrified to see the radical change: Her skin had become gray. Her cheekbones popped out as if she were malnourished, and her nose was crooked with blood gushing from it. Osanna grinned from ear to ear like a hyena as she threw a sudden punch that smashed into his jaw.

Joel stumbled back in a daze, and in that moment of weakness, Osanna hopped up and lunged out at him once more. This time, she was successful and knocked him to the ground. She quickly straddled him and threw a flurry of wild punches at his face. Most didn't connect for heavy damage, but it was enough to disorient him. By the time Joel got his bearings, Osanna had wrapped her cold hands around his neck.

The outlines around her eyes had turned dark like she was undead, and her smile was impossibly large. Joel gagged as he looked up in horror. His eyes darted to the left. The knife! It had fallen to the floor by his feet. He could kick it up to his hand and use it to stop her.

"I do this because I love you, Joel dear," said Osanna. "I can't let you live on as a non-believer! You're garbage, now! Luxian trash!"

Joel's bulging eyes fixated on the knife. She had done so much for him. Even in his darkest times after the death of his birth parents, she had kept him going when he was ready to give up. How could he kill her, especially when he knew that the black gold had caused her radical change in behavior?

"You're all the same! You don't understand his plan! The only solution is to snuff the bad ones out! Those who do not follow his will!" she said while spitting a vile mixture of blood and saliva in his face from the intensity of her words.

As Osanna increased her grip and he gagged some more, Joel realized that she was beyond saving. But did she deserve to die? He couldn't justify it. Even if she had gone mad, it wasn't her fault, he thought. Then, he heard more *thuds* from the basement below, loud enough to bypass the ringing of his ears. Suddenly, he had a change of heart. He had been willing to let himself die, but *not* Pierce. If he was going to do the unthinkable, it had to be for his best friend, his brother. He could still save him, at least.

"Die! Die for the Savior! You scum!" she shrieked as her eyes grew wider; wide enough so that her yellow pupils seemed small in comparison to the sea of white and bloodshot red around them. Her grin turned to a smile of lust; a clear lust for blood.

With his vision fading, Joel let his reflexes take over. He kicked the knife by its handle up to his hand and in one swift motion brought it across a gasping Osanna's neck. Her expression changed to fear and anger. She shouted words that he couldn't understand because of the blood gurgling out of her throat and mouth. Yet, out of some devilry, she somehow kept the pressure on his neck. It may have been too late, he thought, as his oxygen-starved mind became hazy. There was such anger and hate in her eyes, and she continued to scream in his face. How could *this* be his loving mother?

Finally, as Joel's vision dimmed, her grip loosened, and Osanna tumbled over at his slightest push. He savored his breaths and let his eyes readjust for a few moments before looking over at her. She appeared dazed; weak. Joel sobbed as the reality hit: It wasn't a nightmare, it was real.

He turned over to close her eyes shut, but as he tried, Osanna's head snapped back. Joel gasped as she opened her mouth and flung her face forward, biting down on his hand like a bear trap. He cried out in pain as his mother ripped and tore at his skin with her teeth.

Joel tried to push her off, but she wouldn't let go. Osanna wrapped her hands around his neck once more and finally released her teeth from his hand. She looked down upon him with a crooked smile, and blood shot out of her face and throat, spilling all over him. He couldn't understand what kept her alive, save for sheer determination. *Nothing*; not the intense academy training, or even the pillaging of his hometown, could compare to the terror swallowing him up, now.

"Jewl, daaar…" she gurgled out as her jaw let loose and her words became incoherent. Osanna's head bobbled back and forth uncontrollably. Quickly, Joel took the knife and stabbed her in the gut, and then twisted it to finish the job. She did not react to the pain and continued to stare down at him with that horrifying smile, so he stabbed her again.

Finally, her grip loosened, and she tumbled over onto Joel's shoulder.

"For the Savior…" she mumbled before going limp.

Joel sat for a moment, eyes wide and stutter-breathed. His face had been bloodied and battered. He wanted to let out a sigh of relief, but nothing came out. He opened his mouth to call out to Pierce, but again, no noise left his mouth. He looked at his mother and brushed her dark hair back.

"I'm sorry," he mouthed, but the words refused to take shape.

There was no time for self-pity, however. Joel was certain that Pierce was in as much danger, if not more. He grabbed the knife out of Osanna's stomach and ran for the basement door.

He flew down the stairs to see a bloodied Pierce cornered by Jed. He struck his son several times but hadn't noticed Joel behind him.

"You fool! Do you not realize our true role in this conflict?" Jed shouted as he kicked a doubled-over Pierce in the gut.

"I had wanted to give you this dagger as a gift one day, when you were worthy…" said Jed as he unsheathed a gorgeous luxmortite blade, longer than any dagger Joel had ever seen, yet shorter than a sword. "But I can see now that you'll *never* be worthy."

Pierce remained silent as he looked up at his father from the ground with those daggers for eyes. Joel observed a silent rage within him that he refused to unleash; much like the hesitation he had felt in stabbing Osanna.

"Do you know what happens to non-believers? They get stuck like the pigs they are!" Jed said as he pointed the dagger at his son. "Are *you* a pig? Do I have to gut *you*?" Again, Pierce stayed quiet. "Yes, I think I will…"

Joel had heard enough. He rushed Jed from behind, jumped up on his shoulders, and plunged the knife into his neck. Before his father could react, Joel pulled the knife out and stabbed him in the heart, as the academy had taught him. Then, as the horrifying gurgles of Jed filled his ears, he landed another blow in the middle of his chest before finally being thrown off.

However, the damage had been done. The stab to his neck had been more than enough. Blood shot out of his throat and he puked red as he fell to one knee. Joel didn't want to leave it to chance like with Osanna. Jed started to turn in an attempt to strike Pierce one last time, but he was met by Joel once again before he could do anything. He lunged out and stabbed him in his yellow eye, stopping him in his tracks.

Jed fell to the ground, lifeless. Joel breathed heavily and fell to both of his knees. He had just killed half of his own family. It was either him and Pierce, or his mom and dad: an impossible decision.

"You killed him…" Pierce muttered. Joel's head began spinning and it became impossible to breathe. He fell to the ground. All he could see was Jed's corpse and his friend crying over it.

"You killed them!"

Joel's vision faded to darkness as the voice became distorted by echoes.

"You *killed* them!"

CHAPTER 2
THE LETTER

Joel awoke in a deep sweat. He was back in Aldous' cozy hut, and it was morning. *That nightmare again*, he thought. It was becoming more prevalent as the years went by. Part of him wanted to let it go, but it was also the driving force behind his refusal to ever kill again. He kept replaying it in his head, hoping that on that day, something could have been different. On his worst days, he wished that Osanna could have killed him instead. But the result was always the same. No matter how he looked at it, someone was going to die on that day.

It had been a year since the Mt. Couture disaster that saw over 100 Faiwell miners perish, but life had been surprisingly humdrum after what should have been life-changing events. Joel feared that the unaccounted-for black gold would be unleashed onto Faiwell, but to his knowledge, it was nowhere to be found and no one had become infected by Gold Fever since their return. Even more concerning was that the key to the Greed monolith at the heart of Mt. Couture was still at large. Without it, the portal to Greed's prison remained open, and there was always a possibility that he could escape and wreak havoc upon the world. However, all had remained quiet in the village.

Aldous believed that the Council of Wizards had stepped in to keep Greed from escaping, but it seemed like a temporary solution. At least the formidable Nightcrawler would be there to fight him off, he thought. The memories came flooding back as he pictured the other-

THE LETTER

worldly terror charging at him and his friends. He had never seen a creature attack with such speed and ferocity before.

Joel flinched when he heard the door creaking open, but let out a relieved breath to see that it was only Aldous entering the hut. The mute crawled out of bed and Aldous smiled at him in a grandfatherly way. He wore his usual dirty blue tunic but sported a longer gray beard than before. He was falling into the typical 'Wizardly' look, and the thought made Joel chuckle in silence. Aldous was well outside the norm compared to his fellow Wizards.

"Another sleepless night, eh Joel?" he asked with a chuckle. "You've been havin' more nightmares ever since we returned from the mountain."

Joel made hand signals back at him.

"No, I'm afraid I've not heard from the Council, yet. It seems I'm still on probation. I only hope they don't excommunicate me!" Aldous said with cheer. The Council had taken their sweet time deliberating on their status as protectors of the Greed monolith, and Joel wasn't sure how he could remain positive throughout the process. Not knowing what exactly was happening drove him up a wall. He signed some more to him. "No, unfortunately, I haven't heard from my *contact* in some time, either."

"But all of this sitting around and waiting has become tiresome. How's about you and I take a lil' trip to pass the time?" Aldous asked out of the blue.

Joel raised an eyebrow and made some more hand signals in return.

"We promised Alistair that we'd visit him in his home country, remember? I have'ta say that I've missed the big feller. He appreciates Wizards more than anyone I've ever met!" he said, cracking a smile.

Joel's face lit up. He also missed Alistair, big mouth and all. It had been too quiet without him around. He was also interested in traveling to faraway lands so that he could draw more maps. He hadn't traveled in a long time, and even back when he had, it was to avoid the death and destruction of war.

"Mayhap we should ask the others if they want to come along, too," Aldous said.

Joel looked up in thought. Lucia acted like she hated Alistair, but he could tell that she had some respect for him; even if it was only for his bravery in the face of battle. Dalton would certainly go, too, as he'd taken a liking to the big man. Oddly enough, he hadn't seen Conrad around in months, so in addition to the invite, Joel wanted to drop by and say hello. He was certain that Baltr would be unable to make it. As a new group leader of the Miner's Guild, he was busier than ever.

The mute flashed hand signals that he would go and check with the others.

"Great! I've got a few other thingy-jiggers 'n such to take care of while yer gone, so it works out," Aldous said.

After eating a quick breakfast, Joel left the hut and strolled out into the sunny streets of Faiwell.

∽

LUCIA DE VESCI took a staggered step forward, holding a wooden baton outstretched with long, sturdy arms. The wind blew through the spacious, fenced-in backyard of Dalton Rayleigh, her mentor; *her opponent*. Her nose crinkled as the gust fluttered her dark hair, done up in a ponytail. It also fluttered her skirt at the knees, which was tucked into a specialized leather torso armor that covered her up, but was not as form-fitting as it had been during the Mt. Couture disaster. Even one year later, the burns she'd received at the vile hands of Wolfgang could still be irritated by the wrong clothes or ill-advised movements, and she could not afford such distractions; not against the man standing before her.

Under the veil of his mid-length, dark brown hair, Dalton stared back at her with focused eyes, but she was sure that it was only for show. He wore an old and dirty green tunic with big, black boots: his uniform when on guard duty. He'd just returned, and she knew her mentor well. He'd probably been drinking heavily to pass the time, as usual. She could smell the booze radiating from his well-trimmed beard and mouth. In his hungover state, she had a fighting chance to win their practice duel.

Why was it, then, that as she neared him, he felt more and more like an impassable wall? Dalton was tall and seemed to be built out of solid stone, but it was not only those traits that filled Lucia with hesitation. After all, she was a bit taller and had a clear reach advantage when they dueled with the wooden batons. No, it was his form; his poise; in addition to his superb physical abilities that made him seem unbeatable.

She shook the doubts out of her head. *Today is the day*, she thought; the day she'd score a win against her teacher and, with his aid, be granted permission to assassinate Drake Danvers. Alone, she was sure to be killed in the attempt, but with Dalton at her side, they stood a chance of making it out alive.

Although the expedition to Mt. Couture had been a catastrophe, the sympathy generated by the supposed loss of his daughter Edith had catapulted Drake into gaining even more power within Faiwell's community. That, combined with the successful expeditions that had followed at other mountains, ensured that Drake continued to be the most famous and beloved man in the village. After all, the Mt. Couture disaster had only been a mistake in the minds of Faiwell's citizens. They couldn't have imagined that Drake had been deceiving them all along.

"Well, this is a new strategy…" Dalton trailed off, brushing his hair back and out of his eyes. "Do you aim to put me to sleep?"

"Just savoring the moment," she replied with a smile.

Lucia closed in on Dalton and kept her wooden baton completely outreached. He remained motionless but ready. When within range, she brought her practice sword to his and tapped it lightly. It was meant to lure him into a false sense of security, so he would attack. She could then easily block with the outstretched baton, and land a stab.

However, Dalton didn't take the bait and instead took steps backward. Lucia's eyes widened.

"Using the long form, eh?" Dalton asked as she closed in and he backpedaled slowly. "A fine idea, to make use of your reach advantage, but I can't recall ever teaching it to you… something you learned in Lunia?"

"Luneria," she corrected in a bothered tone.

Lucia continued forward, tapping the batons together, but Dalton refused to attack and moved back once more. She smirked. He may have picked up on her new strategy, but he had no response for it. Soon, he would be cornered.

As Lucia had predicted, after some time, Dalton ran out of space and his back touched the wooden fence at the border of the yard.

"I've got you," Lucia said as she pushed the baton ever closer to his.

Suddenly, Dalton switched his stance: He held his wooden sword straight up and from the chest, then placed one leg, slightly bent, behind. Lucia cocked her head. She'd never seen him use this guard before, nor anyone else, for that matter.

Still, the time to strike was now, while his back was to the proverbial and literal wall. She lunged out for the stab as soon as the batons touched again. Dalton kept his stance, and directed her sword to his right, throwing her off balance. As Lucia stumbled forward, she felt the stinging blow of Dalton's baton at her ribs. She focused her eyes to see that he was dashing to his left, but Lucia wasn't about to let him escape unscathed. She arced her wooden sword and swung to the right, tagging Dalton on his wrist as he fled from her reach.

After the exchange, the two remained motionless, aside from Dalton shaking his wrist and Lucia rubbing her ribs. That would turn into a bruise, she thought. It was nothing new to either of the combatants. Even training with the batons was guaranteed to cause injuries, albeit safer ones.

"That's three points for me and one for you," Dalton said as he took the same pose as before and inched his way toward her.

Lucia felt disappointment building in her stomach. She had thought the long form combined with her great reach would throw her hungover mentor for a loop, but it seemed that he had an answer for everything she threw at him.

She held her sword straight out once more. If it wasn't successful in attacking, she could at least have a strong defense while keeping her distance.

Dalton approached and their batons met once more, slowly and but a tap. However, something about his new stance told Lucia that she shouldn't attempt to reply with an attack, even though it seemed like she would have the advantage. This time, it was she who backpedaled as Dalton followed, occasionally catching up and lightly touching swords. The situation had reversed: It was *her* being backed into a corner now, except she didn't have a response in mind.

Now, Lucia was ready to resort to desperate measures. She would have to try something unpredictable. Rather than continue to back down as Dalton had probably come to expect, she decided to go on the offensive the next time their batons met.

Dalton smiled as she planted her feet and prepared herself. In a flash, their swords clashed again, but this time, Lucia pushed through and attempted a stab. Dalton directed her baton to his upper left, but Lucia's reach proved effective and caught his hand. In response, with the swords now snagging, he brought his baton forward and to the right in one swift motion, preventing her from landing a follow-up blow while also tagging her where her shoulder and chest met. Both backed away after the exchange.

"That makes the score six-to-two in favor of me," Dalton said as he rubbed his hand.

"Damn..." Lucia muttered as she massaged her shoulder. "I thought that if I tried something different-"

"A fine idea, but just because I taught you nearly everything you know, doesn't mean I taught you everything that *I* know," Dalton said with a chuckle.

"What was that form, anyway? Why have I never seen you use it?"

"It's called 'crown form'. Great for blocking and responding to attacks with speed, but it's risky, as I'm sure you noticed. As for why I never use it..." Dalton said, staring off into the distance. "Your father was much better at it than me. He wouldn't have been caught in the hand and wrist like I was."

Lucia frowned. "Don't you think you should have taught it to me, then? To pass it on in his honor?"

Dalton shrugged. "The thought never occurred to me."

It had always bothered Lucia how Dalton was quiet about her father, except when they were in the heat of battle. It was almost as if it were a tactic to distract her for the easy win. Or perhaps combat was what reminded him the most of her dad. He had been Dalton's mentor, after all.

"Why is it, I wonder, that you never tell me about important techniques; or my own family who I can barely remember as it is?" Lucia asked with a grimace. Dalton let out a snorting chuckle.

"Is something funny?" she asked, her brow now twitching. He was probably laughing about the red crescent-shaped tattoo around her eye yet again. Despite living together for a year now, he would often laugh at or mock the mark of the moon, making it all the more infuriating that she couldn't defeat him.

"It's nothing," he replied, lowering his baton. "What do you want to know about your parents?"

"For starters-" Lucia cut herself off. Out of the corner of her right eye, she noticed Joel sitting atop the wooden fence. She turned to face him with hands on her hips.

"Ah, Joel! What brings you here? Want to join us in some training?" Dalton asked.

The mute shook his head and responded in sign language.

"Oh no, it's not a bad time to talk at all!" Dalton said cheerfully.

"Well, actually..." Lucia muttered.

Joel made more hand signals in return. He went on for a while, and Dalton stood there, nodding.

"What's he saying?" she asked.

"He wants to know if you, Conrad, Baltr, and I would like to travel with him and Aldous to Alistair's home country, Currencolt," Dalton said as he stroked his beard. "I'm certain that Baltr will be too busy to journey with us, but I'd love to go. I've missed the big fella. What do you think?" He looked at Lucia with enthusiasm in his eyes.

"Not interested," she coldly replied. Both Joel and Dalton frowned.

"You don't have to keep actin' like you hate him. Besides, I bet he's dyin' to see us all again. It has been far too long," Dalton said.

"It has hardly been a year since he left," Lucia said with an eye roll. "But that's not why I'm declining."

"Ah, right… Conrad…" Dalton trailed off.

Joel cocked his head and then signed to the warrior.

Dalton eyed Lucia. "Would you like to tell him?"

"All was well with Conrad until a few months ago. I'm not sure what happened, but he began acting strange. Then, out of the blue, he handed me a sealed letter, and told me only to open it if he didn't return within three months' time," Lucia said with a frown. "I worry for Conrad's safety, but he made me promise to wait the full three months. I am a woman of my word… so I haven't opened the letter. Two weeks remain before I can open it…"

Joel signed again to the pair. Lucia looked at Dalton for translation.

"He suggested we take a look at the letter, in case he's in trouble."

She shook her head. "Absolutely not."

"He has a point, though. What if an extra two weeks are instrumental in saving him?" Dalton asked.

"I cannot open it for another two weeks, and that's the end of it," Lucia replied with crossed arms. Dalton let out an exasperated sigh.

"Your father was stubborn like that, too!"

"Oh, don't you *dare* try to use my father to soften me up!" she shot back.

"Damn…" Dalton muttered.

He walked over to Joel by the wooden fence and the two communicated via sign language some more.

"What are you talking about over there?" Lucia asked before snorting. She had been meaning to learn USL so she could understand Joel, but Conrad had left before he could teach it to her. Dalton wasn't good at teaching anything but swordsmanship, either.

"Oh, nothing, just seeing if they'll wait a couple more weeks for us," Dalton said without looking back at her. After a few more hand signals from Joel, he added, "Couldn't you simply take the letter with you on the trip?"

"And risk opening it when I'm in a far-off land? What if he needs my help *here*?" Lucia asked with little patience.

"Ah, right…"

Dalton and Joel continued to exchange hand signals, which started to get on Lucia's nerves. She resented not being able to understand them and turned to leave.

"You boys have fun chatting. I'm going inside," Lucia said grumpily. She marched through the yard and into Dalton's home.

∽

DALTON LOOKED BACK. A smile crept onto his face. Joel made more hand signals toward him.

"Do I think they're *together*?" he asked, raising an eyebrow. He then leaned in and whispered, "Well, between you and me, I'm the one who started that rumor in the first place."

Joel gasped and put hands to his cheeks. Although he was 19 years old from what Aldous had told him, Dalton felt he had the face of a child, so it always made him chuckle to see his expressions.

"Y'see, they were spendin' so much time together that I wanted them to admit their feelings for one another. But even after I started the rumor, they refused to confirm it!" Dalton said in an annoyed tone.

Joel crossed his arms and frowned before sending more hand signals back.

"Exactly! It's such a bother to keep havin' to ask! Every time I bring it up to her, she neither confirms nor denies, and then says…" He took a deep breath, then in a faux high-pitched voice continued, "'Noooo, he's too short for me!'"

Joel inaudibly giggled and then signed back to him.

"I know my impression is bad, but you get the point."

The mute made more hand signals.

"Mind my own business? It *is* my business! I'm her mentor, y'know! I can't just allow her to become entangled with any scrub in the village. He must be a fierce warrior, like me… though preferably less of a fool when it comes to relationships," Dalton replied before they both let out hearty laughs. "Now, about that trip... consider our answer a tentative 'yes'." He grinned and rubbed his hands together.

∾

Later on, Dalton returned home from a night out at the pub. The alcohol's effects were beginning to wear off, but he still felt tipsy enough to be up to no good. *Time to bother Lucia about the letter*, he thought with a chuckle to himself. He approached her room to find the door open, and her back was turned to him. She was putting something under her pillow.

Foolish student, he thought, walking past her room nonchalantly. He wouldn't have to bother her after all. She could be mad at him all she wanted; opening the letter was for the best.

∾

Lucia walked to the bathing area of Dalton's spacious home. Although he didn't make it obvious, her mentor was more than taken care of after serving in the War of the Bird. He had taken home many rewards and plundered spoils from the enemy.

Most residents of Faiwell needed to use public bathhouses if they wished to clean up, but he had his own private bath. It required constant maintenance and that was one of Lucia's jobs while living there. It was worth the effort, as the burns she'd sustained from her battle against Wolfgang had bothered her every single day since. The doctor had told her there was a chance that they may one day subside, but it would take years, not months. In the meantime, she took frequent baths with herbs that soothed the skin. Constantly training and dueling had only further irritated her burns.

She entered the bathing area and caught a glimpse of the grand mirror to her right, on the tabletop. As a rare and valuable spoil of war, it had first been passed down from her deceased father to her mother, and after her death, it had been given to Dalton. He liked to joke that Lucia had only returned to Faiwell so she could retrieve her 'family heirloom', but in truth, she had no attachment to it. She hardly remembered anything about life with her parents and could find no meaning in their possessions.

Lucia removed her clothes to see the same burns covering her body as always, irritated and inflamed from brushing against the fabric of her clothing. As she had predicted, a bruise was taking shape at her ribs, but on the opposite side of where her burns were. Her eyes widened. Had he taken care to avoid striking her irritated skin? *Damn him*, she thought. No matter how much she was improving, he seemed to always be 10 steps ahead. With a sigh, she hopped in the large wooden barrel, filled with herbs and fresh water, and did her best to relax.

Outside, she could hear Dalton's drunken footsteps. He was approaching her room. *Foolish teacher*, she thought with a smirk. She leaned back in the bath and breathed in the warm fog around her. Eventually feeling a deep relaxation, she closed her eyes, and all seemed to melt around her.

Suddenly, the door burst open. Dalton stood in the doorway, wide-eyed, with the letter opened and in hand. Lucia crossed her arms to cover up. Her cheeks reddening to the same shade as the red crescent-shaped moon around her eye, she said, "I hope that someday, you will learn to knock…"

"Finish up. You need to read this."

CHAPTER 3
THE MISSION

About three months before Dalton opened the letter, Conrad had been doing his best to settle back into everyday life in Faiwell. He and Lucia had formed a strong bond, he got back to work at the bank with his parents, and he helped Henic's widowed family with the never-ending tasks that made a farm thrive in his spare time. However, whether it was his natural curiosity or the haunting memories of Mt. Couture, Conrad couldn't bring himself to leave it alone. He *had* to know what was going on.

It was natural to be worried. After all, there was a stockpile of black gold that had gone unaccounted for, and there were many questions that needed answering. Conrad had hopes that he could get his answers from Aldous, but the old Wizard claimed he had been cut off by the Council, and now knew very little about the situation himself.

Over the months, he'd been pressing some of the surviving miners for more information, but often came up empty. Peter refused to speak with him, as was his usual grumpy way. Brice and the hooligans had disappeared without a trace after the expedition, and the formerly Gold Fever-infected workers had hazy memories of it all at best. Most of the others had refused to speak with Conrad, save for William, the gangly man who was prone to ramble on about things of little importance.

Most concerning to Conrad was that recently, Drake Danvers had acquired even more power thanks to the sympathy generated by his daughter's supposed death. He was named a Village Elder, the youngest in Faiwell history, and promoted along with him were his two new assistants: Hector Brix and Ned Prescott. They were the pair who had attempted to leave along with Brice's group back at Mt. Couture, but the thunderstorm conjured up by the Mountain King had blocked them. Conrad felt that if there truly *was* a Dark Wizard in disguise as Cyriack and Aldous had thought, it had to be one of those two: He was certain that, given Lucia's story, Drake and the Dark Wizard had to have been working together. How else could he have known about the black gold?

Today, Conrad had decided to check in with Peter again. Since he was the toughest of the bunch to get talking, that likely meant he had the most to say. He strolled down the dirt road with his stately tunic and boots, but there was a change in him over the months: He had become less friendly and talkative, and especially untrusting. His warm and welcoming expression had changed to one of suspicion, but otherwise, he kept the same clean-cut look that had made him stand out on the Mt. Couture expedition: Messy beards were the norm amongst most miners.

Upon arrival, Conrad was surprised to see the long, gangly form of William standing outside Peter's door. The two were having a minor argument.

"Will you shaddup?" Peter asked with a snarl. He was tall but older; having grown balder and rounder over the years. He wore a permanent frown upon his face, and now that he was thinking of it, Conrad had never seen him smile without ill will before.

"Well, I was only tryin' to get you talkin' with the older folk… maybe you'd like 'em!" William said with cheer.

"I don' wanna talk with any of you looneys, and that's final!" Peter screeched and then went back inside. William opened his mouth and raised a finger, but the door slammed in his face before he could say anything.

Conrad approached from behind. The gangly man turned to face him, still smiling.

"Oooo, hello there, Conrad! So nice to see you again!"

"And you as well…" he trailed off with a half-hearted smile. "Why did he slam the door in your face? I'm used to him doing that to me, but I thought you two were on good terms."

"Ah, Peter is only in a grumpy mood, that's all!" William said as he brushed back his thin ginger hair. "I was tryin' to cheer him up. I noticed a couple of old men on the outskirts of the village chatting, and I thought he might like to speak with them, being old an' all. Oh, but I fear that I may have phrased it poorly! He took it as an insult..."

"Two old men, you say?" Conrad asked, both eyebrows raised.

"Yeh! They were chatting just inside the Dead Woods. I think they were tryin' to talk in secret. Perhaps it is an old gentlemen's club? Oooooo how exciting! I wish I were old!" the gangly man said while clapping his hands together.

Could it have been two *Wizards* that William had happened upon? The chances seemed slim, but Conrad was curious and growing desperate. He was ready to follow any lead at this point, no matter how weak it seemed.

"Will you show me where they spoke?"

"I wager they're still talkin', now!" William said cheerfully as he walked past Conrad to lead the way. They passed through the slums and then into the center of Faiwell, where small crowds of people walked to and from jobs, markets, and such. Most traffic was headed toward the Miner's Guild Headquarters up north, as per usual. It was a hub of trading, socializing, and general activity for much of the village.

As they traveled beyond the western barrier wall and approached the beginnings of the Dead Woods, Conrad leaned in and whispered, "Now William, I don't want to seem unappreciative, but can I ask you a favor?"

William looked back, his cheerful demeanor unwavering.

"After showing me where they are, will you leave me to listen in on their conversation?"

"Well, I suppose... but I wanted to get in on the old gentleman's talk. Imagine the things they discuss!" William replied.

"Please, I'll make it up to you. Just tell me what you need," Conrad pleaded.

"Well..." William trailed off with a smile. Conrad felt a pit in his stomach. Normally, his strategies had been carefully planned out to get what he wanted from William. This time, he hadn't positioned himself well to bargain. "Got any nice rocks around yer house?"

Conrad let out a snorting chuckle. "Yes, of course. I'll give you my finest rocks, in fact."

"Alllllright! We have a deal, then," the gangly man said with child-like excitement.

It wasn't hard to please William. He was a simple man with simple tastes, as Conrad had come to find out through their many conversations after the Mt. Couture disaster. For that same reason, though, he didn't expect his 'discovery' to bear fruit.

Yet, when the pair arrived at the beginnings of the Dead Woods, William pointed him to the clearing off to the left where the two old men resided. They were sitting up against withering trees. Conrad widened his eyes and held in a gasp: One of them was Aldous.

The strategist smiled and nodded at William as silent thanks. With that, he hid behind a tree as the gangly man walked back toward the village. He focused his ears and peered around the edge of his hiding spot.

"So, the key is still missing, eh?" Aldous asked.

The Wizard across from him inhaled smoke from a pipe and let some rings out. He appeared old and frail, and had a long mane of gray hair and a trimmed goatee. His dark green robe would have felt appropriate for the wooded area if all of the trees weren't dead, Conrad thought with a smile.

"Yep. You an' the boy sure made a mess of things," he replied.

"Well, I wouldn't say it was entirely our fault," Aldous said in a defensive tone.

"Oh no, not at all. I had only heard stories of him, but that Mountain King... such a handful, oh yes indeed."

"He wasn't always like that. The black gold tainted his mind."

"Yes, but that doesn't change the problems he's causing now. He has already maimed and killed several Wizards who were dispatched by the Council to apprehend and replace him," the frail Wizard said as he inhaled more smoke from his pipe.

"Oho! You'll need an army to bring him down!" Aldous replied.

"Hm... between him and Greed, I don't know who is worse. I fear the Council isn't taking this seriously enough..."

"Bah! An entanglement of bureaucracy, that's what they are. Greed is closer to being free than he has been in thousands of years, yet they do the bare minimum."

"Indeed," the frail Wizard said before pointing his pipe at Aldous. "I think that's why they don' like you much, old friend. You're a man of action. They'd rather sit around and talk all day."

"So then, they haven't done much about the Mt. Couture problem... but how about the unaccounted-for black gold? Why haven't they confronted Drake Danvers?" Aldous asked.

"I'm sure you already know the answer: They do not like to

entangle themselves in human happenings if they can avoid it. Besides, what evidence do they have to do such a thing?"

"How about my word?"

"Your 'word' comes from the mouth of a human woman who claims to have overheard his plans. Surely you realize how easily that could be portrayed in whatever favor you wished. Besides, with each passing of a story, it becomes more and more fictional," said the frail Wizard

"Which means they don't trust me," Aldous said with a frown.

"In my opinion? Indeed, they do not trust you."

"Bunch'a useless fools, they are… what about Zequim? He usually listens to me; to reason…"

"He has argued in your favor, as per usual, but the top Council members have overruled him," the frail Wizard said.

"I can hardly see the point in leading a Council that is constantly limiting his authority and power!" Aldous said as he threw his hands up and scoffed.

The frail Wizard took another draw from his pipe and then smiled as the smoke shot out of his nose. "I believe that *is* the point."

"Well, if they won't do anything, I'll-"

"It would be unwise to insert yourself into any more conflicts. You're already on probation… you wouldn't want to be *excommunicated*."

The pair remained silent for a moment. Conrad wasn't sure whether to feel relieved that Aldous shared his concerns, or horrified that he was powerless to do anything. Despite his impressive abilities and knowledge, he was forced to adhere to rules that limited him severely. Perhaps being a Wizard wasn't as glorious as he had thought.

"I understand your concern in regards to Drake, though. The fact that he's gained so much political power in a short time is not lost on the Council," the frail Wizard said.

"It is not his political power that worries me at the moment," Aldous replied. Concern swept over his face. "There are six more seals that can be broken. I believe he wants to break them all."

"The seals are well-hidden across the world. Even the Council does not know where one of them lies. Why would a mere human know where they are?"

"I believe he is working with a Dark Wizard. I felt a malicious presence at the mountain, and I'm sure you've sensed the dark cloud hanging over Faiwell," Aldous said.

"I was under the impression that the Mountain King was responsible for the dark presence?"

"That is what the Council believes, mayhap. However, even in his reduced state, Olivier never exuded such malice and hatred. I've not felt such a horrid presence since…"

"The Oppressor?" the frail Wizard asked, raising an eyebrow.

"Yes…" Aldous said, although Conrad could hear the hesitation in his voice.

"I never encountered him, myself. He was before my time as a Wizard."

"I did, once. I'll never forget it. I have never since been around someone who struck such dread into my heart. I must admit that what I feel now is diminished in comparison. Yet, even if it is not him, it still means a Dark Wizard is trying to influence human happenings. It is worth looking into," Aldous said.

The frail Wizard nodded and then stood. "I agree. This shroud of darkness I feel is troubling. I will report it to the Council immediately."

"I appreciate that. Shall we meet in this same spot next month?" Aldous asked as he also got to his feet.

"Perhaps. A new mission has been assigned to me, so that may interfere. But for now, let's assume we meet at the same place, same time." He frowned and then began to wipe a hand on his robe.

"Something wrong?"

"Tree sap," said the frail Wizard, holding his hand up and crinkling his nose.

"Oho! Now, that's odd!" Aldous replied, stroking his beard. "I didn't think these withered trees could even make sap. Then again, Mother Nature always seems to surprise us, doesn't she?"

"True enough," he said, nodding his head back, westward. "I don't suppose there is a water source nearby?"

"We'd need to cross through the village, I'm afraid."

"Too risky. The Council may well have someone tracking you. I cannot be seen with you while you're on probation." He turned and then puffed a great ring of smoke.

Unlike the previous puffs of smoke, this ring stayed in place and refused to dissipate. In fact, it grew and grew, at the same rate as Conrad's eyes were widening from his hiding spot. Soon, the smoke turned into a portal, and it roared and whirled like a contained tornado. Yet still, it was nowhere near as frightening as the portal to the Cold World had been nine months prior.

The frail Wizard started for the portal, but he stopped short and then looked over his shoulder. "Be sure to keep a low profile, Aldous."

Aldous nodded back as he walked into the portal. Soon after, it lost its shape and the smoke dispersed. The old Wizard stood in silence for a moment before walking away from the clearing. Conrad waited for a short while to ensure that he was alone, then made his way out as well.

However, as he reached the main trail and hung a right to begin his brief trip back, a portal opened in front of him. Out stepped the very same Wizard who had been speaking with Aldous just moments ago. He wore an amused smile.

"Well, hello there..." the frail Wizard said.

"Erm... hello..." Conrad paused. Now, it was best to play dumb. "How'd you do that?"

He snickered. "Don't be coy. I could tell you were eavesdropping on our earlier conversation."

"If that was the case, why didn't you stop talking?"

"Because there is something interesting I'd like to discuss with you... but first, allow me to introduce myself: I am Utrix, a member of the Wizard's Council," he said.

"A pleasure to meet you. I am-"

"Conrad Mercer. I know who you are, as does the Council," Utrix said, raising a finger. "Your curiosity caught our attention... and I'm afraid it is not the sort of attention that you'd desire. Do you understand that action will need to be taken if you pry any further?"

"After all that happened in those mines, how can I be expected to sit back and accept that everything is alright?" Conrad asked with growing anger in his voice.

"The other survivors seemed to have kept quiet."

"And I'll never understand why. The black gold remains missing, a monster capable of enslaving us all could be turned loose at any moment, and the man who came up with the nefarious plan not only walks free but has gained *more* power in our village," said the strategist.

"Ah, but that is where folks like you and I differ from the others," Utrix replied with a smile. "Wizards are a strange breed; always wishing to know, or to understand. You possess those same qualities that many other humans do not have. For most of them, 'Life goes on'."

"Aldous said the same thing."

"In many ways, Aldous exemplifies the Wizardly way. Unfortunately, he and the Council do not see eye-to-eye, an' now he is on probation. You've overheard how they treat their own when they are displeased with their actions, but I wonder how they will receive a *human* meddling in their affairs?" Utrix asked in a barbed, yet aloof tone.

Conrad narrowed his eyes. He had such difficulty in reading him. Was he threatening him? Or was he warning him? His demeanor suggested it was neither, to make matters more confusing.

"What's your point?"

"Since I have discovered you spying on Wizardly happenings, there are two options…" Utrix trailed off. "One: I can bring you before the Council and have your memory erased, as per their policy." Conrad shuddered. He didn't want to forget. "Two: You work with me on a top-secret mission."

A great wave of relief swept over Conrad. "I'd prefer option two."

"I thought as much!" Utrix said with a chuckle. "But y'see, my dear boy, you may well wish you had taken option one in the future."

"What's the mission?" Conrad asked, demanding in nature. Utrix raised an eyebrow. "I don't mean to seem unappreciative, but I am curious as to what a mere human could do for an all-powerful Wizard."

"A fair question. Wizards like Aldous and myself are monitored closely by the Council. They wish to make sure we won't abuse our abilities, or meddle in human affairs unnecessarily. Doing so results in the harshest of punishments."

"I get the feeling that they're the ones who decide when it's necessary. Am I correct?"

"Exactly. Even though it was obvious that Aldous had a duty to infiltrate those mines and interfere nine months ago, he and the Key Keeper were supposed to do little aside from play supporting roles. The reason both of them are on probation is because they joined the expedition and tried to discourage you lot from taking the black gold," Utrix said as he looked up at the sky. Gray clouds passed overhead and a metallic smell signaled that rain was soon to come.

"What were they supposed to do, then?" Conrad asked.

"Aldous' role as Wizard Scout was to inform the Mountain King of impending danger and follow his command from there. Only a Wizard King is allowed to act of their own accord in a situation where a monolith is possibly in danger. The Keeper of the Key is even more restricted. They are to avoid contact with others if able, and their only role is to keep the monolith key safe, or if the situation calls for it, repair the monolith," the frail Wizard said.

"I must admit, from the Council's perspective, they both failed in their roles," Conrad said.

"That is true. And in the case of us Wizards, the Council doesn't care about 'doing the right thing', even though it was kind of them to help you all. If it weren't for them, after all, there would have been no survivors from your expedition."

"Agreed," Conrad said as he rubbed his chin. "So then, you want my help because I'm not under the watchful eye of the Wizard's Council?"

"Don't get the wrong idea," Utrix said with a smirk. "Without a doubt, you and the other survivors are being observed by the Council. You are simply *less visible* than I am, and what I wish to do requires finesse."

"If we're being watched, why is it that some of the survivors have disappeared?" Conrad asked.

"Because they too were given missions by me," Utrix explained.

The strategist's eyes widened. "What missions were they given?"

"I'm afraid I can't tell you."

"How am I supposed to trust your word in all of this? I've already seen a Wizard who was supposed to be the best of you turn bad. How do I know you aren't tricking me?" Conrad asked, crossing his arms.

"M'boy, do not forget it was *you* who sought *me* out," Utrix said in a stern tone. "Think about what you know: I am a friend of Aldous, and your two options are to have your memory erased or to work with me in secret. Use that information and come to a decision."

"Well then, I'll just speak with Aldous-"

"Not an option," the frail Wizard interrupted. "He cannot find out about any secret missions, or he'll want to get involved."

"And why can't he?"

"Because the Council has him on probation. If he takes any further action outside of their guidance, he'll be excommunicated," Utrix replied solemnly. "Excommunication means he'll be classed a Warlock, or worse: a Dark Wizard. You may not know this, but the Council actively hunts down and kills Dark Wizards, as they are deemed too dangerous to be left alive. I do not wish to see that happen to my friend."

Conrad remained silent, and his mind raced. He would be taking a great risk in trusting a Wizard he'd just met without confirming anything with Aldous. The idea made him uneasy, but it was his best chance to understand what had happened to the black gold. At least, he hoped as much. The alternative was far worse, in his estimation.

"What's the mission?" he asked.

"I have strong reason to believe that the missing black gold was sent to a country called Gentorgul. Have you heard of that place?"

"Yes, I read about it some time ago. Many countries have tried to conquer them, but all have failed. It's what they are best known for," Conrad said with an extended index finger.

Utrix smiled back at him. "Correct. Not even Sigraveld can conquer them because they are a hardy people with great natural defenses by land and sea. There is a settlement within Gentorgul called Bosfueras. It lies deep in the woods along one of Gentorgul's coastlines. I have reason to believe that this is where Drake has stored the missing black gold."

"So, my mission would be to infiltrate this place and find the black gold, I presume?" Conrad asked.

"Yes. I can only get so close. I have detected a dark presence there, ever watching. In addition, the townsfolk are not open to newcomers; an' of course, the Wizard's Council forbids me from taking any action against humans without their permission. That is where I need your help."

"I see..."

"I won't lie to you: Your life will be in grave danger as an outsider trying to infiltrate the Bosfueras community. They have never taken kindly to strangers, but even more so lately, they have turned violent against intruders. And of course, you have the black gold to worry about, as well. Because of this, the infiltration will be slow; *at least* a couple of months," Utrix said.

"Can I bring anyone along with me?" Conrad asked. He smiled as the memories of fighting side-by-side with Lucia and the others in the Mountain King's throne room came flooding back.

"No, Conrad. It can only be you," he replied in a stern tone. "As I said before, you have a certain instinct that the others lack. Aside from that, I can't get away with taking *another group* of survivors on a mission. It will raise too much suspicion."

The strategist sighed and said, "Very well."

"Before I give you any more details, I need you to promise me: You will not tell *anyone* of this meeting, as doing so will put them in great danger," the frail Wizard said with sharp eyes.

"I promise. Not a word to anyone."

"Even to those dearest to you?"

"Yes."

"And for the sake of the mission, are you willing to throw your life away if or when it is necessary?" Utrix asked. His tone became more demanding with each word.

"Yes."

"And should you need to, are you willing to kill those who stand in the way of your mission?"

Conrad nearly gasped and looked down in silence. The memories of his duel to the death with Wolfgang were still fresh in his mind. Even though he had vowed never to show mercy to the merciless again, something Wolfgang had said back then stuck with him: *Once you start killing, it's hard to stop.*

"Y-yes." He winced at the hesitation in his voice.

"Alright," Utrix said, now flashing a warm smile. His tone became light-hearted once more. "Meet me in this exact spot in one week. That should give you time to make arrangements for your departure. Then, I will take you to Gentorgul."

"But how will we get there?"

"Ah, I see Aldous never explained different types of Wizardry to you," he said with a chuckle.

"He told me that he was an Elemental, and the Mountain King was a Conjurer."

"And I am a Summoner. That means I can send things to and from where I wish. That includes myself and *you*, as well. In other words, I can take you straight to Gentorgul, so long as I know it well enough. That's one of the reasons we'll need preparation," Utrix explained.

"You've never been there?" Conrad asked.

"Only twice in my long life," the frail Wizard replied with a chuckle. "This is only a precaution. Y'see, if I foul up while summoning, I could send us hurdling through time an' space. Not something we'd like to experience, agreed?"

"Agreed. I will meet you here again in a week."

"Take care Conrad, an' remember… you are not to tell anyone about this. Especially not Aldous. His very life depends on it," Utrix said as he turned and a portal opened up before him.

"Understood," the strategist said. Utrix walked through the gateway while waving goodbye over his shoulder.

After the portal closed, Conrad let out a long, strained breath.

Although he had put on a brave face, it was a stressful conversation. He found it remarkable how Utrix could go from calm and nice to serious and demanding at a moment's notice. It made him uneasy. He also didn't like that he couldn't tell anyone what he had found out, or about his mission. In the short time that he'd known his new friends, especially Lucia, he had always told them the truth. He would have to get used to lying for the next week.

He could at least find some relief in that he would soon find answers, or so he hoped. In the back of his mind, Conrad understood that there was much that could go wrong. Even still, it was a risk well worth taking. What Utrix had said was true: Everyone else seemed fine with continuing their lives as if nothing had happened, but not Conrad.

∼

As the following week went on, Conrad prepared for his departure in secret. He lied and told his parents that he'd been approached for a high-end job overseas and that he would likely be gone for some time. He also continued to probe the Mt. Couture survivors for information. Any sudden changes in his behavior might raise suspicions.

One of his most difficult tasks was informing Henic's family that he could no longer help on the farm. Conrad used the same excuse that he had used with his parents, and they accepted it happily. He hoped that they could stay afloat while he was away. The good news was that Henic's oldest son, Milo, had learned quite a lot in the months he'd been helping. He was sure that the boy could run the Foreman farm, and without Wolfgang or the hooligans around to trouble them, they stood of fighting chance of thriving.

The most difficult person to lie to was Lucia. Despite his efforts to act natural, she asked him many times throughout the week if something was wrong. Somehow, she could tell that he was stressed when even his parents hadn't realized. On the day of his departure, he left her a letter and asked that she not open it for three months. By Conrad's estimation, if he hadn't infiltrated Bosfueras by then, he was probably dead. It was meant to be a failsafe of sorts: In case the villagers got him or Gold Fever took hold. If he were to disappear, never to be seen again, at least Lucia would know what happened.

With the note passed on and a near-tearful set of goodbyes, Conrad met Utrix at the outskirts of the Dead Woods. There, the frail Wizard called upon a portal that swirled around violently.

"After you," Conrad insisted.

"Do not be afraid, m'boy!" Utrix said with cheer. "It's not as scary as it looks. Where you're going will be a much less friendly environment."

With tepid steps, Conrad walked toward the swirling pool of darkness. All of his instincts told him to turn back and call the whole thing off, but his curiosity persisted. He had to know the truth. The fear vanished as he entered the portal. It reminded him much of when he had entered the Mouth of Hell at Mt. Couture, swallowed by the dark.

CHAPTER 4
PORT CITY

Joel, Dalton, and Lucia sat around a campfire just off the dirt road in the plains of eastern Federland. It was night one of their planned eight-day journey to Port City, and so far, it had been a smooth ride. Dalton's horses snored loudly behind them, laying before Aldous' carriage, which he was currently inspecting the wheels of with the aid of a contained fireball in his palm. It was his hobby to collect different carriages, and he took their maintenance seriously.

Lucia looked over her shoulder and snorted. "I think the carriage is just fine, Aldous. Why don't you join us? We have much to discuss."

"Just a moment!" he called back.

"Don't be so eager. He'll become suspicious and go to sleep before we can question him," Dalton whispered.

"Oh?" she replied, narrowing her eyes and smiling. "Are you saying that I can't be subtle? Because I daresay we wouldn't be on this trip if I hadn't played you like a fiddle a few days back."

The warrior groaned and Joel inaudibly chuckled. He'd heard all about how Conrad's letter had been opened. Lucia had kept her oath to him while finding out early what had been in the letter.

Conrad's letter detailed his destination, his meeting with Utrix, and his mission. After first reading the letter, Dalton and Lucia had confirmed with Aldous that Utrix was who he claimed to be. He told them that he had indeed been meeting up with the frail Wizard and that he would likely be able to take them to Gentorgul instantly with his abilities. He also said that what Conrad had described was within his friend's usual behavior, with one glaring exception: Utrix and most other Wizards were vehemently against asking humans for help. Most troubling, however, was that Aldous had not seen him since their meeting nearly three months ago.

"By the way, there's something important I wanted to talk with you about," Dalton said, leaning in. The orange and yellow of the flames reflected off of his face, filled with focus. "Did you forget to pack the booze? I can't seem to find it anywhere!"

"Perhaps I hid it..." she muttered, her voice cracking and her cheeks flaring out.

"Don't say it."

"Under my pillow!" Lucia and Joel burst out laughing as Dalton sulked.

"You'll never let me live it down, will you?" he asked with tired eyes.

"Well, someone has to keep your ego in check without Baltr around," she replied.

Dalton smirked. "He's too important to be spending time with us, these days. With how much gold and silver his teams keep on bringing home, he'll be running the Miner's Guild in no time."

Joel signed to Dalton, noting that out of all the Mt. Couture disaster survivors, Baltr had been the only one to really make the best of his situation.

"True," the warrior replied with a nod. "And in his case, the success is well-deserved. I'm only sad not to have someone so fiercely loyal and competent on our journey. Given that *at least* two of us are headed for Gentorgul, a land so fierce that it cannot be conquered, we can use all the help we can get."

The mute glanced back at Aldous, uneasy. He could sense that Dalton and Lucia were unhappy with him. For some reason, the old Wizard had refused to elaborate on whether or not they'd be joining them on the journey to Bosfueras. As much as Joel had been excited to visit Alistair, was it not more important to ensure Conrad's safety? He was beginning to suspect that something more was at play.

"Then again, we may not even make it to Bosfueras," Dalton continued, eyeing his student. "You're sure that these mysterious contacts of yours will take us aboard?"

Lucia shrugged. "I'd hardly call them contacts, but when you are closely connected to King Cedomir II, as I am, it tends to earn you some favors. There are bound to be some Lunerian trading ships in Port City. All I need to do is show them the mark of the moon, and they will take us aboard."

"Oho! That's a relief! Taking us across the sea with my command of the water would have been exhausting!" Aldous said, finally sitting by the fire.

"So, you do plan to join us on the trip to Bosfueras, then?" said Dalton.

"Well, I never said that…"

"Why won't you give us a straight answer?" Lucia asked with impatience in her tone.

"Let's just say there are other things I have to consider…" the old Wizard trailed off with a half-hearted smile.

"You seem to have something on your mind. May as well tell us," Dalton said, crossing his arms.

Aldous let out a weary sigh. He looked up at the clear night sky. "The truth of the matter is that when I first asked you all on this trip, I hadn't only wished to visit Alistair. He was merely meant to be a stop along the way to my true destination of choice."

Dalton smirked. "You're giving me a bad feeling, Aldous."

"I assume you remember the story I told you about the Dark Savior, and how he split himself into seven different identities that were all sealed away in monoliths 'n such," the old Wizard said as his eyes became fixed on the flames flickering before him. "I have reason to believe that more of these monoliths are in danger. Seven seals in total hold the Dark Savior at bay, and as of now, someone seeks to break them."

"Could it be Drake again?" Lucia asked.

"It is. Over the past year, I had been keeping a close eye on him and managed to intercept a letter that he'd intended for one of his assistant-fellers. It confirmed my worst fears," Aldous replied. "Based on what Conrad had told me and the dark presence I had sensed near Mt. Couture's base, I suspected that a Dark Wizard had been aiding Drake in his efforts to release Greed, and it seems to be true… they are acting quickly."

"Why not inform the Wizard's Council of the letter?" Dalton asked. Joel made hand signals in response.

"As he said," Aldous nudged his head toward the mute. "The Council will do nothing because they don't trust me. They are the kind of bureaucratic filth that would question how I obtained the letter, or if it was a forgery. But I have sat back for long enough. With Greed under the direct supervision of the Council, Drake and the Dark Wizard wouldn't dare return there. No… their next target will be the *Famine monolith* in the land of Mithika."

A tense silence overcame the group.

Lucia leaned in. "You're telling us that the Dark Savior possessed the ability to starve us all?"

"Yes, but only if he came in direct contact with a food supply, and only if he willed its destruction. But truthfully, there would have been no purpose for him to do such a thing, even to his enemies. To render farmlands infertile would hinder his precious melior species after conquering all lands," Aldous explained.

"Between his ability to destroy entire cities and being able to ruin farmlands, I almost get the impression that his war against the luxians was like one big game to him…" Dalton trailed off.

The thought sent a chill down Joel's spine. What if everything that Stalmoz had done was for little more than his own entertainment?

"Mithika neighbors Alistair's home country, Currencolt. I thought that we could stop by, pick him up, and then intercept whoever is being sent to destroy the Famine monolith," Aldous said before sighing. "But now I must choose between helping Conrad and the possibility of another broken seal."

"Hold on," Dalton said as he held up a hand. "You're leaving something out. You said, 'Whoever is being sent.' Is Drake not handling it himself?"

"No. He referred only to his 'new team' in the letter. He did not specify who it would be, but Mithika is merely a detour for them. Drake is traveling to the land of Sigraveld as we speak. He knows the general location of the Degenerate monolith. It lies in the sewers of Endoshire."

"You lot placed a monolith in the middle of the busiest city in the world?" Lucia sneered. "What kind of decision is that?"

"It is well-hidden, believe me. Few humans know of its existence, and none know of its exact whereabouts," Aldous said. "Besides, Sigraveld's rise to power is fairly recent, at least to us Wizards. The Council from all of those years back never could have predicted that their hiding spot would become the world's trading hub."

"This Dark Wizard is a real pain in the arse," Dalton said with a laugh. "He's telling Drake everything he needs to know."

Joel made hand signals toward the group. Dalton raised an eyebrow.

"He makes a good point. What does a Dark Wizard have to gain by unleashing more spawns of the Dark Savior? If all of the split identities combine back into his original form, will he not try to destroy all Wizards, good or bad?"

"I'm not sure what the Dark Wizard's motives are, but I can be certain that it involves power. *Greed* is mayhap the ultimate way to control people, and from a distance, too. With that off the table, though, starving people is a good way to make them desperate... desperation leads to violence, and through that violence, there comes an opportunity to gain power. The same goes for degeneracy. If that were to spread, violence would become frequent, and fear would be at an all-time high. Another great way to take control," Aldous said.

"Alright, so if we know Drake is headed to Endoshire, why are you going to Mithika, first? Shouldn't you take out the root cause of all this nonsense?" Lucia asked.

"A fair question. The sewers of Endoshire are like a giant maze. I visited the site many years ago, but never made it to where the monolith lies. And I should also mention that, much like Mt. Couture, Endoshire has a Wizard Scout, Keeper of the Key, Guardian, and Wizard King to watch over it," Aldous said, nodding with confidence. "It would take Drake a considerable amount of time to find the monolith, and that is only if he can find the manpower and resources that he possessed back in Faiwell. In the meantime, I believe he's sending some of his new team to the Famine monolith. I do not yet know the full scale of their operation, but it is clear what their target is at the moment, and I can't ignore that."

"It seems to me like we should split up, then," Dalton said. All around the fire eyed him with visible surprise. "Conrad is in grave danger, and so is the Famine seal. We cannot leave either of those things to chance."

Everyone nodded in agreement.

"Lucia and I will travel to Bosfueras and find Conrad. You two go to Currencolt, bring Alistair along, and then stop Drake's team from destroying the monolith in Mithika. Then, we can all meet in Endoshire to finish Drake off, once and for all. We'll be in luck then, too. Some of my good friends from the war live there, on the outskirts. They will give us a place to stay and provide aid," Dalton said.

Aldous glanced at Joel. The mute nodded to signal that he was game for the journey. Why the old Wizard had withheld all of this information from him up to now, he couldn't say for sure, but the more important matter was ensuring the safety of the six remaining seals.

"Very well," Aldous said, leaning in. "We shall split up, and then meet in Endoshire after our tasks are complete. We can go over more details tomorrow. For now, my friends, I suggest we get some rest!"

∼

THROUGHOUT THE WEEK, Joel and the others traversed a series of connecting paths through lush green forests, fields of grass and plants teeming with harmless wildlife, empty plains, and mountainous regions where they would go in and out of tunnels, bringing to mind the haunting memories of Mt. Couture. Dalton's horses and Aldous' carriage were of high quality and had made it through the variety of terrain with few issues. As dusk settled in on the eighth day of the trip, their destination loomed on the horizon.

Port City, while not being the only port of Federland, was unique for its great size, and most of all for how it was built: Half of the city was on land, but the other half resided entirely on sturdily-built docks over a bay. As Aldous had described to the others, there was a time when the city had been entirely on land, but when sea levels began to rise, the Wizard's Council had wisely stepped in to help them prepare for the flooding. It was one of Aldous' favorite examples of how the Council had been a force for good in the world before implementing their strict rules on meddling in mankind's affairs.

As they reached the city limits, the road narrowed and became packed in with many people coming and going: From fishermen and sea captains to vendors and performers. Various stone buildings stood tall, and the strong smell of salt water filled the air. At the midway point of Port City, the land ended and became a series of interconnecting docks that not only supported their horses and carriage but dozens of other people and horses as well. Most buildings on or along the docks were wooden and small, but some stone structures towered out of the water below, the green of the seaweed and algae build-up near their bottoms catching all of their eyes.

Joel was drawn in by the ships setting sail at the ports far ahead. There was a complex system of waterways that allowed the vessels to come and go with ease, avoiding overcrowding of the busy ports. He couldn't even imagine navigating such watery paths, let alone having built the system around them.

The group of four stopped at a stable to board their horses and carriage at the rightmost edge of the docks. Next, they turned back and made way for solid land once more, to grab food and drink at the local pub. On the return trip into the heart of the city, many avian flying in and out of the ports with goods strapped to their backs caught Joel's attention. They seemed to always be heading south, and it made sense: That was where the Birdlands lay. Merchants and vendors called out to him as they walked by, and he put his head down without replying. He didn't know much about life in the big city, but he'd heard plenty about the aggressive nature of salesmen in such places.

Inside of the pub, the decor was old and uninviting: The wood seemed even more rotted than the support beams of Mt. Couture had, and the stools felt designed to grind one's spine down into a fine powder.

In short order, Lucia found groups of Lunerian sailors in the pub and managed to set up meetings with two different ship captains for later in the night. One ship was headed to Gentorgul, a trip that would take about 40 days. The other planned to set sail for Currencolt, which would take around a month.

As they enjoyed their food and drink, Dalton told some stories of his adventures and time at war, yet Joel couldn't help but be distracted by something: Every once in a while, between hearty laughs and great gulps of his drink, Aldous looked over his shoulder. Were they being followed? At first, Joel had been taking in the atmosphere of Port City, but now the densely packed surroundings felt like hiding spots for a spy, or worse.

After Dalton finished up with his latest story, Aldous stood and declared, "I gots to find the outhouse-majigger!"

"Uh-oh, guess more than one seal has been broken! Eh, Aldous?" Dalton said as he slammed his fist down on the table and laughed.

Aldous laughed along as he stumbled out of the pub. Joel looked through the window to see that his stumbles immediately ended and his strides became quick and calculated. Something wasn't right. He wanted to leave and see what the old Wizard was up to, but Dalton kept loading him up with drinks.

"Another for my quiet friend over here!" he shouted to the bartender.

The mute returned a half-hearted smile. Throughout the trip, Lucia had mentioned often that Dalton had more money than he knew what to do with. Tonight, he was certainly proving her point.

∼

ALDOUS CUT through the busy streets of Port City and into an alleyway. He walked for some time, enveloped in darkness and equally dark thoughts. Near the alley's end, he came to an abrupt stop. He swiftly spun around with his walking stick ready to attack, but no one was there.

The old Wizard shrugged and then turned back to exit the alleyway, but his breath was taken away when he found someone standing before him. He stumbled back in a panic. Aldous narrowed his eyes, and out of the shadows, dark and sleek as the night sky, appeared a man in a dark blue cloak. He pulled his hood back to reveal his face: He had a white beard that was expertly trimmed, and brown eyes that looked warm and comforting.

"Zequim…" Aldous muttered. His surprise was quickly overcome with annoyance. "How many times have I requested that you *not* sneak up on me like that?"

He chuckled in a grandfatherly manner. "My apologies, old friend… but I must say that your reaction is worth it every time."

Aldous let out a great sigh. Zequim's voice had a quality to it that provoked calm, rational thought. It was one of the reasons he had risen to leader of the Wizard's Council hundreds of years ago. When he spoke, people listened, and often agreed with what he had to say; unless they were stubborn Wizards, anyhow.

"You seem tense. Is everything alright?" Zequim asked.

"I had the strangest idea that I was being followed," he said and then let out a nervous chuckle. "You and I both know that the situation is dire."

"And you know that my hands are tied," the Council Leader replied.

"You are the highest-ranking authority of all Wizards. Your hands are *not* tied!" Aldous shot back.

Zequim raised an eyebrow, but he did not falter. "It is the way of the Council. I cannot act unless the majority agrees. You know that."

"Indeed. And if you, the most powerful of Wizards, were to tell them they had no choice, what would they do? Sit around and talk about *that*, too?" Aldous sneered as he threw his hands up in disgust.

"Such heresy... sounds like the talk of a Dark Wizard," a deep voice called out from behind Zequim. Out of the shadows appeared another Wizard who was tall, bald, and striking in his ability to blend in with the shadows. His brown eyes, unlike Zequim's, were filled with intensity and an ill will that made Aldous nervous.

Zequim held up a hand. "Settle down, Axar."

"You brought *him* along?" Aldous asked with betrayal in his voice.

"Well, how else would I get here?" Zequim replied with an amused snort.

"You'd be better off walkin', methinks," the old Wizard replied.

"May I remind you that you are on probation, Aldous?" Axar said, snickering. The moonlight reflected perfectly off of his dark, bald head. "I would *hate* for you to be excommunicated."

"You see?" Aldous asked and then gestured toward Zequim. "This is why I don't like him. He has never been afraid to abuse his powers n' such."

"Why you worm-"

"That's enough out of both of you," Zequim said. Silence fell over the trio of Wizards. It was that calming voice of his at work, Aldous thought. The Council leader sighed. "Axar is correct, Aldous."

Aldous raised an eyebrow and then pointed at himself, shocked at whose side he was taking.

"You *are* on probation, and while you are not currently in danger of excommunication, meddling in the affairs of other Wizardly operations could be grounds for it," Zequim said. His expression suddenly turned grim.

"I'll have you know that we are setting sail to visit a survivor of the Mt. Couture disaster," Aldous said as he conked his walking stick off the cobblestone ground angrily.

"How nice of you to visit a survivor of the tragedy that *you caused*," Axar said with a sly smile. Zequim looked back at him with raised eyebrows, and Aldous grimaced.

"'My fault', you say? Tell me, did the Wizard's Council know that the black gold wasn't properly contained? Did they know that it could taint a Wizard's mind? Or did you simply *not care*?" Aldous asked. Axar narrowed his eyes. "Olivier told me that he was left there to die slowly. What did you expect?"

"We expected him to do his duty, like you. But all of you failed. Only the Guardian did its job," Axar replied.

"So be it!" Aldous shouted as he threw up his hands in frustration.

"At least I tried to help. What did the Wizard's Council do in the face of these problems? What are you doing *now*?"

Zequim cleared his throat. "We are taking measures-"

"Oooo 'taking measures'! I've heard that one before!" Aldous interrupted.

"Know your place, you worm! No one speaks that way to our esteemed leader!" Axar said as he started toward him. Zequim held a hand out and stopped him by his chest.

"I think that we all need to calm ourselves," he said in a soothing tone. "Aldous, we are not here to spy or do anything other than make sure your trip is leisure and not business."

"As I said, I am visiting a friend," Aldous replied.

"And I'll believe you," Zequim said with a knowing smile. "But please, don't do anything rash. For your own safety, and the safety of the monoliths, let the assigned Wizards do their job. They're trained for this sort of thing."

"So was I…"

Zequim put a hand on his shoulder. "I understand your frustration with the Council right now. But certain processes must be followed. I'm working on it."

"I've heard that one before, too," Aldous said, a wave of exhaustion overcoming him. Talking to other Wizards was often not so different from speaking with a stone wall.

"We'll talk again when your probation ends," Zequim said as he raised a bent arm and made a fist. Axar nodded and then turned while gesturing with an outstretched hand. A portal appeared before him, and it blended in with the shadows of the alley so well that Aldous could only see it thanks to the swirling dust and trash that had been caught up in it.

"And when might that be?" the old Wizard asked as Zequim turned and walked toward the portal.

"Soon!" he said while looking over his shoulder and smiling.

After Zequim had passed through the gateway, Axar stayed behind and sharpened his eyes at Aldous.

"Stay out of trouble," he said with venom on his tongue. "We don't have time to watch over you like a reckless child."

Aldous crossed his arms, but otherwise, he remained quiet and still. After a few tense moments of staring at each other, Axar shrugged and walked into the portal. It closed soon after, and Aldous felt a wave of relief sweep over him.

"Bunch'a busybodies, they are…" Aldous muttered as he shook his head and began walking back to the pub.

∼

The rest of the night went on without incident, and Lucia met up with the two ship captains. They agreed to take them to their destinations and even allowed them to sleep on their ships for the night, as both were set to depart early the next morning. Dalton in particular was impressed with how much sway his student had over the Lunerians. She had to have been one of the top mercenaries to be recognized and respected by complete strangers. Just for that, he bought several more rounds of drinks for everyone to enjoy in celebration of her achievements.

The group said their goodbyes and finalized plans to meet up at Endoshire in two months' time. It was all happening so fast from Joel's perspective. One moment it felt like all was returning to normal, and then the next he and Aldous were rushing to a far-off land; aiming to stop another seal from being destroyed. It was sure to put their lives in danger, just as Mt. Couture's trials had, but at least he would get to meet up with Alistair once more, he thought.

CHAPTER 5
CONSPIRING MINDS

At midday, a majestic ship that flew the Federland flag carved through the calm waves of the sea. It was about halfway through its journey to Endoshire, Sigraveld, and it carried with it precious cargo: Mining Guild president and recent Village Elder appointee Drake Danvers.

He sat in his cabin at a sturdy desk, sipping wine while flanked by his assistants, Hector and Ned. Drake was as well-dressed and groomed as ever, sporting slicked-back blond hair and a flower-patterned tunic made of the finest fabrics that only the rich could afford. While swirling his wine in the fancy glass, a commotion out on the deck distracted him, causing a few drops to spill.

His sharp, green eyes shifted to Hector and Ned, who were already looking to him for orders. Both were burly men with brown hair and eyes. During the Mt. Couture expedition, they had both donned long, messy hair and scruffy beards, but since becoming his assistants, Drake had ensured that they were well-kept and shaven at all times. Both wore red, baggy uniforms that were ideal for concealing weapons.

"Check on it," said Drake. The pair nodded and exited the cabin.

However, the chatter and commotion continued. After some time, Drake grimaced. He placed his glass on the desk that swayed up and down gently with the ship and then went to investigate for himself.

"S-stay back, sir! For yer safety!" one of the crew members cried to him as he exited the cabin.

A crowd had gathered at the deck's center and the men grew louder and more panicked with each passing moment. He ignored the warning and continued ahead, brushing past several of his men. Eventually, the crowd picked up on who was coming through and parted to let the Village Elder pass.

Finally, he came upon the culprit that had riled his men up: Before them was a snake with human body parts. Muscular arms sprouted from its slithering, serpent body, but more striking was its mouth; which had two rows of straight, rectangular teeth. As it grinned at them all with malice, a couple of fangs from the top row of teeth became apparent, and they were dripping with poison.

Drake scoffed and then said, "A tad overly theatrical, wouldn't you say?"

The snake glared at him, and the crowd suddenly fell to silence.

"I do prefer to entertain myself…" the snake hissed. Many gasps came from the crew. Drake's assistants snuck up from behind the snake and drew their daggers. They looked to the Village Elder intently, as if waiting for his command to strike.

He shook his head while waving them off. "Those weapons wouldn't do you any good."

The assistants watched on with mouths agape as the snake transformed into a large man wearing a dark cloak and robe with odd symbols on it. He turned and locked eyes with Hector. His dagger bobbed, not from the motions of the sea, but from all of his trembling.

"Put that toy away, boy," he said with great depth and bass. Hector shuddered and looked to Drake once more, who nodded in reply. The assistants withdrew their weapons.

"Nothing to worry about, gentlemen!" Drake called out to the crew with as much cheer as he could muster. "This is a friend of mine; a Wizard. He has a strange sense of humor, as you can see."

The worry of the crowd immediately dispersed, and the crew went back to their business.

"That's Mr. Danvers for ye…" one of the crewmen muttered.

"How does he have so many connections?" asked another.

"I thought Wizards used sleight of hand ta play tricks, but that looked real ta me!"

"Why would a Wizard play such a nasty trick, anyhow?"

Drake smirked at the buzzing of the simpletons as he led the cloaked man to his cabin and held the door open. He motioned back to his assistants, who had followed him like well-trained dogs.

"Leave us." They nodded and departed for the bow of the ship.

After closing the door behind him, Drake's demeanor fell to freezing temperatures, and he crossed his arms while holding his chin high: a regal, if demanding posture.

"Could you not have appeared *in here*?" he asked while eyeing the symbol on his wrist. It resembled a skull.

"It isn't easy to pinpoint a ship's location in the middle of the sea and summon myself there; even with that mark on your wrist," the Dark Wizard replied. "You seem good at explaining things away, so what does it matter?" He cracked a smile, which was barely visible under the hood of his cloak.

"Fair enough. Can I offer you a drink?" Drake asked as he walked around him and sat back in his chair.

"I only accept *celebratory drinks*. What have we accomplished, lately?"

"Have patience, my friend."

"I don't see why I couldn't have summoned us to Endoshire. Why make this long trip?" the Dark Wizard asked.

"Because I'm on a 'diplomatic mission' to Sigraveld," Drake said with a chuckle, followed by a sip of his wine. "We need to keep up appearances for now, while they still suspect nothing."

"Don't forget, there are some who *do* suspect."

"*Them?* Inconsequential. No one believes them. Not even the Wizard's Council, from what you have told me," Drake replied with a confident smile.

"I received word that their little group left Faiwell nine days ago. They may be coming to stop us," the Dark Wizard said.

"Ah, so that wily old man Aldous took the bait. What a fool…" Drake said with a grin. "That brings us to the matter of *taking care of them*, then."

"A risky strategy…"

"I *live* for the risk!" the Village Elder said, raising his glass in a grand gesture. "If we take those rats out now, no one will stand in our way. With the black gold on our side, we can't lose. Besides, you've had opportunities to kill that Mercer boy and let him live. I am not the only one taking risks."

"I have something special planned for him in Bosfueras," the Dark Wizard said with a deep chuckle. "I take it you've brought up the black gold for a reason?"

"Yes, I think it is time we imbue my assistants with the *dark essence*, wouldn't you say?" Drake asked.

"If I do that, you'll be without them for a couple of weeks. Don't forget that I lack the power or sacrifice to summon even small pieces of the Dark Savior, for the moment. Your men will have to travel from Gentorgul to Sigraveld on their own."

"Yes, yes, that's fine. Once we succeed, I'm sure summoning will no longer be an issue. For now, we'll have to deal with it," Drake said as he took another sip of wine. "That reminds me, how are the other subjects fairing?"

"Although the first few tests gave… less than desirable results, I have found uses for them. The team that you handpicked, on the other hand, turned out perfectly: All are now endowed with their own abilities that have brought them beyond the limitations of their humanity. I think you will be impressed with our top candidate to lead the team. He has gone beyond the threshold of a mere man. I daresay he could challenge nearly any Warlock or Witch and come out victorious," the Dark Wizard replied.

"Excellent. It seems the big fellow will be of some use, after all. With his prowess, the Famine monolith is as good as destroyed," Drake said as he swirled his wine in the glass.

"He and his partner are ready. Shall I send them?"

"Yes, the time has come. They have their instructions, so let's give the order."

The Dark Wizard let out a low-pitched chuckle and turned to leave.

"Oh, and be sure to pump Hector and Ned with as much dark essence as they can handle. I'll need my assistants to be strong and ready for future conflicts," Drake added.

"Naturally," the cloaked man said without turning around. However, upon reaching the door, he stopped and looked over his shoulder. "Although I do wonder… are you sure you don't wish to receive the power for yourself?"

"Don't be silly. We both know there is an *inordinate power* to be had elsewhere," Drake said as he emptied the last of the wine into his mouth. "I'll be seeing you soon."

The Dark Wizard opened the door and exited the cabin. Soon after, Drake heard the harsh, windy sounds of his portal. He had taken Hector and Ned to be *enhanced*.

The Village Elder leaned back in his chair, smiling smugly. All was coming together perfectly thanks to his strategies. Like an unsuspecting boat on a calm sea, about to be swept up by a sudden storm, the world was soon to go through radical changes; all according to the design of conspiring minds.

CHAPTER 6
MANY ALISTAIRS

The shrieks of a woman and the violent gurgling of blood awoke Joel with a start. Near-breathless, he surveyed the area but found no one save Aldous sitting across from him at the modest campfire. He hadn't even reacted to his startled awakening; though at this point, it was becoming the norm. Nightmares and disturbances had dominated Joel's nights for the past year.

He and the old Wizard were off the beaten path and behind a grassy hill. Nightfall had brought upon them an eerie quiet. Not even crickets had come out to sing, as they tended to back home. As predicted, the voyage to Currencolt had taken about a month. Joel had enjoyed the trip at first; often helping crew members and observing creatures of the sea that had come up for air as they sailed along. Yet, by about the halfway point of the trip, Aldous' dire demeanor had him itching to reach Mithika as soon as possible. He had never seen him in such a state of despair before.

However, after arriving at the rocky shores of Garradh-Shoit and checking in with the proper authorities to state their business, Aldous had taken his sweet time while at the local stable. For as painstakingly long as it had taken him to choose horses, it had taken him doubly as long to choose a carriage. The only reason they'd been able to afford such luxuries was thanks to Dalton: He had gifted them half of the gold he'd taken for the trip before separating in Port City.

The mute narrowed eyes at his Wizard cohort. If he hadn't been so picky, they could have made it considerably further by nightfall, he thought. Thus far, it felt like they hadn't gotten anywhere; although in reality, they had passed through a couple of settlements. All were spacious, with a focus on farms that differed greatly from the ones back at home. Most seemed to harbor sheep, goats, and tall grass exclusively. Joel wondered if Alistair spent most of his days herding sheep. The thought of him screaming at the little wooly creatures to keep them in line got him chuckling.

"They were followin' us, y'know," Aldous said, snapping him back to reality. The mute cocked his head. "The Wizard's Council, I mean."

Joel made hand signals in return.

"They wanted to ensure that I won't interfere in other monolith operations," the old Wizard said with a sigh.

More signals were sent by the mute.

"Did I show them the letter-majigger? No, I couldn't keep it. Otherwise, Drake would have become suspicious. Besides, they wouldn't trust me, anyway. Bein' on probation n' such."

Joel sulked. At the rate things were going…

"I'll probably be excommunicated soon," Aldous said, as if reading his mind.

More sign language was exchanged between them.

"Ah, a good point. If we prove that I was right, and we are successful in defending the monolith, then maybe they'll give us a much-deserved reward…" Aldous trailed off and then leaned in. "Between you an' me, I'd take the permanent removal of Axar from the Council as a reward." The two of them laughed.

Joel remembered Axar from his brief time meeting up with the Council leaders. Even back then, it had been obvious that he and Aldous were at odds. Axar put forth an aggressive disposition, but always seemed to be against taking action. The more Joel thought of it, the more it seemed a contradiction.

"I know that your nights have been restless, but you really should try to get back to sleep, m'boy! I'd say we still have another day or so to go before reaching Ghobmor."

∽

AT THE DAWN of their third day traveling, the duo arrived at the top of a hill that overlooked Ghobmor. It was the largest town they had found in Currencolt yet, but it looked similar to the other settlements they'd passed: There were many farms; all filled to the brim with sheep and goats. Some stone towers were mixed in here and there, but most common were sturdy houses painted in washed-out white or red.

They had seen very few Curren natives on their trip thus far, but, from their vantage point high up on the hill, Ghobmor showed the most activity of any town they'd passed through. It excited them so much that they stopped next to the first person they came across.

"Excuse me, sir," Aldous said to a big, brown-haired man hauling a bale of hay across the dirt road. He turned and looked at the pair with a scowl, eliciting a couple of wide-eyed expressions from them. "Er… would you happen to know Alistair?"

The big man raised an eyebrow before dropping the hay. "Yer gonna have'ta be more specific than that. There are many Alistairs 'round here!" His scowl turned to a smile, and then he let out a big laugh.

Joel and Aldous looked at each other, both flabbergasted.

"There's Alistair Catan, Alistair Lathurna, Alistair Greum, Alistair MacAnndra, Alistair O'Cain-"

As the big fellow continued to speak, Aldous leaned next to Joel's ear and whispered, "There must be something we can tell him about *our* Alistair that wouldn't apply to the others…"

Joel looked up in thought for a moment and then smiled. He made hand signals in return.

"Alistair Sgot, Alistair Druiminn, Alistair-"

"Our Alistair is a large feller, with red hair and a big noggin," Aldous said.

The big man cocked his head, as if contemplating, and then he laughed in his face. Spit spewed from his mouth as his heavy cackles seemed to shake the carriage and horses alike. Joel narrowed his eyes, but the smile on Aldous' face did not waver.

"You'll have ta be more specific than that! Nearly all of the men look like that 'round here!" he said between laughs that tapered off into chuckles.

Aldous turned his gaze to Joel once more. He already had another idea, and signed some more to the old Wizard.

"What's that yer doin' with yer hands, lad?" the big man asked.

"Oh, well-"

"Are ya too good ta talk with me? So, yer just gonna talk to him? That's rude, ya know!"

"No, no, my friend here is a mute. Y'see, it's the only way he can communicate," Aldous explained.

"Oooo, I see. Sorry fer the misunderstandin', lad! I can be a bit hard-headed at the worst o' times!" He laughed and then slapped the top of the carriage, rattling it to its very core.

Joel laughed along with him. It wasn't hard to see where Alistair had gotten many of his tendencies from. Aldous, meanwhile, was white as a ghost, probably from the mistreatment of his painstakingly hand-picked carriage. It looked as if his soul had departed his mortal body, and it made Joel laugh even more.

Aldous cleared his throat. "Our Alistair returned here after living in Federland for a few months."

"Oh, ya meant *that* Alistair..." the man muttered as he turned and pointed. He directed them toward a farmland in the back-left corner of town, next to a windmill. "Yer lookin' fer Alistair MacRae. He an' his family live there."

"Thank you for the help, sir," Aldous said with a nod. The big man waved and then returned to carrying the bale of hay across the road.

The pair continued down the hill and then through the flat portion of town. Perhaps for looking so different, they received some stares from the townsfolk who were out and about, but none stopped them or gave them any trouble. It seemed more like a playful curiosity. Joel imagined that Ghobmor didn't receive many visitors from outside the country, and the thought amused him. He figured it had something to do with why Alistair hadn't adapted quickly to Faiwell's customs.

After leaving their horses and carriage at a stable and walking to the back end of town, the pair found themselves around the windmill and up a long dirt path toward a farm. There were big, wooden fences on each side of the trail, both housing farmland that was being attended to by men off in the distance.

The MacRae house was a faded white like many of the others, but the biggest they'd seen thus far; so big that it was almost intimidating. At three stories tall and nearly twice as wide, Joel was impressed. Sure, he'd seen larger buildings before, but those had been the efforts of dozens, if not hundreds; while this one had probably been built by Alistair's family alone. He was certain that it had taken a valiant effort from burly men. They walked onto a porch, which was adorned with a few rocking chairs and tables, and approached the front door. Aldous looked back at Joel and nodded his head toward the entrance.

The mute timidly knocked on the door. There was no response. Joel tried knocking again; this time with more power behind it. Even still, no one came. Joel stroked his chin while searching his mind for a solution. Should they go out to the men working the farmland? *No,* he thought as the memories came flooding back to him: So many funny moments had come about from Alistair's lack of volume control and difficulties with hearing on the Mt. Couture expedition. Perhaps his family was the same and only reacted to similarly loud noises.

With that in mind, he pounded on the door at full force, and even the sturdy foundation of the MacRae home seemed to shake a bit. Aldous flinched with each knock. He brought a hand to Joel's shoulder, and the mute finally stopped.

Suddenly, the door flung open, and before them stood a big redhead, but not Alistair. He was a little shorter, sported mutton chops along his strong jawline, and had mid-length hair. His head was also normal-sized, and it threw Joel off. He had expected the thumb-like proportions of Alistair's head from all of his family members. He wore typical farmer's clothes: brown, baggy pants that were held up by suspenders, bulging in and out with each angry breath that he took; and a tight white shirt that had been dirtied.

"WHAT DO YA WANT?" he shouted. The pair looked at each other with mouths agape. "It's rude ta go bangin' away on people's doors like that! I heard ya the first time, ya know!"

Aldous smiled. "We're sorr-"

"But no, ya think yer more important than anythin' else I've got goin' on, don't ya? Ya look like a couple o' high an' mighty jerks from Sigraveld. Fancy-schmancy knobs from the big city! Ya think yer *so* important! But I gots news fer ya! There are other people ta consider besides yerselves!" the big man shouted. Spit had practically drenched Joel and Aldous during the tirade.

"Well, actually-"

"So? Go on, then! What is it that was so important?"

"You see-"

"I'm waitin'!" he interrupted.

"If you would just let me speak-"

"On second thought, I don' care what ya have'ta say!" The big man let out an obnoxious laugh. "You were rude ta me, so I don't gots ta be nice to ya!"

Joel and Aldous frowned at one another.

"We're friends of Alistair," the old Wizard said in an annoyed tone.

The big man widened his eyes. "Wait, yer the friends from Federland he's been talkin' about?"

"Indeed," said Aldous.

"I thought he was makin' all o' that up!" he said and then laughed some more. His crinkled brow loosened, and now he seemed cheerful, if a tad curious. "So, the story about that terrible mountain ya had ta mine in…"

"It's all true," Aldous said with a nod. Joel shot a surprised glance at his Wizard cohort. Even if this man was related to Alistair, he was still a stranger to them. Why was he being so lax?

"This is excitin'!" The big man clenched his fists. "Then, you must be tha Wizard Aldous, eh?" Aldous nodded, a proud smile spreading across his face. "An' I suppose that makes you the quiet fella, Joel?" he continued. Joel also nodded along.

"The name's Triston! I'm Alistair's big brother," he said. Joel extended his hand for a shake but gasped as Triston gathered both he and Aldous up in his bear-like arms and hugged them while lifting them off their feet. "Oh no lads, no handshakes fer you! Ali told me about how you all saved 'im and kept 'im outta death's grasp! Fer that, yer family, now! An honorary MacRae!"

Aldous and Joel looked at each other and did their best to smile as Triston squeezed the air from their lungs. After what felt like an eternity to their comparatively small bodies, he let them down. His smile was as big as ever.

"Come on in! I'll go an' fetch Alistair for ya. He's workin' out on the fields," Triston said as he turned and led them into the house.

Joel looked on in wonder as they walked through the MacRae home. While not particularly clean, it was the biggest house he'd ever been in. The ceilings were higher than he was used to seeing, as were the hallways wider, giving it a grand feel; almost like being in the Miner's Guild Headquarters or the Hall of Elders back home, except built entirely of wood. The scale of the house made sense for a family that he had to assume were a bunch of giants.

Eventually, they reached what looked to be a dining room. There was a great wooden table at its center with large, spacious chairs along each side and at the ends of the table. The scale of the room and furniture did not surprise Joel in the slightest. Alistair had told him how huge his family was, and the dining room looked as if it could seat *at least* a dozen, if not more.

"Have a seat!" Triston said cheerfully, pulling out a couple of chairs. "I'll go get 'im, now."

The pair sat as he exited the room and shortly after, they heard a door slam. Joel and Aldous chatted for a bit, until hearing the back door fly open and shortly after, heavy, fast-paced thuds against groaning wood.

Into the dining room charged Alistair, whose round face was alight with joy. He was just as much a titan of a man as Joel remembered, and that red hair of his was as curly as ever. He did, however, notice that he was starting to grow some stubble on his face. He wore the same farmer's clothes as his elder brother.

"I-I don' believe me eyes! Yer here!" Alistair shouted. He ran over to Joel and gave him a spine-crushing hug that made Triston's seem like a gentle breeze in comparison. The mute gasped for breath as Aldous looked on, chuckling.

Alistair then turned to face the old Wizard.

"Don' think yer missin' out on a hug, mista Wizard!"

Aldous put his hands up in protest, but there was no avoiding it; Alistair squeezed the life out of him too, and Joel let out snorting laughs as he watched on.

"I was hopin' you'd come an' visit soon-" Alistair paused and then looked around the dining room. "Hold up. Where are the others?"

Joel started to make hand signals, but Aldous spoke over him.

"They had to make a stop in Gentorgul, first; but don't worry. Soon, they will meet up with us."

"Oh... why tha hell would they wanna go thar? Such an unfriendly place, Gentorgul! Not like here! We treat everyone like family in Currencolt!" the big man said.

"'Cept them jerks from Sigraveld!" a voice called from behind. It was Triston.

Alistair rolled his eyes. "Er... right."

"Do you hate Sigraveld because they have encroached on your land?" Aldous asked as he turned to face the elder MacRae in the doorway.

Triston's face turned sour. "Yer damn right! Our king is a gutless coward fer lettin' 'em in!"

Joel made hand signals to Aldous in search of clarification.

"Y'see, Currencolt was struggling for a wee bit, and Sigraveld swooped right in and started taking the land. Instead of fighting, the king gave in. Officially, it was billed as Sigraveld 'helping out a country in need', but off the record, they control this place. Currencolt is now one of their satellite states," he said.

"Right, and they've been ruinin' our lovely land, slowly but surely, with all that trash they're buildin' up north. It'll only be a matter a' time before they come down here an'-"

"They'll take this land over me dead body!" a husky voice called out from behind Joel.

Everyone turned to see a redheaded woman so wide that she nearly filled the doorway. She wore an old red dress and just as red was her face, which held a scowl that sent shivers through Joel's spine. It was easy to see where Alistair got his looks.

Alistair smiled and then stood from his chair. "Ah! Mum, these are my friends-"

"I know who they are," she said in a scornful tone.

"What's the problem?" Triston asked, crossing his arms.

"They're here to stir up trouble fer me baby boy! I can tell!" she bellowed back.

"Nonsense! Alistair told us of his adventures with them, and they saved his life on many occasions!" Triston said.

"I saved 'em sometimes, too…" Alistair muttered, but his voice was drowned out by the other two.

"All I'm sayin' is ya should give 'em a warm welcome, mum!" the elder MacRae argued. Alistair looked down while shifting in his chair. Joel's cheeks flared out as he did all in his power to stave off laughter. He reminded him of a young boy, embarrassed by his parents fighting in front of guests.

His mother's gaze shifted to Aldous, and she grimaced at him. "Yer the Wizard he told us so much about, ain't ya?"

"Well, I'm on probation n' such, but yes…" Aldous replied.

"Ya see? He's tryin' ta take my lil' Ali off on another dangerous adventure! That's what Wizards do!" she shouted while pointing at him.

"Don't be ridiculous, mah!" Triston shot back, putting hands to hips. "They came fer a visit and nothin' more! We should throw 'em a big ole' MacRae feast and show 'em a good time!"

"Well, actually…" Aldous muttered. Suddenly, the dining room fell silent and all eyes were fixed on him. "Erm… we *were* going to see if Alistair wished to accompany us on a journey."

"OUTTA THE QUESTION!" said Alistair's mom.

"ABSOLUTELY NOT!" cried Triston.

"SIGN ME UP!" bellowed Alistair. His mom and brother were staring a hole through him, now. "What? It's about time I did somethin' a lil' more than herd sheep on tha farm!"

"It's too dangerous! This is where you belong!" she replied. Alistair looked over to his brother with puppy-dog eyes.

"Sorry brother, but she's right. Dangerous adventures an' the battlefield are no place fer you. Yer best off here, takin' care of the farm. Ya don' have the right instincts. Take it from me, I've seen me share of battle. You were fortunate to have skilled warriors and a Wizard on yer side, last time. This time… yer luck may run out!" Triston said.

"With all due respect," Aldous interjected. "I think you are both underestimating Alistair. We wouldn't ask him to come along if he was not up to the task. He may need some more work in combat, but his fighting spirit is among the best I've seen."

The room remained uncharacteristically quiet for a moment. Alistair smiled at the old Wizard, and it almost looked like he had a tear in his eye. Joel gave him a nod to show that he agreed.

"I know my brother," Triston said, shaking his head. "And I tells ya, we can't keep puttin' 'im in danger!"

"Says you! Just let me go! What do you care?" Alistair asked.

"I know ya don' wanna hear this, but someone's gotta say it. Battlin' an' adventurin' just ain't yer specialty. Even you have to admit that yer friends saved yer hide time and again because ya don' have the street smarts or the battle instincts," Triston replied in a somber tone. "So yeh, ya should stay here an' herd sheep. It's fer yer own good!"

"But I can-"

"Ya ain't goin' nowhere, an' that's the end of it!" his mom said.

Alistair slumped over and wore a child-like frown.

"Fair enough," Aldous said, outstretching and bobbing his hand. "We won't forcibly take him anywhere, after all. Consider this little more than a friendly visit!"

***

Throughout the day, Alistair and Triston gave Joel and Aldous a tour of the MacRae farm while also introducing their siblings. Working out on the fields were their brothers, Rory and Owen: Two burly men who didn't share the redheaded traits of the others.

"They take after me dearly departed papi," Alistair explained.

Herding the goats and sheep were their other brothers, Adair and Donald. They looked a bit more like Alistair and Triston, although they were shorter and stouter. Normally, Alistair would have been helping them herd, but since his friends had arrived, he'd been given a rare day off.

Over the years, the farm had changed slowly but surely in its approach. They wished to focus more on livestock and selling food. After the Sigraveld takeover, it was becoming a more precious commodity. Three of the siblings worked exclusively with the animals that were to be slaughtered and sold for food: Brien, Arthur, and the youngest of the MacRaes, Lina.

As Aldous was chatting with Lina about how baby chickens were raised, Alistair leaned in, next to Joel.

"I know what yer thinkin'," he said. Joel raised an eyebrow. It sounded like he was trying to whisper, but it had come out at normal volume. *Same old Alistair*, he thought with a smile. "Yer thinkin' she's cute, ain't ya? I'd be honored if ya took me lil' sister's hand in marriage one day."

Joel had to arch his neck all the way up just to look Lina in the eyes. She was nearly as tall as Alistair, although slender; almost to the point of being dainty. In many ways, she was the opposite of her brothers, save the red hair and height. They would have made a funny couple, he thought. The mute shook his head and then sent hand signals.

"Ah, right! I fergot about that mystery gal of yers…" Alistair trailed off. Joel nodded and his smile grew twice as large. The big man had learned the basics of Universal Sign Language while living with him and Aldous, but it seemed like he had perfected his understanding of it since returning home.

"I suppose there's only one more sibling to introduce you to…" Triston muttered, his face and tone reflecting dread. *"Gwen."*

Alistair gulped.

"Something wrong?" Aldous asked.

"Nothin', it's just… my big sister can be a *wee bit* difficult ta handle," Alistair said.

"But I'm sure she'll be no problem for a Wizard!" Triston added.

Alistair's expression said otherwise. As they reentered the house and walked up a long and wide set of stairs to the second floor, Joel let his imagination take over. He pictured a giant of a woman with an angry temperament, like Alistair's mom. But if they *feared her*, she must have been even scarier than that.

Triston knocked on the door so gently that it almost sounded like the scurrying of a mouse.

"Who is it?" a delicate voice called back.

"It's yer brother. Come out an' say hello to Ali's friends," he said calmly. Joel had never heard Triston at such an even temperament in his short time knowing him.

The door opened, and before them appeared a petite woman with long brown hair and a lovely blue dress. She was the only one save for their mother to not wear typical farming clothes. She did, however, wear a demanding look on her face: not outwardly angry like her mother's expression, but a curious one.

"You're my little brother's friends? The ones who kept his sorry arse alive on that mining expedition?" she asked. Alistair sneered and opened his mouth, but Triston held up a hand. The big man let out a sigh. "I thank you for gettin' him back safely. Even if he is dimwitted and reckless, he is still my brother, and I love him."

"Erm… you're welcome…" Aldous muttered, the awkwardness shining through in his words.

"Let me guess: You're the Wizard he couldn't stop talking about," she said.

"Well, I'm on probation, y'see-"

"Skip the pleasantries and show me somethin' magical," Gwen demanded as she placed hands to hips.

Aldous looked back at the others. Alistair and Triston smiled and nodded with palpable excitement.

"Alright, how about *this*?" said the old Wizard as he pointed a finger at her. From her body came a small current of lightning that gathered into the palm of his hand in the form of a ball.

"Whoaaaa! Is that lightnin'?" Triston asked.

"Indeed, it is. And from *her body*, no less." Aldous nudged his head in Gwen's direction while smiling. "Y'see, I discovered that we all have little bits of lightning n' such stored in our bodies-"

"Big deal!" Gwen interrupted.

"Beg your pardon?"

"I said, '*Big deal.*'" Gwen rubbed a hand rapidly on her dress before walking up to Aldous and poking his shoulder. He recoiled back at the static shock, and the ball of electricity dispersed. "See? I can do that, too."

Aldous snorted. "Well, if I had some water-"

"Ya need water to do magic tricks? How sad!" Gwen replied before flipping her hair back and scoffing.

"If I could just-"

"Next!" she said with impatience on her tongue while turning to the mute. She crossed her arms and inspected him up and down. "You must be Joel." A sly smile grew on her lightly freckled face.

He took in a gulp and then nodded.

"Not one for talkin', eh Joel?" she asked. He shook his head in response. "Is it because you can't, or because you have nothin' useful to say?"

Alistair frowned at the question, but he remained silent. Joel, on the other hand, had heard much worse before, and he signed back to her, undeterred.

"What did he say?" she asked, looking back at the group for clarification.

"Erm…" Alistair trailed off. He looked over at Aldous, who returned an encouraging nod. "He says that he is unable to speak, but has plenty to say."

"Ah, so you learned how to communicate with him, Ali? That makes you seem cultured. I like that," she said with a smile. "The two of you make an odd pair, though. A quiet, small boy with a bigmouthed giant like yourself?"

"What're ya talkin' about?" Triston asked. "Alistair's the *quiet one* in our family!" He let out a hearty chuckle.

"True, but outside of our family, he's a loudmouth," Gwen replied before turning back to Joel. "Anyhow, it was nice to meet you, Joel. You impressed me more than the so-called 'Wizard'." She turned to leave. Aldous' face turned red, but he kept quiet.

Gwen returned to her room and shut the door. The four men let out a great sigh of relief.

"Your sister is certainly… unafraid to speak her mind!" Aldous said as they walked downstairs.

"Gwen is tha troublemaker of our family. She may be small, but she's got a sharp mind. Unfortunately, she doesn't use it fer much good!" Alistair said with a laugh.

"She's always scheming and gettin' away with things. We learned over the years not to cross her. She *never* gets caught. Never," Triston added. The brothers looked at each other and laughed some more.

Aldous stroked his beard as they reached the first floor. Joel knew that he was up to something.

That night, the family gathered and cooked a great feast in honor of Alistair and his friends. There was much drinking, eating, and noise that filled the entire house. Throughout the commotion, Joel noticed that Aldous had sat next to Gwen, and they chatted quietly as the others cheered, ate, and drank loudly. Even the mute joined in on the fun as he, Alistair, and a couple of the MacRae brothers jumped up on the grand table and danced to music played by Triston.

As the night began to quiet down, Aldous cleared his throat and stood.

"I wanted to thank you all for the wonderful dinner and entertainment. I wish we could stay longer, but I'm afraid we must depart tomorrow morning," he said with a smile.

"Aw, but ya just got here!" Alistair sobbed, his words slurring and his cheeks rosy.

Joel made hand signals to let him know they would stop by on their way back.

"Not good 'nuff lad, not good 'nuff…"

As Joel and Aldous lay in Alistair's room on nap sacks and the night wound down, the big redhead continued to complain aloud from up on his bed.

"It ain't fair! No one ever gives me a chance ta prove me'self 'round here!"

"Relax…" Aldous whispered. "You are coming along with us."

Alistair gasped. "Ya figured somethin' out?"

"Yes. When the time is right tomorrow, be sure to listen to your elder sister n' such," Aldous said.

"Aye…" Alistair trailed off. It seemed as if he were dozing off, but then he sat back up in shock. "Wait, how tha hell did ya get 'er ta go along with it?"

"Erm… let Joel and I worry about that…" the old Wizard muttered, rubbing the back of his head.

Uh-oh, Joel thought. He turned over and looked at Aldous, who avoided eye contact. He made hand signals to ask what he'd gotten him into.

"Well… er… y'see… his sister appears to be infatuated with you…"

Aldous trailed off. The mute cocked his head. "I don't know why, but she is. I *may* have promised that you would give her a kiss in exchange for her help."

Joel's eyes widened and then he shook his head emphatically. He signed faster than usual to the old Wizard with a crinkled brow.

"Yes, yes, I know you have someone already. But she isn't around, and we want Alistair on this trip, don't we?" Aldous said, putting his hands up in defense.

"Now that you've told her somethin', ya best be keepin' yer promises to Gwen, lads," Alistair added. "Trust me, ya don' wanna cross her. Besides, if she really is gonna help, I can get outta here fer sure!"

Joel crossed his arms and rolled over.

"Oh, don't be sour, now. We must all pitch in and make sacrifices on this journey," Aldous said. Joel didn't bother to respond.

"Speakin' of tha journey, where are we goin'? What's all o' this about, anyway?" Alistair asked.

"I'll keep this short and explain more to you while we travel. I want to get some sleep, after all, and I could be up all night telling you every detail," he replied with a chuckle. "Remember how Greed had a monolith sealing him within Mt. Couture?"

"How could I ferget?"

"There are six more monoliths sealing the split identities of Stalmoz away, and we know that two more are in danger of being broken: One in Thironas, Mithika; and one in Endoshire, Sigraveld."

"ENDOSHIRE?" Alistair asked aloud. Both Aldous and Joel angrily shushed him. "Oh, right… sorry, lads…"

∼

OUTSIDE OF ALISTAIR'S bedroom and propped up against the wall was Triston, trying to listen in on their quiet conversation.

"Endoshire, eh?" he whispered to himself.

Obviously, they were up to something, but having heard that *Gwen* was involved, he didn't want to cross her. Instead, he would intercept them before they could reach Endoshire, or ideally, before leaving Currencolt. After all, it was Triston's duty to protect his little brother.

∼

The next morning, all seemed normal. The big family had breakfast, Joel and Aldous said their goodbyes; vowing to return soon, and then everyone got to work. Alistair waited for what felt like an eternity to be approached by Gwen, wondering what her plan would be.

Meanwhile, Joel and Aldous would be waiting at the horse stable in their carriage. They were all packed up and ready to go, and had even smuggled out most of Alistair's belongings, so he wouldn't raise suspicion when sneaking away.

By lunchtime, Gwen finally approached her brother while he was eating alone at the grand dining room table.

"The time is now," she whispered into his ear. "Are you sure about this? Mum is being over-protective for sure, but Triston? He tends to be right about these sorts of things."

Alistair nodded and then stood. He turned and looked at his sister, who was well-dressed, even more so than usual. No wonder it had taken so long for her to approach him, he thought. She had applied makeup, and her long, brown hair was braided; pristine.

"Is my departure such an occasion?" he asked and then laughed. The big man almost slapped her on the shoulder but he stopped himself. That would be asking for trouble, he thought.

"Consider it a backup plan."

Quickly and quietly, the two snuck through the house. True to form, the entire family seemed to be obstacles in the way. With each room passed through, Gwen told Alistair to walk ahead of her and then to wait. After a long enough interval to avoid suspicion, she passed through. The final room was the hall leading to the front door, where their mother stood, blocking the exit.

"Let me do the talking…" Gwen muttered.

Their mother crossed her arms as they approached, and said, "Where do ya think yer goin'?"

"Oh, hi mum," Gwen said nonchalantly. "I've got a date this afternoon with that man from up the road. You remember Nigel, don't you?"

"Oooo, so that's why yer all gussied up!" she said and then clapped her hands together. "Am I finally gonna get grandchildren out of ya?"

"We can only hope!" she replied with forced excitement while walking past her. As she opened the door, Alistair attempted to follow, but his mom blocked him.

"And where are *you* goin'?" she asked, putting hands to hips.

"Uhhhh…"

"He's walkin' me over to Nigel's house. To show that we are serious. Nothin' like the biggest of the MacRaes to make him start takin' the idea of marriage seriously!" Gwen explained.

Their mother remained quiet for a moment and then suddenly seemed to be overcome with joy. "My wonderful children are so sweet ta one another! I knew I raised ya right, Ali!" she cried while pinching his cheek.

Alistair flinched and groaned. "Mahhh…"

"C'mon Ali, we need to move along, or I'll be late!" Gwen squeaked with so much cheer that it was obviously forced. It took all of Alistair's willpower not to laugh.

The pair exited the house and then strolled down the long dirt path, along the farmland.

"Not bad, sister!" Alistair said.

"Don't expect me to be that nice from now on," she replied.

Although she could be quite mean to him at times, he got the feeling that when it truly came down to it, Gwen would do anything for him. He smiled down at her as they walked.

"So, ya really wanna kiss Joel?"

"That's right."

"Ya know he has a girl-"

"Don't care," Gwen interrupted.

"Ya know yer about a dozen years older than 'im too, right?" Alistair asked.

"Still don't care," she said, then rolled her eyes as they made their way around the windmill. "I want a kiss from him, and it better be a good one… or I'll tell mum that you forced me to help you."

"Why you-" He held his tongue. Perhaps Gwen wasn't going soft, after all. She held all of the power in their present situation. If she told their mother before he could gain any distance, Triston and the other brothers would hunt him down and bring him home. They were like hound dogs, most of them.

Soon, they arrived at the horse stable, where Joel and Aldous were waiting in the carriage. Alistair felt the excitement build up in his chest. It had only been a year, and yet it felt like a lifetime since he last got to adventure with his friends; people who appreciated and respected him. There wasn't much of that to go around at the MacRae farm.

∼

Joel and Aldous hopped out of the carriage to greet the MacRae duo.

"I held up my end of the bargain. Now, about my *payment*," Gwen said as she eyed Joel and shot him a sly smile.

Alistair leaned in and tried to whisper, "Sorry lad, ya gots ta take one fer the team," but it came out at regular volume, and Gwen smashed her fist into his ribcage, stunning the big man.

Aldous patted Joel on the back. "I'm sorry to have put you in this situation, m'boy. It was the only way."

Joel eyed his Wizard cohort, but he made no attempt to reply. His frustration with him was mounting, now. The lack of communication or clarity in his plans could be chalked up to him being a Wizard. It was the Wizardly way to keep secrets, after all. Yet, he had no problem disclosing valuable information to Alistair's family members, like Triston. And now, he had put Joel in this situation without his permission. If he was acting this way about a mere kiss, then what else was he withholding about the Famine seal in Thironas? The mute worried that Aldous' desperation had turned him reckless.

His gaze turned to Gwen. She wore beautiful makeup and the dress fit her like a glove. The thought slipped into his mind that at the very least, he'd be kissing a beautiful woman. Yet, there was a stubborn pit in his stomach that told him *no*.

Joel crossed his arms and shook his head.

"C'mon, Joel! Ya have'ta do this!" Alistair said through gritted teeth.

Gwen snickered and walked up to him. She smelled lovely; the perfume reminded him of a warm spring day, and it was almost intoxicating.

"Sticking to your principles…" she trailed off, leaning in for a kiss. Joel closed his eyes, but he was surprised to feel it land on his cheek. "I like that. You pass again, Joel."

"'He passes'?" Aldous asked, eyes wide.

"I like Joel because he is principled, and sticks to what he believes," Gwen said, crossing her arms. "If he had decided to kiss me and betray his true love, I woulda ratted you out to mum, anyway." She glared at Alistair.

The mute smiled back at her. He was glad that she understood and that there were no hard feelings.

"A Wizard who needs water to do tricks and my bigmouthed brother… I wouldn't trust 'em out on their own, but with *you*…" She pointed to Joel. "You lot may have a chance with him by your side, on whatever this big adventure is."

Aldous and Alistair groaned and grumbled to themselves as Gwen leaned in and whispered to Joel, "I meant it, though. I do like you. If you and this girl ever end your entanglement, you know where to find me… take care of my foolish little brother…"

She winked at him and then turned to leave. Joel was stunned yet again. *What a handful*, he thought. Although he felt quite a respect for her, too. She was confident and cunning in every decision, and something about her personality reminded him of royalty. Not in a snobby way, but in an 'educated' sense; she had *class*.

Most importantly, he and Alistair were finally reunited, set to go off on a grand adventure. Or so he hoped. In the back of his mind, Joel still worried about the dangers: Aldous' increasingly erratic behavior, the Guardian of the monolith that would almost surely try to kill them as the Nightcrawler had, and the possible dangers of Drake's new team couldn't be ignored. He was sure that tough times lay ahead for them.

CHAPTER 7
INFILTRATION

Conrad Mercer looked up at the dull, gray sky from the ground, his back against a tree. His heart raced and he couldn't seem to catch up with his own breath, but he'd escaped yet another Gentish mob with his life and limb intact. He felt a scar on the back of his head, under a patch of hair. At least they hadn't pelted him with rocks this time.

The strategist looked over his shoulder at a path that cut into the woods. He had finally found the trail that would take him to Bosfueras. Even if he hadn't been learning Gentish over the past three months, it'd have been an easy guess: Dozens of signs were nailed to the trees and all messages were in big, bold letters. They reminded him of the warnings that had been posted on the way to Mt. Couture.

He snorted while struggling to his aching feet. The signs hadn't deterred him then, and after the hell he'd been through while traveling across Gentorgul, they certainly wouldn't stop him now. Conrad walked over to a nearby creek, still alert and looking for potential enemies. After ensuring that no one was around, he knelt over and cupped some water in his hands, splashing it in his face.

As the water settled below, the reflection showed a changed man. To fit in with locals and learn the language, he had grown a full beard and began dressing in dirty white and brown farmer's clothes. It hadn't worked. From the day that Utrix had dropped him off on the east coast, the locals had been wary of him. It hadn't just been how he dressed, or the fact that he was fair-skinned and blond compared to their tanned skin and almost exclusively dark hair; it was how he carried himself. As he traveled to new towns, Conrad had experimented with changing how he spoke and acted, but like watchful dogs, they had always sniffed him out.

A rustling in the nearby woods took his breath away, and he drew upon his saber: A curved blade that he'd never seen up close before until this trip. Though he had still brought his trusty rapier and concealed dagger along, Conrad felt the saber would help ward off groups with its speed and cutting ability. Even early on in his travels from town to town, his hunch had been correct. Whether it was in protest of him, a leader, or some other unfortunate soul, it hadn't taken much for the Gentish to gather into angry, violent mobs. It'd have been fascinating to study if it weren't so frightening. Even the royalty of the land dared not risk becoming targets of their so-called 'subjects'.

Conrad let out a relieved breath as a squirrel popped out of the woods. He walked back to his spot under the tree and grabbed his lightly-packed belongings.

The mission was simple: Identify that the black gold was on Bosfueras land. Utrix would then inform the Wizard's Council and pretend it was *he* who had made the discovery. After all, Wizards didn't often trust the word of a human, and working with one on such a dangerous mission would likely see Utrix excommunicated and Conrad's memory wiped. The strategist had also been asked to confirm the presence of a Dark Wizard, if possible, but it wasn't a requirement. The black gold took priority.

A shudder ran through his body as he looked back at the village on the horizon, still buzzing with activity at its latest mob gathering. If he succeeded in Bosfueras, Conrad would need to travel across the country once more to meet back up with Utrix on the east coast. That would be his ticket out of here, but the idea of a return trip filled him with dread. The past three months had nearly pushed him to the breaking point, and while he had avoided killing anyone so far, he worried that there would be no choice in Bosfueras.

Walking toward the wooded path now, Conrad's imagination took over. The warning signs at the edge of the woods painted a violent picture of the Bosfueran people. If even their countrymen feared them, just what kind of a hellish experience was he in for?

INFILTRATION

CONRAD'S JOURNEY through the woods was a lonely one. It not only lacked human contact, but there was a bizarre absence of wildlife, too; or at least wildlife that he could see. At night, he heard wolves howling off in the distance, and at times he was certain that something was breathing outside of his tent, but whenever he checked, there was nothing save darkness and silence. The world around him seemed swallowed up, and it made him uncomfortable. Even in daylight, there were only the trees surrounding the path to comfort him, and they often blotted out the sun. With no true signs that he was getting any closer to his destination, the strategist was becoming nervous. He had only packed enough food for a three-day trip.

Two days into his hike, Conrad came upon a wooden sign that had been nailed to a tree. The writing on it was a dark, crusty red; like dry blood. His eyes widened and all of the air suddenly escaped his lungs in a gasp. *The language was foreign to him.* After painstaking months of learning Gentish, this sign was telling him that Bosfueras residents didn't speak it. It looked vaguely familiar, almost like an old version of what he had learned. Was there such a thing as Old Gentish?

Based on Bosfueras' reputation and how suspicious nearly every other Gentish settlement had been of him, Conrad knew the odds of blending in with the townsfolk and discovering the black gold's location peacefully were low. But this sign was the final nail in the coffin. Without being able to communicate properly, he was down to two options: stealth or force.

Naturally, his preference was stealth. Against a settlement known already for its rejection of outsiders, he felt his death would be assured if he tried attacking them; especially if they were under the Gold Fever's influence.

The strategist continued along the path until the trees became withered and less prevalent, while the terrain became rockier. He began walking up and down rock-filled hills, but still, there was no sign of the town. Instead, as dusk approached, he found a single shack, about 100 paces to his left off the beaten path. It appeared to be abandoned and broken down. Its meager foundations had moss growing throughout, and as he approached, a putrid smell attacked his nose. It could best be described as rotting flesh combined with sulfur.

Covering his nose, he walked into the shack to be greeted by a swarm of flies whizzing past him; the first bugs he had seen since entering the woods. He looked around to see old, yellowed bedding with red stains on his right. To the left, there was a pile of lumpy flesh, where yet more flies had gathered. There were no signs of bone, however. It gave Conrad a slight sense of relief. At least whatever had died in there wasn't human, he thought.

That night, while sleeping in his tent, Conrad was disturbed by some shouting off in the distance. It was faint, but enough for him to investigate. He exited his tent and unlike the times before, the noises continued, and so he walked up onto a rocky hill. At the top, he could see dim light sources far off in the distance. It reminded him of the mobs he had seen throughout Gentorgul. He was close.

∽

AT THE CRACK OF DAWN, Conrad got back on the path. Dead trees and leaves became the norm, and the temperature cooled. He could feel himself descending slowly but surely into a fog. It wasn't long before he encountered another sign with blood-red writing on it. Still, he couldn't understand what it said.

After reaching the top of another hill, Conrad spotted a fenced-off shack down the slope. He could see other buildings far off in the distance, but they were obscured by trees and fog. Had he finally reached Bosfueras?

While plodding down the slope, Conrad began to strategize. This shack, unlike the previous, showed signs of life: The fenced-in area housed some cows and chickens; and atop the roof was a chimney with little puffs of smoke coming out. If someone lived here, and black gold had overtaken Bosfueras, then surely, they'd have some stashed. With some finesse, Conrad could complete the mission without having to plunge himself into the depths of the town, thus bypassing the risk of another mob coming for him.

Conrad hopped the fence, and one of the cows approached. He snorted as she rubbed her head against his shoulder. He had half-expected even the farm animals to attack but was thankful for the kind gesture and returned the favor with some scratches behind her ear.

Crouching now, the strategist snuck up to the side window and peered through. There were no signs of activity. He could see what looked to be a kitchen that transitioned into a small lounge, where the fireplace sat. After waiting some time, he was ready to take the risk and sneak in. The owner of the shack had probably run off on an errand or was wandering somewhere outside. If he broke in and discovered the black gold fast enough, he could easily leave before being detected.

He pushed up from the bottom of the window, but it snagged at the top, and he heard a clicking noise. *Locked*, he thought with a groan.

Conrad jumped back over the fence and approached the front door. He turned the knob slowly, and to his surprise, it turned all the way. Why would someone lock their window, but not their door? Was the owner of the shack *hiding* in there? With only enough food and water left for one more meal, he didn't have time to wait around and find out, especially if his return trip through the woods was to be so long and lifeless. He pushed the door open, and it creaked and groaned as it moved, sending his shoulders up to his ears.

Inside, there was a wall in front of him with a bear's head sloppily mounted on it. To his left, Conrad could see the dust-laden kitchen, and he heard the crackling of the fireplace. In the kitchen area, some old cabinets lined the walls. If he were stashing some black gold, the cabinets would be a decent spot, he thought.

In the kitchen, the strategist tepidly opened one of the cabinets. Inside, there were a variety of forks and knives, and some of the blades had fresh blood on them. Conrad's face contorted in disgust as a ghastly smell shot up at him and down his throat. No matter how badly he wanted to remain stealthy, he couldn't help but choke out a cough, and that was when he heard a stirring behind him.

Conrad turned to see a man sitting by his fireplace in an old wooden chair, staring at him. His coughing fit had ended, but the strategist's mouth remained agape. The man had been so still that he hadn't even noticed him while spying through the window or even when entering.

In Gentish, Conrad said, "Please, excuse my rudeness. I mean you no harm. I am looking for Bosfueras."

The man remained silent as he slumped out of his chair like a lump of meat lifted from a plate. He wore farmer's clothes similar to Conrad's, but they were stained with blood. It was nothing to panic over, he thought. After all, he owned farm animals and had probably slaughtered one of them for food. Despite how short his graying hair was, it still managed to be disheveled, and his face was wrinkled and pale to the point where it almost looked gray.

On his feet and motionless now, the man continued to stare at Conrad, and it was like he was looking back at a blank canvas. It was a certain single-minded expression that felt familiar, but he couldn't put his finger on why until recalling his reason for journeying here to begin with: the black gold. The Gold Fever-infected miners had also been single-minded in their goals and actions.

As the thought occurred to him, Conrad regained focus. The man was now lumbering toward him, rocking slightly from side to side with each step, but his eyes never wavered or broke contact with his. When looking closely, he could see that his pupils were not yellow, but a light tint of *red*. There was no hint of what emotion he was feeling in his expression, and the same went for his body language. The strategist brought a hand to his saber's hilt, just in case the man became hostile.

When he got close, however, he stopped. Conrad raised an eyebrow as the odd man tilted his head back and shouted aloud in a language that he didn't understand. Despite the loud words, there was still no emotion on his face.

The man then shrieked like a banshee, turned back, grabbed a knife off of the table, and came at Conrad with shocking quickness, primed for a surprise stab. The strategist, however, had been prepared, and easily sidestepped the attempt. The crazed man flailed and fell to the floor with a *thud*.

Despite the clumsiness of the attack, Conrad's heart was beating through his chest. Alone, this man was no problem, but if he were to gather more, it would be trouble. Was there any way to resolve this peacefully? After all, *he* had been the one to trespass.

Just then, the front door burst open and another man wearing farmer's clothes stepped in. He had the same grayed, wrinkled skin, but his hair was brown instead. His expression was also blank. The knife-wielding man stood, pointed at Conrad, and then shouted something in a different language.

"Please! I come in peace!" he barked back in Gentish, but neither man acknowledged him. The man at the front door nodded at the knife wielder and then dashed outside with a sudden burst of speed.

"Damn..." Conrad muttered. He was likely headed back to town, where a mob could be gathered to swarm him. He couldn't let him reach the other townsfolk, or the mission and his life would be at risk.

The strategist made a run for the door, but the knife-wielding man jumped in front of him. Conrad scanned for any sort of emotion or tell in his body language or face, but he was like a locked door that couldn't be opened, and it made him all the more anxious.

"Stay back," Conrad said as he drew his saber and held it out in front of him.

The man paid his threat no mind and lunged out for a stab. Conrad redirected the knife blade to his left; and as the crazed man fell off balance, he slashed across to the right and opened a wide gash in his stomach. He screeched while crashing to the floor, where his blood had already spilled. After some moaning, the man went limp, and a pool of red gathered around his body.

Since the Mt. Couture disaster, Conrad had taken Lucia's advice to heart: When someone says or shows that they wish to kill you, believe them; show them no mercy. He had done just that in this confrontation, but it brought to mind his duel with Wolfgang, too. Before the final blow had been struck, the brute said something that had also stuck with him: Once you begin killing, it becomes hard to stop. It truly *had* gotten easier after his first time. Was he on the slippery slope to becoming just like Wolfgang?

He didn't have much time to contemplate such questions, though. There was still a chance that he could catch the other man before he returned to town and alerted the others. Conrad started for the door, but he was stopped by a grip around his ankle tugging back on him.

"No..." he murmured. The strategist turned to see the man on the floor with his arm outstretched, pulling back on his ankle with an iron-like grip. He moaned, as if awakening from a deep slumber, and rose. Conrad swiftly brought his saber down and severed the hand from his wrist, freeing his ankle.

As the crazed man stood fully, blood gushed from his stump of a wrist, but he showed no sign of pain or panic. He yelled something in a different language at Conrad once more, then bent over to retrieve the knife. Before he could make any more moves, the strategist lunged forward and plunged the saber into his throat; a squishy, fleshy noise echoing in the shack as he did. He grunted and then fell to the ground. As he pulled the blade out of his neck, Conrad noticed that the spurting blood was darker than what he would have expected; closer to maroon than red.

"Just what is going on here?" he asked aloud, shaking his head. Finally, he made his way out of the shack and ran back onto the path.

Conrad descended into a thick fog as he ran. The uncertainty of his environment convinced him to slow down. He could hear shouting off in the distance. Had the townsfolk been alerted? Would he be hunted down and killed?

Soon, the shouts grew louder, but the fog had become like a stack of smoke, so he couldn't confirm the source. The strategist elected to continue straight until he saw any more townsfolk, or found a good place to hide. His thought process was that running into the woods would get him lost, and eventually caught. Awareness of his location would be key to surviving.

After some time moving forward, he heard a new noise: running water. Before him was a thin rope bridge that stretched across what appeared to be a ravine. There was a river running at the bottom, but he couldn't tell from sight. The fog was too thick. He took a step on and it swayed and groaned, bringing a sinking feeling to his stomach. Conrad took a deep breath. There was no more time to waste. If a mob was gathering, he needed to find evidence of the black gold quickly. At least the narrow nature of the bridge made a potential confrontation with the townsfolk less dangerous: They would be lined up for him, one at a time, to strike down.

Conrad tepidly walked across the creaking bridge as it swayed in the wind; or was it movement coming from the other side? Lack of vision in the fog kept him on edge as his imagination began to take over. The townsfolk that he had encountered thus far had been quiet and plodding in their movements until getting within range. They could attack him at any moment, and he'd never see it coming. What if there was a whole horde of them waiting under the cover of fog? He drew his rapier, just to be careful.

Soon, a shadowy figure became apparent up ahead, in the thick of the mist. He held the rapier out in front of him and slowed his steps even more. This time, it was a woman wearing old country clothes; a colorful outfit, but dirty. The man from before had been irrationally violent, perhaps due to Gold Fever, but he hoped to have better luck with her. He was at least willing to try.

While approaching the woman, who remained still as the night, Conrad said in Gentish, "Greetings, miss. I come in peace."

There was no response. He squinted and took notice of what seemed to be her gray skin. Almost all Gentish folk that he'd encountered before reaching Bosfueras had bronzed skin. She remained motionless and wore a blank expression as he drew closer. She exhibited all of the same signs as the other two. Conrad's stomach was in knots as he pivoted sideways and took a fencing stance.

The woman's eyes glowed red, poking through the haze as she let out a blood-curdling scream. Conrad prepared himself for an attack, but instead of coming for him, she pulled out a knife and began cutting the rope to her right, one of the foundations of the bridge.

"Fool! What are you doing?" he cried while plunging his rapier into her leg. He did so as a warning, but like his previous confrontation with the crazed man, she showed no signs of pain from the attack. She merely continued to carve away at the rope, which became thinner by the moment. The dark red blood pooled in her dirty apron.

With gritted teeth, Conrad pulled the rapier out of her leg and then stabbed her in the temple with one swift motion. The woman gasped and collapsed, but not before getting one last slice in on the rope. Conrad's eyes widened as the strength of the twine gave way and snapped. He swiftly stuck his feet in between the vertical ropes and held onto the rope on his right as the sliced-up side split and the bridge flipped. The crazed woman fell into the abyss of the fog.

To Conrad's surprise, he also heard the screams of others from further along the bridge; they must have fallen too, he thought. Seconds later, he heard splashes from below. It seemed like a long drop to him. Luckily, he had positioned himself well, and laterally made his way across the bridge, taking steps in between the vertical roping that remained.

When he was close enough to see the end, Conrad spotted three more shadowy figures approaching. He increased his pace, knowing that he would have to beat them to the ledge to stand a chance. There was no turning back, now. They'd cut the rest of the bridge down before he could return to the other side of the ravine.

With an intense focus that drowned out any nerves, Conrad rushed across the remainder of the bridge and made it to solid ground before they could reach him. He drew his saber once more, but while taking a stance, he noticed something behind the three men: flickering flames in the fog. They must have been torches or lanterns, he thought; and there were *dozens*. As he had feared, the mob was coming for him.

In that moment of distraction, one of the three men swung a wood axe at Conrad. With a sudden jolt of energy and awareness, the strategist deflected with his blade, but it left him wide open to the other two, who were in the midst of their own attacks.

The man to his right swung a meat cleaver, which Conrad narrowly avoided by shifting to the left. However, the dodge had left him vulnerable to the crazed man with the pitchfork, who thrust it at him with a delirious cry. He did his best to avoid it at the last second, but one of the prongs of the fork tore into the side of his arm and ripped his shirt.

Conrad pushed the burning pain out of mind as he struck back with a slash of his saber. He felt the blade chop down into the bone of the man's arm, which left it dangling by a thread. He dropped the pitchfork but otherwise showed no signs of pain.

"What is wrong with these people?" he muttered. The Gold Fever-infected back at Mt. Couture had normally been happy to die for their Savior, but they still felt pain. The folk he had encountered thus far were like blank canvases, reacting only to him. He had never seen such single-minded focus before.

There was little time to consider what was going on, however, as the man whose arm he'd chopped lunged out at him, flailing his dangling arm around with reckless abandon. Conrad sidestepped, then nailed him in the back of the head using the butt of his saber. He crashed to the ground and considering the situation for but a brief moment, the strategist understood that it was time to run. He could hear the chanting hordes approach from down the path, and the two other men were still a threat.

And so, Conrad dashed into the fog-filled woods on his right. He heard shouts from the two men behind him, and out of the corner of his eye, noticed the flickering flames shift in direction: The manhunt had begun.

∽

NEAR THE RAVINE, the man with the dangling, bloody arm stood slowly, like an accordion folding outward. His red eyes focused on a tattered and bloody piece of fabric on the ground. It was from that *filthy outsider's* shirt; a result of the pitchfork connecting with his arm. The dazed man picked up the fabric, and rather than give chase along with the rest of the mob, he lumbered down the path to town, disappearing into the haze.

∽

CONRAD RAN straight for as long as his poor lungs would allow. He had to take early advantage of the mob's lack of speed, and a sprint, followed by a long jog seemed the best way. After an hour of jogging, he finally stopped at a small rock face. The strategist took a mental note of the cliff as a way to track where he was, then made his way to the left, back in the direction of the path into town. Unless they spread out at an individual level, he could reach Bosfueras on an unbeaten path while avoiding the horde.

Although already in dire straits, Conrad wasn't ready to abandon his mission. He had enough supplies for another day if he was conservative, and he'd learned enough over the months to find more if need be. His main concern was what to do upon reaching the settlement.

As he walked in what he hoped was the direction of town, Conrad noticed the fog was beginning to lift. Although the environment became less eerie as a result, his anxiety shot through the roof. It was his best form of cover, and with their torches, he could see the townsfolk coming from far away in that fog. The knots in his stomach quickly turned to hunger, however, and he felt an intense thirst come over him, too. He'd been running non-stop for an hour, after all. Despite the risks of stopping, it would be even riskier to press on and potentially lose all of his energy.

Conrad sat up against a tree trunk, facing in the direction of where he had originally fled from, and ate as quietly as he could. Just as his breaths calmed and relaxation started to come over him, his arm flared up, eliciting a brief gasp that he quickly snuffed out like an ember under water. He scanned the woods and focused his ears. No movement. No sounds, save for his own strained breaths.

In the excitement and tension of escaping, he had completely forgotten about the wound. He looked down at his arm while taking in a gulp of water from his canteen. The strategist retrieved some fabric from his pack and began wrapping the wound up, as it was fairly deep and still bleeding; but it was nowhere near as bad as the damage he'd sustained at Mt. Couture, to his relief. He *still* felt aches and pains in his shoulder and chest, at times.

A wave of exhaustion hit Conrad as his eyes began to close and his head sagged. He knew that this was no place to fall asleep, but the food and drink had not yet given him an energy boost, and the blood loss and hour-long run had drained him. Instead of worrying, though, he thought back to his fateful duel with Wolfgang over a year prior. He remembered every detail, down to the searing pain when the brute's blade had ripped into his arm. Even more painful had been when Greed shot his own rapier back out at him, piercing his chest. The permanent, vile grin of the monster was something he would never forg-

Conrad snapped back to reality when a great howl echoed in his ears. A wolf, perhaps? It didn't sound too far away, and it was a startling reminder that the mob might not be his only obstacle. The lack of wildlife on the trip to Bosfueras had concerned him, and now he began to suspect that an overwhelming predator had been responsible. If a pack of wolves happened upon him while bleeding and tired, he was certain that they would attack. Or could it have been that the townsfolk were using dogs to track him?

Either way, he didn't wish to find out, so Conrad packed up his belongings and jogged once more. His current situation was favorable if he continued to move. Many tracking dogs were fast at short range, but they were not adept for long-distance running: A useful piece of information that he had picked up over the years while reading whatever he could get his hands on.

After another hour of walking and jogging, Conrad emerged from the bushes and stopped short of a great cliff face. Far below and to his right resided Bosfueras. The town sat in a grand basin that almost seemed carved out just for them and had a rural feel to it. Various stretches of farmland and stables mixed in seamlessly with unobtrusive shacks and small stone foundation buildings. Many diverse areas drew his eyes, but the most noticeable was on the other side of town: A grand cathedral sat atop a rocky hill, poking out the top of a walled-off citadel that buzzed with activity. It was by far the largest building in town and well-decorated to boot. If there *were* a Dark Wizard, Conrad thought, that was where he would be.

With no clear entry to the town from his location, Conrad scouted a path along the cliffs further to his right. It was a steep route that had been carved into the cliffs and dropped directly into Bosfueras. The bad news was that it would be difficult to reach the cathedral from there, undetected. Atop the walls of the citadel and all around the church, he could barely make out figures moving back and forth. They were most likely armed guards on patrol, he thought. As the strategist had it figured, his best bet was to trek through the farmlands and use natural cover to avoid detection. The townsfolk would likely be on high alert, so he resolved not to take any risks unless absolutely necessary.

Conrad traveled along the cliffs for a while longer until reaching the edge of the woods, where he turned left onto a dirt trail. Soon after, he reached the steep cliff path, and below, he could better see how active Bosfueras was. Despite a mob having gathered to find him, there were still many people out and about, traversing the roads and tending the farms. If he took the ledge path into town now, he would almost certainly be spotted. There were too many people.

He returned to the beginnings of the woods and hid behind a set of bushes, spying on the dirt trail to see how often the Bosfueras townsfolk walked it, and more importantly, to stall until nightfall, when he would be difficult to spot. As dusk gave way to darkness, Conrad had counted less than ten people traveling up or down the path, and all of them did so while it was light out. An odd detail that he'd picked up on was how ordinary they had acted while traversing the path. They spoke in what he believed to be Old Gentish while carrying supplies like wood or fish, and some were even cracking jokes with each other. It was an unexpected departure from the townsfolk he had encountered so far. It was almost as if his presence had triggered something; made them single-minded.

When the moon fully shone down upon him, Conrad exited the bushes and checked a few times for possible townsfolk traveling the path before making his way down and into the town. That trail weaved back and forth as it steeply descended, and it made his boots drag against the pebbles and dirt. Each gravelly sound was like a punch to Conrad's gut, and worry overcame him. The noises had probably carried down and into town. Eventually, however, he reached the bottom, undetected. To his left was a small piece of farmland and a stable filled with animals such as chickens, horses, and cows.

The strategist found a large stack of hay that looked like a good place to sleep for the night after doing some scouting. Keeping the location in mind, he returned to a path and snuck between the crevices of the shacks until he reached what looked to be the main street of Bosfueras. It was a dirt road much like the others, but wider. His eyes also picked up on some patrolmen walking the streets. While all others beforehand had worn farming clothes, these men had full suits of armor that gleamed under the rich moonlight, and they carried spears, poleaxes, swords, and shields.

At least five guards were walking along the main street by Conrad's count. Wanting to avoid their gaze, he wandered further into town by sneaking through dark alleyways. The prominent cathedral likely meant that a strict curfew was enforced; a common practice in places where religious factions had control.

As he explored the tight alleys of Bosfueras, a plan began to take shape in Conrad's mind: He would scout out the guards' patrol routes tonight, spend tomorrow morning in the haystack, and then infiltrate the church tomorrow night when their guard would hopefully be down. The armored men atop the citadel walls were his biggest concern. If they were out at all hours of the day, then no amount of sneaking would matter. They would always catch him. He had to hope that-

A desperate scream interrupted his thoughts. Grunts and whining soon followed. Conrad rushed through the alleyways and back to the main street to see what the commotion was. A struggling man, face bloodied to a pulp, was kicking and screaming as a couple of armed guards dragged him along the unforgiving dirt road. Conrad couldn't understand him, but it sounded like he was pleading. The guards responded, once again, in a language that he couldn't understand, except one thing had caught his ear: a name.

Willoughby

The pleading man reached a fever pitch of panic and began flailing like a fresh fish out of water while crying and screaming like a toddler. One of the guards turned back and elbowed him in the nose, and the pleading man slumped as he continued to be dragged along. His panicked pleas continued, but he had become quieter; a fearful acceptance of whatever was to come. Conrad was stunned. All townsfolk who had attacked him earlier showed no fear and felt no pain. Yet, this man was so intimidated by a name?

'Gentoure Willoughby.' He was certain that's what they were saying. In Gentish, 'genter', meant 'mister'. Could that have been the Old Gentish way of saying it?

"Mr. Willoughby…" Conrad muttered. For some reason, the name felt familiar. He followed the pleading man and guards by crossing through the alleyways until they finally stopped at a wide and one-story tall stone structure.

As one of the guards fumbled with his keys to open the great iron door, Conrad peeked around the corner of a shack to get a good view of the cathedral: It was propped up on a rocky hill within the fortified citadel and beautifully crafted with many murals that were visible from the outside. He noticed too that while there were no guards atop the citadel walls tonight, they had instead gathered near the entrance of the church. With so much security, there was bound to be something of great importance in there. Still, with all of the guards swarming around, how could he sneak inside, undetected?

Conrad heard the groan of the great iron door and turned his attention back to the pleading man and his captors. Inside, he could make out a stone set of stairs that descended into darkness, but little else. The man cried aloud once more and fell to the ground. The guards dragged him into the dark as he shrieked, but it did him no good. The door closed behind them, and Conrad shuddered. It felt like he'd just witnessed a man walking to his execution.

About a quarter-hour later, the same guards exited the stone building, and then closed and locked the door behind them. To Conrad's complete lack of surprise, the pleading man was nowhere to be found.

Who was Mr. Willoughby? The Dark Wizard, perhaps? Did he reside in that dungeon of sorts? It seemed to him that the church was too well-guarded for there not to be something important in there, however, so he decided that it was still his target. He crept his way back through the alleyways and returned to the stable he had picked out earlier. Conrad burrowed himself into the pile of hay that he had scouted and began to doze off. Bosfueras was a deceptively large town, and sneaking around it had taken longer than he thought. Dawn couldn't have been more than a few hours off.

As his dreams started to overtake him, Conrad wondered how he could fall asleep in such a hostile place so easily. Perhaps the journey through Gentorgul had been beneficial, in that regard, after all.

CHAPTER 8
MR. WILLOUGHBY

That night, Conrad dreamt of his harrowing experiences at Mt. Couture. It had been common for him to have nightmares about his duel with Wolfgang, the conjured-up thunderstorms of the Mountain King, or the disturbing behavior of the Gold Fever-infected. This time, however, he found himself entrapped in a dark mineshaft with no torch. Nothing odd was happening to him, but there was one thing save for the pitch black that sent shivers down his spine: *the breathing*.

They were high-pitched, long breaths; stuttering, as if coming from a bloodthirsty monster who was trying to hold back its cruel laughter. There was a certain excitement to the tone of each breath, and it grew louder with each passing moment. It was rabid; primal. Conrad shook in the darkness as one last breath penetrated his ears. It was close; within an arm's length.

That was when he remembered: He hadn't experienced anything like this in Mt. Couture, and all of his nightmares had been memories of that place. The environment was the same, but the experience was not. Every time he was in a dark, confined tunnel, he was with others, had light sources, and it was eerily quiet. Something wasn't right. Never before had he experienced 'the breathing'.

Conrad opened his eyes and saw nothing but the hay that he had burrowed under. No light shone through, so it must have still been nighttime, he thought. He calmed himself, realizing it had only been a dream, and then he heard it: the stuttered, high-pitched breaths. They were just like in the dream, which meant that *he had been hearing them the whole time*. It was a similar phenomenon to when crowing roosters would make their way into his dreams back in Faiwell.

The noise was coming from right in front of him, so the strategist slowly shifted the hay, not wanting to bring attention to himself, and peered out into the night. He had hoped it was simply one of the farm animals, but one look confirmed it was something else entirely.

Before him stood a dark and tall human-like figure. It had arms that stretched down to the knees, and its legs were puffy and without shape. It wasn't wearing any clothes, yet didn't look like a nude human. Instead, it resembled a man that had been covered in tar, or some sort of chunky, spoiled meat. Strangely, the figure looked familiar.

As Conrad's eyes adjusted, he began to understand why: The creature's face was skull-like; missing features that made a man complete. Its lips had receded into its maroon-colored gums, and its teeth were long and rectangular, making its head and jaw too tall to be human. Its nose looked to have been pushed in and upward, while its eyes were several rings of glowing red in a sea of black.

The creature reminded him of Greed, aside from the normally yellow, solid pupils being several rings of red. At that moment, the realization hit Conrad that it was standing there, staring down at him with those twisted eyes. There was no doubt about it: The monster knew that he was in the haystack.

However, it did nothing save stand still as the night and look down at Conrad. It occasionally took its goosebump-inducing breaths, but nothing else. The strategist trembled and struggled to keep his composure within the hay. It had become clear that what stood before him was not simply a monster or a man: it was an experiment. He saw what little left of humanity it had: Patches of dark hair on its otherwise bald scalp and small stretches of skin that didn't look like the organic, gelatinous tar that had overpowered its body. Even its quivering lips, which looked desperate to say something; to cry out in pain, had mutated too far. All it could do was make disturbing noises.

He had to put it out of its misery, if that was even possible. The fact that it looked similar to Greed, who had been invincible to his weapons a year prior, was not lost on him. Either way, the creature knew of his position and he needed to make a move.

With a surge of energy, Conrad jumped from the hay and drew his saber in one swift motion. The beast before him let out a shrill cry that rang in his ears like nothing he'd ever heard before. It felt like his brain had been scrambled. The monster's eyes expanded into many more rings and then focused and shrunk; combining into small, red circles. It then opened its gaping mouth and unleashed a dark red tongue, and from that came a great organic web that branched out into many different directions. Before Conrad could take a swing, his blade was caught up in the sticky, disgusting web. He found his arm and blade completely restricted, and some of it had landed on his left leg, too.

His right side remained free, however, and that was the pant leg where he had stashed his dagger. He flexed his upper body awkwardly to the side and reached down as the monster closed in on him, continuing to breathe excitedly. Its walk was hobbled and jerky as if it didn't fully understand how to use its knees, and its arms swayed too much for such a slow walk.

The unsettling movements struck panic into Conrad, and he fumbled around while trying to obtain his dagger. He felt the putrid breaths of the beast smack his face, and he turned to look at it. Its giant mouth was agape, and it was about to take a bite out of him. The monster lunged forward, and as it did, the strategist brought his dagger up and into the side of its head.

Thinking quickly, he then sliced at the organic webbing on the left side of his body to free himself. Dark red blood spurted from the creature's head, and it stumbled back for a moment, but it wasn't long before it glared back down at Conrad once more with killing intent.

Out of the corner of his eye, Conrad noticed that the monster was holding a piece of bloodstained fabric in its long, deformed hand. Had it belonged to the pleading man from earlier in the night? Was *this* Mr. Willoughby?

The strategist took several steps back, put the dagger under his pant leg, and then drew his rapier. He kept the saber out as well, so he would be dual-wielding and harder to reach. The monster lumbered toward him, continuing its shrill breaths and never once breaking eye contact. Much like the crazed townsfolk, Willoughby was obviously single-minded. Conrad swung the saber at the monster's arm: a deliberate tactic, to see if it could regenerate lost limbs, like Greed.

The saber cut straight through Mr. Willoughby's arm. It flew through the air, but no blood spurted out. Only more strains of the red, organic web that had been stuck on Conrad earlier. As soon as the arm hit the ground, however, the webbing from within it shot back up at the monster and reattached itself in only a few moments.

Conrad quickly ran through his options. There was no way some sort of human experiment could be as powerful as Greed, he thought. What would it take to kill Willoughby? He had a few ideas, but as he thought them out, the monster let out another cry. It was a disturbing sound; like the whines and roars of several animals at once. Soon after, Conrad took notice of torchlights off in the distance. It was alerting the townsfolk.

"Smarter than you look…" he muttered with a nervous smile and a sweat building on his brow. The creature began walking again.

However, instead of traveling toward him, it went to the right. Its sights were set on a cow.

"No…" Conrad said, his eyes wide with fright. He started for the monster, looking to intervene, but the loud voices of the townsfolk nearby stilled him. More torchlights could be seen off in the distance. At this rate, there was no time to stay back and help the animal. It wouldn't be long before they found him if he didn't make a run for it now. His new plan was to return to the woods at the top of the cliff face and scout the situation out from there.

As he ran up the steep path, Conrad heard the cow wailing out in pain, and then the grotesque crunching of her bones. He paused and then looked down to see Mr. Willoughby feasting upon the downed cow, who had been ripped in half. Between violent chomps of the raw meat, the beast let out shrill, excited breaths. Conrad shuddered. The carnage below was a peek into his future if the monster ever got its hands on him.

After a tiring sprint up to the ledge, Conrad returned to the same part of the woods he had hidden in earlier, but he didn't take cover in the bushes. Instead, he remained behind some trees. From there, he could see over the cliff face and into Bosfueras. The night was especially helpful in seeing how many townsfolk had been alerted by the cries of the creature and subsequently the cow's mooing and wailing. He counted over 20 torchlights patrolling the area. Two were headed up the cliff path. Would they check the woods?

Not wanting to risk further detection, the strategist ventured further back along the lining of the cliff face until returning to the spot where he had first scouted out Bosfueras. He then took refuge in a set of bushes, where he would have a decent view of town.

Conrad spied for what felt like over an hour. Eventually, the torchlights dimmed and then disappeared. The night fell silent, and none of the townsfolk came for him. He should have felt safe, but there was some feeling of dread he couldn't shake; a malaise that called to mind the feeling of a spider crawling up his arm.

Just then, he heard a shriek off in the distance of the woods. It hadn't sounded like Mr. Willoughby, but the noise had still felt hostile to his ears. Soon after, he heard multiple high-pitched shrieks, closer than before. Now, he could hear rustling in the grass, and whatever it was drew near.

The strategist widened his eyes. Had his location been compromised? As if to answer his thoughts, a twig snapped about 20 paces to his right, behind some trees. Without hesitation, Conrad grabbed his pack and hopped to his feet to make a run for it. As he sprinted aimlessly through the woods, vaguely remembering the direction of the cliff face that he'd made note of earlier in the day, he could hear leaves rustling and the sound of scurrying footsteps behind him. The noises increased in number and felt closer, so he put his head down and moved as fast as he could.

Within mere moments of pushing his hardest, something jumped onto Conrad's back and dragged him down. He crashed to the grassy ground and then winced several times over as the impacts of several others dog-piling on him rippled through his body. Oddly, each strike had felt focused, but heavy; as if the legs of a table had been dropped onto his back. With a grunt, he turned over and flung the attackers off. Silence came over the clearing as he got a better look at what stalked him. Poking out of the darkness were blood-red giant insects that looked similar to spiders. Each was about the size of a dog and had large, pulsating fangs that were black; likely filled with venom, Conrad thought. As he stared down his attackers, the pain on his back intensified and scorched. He gasped and then reached behind to find a couple of holes poked into the back of his shirt.

The effects of the bite were immediate: Conrad felt drowsiness overtake him, but he hadn't lost feeling in any limbs, yet. He still had time to react and escape. One of the spider-like creatures shrieked and then jumped out at him, fangs-first. In response, he drew his saber and then sliced it down vertically with all of his might. The creature was split into two evenly cut pieces, which shot diagonally away without making contact with him.

Splat

Conrad raised an eyebrow and darted his eyes back to the remains of the spider-creature. To his surprise, it had exploded into the same odd webbing that Mr. Willoughby had used on him, earlier.

Even that brief distraction had been enough incentive for the other monsters to attack. Each came at him with frightening speed, and so the strategist swung wildly; diagonally; as fast as he could, to keep them at bay. The spiders slowed to a crawl, but they continued forward as if looking for the next moment of weakness. Soon, Conrad began landing successful hits with his blade.

As blood-red limbs soared through the air and carcasses exploded into red webbing, it became clear to Conrad that the monsters were incapable of coordinated attacks or strategy. They were single-minded in their attempts to either pin down or bite their prey, even when it was to their own detriment. After ripping his blade from the head of the last spider, the strategist felt a wave of exhaustion sweep over him. He was willing to drop where he stood and doze off, but one singular thing kept him from doing so: *the breathing.*

Conrad's eyes twitched as the distorted breaths of Mr. Willoughby drew near. Off in the distance he saw the dark figure approaching with its stiff walk and pale imitation of human-like movement. How? How was the monster able to detect him?

He narrowed his eyes and spotted the same bloody piece of cloth from earlier in Willoughby's hand, and that was when it finally hit him: The monster carried not the tattered clothing of the pleading man from earlier in the night, but *his own clothing.* He remembered back to his confrontation with the townsfolk, where one of them had landed a hit with the pitchfork. It left a nasty cut on his arm, but also a hole in his shirt.

"You can smell me..." he muttered, cracking a nervous smile. Sweat began to stream down his forehead. The toxins were getting to him.

As the monster trudged on, a stirring of the red webs caught the corner of his eye. He watched on, mouth agape, as it began clawing, all on its own, in the direction of Mr. Willoughby. Upon reaching it, the webs shot up and were assimilated into its lumpy body.

A stuttered breath escaped Conrad's lips as Willoughby's red rings for eyes each combined into one, glowing dot that focused in on him. Not only could it regenerate and track him by smell, but it could even create little minions to attack and weaken him.

With a grimace, Conrad re-sheathed his blade and made a run for it. He had a new idea. Instead of hiding, he would test Mr. Willoughby's abilities, and if it wasn't up to the test, then at least he would have escaped.

Throughout the jog, Conrad's vision blurred. He blinked to try and get his sight back, but everything was going dark. He then smacked himself on the head. The darkness still overtook him. He stopped for a moment and then retrieved the canteen from his pack. He poured water on his face, and that woke him up.

With a second wind, the strategist pressed on until he reached the rock face that he'd made note of earlier. Mr. Willoughby was sluggish and awkward, so he got the impression that it wouldn't be able to reach him high up. He began to climb, but the toxins took effect once more, and his fingers felt weak. Making matters worse, his back was on fire, and all around him started fading to black.

Against all odds, he made it to the top before collapsing to the rocky ground. With what little consciousness he had left, the strategist scouted the area to see that it was flat at the top. If the monster was able to reach him, he'd at least have a fighting chance to escape. With that last thought, he faded into darkness.

In his dreams, Conrad could hear a deep, dark voice echoing off in the distance. It chanted the same thing over and over, but it was too far away to make out the words. With each passing second, however, the sound got closer. After some time, he was able to make out the words:

Slara teat feinum
Pleite an chroide
Glabris adtu vaor

Then, the chant became louder; enough that his ears rang and his head pounded. In his dream, Conrad covered his bleeding ears and cried out for it to end. As he began to feel truly overwhelmed, the chanting ceased, and all went dark.

Conrad awoke to the sound of shrill, excited breaths. He snapped up and looked around the cliff top to find no one, but he could still hear the breathing. He crawled forward and then gazed over the ledge to see the face of Mr. Willoughby staring back up at him with those glowing rings for red eyes. He hopped to his feet with a gasp, but never took his eyes off of it. The monster before him had changed form. Instead of the big, lumpy body that he'd grown accustomed to, it now resembled a kraken: With long, dark tentacles whipping around and holding onto the rocks as it slowly climbed. Its head mostly remained the same, but the mouth had deformed in such a way that it looked to be able to open either upward or sideways, and the top of its scalp had grown larger.

The strategist drew his saber as one of the tentacles reached the top. His first thought was to cut it in the hopes that the beast would fall, but he stilled his blade when a new idea came to mind. It would be risky, but he had to find a way to kill it.

More tentacles rose and clasped down onto the rocks as Conrad readied himself. Slowly but surely, the deformed head reached the level of the ground at his feet, and as it continued to ascend, he charged Willoughby. The monster only hissed lightly as he swung the saber horizontally at its neck with all of his might.

A wet, muddy sound echoed in the wind as Conrad watched Mr. Willoughby's disembodied head spinning and falling. It struck the ground and splattered like an old watermelon. The body followed suit and fell afterward, also splattering on impact with the ground. The vile remains were a combination of Willoughby's odd web-like makeup and liquid darkness, but no one could have guessed that it was once a living creature unless they'd witnessed it first-hand.

Conrad climbed down the rock face and went over to investigate the abomination. He knelt over and found no sign of vital organs that a human would have, but he did see hair and human skin patches here and there. It once again reminded him of tar or rotted meat, mixed with a dark shade of red. He normally would have thought it was the creature's blood, but he had been *attacked* by little red extensions of it several times and in different forms.

As he was inspecting, he noticed an oddity toward the center of the splattered remains: The red material started to bubble, as if it were boiling. The dark, red, and human patches spun like a whirlpool, and in the middle of it all, something was building. It was like watching the making of a sculpture in double-time.

"No…" Conrad muttered. He watched on as the bottom half of Mr. Willoughby took shape, and the rest of the mush materialized into a deep, dark red webbing that slowly crawled up its body and excreted juices that smelled of rotten flesh.

Having seen enough, the strategist ran past the regenerating monster in the direction of the rope bridge. Now, there was no choice but to retreat. The sky was brightening and he was certain that a confrontation with the townsfolk in daytime would spell his doom. With a monster able to track his every location, his only option for the time being was to leave.

While running, there was a creeping feeling in the back of Conrad's mind that he couldn't put his finger on. As if he were itchy, but didn't know where to scratch. It was a discomfort that felt vaguely familiar to him, but he tried to push it out of his mind. He had to escape now, or it would be the end for him; whether the townsfolk or Mr. Willoughby finished him, it didn't matter.

The run soon turned into a jog, and as beams of sunlight peeked into the woods, the fog from yesterday returned. It wouldn't be helpful for finding his way out, but at least it would be an advanced warning for approaching enemies and their torches.

After an exhausting jog, Conrad found himself back on the dirt path where he had been attacked the day before. He ran to the left through the thick fog in hopes of finding the bridge. Soon, he heard running water, and even sooner after, he reached the ravine. However, there was no sign of the rope bridge. Had he inadvertently found a different dirt trail?

Conrad let out a stuttered breath when his eyes caught the wooden posts that normally would have made up the foundation of the bridge. One of the ropes had been cut by the crazed woman yesterday, but now, even the rope from the other side was missing, and the bridge was gone.

They intended to trap him, and now his options were limited. Running back to where he had just come from was risky. Mr. Willoughby would be chasing him, perhaps with the odd spider creatures in tow. Meanwhile, the path straight into town seemed downright suicidal with the townsfolk on high alert.

His best option was to try the woods on the other side of Bosfueras, or directly across from where he had come from. However, from what he could make out, the area seemed to have residents living in it. He could spot at least a few cabins nestled between trees and bushes off in the distance.

There was little time to debate with himself, though. That was his best chance at survival, so the strategist walked into the woods, slowing his pace for the sake of his racing heart and hoping to avoid further detection.

As he traveled through the misty woods, Conrad heard a commotion behind him. He could see from the flickering lights off in the distance that a new mob had gathered back on the main path to town. The lights gave him an idea; a solution to finally defeat Mr. Willoughby. He would have to exploit one of the townsfolk when they were on their own, though. He couldn't take on all of them at once. From what he could tell, there were at least 10 people in the mob. Instead, he planned to invade a few of the cabins up ahead. He had already passed by some, but couldn't tell if anyone was inside and hadn't wished to find out.

At the next cabin, he found no signs of activity and snuck through the front door. The inside was similar to the shack he had invaded yesterday: deceptively large inside and packed full of the essentials, like a kitchen and living room. In the kitchen, the strategist knelt and opened a cabinet.

"Perfect," he said, reaching in to grab a lantern. He opened the hatch to see that it contained plenty of oil. Hope crept onto his tired face.

His excitement was spoiled, however, by creaking footsteps behind him. Conrad spun around with a light gasp. However, he was surprised not to find an angry man, woman, or monster, but a young boy. He too wore farmer's clothes and the same expressionless face of the others who'd attacked him earlier. Gray, wrinkled skin and red eyes told him that he'd also been infected by whatever was plaguing this town.

"Hello, little one," Conrad whispered in Gentish. It was in vain; the boy didn't acknowledge his speech. They may as well have been in different worlds. He slowly approached Conrad.

The strategist placed a hand on the hilt of his rapier but stopped himself from drawing it.

"How could I?" he muttered, releasing his grip from the hilt. He was only a child, after all. What could he possibly do to him?

The child reached into his pants pocket, to which the strategist tensed up. A weapon? No. He gasped as a black ore greeted his eyes with magnificent sparkles. The boy held it out for him in both hands. He placed the lantern on the kitchen table and then approached. It called to him, and that strange feeling from earlier came back: the itch. Conrad's eyes glazed over as he reached out for the dark ore. He felt a calm sweep over his mind.

Just as he became cognizant of what he was doing, Conrad grabbed the black gold and held it out in his hands. His mind told him to drop it, throw it, give it back; anything to rid himself of it, but his heart told him to gaze upon its magnificence in wonder. And so, he and the boy did look upon it, with slacked jaws and mindlessly happy expressions. Darkness washed over the room, but not a frightening one; an empty one. It was soothing. The troubles on his mind faded away just as his vision had, and he imagined this was what it was like to travel amongst the stars. It was a blissful eternity to him; a never-ending dream.

∼

CONRAD SNAPPED out of his stupor upon hearing shouts from outside the cabin. He widened his eyes and dropped the black gold. As it thudded off the wooden floor, the child ran forward to pick it up, and the strategist rubbed his eyes. How much time had passed?

There was little opportunity to contemplate, as he heard footsteps and grumbling over by the front door. Conrad rushed over to the table, grabbed the lantern, and made a run toward the door. However, it flung open as he neared it, and four men entered the cabin. They all stared with their blank canvas faces while lumbering toward him. In a panic, the strategist looked to his right and spotted a window.

Rather than attempt to fight off the horde, Conrad made a run for the window and jumped straight through it, cradling the lantern as he came crashing down to the ground outside. On his hands and knees now, he looked up to see a dozen more townsfolk standing before him, weapons in hand. He couldn't help but chuckle. Bosfueras was living up to its horrible reputation.

Time to run, he thought while hopping to his feet. Conrad dashed to his right, aiming to reach deep enough into the woods that they'd lose sight of him. The townsfolk, however, weren't ready to let him go. His shoulders tensed up to his ears as a spinning sickle flew past him and landed on the grassy ground ahead. In response, Conrad began running in erratic patterns: Sometimes it was zigzagged, and other times it involved stutter-stepping to trick the mob behind into missing. Early on, the new strategy worked. He'd avoided several rocks and sharp farming tools.

From behind, he heard a crazed woman screeching, and then several loud *whooshes* rapidly approaching. A split-second later, fiery pain overtook his right shoulder and a horrible, fleshy sound pierced his ears: it had sounded like a juicy steak being cut. He stumbled momentarily but managed to keep his footing. A tumble to the ground right now likely meant his death. He couldn't allow the mob to gang up on him.

Conrad continued off into the woods with the weapon hanging out the back of his shoulder, waving as he moved and paining him all the more. He suspected that it was an axe, but dared not reach back until completing his escape.

The next cabin he passed had yet more of the crazed townsfolk waiting for him. One man held a bucket of dark, bubbling substance. Tar? Or whatever Mr. Willoughby was made of? Conrad couldn't be sure, but he didn't wish to find out. The man ambushed him and flung the bucket forward. The strategist's eyes narrowed as the dark liquid flew his way, and in a split-second decision, dove to his right, dragging through the grass and dirt as he heard the substance splash nearby.

His body ached and his eyes desperately wanted to shut from exhaustion, but Conrad knew that he couldn't be still for long. He observed the dark material oozing toward him through the leaves and grass for but a moment before clawing up to his feet once more. He could hear footsteps and angry voices all around but had no intention of looking back.

Out of the corner of his eye, he spotted the man with the bucket winding up to swing it at him.

Whoosh

Conrad ducked the swing, and the man grunted as he flailed and fell to the ground in a sad heap. Up ahead, he could see no more cabins. Only trees, bushes, and grass beckoned him. This was his best chance to escape.

Putting his head down and pushing through strained breaths, Conrad jogged into the depths of the woods until he couldn't move anymore. He was too exhausted, sore, thirsty, and hungry. He collapsed against a tree and looked all around. There were no signs of life; not even a noise. He had lost the mob, for now. The pain in the back of his shoulder had become unbearable, and every movement of his upper body felt like a new stab wound. With a trembling hand, Conrad reached back and slowly pulled the axe out of his shoulder. Despite his best efforts to remain quiet, a subdued cry escaped his lips. Oddly enough, it wasn't as painful as he had been expecting. The injuries sustained in his battle with Wolfgang a year prior had pained him far more.

After pulling the axe out, Conrad dug into his pack to retrieve food and water. It wouldn't be long before *someone* caught up with him, but for now, he was content to be still. He desired the same relaxation as when he had held the black gold in his hands.

His eyes widened. Why would he think such a thing? He had been able to resist black gold's effects before. Why not now? The strategist could only sit back and wonder as he ate. The gash on his shoulder needed further attention, but for some unexplainable reason, he felt no urgency in addressing the wound. Now that he was thinking about it, the stab wounds from the spider-creature's fangs and the cut on his arm probably needed further treatment, too. The injuries were starting to pile up. He let out a deep sigh. As things were going, it wouldn't be long before he was caught.

※

BACK ON THE main path outside of the woods, Mr. Willoughby crept into the large mob of men and women. They all spoke in Old Gentish, something no one from the outside would understand. Of course, the monster itself never spoke. Instead, it watched on as the others laid out their plan. One of the men said something that seemed to displease the beast, so it walked over to him and stared down, its ringed eyes focusing into single, red dots.

The man stared back at the monster, his expression defiant and cocky. Mr. Willoughby slowly tilted its head back, and its jaw opened inhumanly long and wide; enough that a full-sized turkey could be taken in with one gulp. Its shrill exhale seemed to disturb the defiant man, along with a variety of birds that stirred and then fled from the thick of nearby trees. He reached down to draw his weapon, but in a split-second, Willoughby jerked its head forward. The man didn't have time for his next breath before his head was enveloped by the over-sized jaws of the monster. A loud *crunch* echoed off the trees, followed by a series of other crunches. The defiant man's body fell, decapitated. The stump of where his neck had once connected to his head squirted and then pooled dark blood. None of the horde reacted to the gruesome display. It was as if they hadn't even noticed.

Mr. Willoughby plodded off into the woods as it chewed and crunched on the skull some more. In a short time, it had swallowed the whole thing. Most of the horde followed it with their weapons, tools, and torches in hand. They wanted blood.

※

AFTER OVER AN HOUR of following the beast, it stopped in its tracks. The townsfolk held up behind it and did not question the decision. Mr.

Willoughby's glowing red-ringed eyes focused in on a tree up ahead. It *reeked* of the outsider's blood. It could also see that he was trying to hide, but a bit of his shirt was sticking out from the spot, and he was shaking. The monster let out a pained, hoarse chuckle and lumbered in the direction of the tree.

The horde behind remained silent and motionless as if waiting for a command. The creature stopped in front of the tree, facing Conrad's back, and held one of its long arms out. It morphed into a sharp, dark spear. It pulled back, then thrust the spear into the trunk of the tree and entirely through it to pierce its prey on the other side. It made sure to twist it around after stabbing through for maximum damage.

Mr. Willoughby then pulled the spear out of the tree and reformed it into its arm. It peered through the hole in the trunk and saw no sign of its target.

∼

JUST THEN, a shirtless Conrad dashed out of some bushes to the left with a lit lantern in hand and threw it at the monster. There was no time for it to react, and the lantern erupted into flames upon impact. The fire spread over Willoughby's body like oil in water. The monster let out one cry, and one cry alone: A twisted concoction of human, animal, and monster all at once. He had never heard anything so unnatural in all of his life. Not even the Nightcrawler compared.

After a few moments of burning, it became clear that the flames weren't going to let up, and Conrad smiled confidently as he retrieved his shirt from the tree. It had been pinned there by the axe pulled from his shoulder earlier.

Smoke plumed from the raging fire on the motionless creature. It had ceased any sort of noise or reaction. It only stood there, staring at Conrad as it had the night before. Behind it, the mob of townsfolk also remained still, only watching him with their vile, red eyes. Something wasn't right. Why weren't they attacking?

Then, Mr. Willoughby began walking in its usual jerky motion, despite being lit ablaze. However, it wasn't headed toward Conrad, but further southwest. As far as he had seen, that led to nowhere except another cliff.

The river, Conrad thought. It was going to put the flames out by jumping from the ledge. He started for the monster and began drawing upon his saber, but stopped when the horde began shouting while advancing on him with their weapons at the ready. He couldn't afford another blow from the mob.

A fiery Mr. Willoughby walked up to the cliff ledge, and without hesitation, jumped off. After confirming his suspicions, there was no more reason for Conrad to stick around. He turned and ran as fast as he could. He hoped to either stumble across an alternate route around Bosfueras or find a path to sneak into town.

After some jogging, he reached the end of the woods and came upon a dirt road. He could hear running water to his left, which he figured to be the river. He preferred not to go that way, in case Willoughby had survived its plunge. Instead, he made a right turn onto the path and crept along, thinking it would lead him into town.

However, it wasn't long before Conrad encountered more than he had bargained for: There was a whole new mob of townsfolk waiting for him on the road, and they immediately spotted him when he approached. There were at least a few dozen this time, and they were armed to the teeth from what he could see in the lifting fog. They had flanked him, he thought. An ingenious move that he hadn't anticipated from such sluggish foes. How had the previous group managed to inform this horde of his general location? It mattered little, as he was now like a rat trapped in a maze. As Conrad turned to run, he heard a loud *whoosh* go by his ear and he paused, in shock. An arrow landed a few paces in front of him. Its tip was dipped in something dark.

The strategist ran to his left, into the woods, but stayed along the path. He was using the trees for cover. Currently, he had three options: travel back into the woods and risk being killed by the horde in there, return toward the town and try to sneak by an even bigger and more alert group of townspeople, or head down by the river and see if the stream could carry him somewhere safe.

The last option seemed the most hopeful, although he didn't like the idea of potentially being met at a riverbank by Willoughby. Still, it was probably the safest choice.

Conrad crept along for some time on the declining path down to the river. He hoped that keeping quiet would make the other group think that he'd run back into the woods, but he would often hear loud shouts behind him, off in the distance.

When he finally reached the riverbank, Conrad stopped in his tracks. The current looked strong. He wasn't a bad swimmer, but he was injured and dazed. It would be another risk, especially since he didn't know where it would take him. For all he knew, it might dump him out into the ocean.

Then, he saw it: Steam coming up from the middle of the current. After the steam followed a dark, charred head. Fear struck him like a bolt of lightning when the red rings for eyes emerged from the depths.

"No way..." Conrad trailed off before letting out a defeated chuckle.

He watched as Mr. Willoughby rose from the river and walked toward him. It appeared sleeker; having shed some of the chub in its mid-section and legs. It was also missing the bottom half of its jaw, but it still managed to breathe with its usual excited strain.

"Now what?" Conrad muttered. Before he could contemplate anything further, something sharp struck his back, and much like the axe from earlier, it wasn't as painful as he'd expected. A strained gasp escaped his mouth as he reached back and felt the shaft of an arrow. His hand had not the strength to even grip it, let alone pull it out, and his head began swimming as he lurched forward, stumbling into the water.

Conrad felt the darkness taking him once more, and after being battered and broken, he didn't feel like fighting. The last thing he saw was the flowing water, mere inches from his face, as he fell and all faded to black.

CHAPTER 9
PREY

Conrad faded in and out of consciousness as the strengthening current carried him downstream. After some time adrift, he was able to see that the river branched off two ways: To his left, it appeared to dump out into the ocean. Due to his positioning, he stayed to the right, and caught wind of a man-made drainage system even further to his right; coming from what appeared to be the rocky foundation of town. He had insufficient strength to swim for it, but he made a mental note that it was there.

Not long after, he noticed another man-made dumping slide off to his right. It led to an open cylinder with muddy water pouring out of it. This time, he suspected, it had to be a sewage system. Once more, however, he lacked the strength to swim over and inspect any further.

After some time, the current swept him under a great wooden bridge, and finally, he was dumped out into the ocean. To his right, Conrad could see a dock, but it was at least a few hundred meters away, and he was exhausted. However, the strategist could swear that he was feeling *better* since the arrow had pierced his back. Perhaps it was a second wind. Despite having little strength in his arms and legs, he paddled toward the dock. There was no time to drift, as Willoughby and the mob had proven themselves persistent in their tracking of him.

Luck was on his side, as the current and tide helped push him toward the dock faster than his meager strokes normally would have allowed. Soon, Conrad found himself underneath the dock, clinging onto a ladder and resting. After a short breather, he climbed and was shocked upon reaching the top to find no one in sight. More surprising still was that he was able to walk. The damage he had taken prior and lack of sleep made him weary, but after an arrow to the back and an axe to the shoulder, he had assumed movement would be out of the question for some time. Yet, the wounds now felt more like bothersome cuts. The arrow had come out on its own at some point during his trip downstream.

Conrad didn't want to stand around and contemplate, though. Despite already having completed his mission by confirming the black gold's existence in Bosfueras, it seemed different from what he had encountered at Mt. Couture, and it had him curious. It was certainly an option to turn tail and flee town, but while he was here and going through all of this trouble, why not also confirm that it was a Dark Wizard who was responsible for all of this madness? Conrad was tired of being in the dark, and for every answer he'd found so far, 10 more had come to mind.

He had already come up with a plan to sneak into the citadel. It was based largely on a hunch, but there was little left for him to go on and with Mr. Willoughby still on the prowl, he needed to keep moving, anyway.

Upon reaching the path perpendicular to the dock, the strategist took notice of a tall stone wall across from him. His best guess, based on positioning, was that it blocked off the rocky shore where he had seen the two man-made slides for sewage and drainage upstream. There was no chance he could climb it, being at least 10 meters high and without anywhere to grab onto. Instead, he had every intention of returning to the river, traveling downstream once more, and then entering the drainage system. Through there, he was certain that he could infiltrate the citadel from below and then sneak into the cathedral. There, he was sure to find the Dark Wizard, and perhaps even the stockpile of black gold that had gone missing one year ago.

To his left was a path that climbed high up onto a hill filled with trees. Conrad believed that it would take him back to the same ledge where he had first scouted out the town. To his right was a bridge off in the distance; the very bridge that he had gone under before being dumped into the ocean.

Aside from the small beach where he had been struck by the arrow, Conrad hadn't encountered a spot where he could safely jump into the river. Most of the time, it was too high up. The bridge that he had initially crossed to reach Bosfueras was at least 50 meters above the water in his estimation, if not more.

The safest and most logical option was attempting to find the river source. There had to be a mountain where the river began, and along the way, he would be sure to find a safe place to enter the water. From there, all he would have to do was let the stream carry him.

At the end of the dock, Conrad took a left. Shivers of paranoia ran down his spine faster than he himself could move; knowing that until reaching the trees at the top of the hill, he was virtually defenseless. He may have had his weapons, but without cover of any kind, swarming him would be easy for the townsfolk. However, to his surprise, he didn't run into anyone as he lumbered up the hill.

When he reached the top, the path turned to the right. He was certain that it would lead directly to the steep path into town, so instead, he continued straight into the woods. Relief swept over him, just as the protective shadows of the trees had. It was the first time he hadn't felt chased or attacked in hours. Of course, Mr. Willoughby could track him down if he didn't keep moving, but at the monster's slow pace, even walking would help him gain ground.

Conrad traveled through the woods for about an hour until he noticed a cliff to his right. He was positive that it was the same cliff he had climbed and slept on top of earlier, but from the other side. Further off to his left, there was another cliff, even bigger. The strategist suspected that he was entering a mountainous region; a sign that a river source might be nearby.

He reached and felt his back. The wound from the arrow had closed up and become itchy. The axe wound had also healed, and the scabs were black. Conrad shivered, wondering what it meant. In his wandering thoughts, he kept coming back to his moment with the black gold earlier in the day. Why? Why had he reached out and taken it? After all of the grief it had caused one year ago?

It was then that a startling realization struck him: He desired to hold the black gold once more. Never before had he felt such clarity and peace of mind. In that one moment when he had held it, the pain went away. The headache from lack of food or drink, the aches and pains from earlier battles: They were all gone. It was unfair; why couldn't he have the black gold? His mind jumped around, trying to justify it, but he knew from all of the pain, death, and suffering of the past that he couldn't have it.

Then, through the fading light between leaves and branches,

Conrad observed that the sun was setting. It was another phenomenon of the black gold: Time seemed to pass in an instant when his mind was on it, or when he held the cursed metal. How long had he been thinking about it? How long had he been *walking*?

As these thoughts bounced around in his mind, a howl echoed from off in the distance. He increased his pace, for he knew what those sounds meant: Wolves or perhaps dogs roamed the area.

Soon after, he entered a clearing to see several mountains looming from off in the distance. The river couldn't have been far off. The problem, however, was that his eyes were heavy and his body felt even heavier under the strain of his newfound exhaustion. He couldn't jump into the river in this state. Rest was needed, and with that need came a new idea.

He walked for another hour, gathering stray branches along the way. Just because he was being hunted, didn't mean he couldn't get some rest. At the edge of a clearing, Conrad found a perfect spot to rest, up against a tree. His plan was to set branches as an alarm for any potential attacker while he slept. At Mr. Willoughby's slow pace, he would have plenty of time to escape after hearing the crunching branches, he thought.

After laying branches in a perimeter about five meters around his resting spot, he lay up against the tree trunk and dozed off. In a pool of darkness, he heard a deep voice echoing from far away. Similar to his previous dream, the noise progressively got closer, but instead of becoming loud and unbearable, it simply became loud enough to hear:

Maut in aibero
Le gachni netute
Glabris adtu vaor

Conrad awoke to the sound of snapping twigs. It was pitch-black out. Even the light of the moon had become obscured by the tall trees. He squinted for a few moments to see a pair of red eyes staring back at him from across the clearing.

"Willoughby…" he muttered, but while standing, he noticed another pair of red eyes appear in the infinite shadows of the night, and yet more twigs snapped in their presence.

Moments later, another pair looked at him, and then two more in succession. He could hear breaths, but not of the monster he'd come to expect: They were the breaths of a canine. Were they wolves? Or tracking dogs of the mob?

The answer came soon after when a wolf stepped into the middle of the clearing. It had mangy fur, and appeared larger, both in bulk and length, than any wolf he'd ever seen. Its single-minded gaze was fixated on Conrad, but what filled him with more worry was the fact that its eyes were red.

If the red-eyed townsfolk were dangerous, violent, and resistant to pain, then what did it mean for the wolves? Would they be the same? Had they been influenced by the black gold, somehow?

Conrad stared down the wolf, showing no outward fear. He put a hand on his saber hilt and stepped onward. The wolf growled as it lowered itself and crept ahead. The others stayed back, but the glow of their eyes could still be seen in the black of night. The strategist drew his blade.

"Stay back!" Conrad shouted as he swung his saber horizontally.

The wolf backed down, but it could almost certainly tell that the swipe had only been for show; as it hadn't come close to landing. After a pause, it closed in once more, this time baring teeth. Conrad took a defensive stance, knowing that an attack was imminent.

Behind him, the strategist heard a twig snap. They were attempting to surround him, he thought. Conrad pressed his back up against the tree trunk so that an ambush couldn't come from behind. The wolf in front of him bent back on its hind legs, then leaped out with jaws wide open.

Conrad sidestepped the attack and brought his blade down upon the back of the wolf as it crashed into the tree. The canine let out a defeated yelp, causing some of the red eyes in the darkness to scatter. He knew that wouldn't be the end, though; wolves wouldn't give up on a potential meal so easily.

Thinking it best to finish off the most immediate threat, his eyes fell to the wolf whom he'd struck down. It lay on the ground in a prone position, but it still gazed back up at him with killing intent. It then let out a demonic wail that sounded like a dog and screeching cat combined. Conrad took a step back and gasped as the open wound on its back shot out a thin, green tentacle that wrapped around his wrist.

The bloody lesion on the wolf's back grew large, jagged teeth that looked similar to bone, and opened up further as the dreadful sound of tearing flesh filled Conrad's ears. The gaping wound had turned into a giant mouth, and now the tentacle was reeling him in slowly, like a helpless fish on a hook.

Thinking quickly, Conrad chopped at the tentacle with his saber, but to his surprise, it merely bounced off. The beast let out a shriek, so he at least knew that it had caused some pain, and upon closer inspection, the feeler was now leaking green, rotten juices. Once again, he brought his blade down on the slimy, hairy tentacle, and this time, the grip loosened. He had cut all the way through.

Conrad wiggled the sliced-off tentacle from his arm and it squirmed like a panicked worm after hitting the ground. What remained of the feeler retreated into the body of the prone wolf as it let out its loudest cry yet.

Believing the threat to be neutralized, the strategist checked his surroundings. All of the red eyes that had previously surrounded him were gone.

"Great…" he muttered, but then turned when he heard a stomach-churning noise.

The sound reminded him of a simpleton chewing with his mouth open. He gazed over at the source: The same prone wolf that had attacked him with the tentacle. The great mouth on the side of the wolf's body closed and looked to be chewing. After a few moments, the beast wailed and opened its unnatural mouth, shooting out five hairy tentacles in the process. They flailed around in the air randomly, and now Conrad knew that he would have to run. If he were ensnared by more the one, it would likely mean his death.

He grabbed his backpack, then turned and dashed toward the mountains. As he ran, he could hear pitter-patter behind him and to his sides. Just as he had feared, the wolves were stalking him, and now he knew that they were far from ordinary wild animals. No man could outrun a wolf, Conrad thought, so the wisest thing he could do was climb high up a tree and wait them out. Wolves couldn't climb, after all.

With snapping twigs, rustling leaves, and panting canine breaths all around him, the strategist made a run for the nearest tree filled with branches and began climbing.

With some effort, he reached about four meters high: well out of reach for his pursuers. Conrad looked down, feeling triumphant; until realizing that the tree was being circled by four wolves. It had only taken them seconds to swarm. What stood out to him more than anything else was the alpha of the group: It was bigger to a considerable degree; so much that the others looked like pups in comparison. The beast had darker fur and monstrous fangs that it showed while gazing up at him with red, hungry eyes.

Despite the alarming presence of the wolves circling his only safe haven, Conrad chose to keep his mind on other things. He looked up at the sparkling night sky and inevitably began to think of the black gold, its beauty reminding him of the stars. It wasn't like those times he'd held it a year before. Instead of a nervous, angry feeling, he had felt at ease. A darkness had overtaken him when he'd held it back in the cabin, but not one of fear; complete and total relaxation for the first time in his entire life. His mind had been freed of all the problems and conflicts of the world, and he yearned for that feeling once more.

Conrad shook the cobwebs out. He thought of the Gold Fever-infected miners back at Mt. Couture, and how it had driven them all to insanity. Even an all-powerful Wizard like the Mountain King hadn't been able to withstand its maddening effects forever. He had to think of the consequences. No matter how tempting, he could never take the black gold again. But what if *this* black gold was different? The idea lingered like a sweet aroma trapped in his mind.

His thoughts were interrupted by excruciating bone-crunching noises below. Conrad peered down and his jaw fell slack. The alpha wolf was undergoing a gruesome transformation. It hunched over while writhing in pain with a curled back upward. The beast's paws grew outward into fingers with long claws, and chunks of its fur shed to make room for swelling muscle. Its back then arched further upward with a loud *crack*, to which it reacted with a yelp. The alpha had changed its physiology to stand upright, as a human would. It had also given itself massive hands, perfect for climbing.

A shiver rippled through Conrad's body as he watched the alpha sink its claws into the tree trunk and climb. Its neck had grown thick and so too had its chest, making the climb effortless for the beast. It gazed up at him and drooled while letting out demonic grunts.

Conrad kicked the alpha in the head as it got close, but it was undeterred and reached a hand out. The mighty grip of the alpha made him wince, and he was thrown down from the tree with a simple flick of its wrist. The shock of striking the ground momentarily froze him, but it didn't take long for his survival instincts to kick in as he saw three other wolves circling him with lustful red eyes. Still on his bottom, Conrad clawed backward in desperation, but the wolves only mimicked his sluggish speed. They were playing with him, now.

They stopped in their tracks, however, when the alpha hopped down from the tree and landed with a crash, briefly shaking the ground and disorienting Conrad to the point that he fell flat on his back. He looked up to see the beast lumbering toward him with deep, heavy breaths.

Conrad hopped to his feet and drew the saber once more. The alpha stopped and only stared back at him. Now, what? Would a slash from his blade even harm it? It appeared to think so, even if it was a hulking figure that outclassed him in nearly every way.

"Keep your distance…" he muttered, taking a few steps back.

The next thing Conrad knew, his head felt light as a feather, and he was flung forward onto his face. Upon trying to get back to his feet, he realized that he was being pinned down by two paws on his back. One of the wolves had attacked him from behind.

The wolf bit through the protection of Conrad's boot and into his calf. A desperate, pained cry escaped his lips. This would be the end, he thought. They were all going to feast on him. Just as he began to accept his fate, however, he felt a harsh wind overhead and then heard the yelp of a wolf. In an instant, the weight was lifted from his back. He looked up to see that the alpha had knocked it away.

Conrad let out a faint chuckle as the alpha stood over him and raised its claw. He looked down and closed his eyes, knowing that he wouldn't be able to avoid the final blow. Yet, the searing pain of the claws never reached him. He looked up sheepishly to see the alpha with its ears perked up, gazing over to its left, where Conrad had originally come from.

The beast growled, and so too did the other wolves. Conrad couldn't understand what was going on, but he was relieved when the alpha turned to face the direction of whatever it was hearing. After a few moments of what he thought to be dead silence, he finally understood what had disturbed the wolves from their meal: *the breathing*.

The screeching, maniacal breaths of Mr. Willoughby bounced off the trees, carried by the light wind. The wolves and even Conrad remained motionless, waiting for the monster to show itself. After much anticipation, he saw the red-ringed eyes off in the distance, swaying slightly from side to side as it stumbled at its slow pace. Out of the darkness and into the clearing appeared Willoughby. It paid no attention to the wolves, who were all baring their teeth and growling, but instead set its horrid, focused gaze on the strategist.

One of the wolves lunged out at Willoughby, but in mid-air, it slapped the canine down to the ground and then stomped on its body with the force of a swinging war hammer. Conrad winced as the crunch of the wolf's bones rang in his ears, drowning out its pained cry. The alpha growled once more and took a few steps toward Willoughby. The wolf on the ground shot a tentacle out of the gaping wound in its side, grabbing hold of the monster.

However, Mr. Willoughby continued ahead, unhindered, and the wolf was dragged along by its feeler instead of stopping it as intended. The other two wolves and the alpha surrounded the monster, but it refused to take its eyes, now single red dots in seas of black, off of Conrad.

The strategist scrambled to his feet and turned to run, but he felt an iron-like grip on his arm, stopping him. He looked back and gasped to see that Willoughby had extended its arm supernaturally long, like stretchy goo. It used the other arm to swat away at the wolves, who didn't dare make a move but held their circle around the monster.

Conrad flicked his captured wrist, tossing the saber to his other hand, and then slashing at Willoughby's extended arm. It sliced through and the arm dissolved into the same dark red webbing that he'd been trapped in earlier. Without a second thought, Conrad bolted in the direction of the mountains.

While running, he heard the howling of wolves and the screeching of Mr. Willoughby. He hoped that they would tear each other apart.

Over time, the fire in his gut simmered to an ember, and his calf began to burn from the prior wolf bite. His quick-paced strides transitioned into a hobbling jog, and his whole body felt as if it had tripled in weight. The aches and pains of his previous wounds also returned, and all Conrad could think about was how the black gold would dull the soreness.

His thoughts were interrupted, however, by a dark streak shooting by to his left. He had only noticed it with his peripheral vision, but when he turned his head, nothing was there save trees and bushes. Conrad hoped that it had only been his imagination, and hobbled on. His body wanted to stop, but having gotten so close to the mountain range, the river had to be nearby. This was his best chance to escape.

Soon, Conrad caught another dark streak out of the corner of his eye. Whatever it was, it was *big*, and now he heard the trampling of its strides and heavy breaths. The trees to his left rustled, as if a powerful wind were pushing through them, and then, out of those trees burst the large figure. He stopped as it galloped out in front of him, blocking his path.

Before Conrad stood an upright deer with hooks for hands. It was well over two meters tall, including its dark antlers, had the same red eyes as the wolves, and the face of a dead deer. Rotten flesh hung off of its snout and a tongue draped over its jagged teeth. Its body was muscular, especially in its hind legs, which looked identical to any other deer's. Yet, it stood upright, as if it were human. The most alarming feature of the beast, however, was that its fur was coated in dry blood.

"What the hell have they done to the wildlife around here?" Conrad asked aloud.

The deer-beast huffed and kicked up some dirt with its hoof. It put its head down and let out a distorted cry before charging at Conrad with startling speed.

Conrad narrowly avoided the attack by rolling to his right. The deer-beast stopped far quicker than he'd anticipated, and then turned and swung its hook for a hand at him.

With no time to draw a weapon, Conrad ducked the horizontal swing, but the deer came at him with its other hook vertically, forcing him to sidestep and keeping him on the defensive. The deer-beast continued to swing wildly until Conrad's already depleted stamina ran out. He tripped over his own feet and fell to the ground. Instead of attacking, the deer-beast cocked its head and stared down at its prey.

After a few moments of heavy breathing, the strategist sprang to his feet and turned to run. He knew that it was futile, but there wasn't much else he could do. He heard the distorted cry of the deer behind him, then the stamping of its hooves, and finally the charge. He didn't dare look back, however, and instead focused on a tree up ahead. With those hooks for hands and hooves at its feet, perhaps it wouldn't be able to climb, he thought.

Conrad himself was uncertain of his ability to scale the tree after how much damage his calf had taken, but he had to try while the deer-beast appeared to be doing little more than playing with its food. In the brief moments of his awkward strides, he thought about the black gold once again. It brought comfort to him. He no longer thought of his tired and damaged body, but instead the relaxation of nothingness.

It was a feeling that lifted Conrad into the night sky and allowed him to fly amongst the stars; a wonderful sensation that he wished to feel more often. His visions were distracted, however, by a pain in his shoulders. It started off dull, but increased in intensity as each moment passed until it felt like a searing hot nail was shooting through. Suddenly, he realized that his journey through the night sky wasn't a vision, but *reality*.

He looked at each shoulder to see that he was under the tight grip of dark talons. Next, he gazed upward to see what was carrying him: A giant owl, bigger than him, with black spots on its brown wings. The winged beast carried Conrad through the night sky as if he were a fish caught from the river. He couldn't see them for himself, but he was sure that the owl had the same red, piercing eyes as the other nocturnal animals that had attacked him so far.

At first, panic set in. Was the owl taking him back to its nest? To feast on him? To feed him to its young? Horrible possibilities flooded Conrad's mind, but then, something caught his eye down below: the river. As he'd suspected, the source of the stream came from the second mountain in the range, and the owl was taking him in that direction. A new idea crept into his mind.

They flew high in the air for a while, and Conrad's entire body became sore from his own weight as they reached the base of the mountain. As luck would have it, the owl swooped down and then started flying up at the angle of the mountain's base. The strategist slowly reached down and drew his saber. Then, fast as lightning, he struck the beast in its belly. It let out a blaring screech while dropping him.

The drop was higher than he'd expected, and he couldn't help but cry out in fear while crashing through some tree branches. He landed with a *thud* on a patch of dirt that had small rocks sticking out of it. Fortunately, the branches had slowed his fall, and all told, it had only left him with a few cuts along his arms and a dizzy spell after having the wind knocked out of him. Truthfully, he felt relieved to not be held up by his body weight anymore. The flight had exhausted him. The owl let out a distorted *hoot* as it shot overhead.

As he clawed through the pebbles of the mountainside, the sound of running water penetrated a groggy Conrad's ears; enough that it snapped him out of his daze. He looked up to see that the owl had turned around and was coming down for another swoop. He grabbed his saber and took a sideways fencing stance. There was no use in seeking cover; trees were nearby, but they were scattered compared to the woods.

The owl dove with incredible speed and ferocity; so much that wind smacked Conrad in his face as he sidestepped and held his saber out. His blade shot back and flew from his hand as he toppled over in surprise. He heard the distorted cry of the owl as he struck the ground, and soon after came a great crashing noise, along with bouncing rocks.

Conrad took a deep breath to regain his bearings and then stood. He tracked down his saber, which was covered in thick, dark blood, before looking to his right. Further down the incline, against a boulder, the giant owl writhed and struggled. He could see its blood splattered on the face of the rock.

Figuring the owl to be incapacitated, Conrad began hobbling to the left, where the sounds of the river beckoned him. However, the sudden, panicked cries of the owl stilled him. He looked over his shoulder to see that a small group of rabbits had approached the winged beast. The strategist snorted.

"Only rabbits…" he muttered, facing forward once more.

The owl squealed as Conrad walked, once again catching his attention. His jaw hung open. *The rabbits were feasting on the owl.* The large bird squirmed and cried out until moments later when it fell limp. Dozens of rabbits surrounded and gorged on the carcass as its dark blood erupted around them.

They were no larger than ordinary rabbits, Conrad thought, but they also vastly outnumbered the owl. With its injuries, it had been completely helpless. Maybe the rabbits only liked to scavenge. Just in case they were a threat, he decided to creep away. In his current state, he wouldn't be difficult to catch.

As the strategist tip-toed away, his foot caught on a large pebble and knocked it down the hill, along with a few others and some dust. All at once, the rabbits looked his way. Their chubby cheeks were covered in blood, but most horrifying of all were their large, red eyes. They were much like Mr. Willoughby's eyes whenever it focused on him, except bigger.

The strategist froze in place and looked down at the bloodthirsty creatures. They too remained motionless, but their empty gazes remained fixed on him. He looked over to the owl's corpse. It had been reduced to a nearly unrecognizable state; with wings that had been rendered into featherless stumps, a face that had largely been chewed off, and a body that already had bones sticking out of it.

"Killer bunnies…" he mumbled before chuckling. He then pivoted his feet and crossed over in the direction of the river. All of the rabbits shifted slightly so that they continued to look at him. "Stay there…"

After crossing over once more, Conrad shifted weight to his left and bolted with as much speed as his tired and injured body would allow. He heard the chirp-like noises of the rabbits behind him but didn't dare look back. The river had to be close, he thought. Even if some of them caught up, he could make it.

Despite his mad dash, it wasn't long before Conrad felt disturbances on his boots, and then the crunch of skin breaking on the back of his ankle. The next pain came on the back of his left thigh, and then he felt something small jump on his backpack.

With stuttered breaths, he stumbled and fell to the ground, his chest dragging painfully in the rocky dirt and tearing at his shirt. In the blink of an eye, Conrad had been swarmed by a dozen of the demonic little creatures, all nibbling, nipping, and chomping on him at once. He felt a second wind welling up, and with that extra power, he swung his arms and knocked several of the rabbits off of him.

Conrad jumped to his feet and looked down to see that some of the little beasts had been crushed by his fall. Not only that, but most of the bites weren't deep wounds, to his relief. Perhaps his first hunch about them scavenging had been correct. The rabbits had been able to tear apart a gravely injured creature like the owl, but not him; he still had strength left. That wouldn't last long, though. They may not have been deep wounds, but he could feel blood leaking from several of the punctures on his legs and back.

Even though he'd been able to fight them off, the rabbits didn't relent. They stared back up at him as if waiting for the next move to inform their reaction. He gazed past the rabbits, and further off in the distance behind them, saw another pack of the little creatures scampering. There were well over a dozen more headed their way.

"No…" Conrad said as he took a step back. The rabbits in front of him inched forward as the reinforcements from behind drew near.

The strategist readied his saber, and in one swift motion, swiped at the rabbits in front of him. He was successful in hitting a few, but most jumped back to avoid the blow. It had only been a distraction, though, as he turned and hobbled away as fast as he could.

In even less time than before, Conrad felt the sting of a bite on the back of his leg, but he pushed through the pain and pressed on. Several rabbits hopped onto his back, and one even reached his neck and sunk its teeth in. He jerked his neck back in shock before grabbing the rabbit by its foot and throwing it as hard as he could in a side-sweeping motion.

The sounds of the river grew louder with each painful stride taken, and then finally, Conrad laid eyes on what he'd been hoping to find for hours: the river bank. It was a rocky ledge, but this time, he could see the bottom. It was about a five-meter drop, in his quick estimation.

There was no time to think about the height of the drop or depth of the water, as Conrad felt his head grow light from blood loss, and he knew that it wouldn't be long before the tiny beasts overwhelmed him.

Conrad took two large final strides before jumping off the ledge, with several rabbits hanging onto him as he did. They flew through the air together until crashing into the water with a great splash, to be carried downstream by its swift current.

As he floated away, Conrad looked back at the rabbits that remained atop the ledge, gazing with wide, red eyes. For all he knew, the water might swallow him up, drown him; but he didn't care. He smiled defiantly at the little monsters. Tonight, they had missed out on their prey.

CHAPTER 10
WATER HAZARD

His heart racing, Conrad had no choice but to float aimlessly down the stream with nothing save the moonlight to aid his eyes. At first, the current was manageable, but over time, he could feel his speed picking up and the river narrowing. The rabbits that had come crashing in alongside him had all disappeared; either by drowning or swimming away.

After some time floating, the tension in Conrad's mind gave way to a strange relaxation. There was no noise save for the stream, and he laid his head back into the water, muting the sounds even further. It was a nice feeling, to not be hunted; at least for the time being.

As night gave way to dawn, the river bent, turned, and narrowed, increasing the intensity of his trip. Conrad's arms felt heavier than bales of hay, so he decided to take a break. He came across a boulder sticking out of the water and grabbed hold of it.

The strategist's weary eyes wandered up the flowing river. He couldn't see anything out of the ordinary. Even if Mr. Willoughby was slow-moving, the fact that at this very moment, it was tracking him down, headed straight for him; all with the intent of ripping him to bloody pieces; sent shivers down his spine. That trembling only made him more tired, however, and he fell into a daze.

∼

WATER HAZARD

Conrad blinked, and suddenly, the sun began to shine down upon him. He rubbed his eyes and groaned. How much time had passed? He turned, now on his belly, and looked upstream. A chill struck him like lightning. Around the bend of the ravine, a dark figure lumbered downstream, the rapids not nearly strong enough to carry it. Its soulless dots for eyes locked on him, and those familiar, taunting breaths penetrated his ears. In a panic, Conrad scrambled to his feet and jumped back into the water.

After drifting around some bends, Conrad noticed an irregularity in the stream up ahead. The current looked to be spinning like a tornado. *A whirlpool*, he thought. The problem was that the spinning water took up the entire width of the river, and it looked powerful. It was also difficult to tell which way the water was spinning. He hoped that he could simply go along with the current and then break away, but there was a chance he'd choose the wrong way and become trapped.

Since he was already to the left, the strategist chose that way. He paddled as far over to the side as possible and prepared to be swept up by the current, one way or another.

To his horror, he felt the current pushing against him as he slammed into the edge of the whirlpool. In seconds, he was swept up into the swirling water, and traveling around in a circle while simultaneously sinking further into the depths. After only a couple of rotations, he could no longer see above the edges of the whirlpool.

In an attempt to regain his composure, Conrad thought of the black gold once more. Even if it were just to hold it for a final time, he couldn't let this be the end. The newfound determination lit a fire in his gut, and he raised his knee to grab the concealed dagger. He drew in a deep breath and then dunked his head under to take a look: The waters were shallow enough that he wasn't far from the bottom, and the floor was rocky. He could also see which way the current was going thanks to some underwater flora waving around. With strong upward paddles, he resurfaced for air.

Conrad waited until the whirlpool carried him around three-quarters of a circle before dunking under once more and springing for the riverbed. He plunged his knife in between a couple of rocks, and then painstakingly pulled himself forward. It was a slow process; a tug of war between him and the whirlpool.

Realizing that his breath was running short, the strategist pulled with his last iota of strength, finally freeing himself from the current.

Even though it felt as if his chest was about to burst, he could only make small paddles upward after exhausting himself so much.

Upon reaching the surface, Conrad exhaled violently, and after a few heavy, strained breaths, he turned back to look at the force of nature he had narrowly defeated. Instead, what he saw was Willoughby, slowly marching down the river. The monster cut through the whirlpool with ease, as if to taunt him and his struggles. It hadn't even affected the jerky, uncanny motions of its strut. With that, Conrad became convinced that the only conceivable way for him to kill it was with fire, and lots of it.

For now, gaining some distance from the monster was his best option. He put his head down and paddled as fast as he could, dodging rocks and boulders that peeked out of the stream, and going with the flow of the ravine's many bends. After getting far enough ahead that he couldn't see Willoughby when looking behind, he ceased swimming, and let the current carry him once more.

After drifting for a couple of hours, Conrad realized that he was passing the collapsed rope bridge from the other day. It truly was as high up as he had originally thought, but it was difficult to see the foggy landscape above. Ahead, there was a small, rocky beach. After his struggles with the whirlpool, his breaths had become short and his head light. Resting would be wise, even if it meant his pursuer might gain some ground in the process.

Like before, Conrad looked upstream to make sure that Mr. Willoughby wasn't close behind as he rested. He felt his eyes closing, but even more, there was a deep longing in his heart for one thing: the black gold. As he dozed off from the exhaustion of his body and mind, he felt a breeze pass through him. The breeze soon turned into a howling wind, and it felt as if a bunch of arrows were passing him by loudly.

Conrad's eyes opened as he gasped and looked around. There *were* arrows flying at him. He gazed upward to see several dark figures firing black-tipped arrows at him from the veil of fog atop the cliff. He got up and grabbed his belongings, ready to make a dash for the water once more, but then something tugged at his leg. He looked down in horror to see a long, blood-red tongue wrapped around his ankle. He looked back and upward to see the deformed and decapitated head of Mr. Willoughby, carried by eight spider-like legs and hanging from the rock wall of the ravine. Its mouth was open impossibly wide, and was the source of the disgusting tongue holding him back.

The strategist's eyes wandered forward, picking up on an arrow speeding straight for him. As a reflex, he immediately ducked to avoid it, and as the *whoosh* rang in his ears from overhead, he drew his saber. A tug at his leg turned Conrad's attention back to Mr. Willoughby, who, like a fishing line being reeled in, was headed straight for him under the tension of its outstretched tongue. In one swift motion, Conrad cut the tongue with his saber and then drew his rapier and impaled Mr. Willoughby. The blade pierced straight through its elongated mouth so that the back of its throat rested against the hilt of his rapier. The monster's red eyes looked up at him, and its shrill, maniacal breaths continued. He could *feel them* on his hand, nearly causing him to wretch. Instead, he flung the blade forward, sending the spiderhead combination across the beach.

Conrad jumped into the river and looked behind to see that the monster was already showing signs of recovery. The hole in its mouth had closed up, and its spider legs twitched with renewed life. He next looked up to see more arrows flying his way, so the strategist dunked underwater to remove himself as a target. He opened his eyes while submerged to see arrows piercing the surface, only to slow down and then float back up harmlessly.

The strategist held his breath for as long as he could, and when he came back up for air, the arrows had stopped, and there was no sign of Willoughby upstream. With a sigh of relief, Conrad refocused himself. He hadn't only entered this river to survive but to infiltrate the citadel. Now, he aimed to ride the current downstream until reaching the drainage system he had noticed yesterday.

༄

AFTER ABOUT ANOTHER hour of drifting downstream and curving around the edge of what he believed to be the woods at Bosfueras' outskirts, Conrad encountered more arrows flying his way from atop the ravine. This time, it was even more nerve-wracking, because the fog had picked up enough that he couldn't see the tops of the ledges, or who was shooting at him.

Even though none of the shots came close to hitting, it reminded him of a problem soon to come: To reach the drainage pipe, he would have to pass the beach where he'd first been struck by an arrow. It was becoming clear to him that the townsfolk were crafty. Somehow, they'd been able to scout his position and report it to their reinforcements faster than he could move. Would there be a whole horde waiting for him at the beach?

On the sides of the river, Conrad noticed broken tree branches scattered about. Perhaps the result of a storm, he thought. It was perfect, though: He could use a branch and its many leaves as cover. It wouldn't be out of the ordinary to see such things floating downstream.

The strategist swam to the edges of the river and collected branches. As practice, he placed several leafy limbs over himself and floated. With enough leaves, it seemed natural, and he could go undetected.

Conrad collected branches for another half-hour until he determined that it was enough. He floated face-first downstream and placed the pile over his body. It was difficult for him to see, but that had to mean it was good camouflage, too. In addition, he tossed many other branches into the river around him, in the hopes that it would look like natural wreckage from a storm. After all, seeing one patch of branches might be suspicious.

It wasn't long before he noticed a group of townsfolk up ahead on a beach. However, he was surprised to see some of them standing in the water. Conrad grew nervous as he neared them. It was all up to chance, now. If he ran into one of the crazed men, it was all over. From his current trajectory, it was going to be close. He saw one of his earlier 'decoy' branches get pushed aside by a man.

Conrad's eyes widened when he saw that the man he was headed for held a piece of dark ore. *Black gold*, he thought.

Take it.

A deep voice in his head echoed. He shivered and tried to ignore it. He was about 20 meters from the men in the water, now.

You need it.

Only 10 meters from the townsfolk, he closed his eyes and tried to think of anything aside from black gold.

You will be at ease.

Conrad opened his eyes, and time stood still. The man holding the ore was to his right, within arm's reach. He could easily snatch the black gold from his hand. Then, he could make a run for it down the stream before they knew what had hit them. It would only be a minor inconvenience, he thought.

Yes, it is worth the effort.

The deep voice beckoned.

WATER HAZARD

Take it.
Take it!
TAKE IT!

Conrad clenched his fists and let himself float by, undetected. There was not a peep from the townsfolk, but he wanted to scream out loud. He told himself that it would be worth it to avoid the black gold for now. After all, there would probably be a whole treasure trove in the cathedral. No matter how much it pained him, he had to reach his objective first.

After waiting for a while, the strategist threw the branches off of his head and looked back. He was too far off for the townsfolk to see. Although it was all a haze to him, he remembered that the drain pipe had come after the beach. He swam to the right side of the river and waited.

A half-hour passed, and that was when he spotted it up ahead: a watery path carved into a ledge on the right. Some ways up the path was the drainage pipe, sticking out of the town's rocky foundation. He grabbed the ledge and pulled himself out of the water with considerable effort. Conrad once again found himself drained of all energy. All he wanted was to sleep, or have a piece of black gold to himself. However, he knew that halting his progress would invite the challenge of Mr. Willoughby. He was so close to his goal; certain that the drain system would grant him secret access to the citadel.

After stumbling for a few moments, Conrad walked further up the rocky ledge and toward the drain pipe. He looked into the cylinder, and as expected, it was dark and dank. It smelled like old, musty water, and he could barely see, but what other choice was there? At the very least, he spotted two long walkways flanking the waterway within.

Once inside the drainage system, Conrad realized that the pipe served only to funnel the water on its way out. The drain turned out to be more like a large hallway; easily five stories high and several meters wide. He had expected it to be a cramped cylinder inside. Ahead was a shining beacon of encouragement: a streak of light sliced through the darkness off in the distance. For such a closed-off structure as a citadel, a storm drain would be important to avoid flooding. He was certain that his goal lay ahead.

Pulling on a second wind, Conrad walked toward the light on the left-hand walkway, carved of textured stone. As he traveled, drips of water echoed off the walls, and a quiet stream flowed next to him.

Aside from the light up ahead, though, it was pitch black. It reminded him of the dream he had when first encountering Mr. Willoughby.

Suddenly, to his left, Conrad's eyes picked up on a hand shooting out of the darkness. It grabbed hold of his mouth, and he struggled and wriggled while being dragged into the abyss with explosive strength.

Moments later, he was thrown to the ground, a lantern was lit, and then it was shone in his face. Conrad could see the glint of a blade near his neck, and beyond the weapon was a scowling, bearded face. Standing over him was a chubby Gentish man who appeared middle-aged. There was a certain intensity to his eyes that felt familiar.

The strategist put his hands up and, in Gentish, said, "I come in peace! Please!"

A useless gesture, he thought. The townsfolk only spoke Old Gentish, and even if he had spoken it, it was unlikely that the man would listen or care for his words.

The scowling man raised an eyebrow and tilted his dark-haired head. He then withdrew the blade and moved his lantern closer to Conrad's face.

"You're… a foreigner?" the man asked in Gentish. His voice was hushed, yet carried with it a surprised tone.

Conrad's eyes widened. "And you… you're not infected?"

He snickered. "Your Gentish needs work."

"You speak the King's Tongue?" Conrad replied, wide-eyed now.

"Well, it is the most common language in the world, is it not?"

"I was led to believe that all of the Gentish refused to speak anything but their own language."

"Most of us learned other languages in order to trade with other countries. But outside of trade, what you say was once true. Things have changed recently, though. We surely live in strange times," he said before sighing. "And as for whether I'm 'infected', that is the reason why I'm down here. I'm not one of *them*."

"I see…"

"The real question is: What are you doing here in Bosfueras?"

"Let's just say that I'm here to prove the existence of something bad."

"Well, I'd say you've found something bad, alright! I refer, of course, to the crazed people above."

"You must be wondering how they fell to the madness…" said Conrad.

"Indeed. But when I think about it, the answer is obvious. Everything changed once that beautiful dark ore came into our possession. We all loved it so much, but slowly, I noticed a change in everyone's behavior. They became crazed… murderous, even. We have never been kind to outsiders, but when we started killing them needlessly, I knew it was time to get away," the man said.

"Why are you still here, then?" Conrad asked.

"Someone caught wind of my attempt to leave and a mob attacked me. I escaped, just barely, with my life. I've been living in here ever since," he replied. The strategist grimaced. "It is not so bad. No one comes down here anymore. I go fishing outside for food, and there's plenty of water. The river is a great resource."

"Still, to be in hiding in your own country…"

"What other choice is there? If I am caught… I've seen what they do to those who don't align with their beliefs," the man replied.

"You can escape with me if you wish. There's something I must do before leaving, though," Conrad said as he stood.

"And what might that be?"

"The reason I came down here in the first place was to infiltrate that citadel from below, and eventually, sneak into the cathedral," Conrad explained. "The town is swarming with men in plated armor, and many of them are concentrated around that building."

"Sorry to tell you, but it won't work. There are ladders that go up to the surface, but they are blocked off by iron bars. I can't remember if they were always there, or added after the town descended into chaos," the man said.

Conrad sighed. It seemed that for every solution he'd come up with while on his mission, he'd only ever been greeted by failure or rejection.

"I never should have come here," he said with a chuckle.

"That's right. You shouldn't have," the man replied with a frown. "I'm afraid there is no escape for either of us, Mr…"

"Conrad. And you are?"

"Feliz."

"Nice to meet you. I wish it were under better circumstances."

"Yeh, me too. Even still, if you wish to stay here and hide, there's plenty of room, as you can see," Feliz said as he raised a hand and gestured at the vast, empty space.

"If I stay here for long, it would only drag you down," Conrad replied.

"How so? They haven't managed to find me down here, yet."

"They will if I stay," said the strategist. "You see, I am being tracked by a monster, and no matter where I run or hide, it always finds me. I overheard some of the townsfolk, and I believe they call him 'Mr. Willoughby'. Such a familiar name, but I cannot recall why…"

Feliz's brown eyes widened. "Willoughby…"

"You know him?"

"Not personally, no. But before the carnage began, we captured and questioned a group of foreigners who had snuck onto our land without permission. That must have been a year ago, now. One of them had the surname, 'Willoughby'," Feliz said.

"I had a feeling that the creature was once human. There were patches of hair and skin on its otherwise tar-like body," Conrad added.

Feliz stroked his beard and said, "If you cannot stay here, and you wish to infiltrate the citadel, there may be another way…"

Conrad's ears perked up. "I'll take anything, at this point."

"Further down the river, there is another man-made waterway. This is for the town's sewage and trash. It connects to a spot where we used to hold ceremonies for the dead, but I doubt they honor the dearly departed, these days," Feliz said with a chuckle. "Even so, if you can navigate your way through there, you should reach the morgue, which is in the citadel."

"There is no time to waste, then." Conrad turned to leave. "Thank you for your help-"

"Wait," Feliz interrupted. "Shouldn't you stay and rest for a while? You don't look so good."

Suddenly, Conrad noticed his stuttered breathing and how much he was shaking. He had pushed it out of his head, but he *needed* some black gold to feel better. It would ease the pain of his injuries, but especially the strain on his mind.

"Yes, I've been through some difficult situations these past couple of days. I don't suppose you have any of that black gold, do you?" he asked.

"Is that what it's called? I do have some, wrapped up with my belongings. I do not dare touch it, though."

"Can I hold it for a while?"

"You want it?" Feliz asked.

"No, I… just need to hold it, then I'll be alright…" Conrad said, his eyes wandering.

"Alright, follow me," Feliz replied, then began striding down the dark corridor.

As Conrad followed, he noticed the water flowing faster and more steadily than before. It became louder, and he could just barely see it rushing down the waterway from the lantern's light.

"Must be raining," the Gentish man muttered.

Eventually, they reached the end of the corridor and took a right, followed by an immediate left. This led to a dead-end, but there was a half-circle carved out of the wall and some bent iron bars that had formerly blocked entry to the outside. Rays of dull light poked through from the stormy outdoors, and it was sufficient enough that the lantern was no longer needed

"This is my secret entrance and exit, in case of emergency," Feliz said, dimming the flame of his lantern. "Otherwise, welcome to my humble abode."

Conrad looked around the small space. It had the essentials like a blanket, fishing rod, and hunting knife, but there were also some personal belongings. There was an old, dusty book, a framed painting of a family, and a cloth that was wrapped around various objects. The strategist stared at the cloth for some time. It had to be the black gold. Even just thinking of the glorious nothingness to come when he finally laid hands on it made his eyes glaze over in bliss.

"I hope you're not about to go loco, like the others," Feliz said, snapping him back to reality.

He shook out the cobwebs and said, "No, no. I only want to hold the black gold for a moment, that's all."

"Very well. I don't truly want the wretched stuff, anyway," Feliz said as he knelt and unwrapped the cloth. Conrad's eyes lit up when he saw the sparkles of the black gold.

Take what is rightfully yours.

The deep, booming voice made him wince.

Take it.

Take it, and kill him.

"No..." Conrad muttered.

Feliz stood with the black gold in hand. "Is everything alright?"

"Yes, yes... just feeling a little under the weather."

"I can tell. Many foreigners that come to this land are fair-skinned. But you, my friend, look like you're turning into a ghost," Feliz said with a chuckle. He held the black gold piece out for him, but as Conrad reached for it, he clenched his fist around it. The strategist frowned and looked at him with demanding eyes. "Are you sure that you want this?"

You see? He won't give it to you. Kill him!

"Y-yes, of course…" Conrad trailed off, holding a hand out to accept it.

Kill him.
Kill him!
KILL HIM!

Conrad flinched as the ore fell into his hand, and then he felt relaxation. He melted in his skin until his back pressed against the wall, and he sat. He gazed upon the black gold with a sort of careless, thoughtless smile.

Feliz chuckled. "I see you really appreciate it. Wait here for a short while. There is something I need to go and take care of."

Though he had meant to reply, Conrad's mouth refused to move, and he continued to smile stupidly at the rock in his hands. Feliz shrugged after waiting a moment and then left with the lantern in hand.

A familiar darkness overpowered Conrad's eyes as relaxation and peace came over him. It was as if he were quietly traveling through empty space, gazing upon the stars in their finite lifespan, only to watch them burst in spectacular fashion. It was a joyous, yet bittersweet sight; to see something of such beauty shrivel up and collapse under its own weight.

In the aftermath of the exploding stars, a pair of giant, yellow eyes opened out of the dark. They gazed upon him, and they truly made him feel small. However, the eyes stared not with the malice he had come to expect, but a sense of pride. His relaxation had come to an end and been replaced by something else: anger. A new voice spoke to him; powerful, but not as deep as the one that had commanded him to kill Feliz. It was commanding but persuading.

> *The human star grows ever dim*
> *They are weak-willed in the presence of him*
> *Soon, they shall burst like others before*
> *And the Savior will rise to settle the score*
> *To make the traitors and heretics pay*
> *To kill the many pretenders who say*
> *That they are the one, but the truth shall arise*
> *When he who is Witch-born meets his demise*

Conrad awoke from his stupor to the sound of blood-curdling screams bouncing off the walls. He stood and placed the black gold in his pocket, but was surprised to still feel his previous aches and pains. Frustration built as he drew his saber, and in the reflection of his blade, he could see that his eyes flickered a shade of yellow. Before he could even ponder if it had only been his imagination, more screams echoed from down the waterway. Conrad walked into the dark corridor to see what the commotion was all about.

"I must kill him…" he muttered.

CHAPTER 11
ABOMINATIONS

Conrad took a right out of Feliz's temporary living area, and then a left to get back on the corridor where they had first met. The water to the left of the path was flowing stronger than ever, which made him wonder how long he had been holding the black gold. He continued with his saber at the ready, looking for any sign of movement.

The screams of Feliz likely meant that he had been slain at the hands of Mr. Willoughby. Conrad couldn't help but feel guilty. It was because he had stayed for too long. Even still, there was a grander purpose at play that pushed any hint of sadness from his mind: There could be no doubt that a Dark Wizard was behind the madness in Bosfueras. But he was a mere pretender; an imitator of the *one, true Savior*. And for his insolence, he deserved death.

Though fully aware that it was an odd thought to be having while being hunted, Conrad had entered a different state of mind: one of raw emotion coursing through his body. The only way to sustain it was to act out his violent and angry desires. It was like snapping back at another person angrily, but instead of being a momentary emotion, it was all he could feel.

After turning onto the main corridor where the exit was, Conrad observed Feliz's lantern off in the distance. In the waterway and walking slowly toward him against the strong current was Mr.

Willoughby. Its shrill breaths echoed off the walls and assaulted his ears.

Conrad turned and ran for the secret exit from earlier. Even if the flames of the lantern could kill the monster, it would likely jump into the water once more and recover. Instead, he chose to focus on his mission. The strategist made a left turn into a new corridor, and after running for some time, made a right that was followed by an immediate left.

He ran up to the exit, squeezed through the iron bars, and crawled along the muddy landscape until he came out of some high grass and onto the rocky land next to the river. Further down to his right, he noticed a large tube sticking out of the town's rock foundation.

Rain slapped Conrad in the face as he dashed for the tube. He violently pushed through bushes and brushed past some trees until finally, he saw the entrance. It smelled putrid; of human waste and decay. There was brown water coming from it, but before he could even consider whether he wanted to brave the stench, Feliz appeared from the dark, his face reflecting dread.

"You're alive?" Conrad asked, nearly breathless.

"Quickly, before anyone sees you!" he called back, stretching his hand out. Conrad took it and was pulled into the stench.

The inside was similar to the drain system from before: There were two stone walkways on the left and right. In between them was where the waste flowed down and eventually into the river. Conrad followed a fast-paced Feliz along the right walkway.

"You told me that Willoughby had become a monster, but I never could have imagined in my wildest dreams…" he trailed off between huffs and puffs. The air was thick, to make the matter of their location even worse; it was as if they were eating waste.

"I heard you scream, back there. I thought it had gotten to you," the strategist said as they made a right down a new corridor.

"Yes, well… it startled me," Feliz replied with a chuckle. He took another right. The sewage system was beginning to feel like a maze. "I'm glad to see you're in better spirits. I take it the black gold helped?"

Conrad felt the piece of ore in his pocket and smirked. "In some ways, yes. It gave me focus."

"Focus didn't appear to be your problem, earlier on."

"My mission is clearer than ever. I now realize that I don't only need to confirm the existence of a Dark Wizard. I must also kill him. He is a pretender."

Feliz raised an eyebrow. "A pretender of what?"

"The Dark Savior, of course. Is there a problem?" Conrad asked in an aggressive tone.

"No, no... it's just... interesting," Feliz assured him as he took a left down another corridor. "If you don't mind me asking, how do you plan on killing a Wizard? Aren't they supposed to be all-powerful?"

"I'll find a way, as long as you lead me to him," he replied. "You *do* know where you're going, don't you?"

"Indeed, I do. My job before the chaos erupted was to dispose of trash," Feliz said. "I know these disgusting halls like the back of my-"

Feliz froze, and Conrad stopped behind him.

"What's wrong?"

The Gentish man pointed ahead, his finger shaking. Conrad squinted; the walls had little windows carved out to provide light or perhaps alleviate the smell. Through the slivers of light passing through, he could see movement in the muddied water below. It was something long and dark.

"I don't remember anything like that..." Feliz murmured.

Out of the water crawled an abomination that even made a determined Conrad falter. In the slithers of light, he saw a large centipede crawl out onto the path parallel to them, but it was not an ordinary one. Although its body was insect-like, its normally sharp legs had been replaced with human arms that looked to be rotting down to the bone. Its face was a decapitated human woman's head, also deteriorating. Her eyes were crossed and her tongue hung out like a dog's. A piece of her nose had fallen off. She had long, greasy hair.

"Wh-what *is* that?" Conrad asked in a harsh whisper as the monster stopped. She tilted her head as if listening for noises in the dark.

Feliz held up a finger in front of his mouth and looked back at him with urgency. Conrad nodded in return, and yet he felt a fire in his gut. He thought back to the mutated animals of the woods, and now the monstrosity that stood before him. These weren't animals or insects; they were *abominations*, he thought. Abominations that needed to be put out of their misery. They had almost certainly been the handiwork of the Dark Wizard, the pretender. With these fiery thoughts in mind, he drew his rapier.

The beast turned her shaking, mutilated head toward the pair. Feliz shivered and looked back at the strategist.

"The hell're ye doin'?" he asked.

"What must be done," Conrad replied before taking a fencing stance and pointing his rapier at the monster before him.

The centipede let out a shriek that sounded like a woman's harrowing cry, hissing cat, and locust swarm combined. Next, her deteriorating arms scurried toward Conrad with startling speed, but he was quick to react with a stab to her face.

The beast stopped in her tracks and let out another shrill cry. Conrad ripped the blade out of her skull and a black sludge poured out from the wound. However, rather than slump over and die as expected, the centipede-woman let out another roar and reared the front half of her body upright. She swung four different hands at Conrad, all at once; and one of them connected with his rapier and sent it bouncing off the wall.

With no hesitation, the strategist drew his saber and slashed at the monster's underbelly. She let out a distorted cry and flailed backward as dark liquid spilled and splattered against the dim-lit walls. After landing on the adjacent walking platform, the corpse rotted away in rapid succession, as if deflating. The gaping wound in her thorax then decompressed and burst. An explosion of black liquid scattered everywhere, but along with it came several smaller centipedes with human heads. They were each the size of small dogs, and their various limbs, while human-like, appeared to be more dangerous: Each finger had long claws that looked similar to a bear's, and their hide was thick and strong like an insect's. Their faces were also a hybrid of insect and human; with pincers coming out of their human mouths, and antennae poking out of their greasy hair. They had human eyeballs, but their pupils were large and red.

Four in all had burst out of the centipede-woman, and it didn't take them long to set their sights on Conrad and Feliz.

"Sh-she was pregnant?" Feliz asked.

"More abominations to purify," Conrad said as he knelt, careful not to take his eyes off of the little beasts, and then retrieved his rapier.

"By 'purify', do you mean 'kill'?"

"We have to. Do you think creatures like these should be allowed to walk free? What if they reach other parts of Gentorgul or even another country?"

The little monsters cast red gazes at the pair and hissed. They sounded like high-pitched versions of their mother.

"We should run," Feliz said. "It's four against two."

"They're newborns," Conrad argued as one of the little monsters screeched and scurried toward them. "It won't take much!"

The boy centipede leaped in the direction of Conrad, his mouth open impossibly wide. Inside of the mouth were several tongues and rows of jagged teeth. The strategist didn't hesitate and performed a lunge of his own: A stab that pierced directly into the centipede-boy's mouth and skewered him.

He squirmed like a fish out of water for a few moments before grunting and falling limp. With his rapier, Conrad flung the corpse at his centipede-brother and sisters. Another one hissed at the pair; this time one of the girls.

"We need to run!" Feliz shouted.

"We'll go when I've dealt with them," Conrad said while glaring back at him.

Feliz gasped. "Your eyes…"

"What about them?"

The Gentish man gasped and then pointed ahead. "Watch out!"

Conrad turned to see the centipede-girl flying at him. Without any time to evade, all he could do was raise his rapier in defense. The girl wrapped her many hands around the blade and then used some of her free hands to unleash a flurry of swipes at him.

One of the swipes connected, and Conrad felt the sting of three deep cuts across his cheek. Angrier than ever, he shook the centipede-girl off of his blade, knocking her to the walkway ground in front of him. He then stomped on her hard shell, to which the little monster to shrieked, but the armor was strong and did not break.

Out of the corner of his eye, Conrad caught wind of her siblings scurrying over. He drew his saber once more and turned to Feliz. "I could use a hand…"

The Gentish man remained silent, quaking in his boots.

Conrad swung his saber in the direction of the two attacking centipede-children, who halted by rearing the front half of their bodies while hissing at him. In response, he brought the blade around and cut the incapacitated centipede-girl where her head and squirming insect-like body connected.

Dark liquid spewed from the thorax as her head rolled, a blank expression filling her deformed face. Conrad felt justified as he gazed into those lifeless eyes. She may have had a human head, but she wasn't *truly human*, he thought.

The other two centipede children squealed and then scurried off in the direction of the sewer exit.

"They're getting away!" the strategist shouted as he turned to run, but Feliz grabbed him by the arm. "What do you think you're doing?"

"We need to go."

"I already told you-"

Conrad held his tongue when the panicked shrieks of the centipede-children bounced off the walls from afar.

The pair looked at each other in confusion, as a new noise began to overcome the sound of the muddy water and pelting rain outside: *the breathing*. They nodded at each other with urgent eyes and resumed their quick-paced stroll up the walkway.

"It's following us," Conrad muttered through grit teeth. "I had hoped that the stench in here would cause Willoughby to lose my scent."

"We aren't far off, anyway," Feliz said as he picked up his pace to a light jog. "At least that monster is slow-moving."

"When it wants to be…"

Eventually, the pair reached a dead-end, where a ladder ascended into a small opening in the grimy ceiling.

"The next floor is where I used to work," Feliz said as he grabbed hold of the ladder. "From there, we can reach the morgue basement, which is within the citadel."

As they climbed, a loud screech echoed from above. It sounded to Conrad like the distorted wail of a hog. With all of the abominations crawling around, it wouldn't surprise him if a mutated hog was exactly what they had just heard.

"I don't suppose you kept any animals up there?" Conrad asked.

"No…"

On the next floor, they found themselves in a new corridor, free of the running water, but not of the terrible smell. Ahead, in the distance, appeared to be a set of iron bars and a lever next to it. Feliz strode quickly toward the bars, and Conrad followed.

"This wasn't here before," the Gentish man said.

"Well, there's a lever for it, so what does it matter?" Conrad asked with impatience in his tone.

"You don't find it odd? Maybe we should exercise some caution-"

"There is no time to waste. Are you going through or not?"

Feliz snickered while pulling the lever. "Don't think yer in any spot to be givin' me orders…"

Conrad raised an eyebrow and opened his mouth, but he froze when the boar-like squeal reverberated from down the corridor once again. It sounded closer.

The iron bars lifted, and the hall led to a grand room with a light, brick floor. It was covered with large piles of wet, juicy trash that made Conrad want to gag. Feliz was already halfway there; coughing into his arm and wiping his watery eyes with a free hand.

"I thought you'd be used to the smell… having formerly worked here," the strategist said.

"Well, I-"

The hog-like squeal erupted again.

"I don't know about you, but I don't wanna find out what's making that noise," Feliz said as he walked between piles of trash. "Let us be quick."

While navigating the maze of garbage, Conrad frowned. Something about the way Feliz had spoken to him earlier clawed at the back of his mind. Was it that he'd been combative? Or was it simply the fact that he had to rely on this man, whom he had only just met, to reach his destination? He snorted while looking around. Everything in here looked the same. It was almost as if the mounds of trash were taunting him. For their obstruction of his view; of his general direction, perfectly represented how he felt. He had taken this mission to find answers, but so far, had come away with more questions than ever. Then, something caught the strategist's eye. One of the trash piles stirred. Something was about to burst out of it; something *big*.

"Get down!" he cried while tackling Feliz.

The pair fell to the nasty ground while being pelted with garbage, and overhead, a great *whoosh* filled their ears. Another explosion of trash hit them from the right this time, and once again the distorted hog squeal echoed in the chamber. Conrad groaned while wiping the putrid waste from his face, and then looked up.

A single, giant eye gazed down upon him with apparent intensity and hunger. The beast had a wrinkly brown hide for skin, and four wretched arms on each side of its round body, complete with jagged pincher claws at the end of each. More horrifying still was that the monster had *two mouths*: The larger one could almost certainly swallow him up in one bite and contained fangs the size and shape of sabers; while within that mouth was yet another, with more rows of smaller, sharp teeth. Disgusting, putrid fluid swirled from within as the creature let out its squeal.

The strategist stood and drew his saber as the monster scurried its two bottom arms and charged at him. In one swift motion, he swung his blade but was shocked to hear a loud *clang* on impact. The monster had closed its teeth around it. He looked on, his mouth agape, as the groaning steel gave way to loud *cracks*. The beast was chewing up his saber as if it were a common meal. Feliz tugged on his shirt, and Conrad took it as his signal to retreat.

The pair bolted away as the squeal of the monster erupted behind them.

"You ever hear... of anything like *that*, before?" Feliz asked between breaths as they hung a left around another trash mound.

"No... that thing is an abomination... like the centipedes we saw earlier... there are consequences... when a pretender tries to... use powers they don't understand," he replied, the anger shining through in his strained breaths. "That is unless... *you* had kept this creature... as a pet this whole time... I couldn't help but notice... that it went straight for me..."

"No way... it must'a been... a coincidence. I wouldn't do... something like that... yer imagin' things..." Feliz replied.

Conrad remained silent. Something still bothered him about the way Feliz was speaking, but he couldn't put his finger on *what*, exactly. After more navigation through the trash pits, the pair reached an exit. However, it too was blocked off by iron bars, and the lever was on the other side. The beast squealed from behind. It wasn't far off.

"What do we do?" Feliz asked in a panicked tone.

Conrad looked back to see the trash monster staring him down. It squealed while spewing out a vile liquid that steamed upon striking the stone floor. It kicked up a dusting of trash as it used the colossal strength of its bottom arms to charge at them like a raging bull.

"Oi! Conrad! Do somethin', will ye?" Feliz cried out.

Without looking back, the strategist drew his rapier, and then brought it down vertically, to his side. The blade slipped through the iron bars and hit the lever, causing the bars to rise through some slots in the ceiling.

Feliz and Conrad dashed for the exit, but not before knocking the lever back to close the gate behind them. They didn't look back upon hearing a great crash and the groaning of iron. Instead, they kept running forward to where the next ladder was.

As Feliz climbed, Conrad said, "You talk differently when you're nervous, you know that?"

"I don't know what you mean," he said.

"Perhaps it's only my imagination, but I found it funny."

The next floor was smaller in comparison to the sewer and trash areas. It was dimly lit by lanterns hanging on the walls, just enough to see the various wooden crates lying about. Lining the room, in rows of three, were many operating tables. All of them had bodies lying on top, covered by white sheets that commonly dawned blots or puddles of blood.

"The Dark Wizard has been busy," Conrad said.

"It was nothing like this, before…" Feliz trailed off. "This room was once used to honor the dead."

Suddenly, Conrad picked up on some movement, and his eyes darted to the right.

On an operating table further ahead, a bloodied white sheet flew off and floated to the floor. A woman stood, shaking as she did. She wore a gray gown with several bloody holes in it, the largest of which was in her stomach. From that bloody hole flailed several cut-up pieces of her intestines, each wriggling like worms. Her long, dark hair was so greasy that it looked as if she had been in the water, and her gray pupils stretched nearly to her eyelids. Most disturbing, however, was her elongated, twisted jaw. So long and wrenched was the jaw that her chin was level with her prominent collarbone, and the right corner of her mouth aligned with the center of her nose.

The woman lumbered toward them, breathing much like Mr. Willoughby as she did. Her mouth moved, but perhaps due to her unnaturally long jaw, nothing comprehendible came out; only gurgling noises. Conrad drew his rapier as she came within arm's reach of him, her living intestines each coiling like snakes about to strike.

"Another monster?" Feliz asked in a fearful tone.

"No…" Conrad said as he stuck the blade into her chest. The woman gasped while hunching over and the snake-like intestines fell limp. "A cry for help." He ripped the rapier out and then stabbed her in the temple to finish her off.

The woman let out a brief sigh before dropping to the floor, lifeless as her eyes had already been.

"You killed her…" Feliz muttered.

"I ended her suffering," he replied coldly, his eyes wandering about the morbid room. "As a matter of fact, before we confront the Dark Wizard, we should make sure they're all dead. It's only merciful."

Conrad turned to face the first row of operating tables.

"I agree..." Feliz trailed off. Conrad's ears picked up on him unsheathing his sword. Something wasn't right. "All o' the filth in this room deserve a mercy killin'!"

Like a strike of lightning, Conrad turned and plunged the rapier into Feliz's chest. The Gentish man gasped and dropped his blade, which he had also pulled back, as if about to make a stab. Feliz had planned on betraying him.

"You did well in deceiving me until your manner of speaking began to change. And for a man who once worked around so much trash, it nearly had you gagging, back there. Spend enough time with someone and their true nature will eventually be revealed," Conrad said. Feliz slumped over, and it felt as if the rapier was the only thing holding him up. "I wanted to believe I had an ally in this hostile town, but I suppose you were against the cause, too."

Suddenly, Feliz's head shot up, to which Conrad gasped. The Gentish man smiled back at him with eyes as wide as could be.

"Yer smarter than I gave ye credit for." Feliz's mouth moved, but it wasn't his voice. Somehow, it sounded familiar.

Feliz's skin lightened until it was fair, and his hair turned a dark brown. He shrunk down, but, as if to make up for the height decrease, his nose grew long and thick. Conrad's eyes widened.

"Brice..."

Memories from a year ago came flooding back. Brice, the troublemaker and leader of the hooligans; the man who had disappeared without a trace after the Mt. Couture disaster, was standing before him in another country. Not only that, but he had managed to perfectly disguise himself as another man entirely. It was a sight that shook the strategist to his very core.

"Correct!" Brice replied with a venomous grin. He grasped the blade and then pulled it out of his chest. Conrad's brow twitched. How? How had he been able to speak Gentish perfectly, like a native? Why hadn't his rapier left him a bloody heap on the floor? Whatever devilry he'd been using made him dangerous, and with that realization, Conrad regained composure and took a fencing stance.

Brice laughed. "Oh, put it away. It won't do ye any good."

"I'd rather go down fighting than surrender to another abomination."

"I ain't gonna hurt ye, *yet*," he replied with a sly smile. "I'm gonna bring ye to the Dark Wizard. That's what ye want, isn't it?"

"I aim to kill him, and he is your master, is he not? What kind of a fool do you take me for?" Conrad asked in a defensive tone.

"There's nothin' ye can do to hurt him," Brice said before snorting. "He only wants to talk. So, what's the problem?"

"The problem is that I don't trust yo-" Conrad was cut off when Brice extended his arm farther than humanly possible, connecting with a hard punch to the jaw. His vision blurred and his head fell to the weight of a feather, and then all went black as he tumbled to the grimy floor. Yet, he could still hear the big-nosed man, standing over him and laughing.

"I suppose yer gut feelin' was right, eh?" he asked as Conrad felt tentacles wrapping around his body and lifting him like he was a mere child. "Let's pay the Dark Wizard a lil' visit…"

CHAPTER 12
A BLACK MASS

Slara teat feinum
Pleite an chroide
Glabris adtu vaor

Conrad awoke and shook his pounding head. The chants he had heard were not from the Dark Savior, but from another sinister source. It was coming from a crowd, and eventually, a familiar voice, deep and base-filled, joined in. It was then that he realized he was sitting on a wooden bench in a dimly lit church. Upon looking around, he saw several of the townsfolk sitting next to him, and the entirety of the grand cathedral was filled. An organ blared in the background, perfectly in sync with the thunderclaps outside.

Up front, a robed man stood at an altar, flanked by long candle sticks that glowed unnaturally green. The man was tall and his robe was an odd mix of black and dark purple symbols, but Conrad couldn't make out his face, as a hood covered it well. The only hint of his features came in the form of a long, demonic goatee that poked out.

The Dark Wizard, he thought. However, the prior urges that Conrad had felt; the will to assassinate this pretender on behalf of the true Dark Savior; had faded with his consciousness. He could still feel a hatred welling up inside of him, but not nearly to the manic point of earlier. Besides that, any attempt would easily be stopped by the hundreds of townsfolk sitting around him. There was nothing he could do but sit and listen.

As the thought occurred to him, the robed man raised his hands and the organ fell silent. The candles all around the church lit up a dark green, and the townsfolk bowed their heads. Conrad played along.

"The souls of mortal men are easily corrupted," the robed man said. His voice penetrated Conrad's ears as if they were whispers right beside him. It was the same deep voice that had encouraged him to kill for or steal the black gold at any cost. "We must divide and control to bring order and balance."

The townsfolk bowed their heads once more, and in unison said a quick prayer in Old Gentish that Conrad couldn't understand. He did his best to blend in.

"I have come to free our minds of pain, suffering, and choice. It is for the betterment of the world to not fear, but embrace, the darkness," the Dark Wizard said as more chants erupted from the crowd. "Tonight, we have a special guest…"

The strategist broke out into a nervous sweat, assuming he was to be the 'guest'. The last thing he needed was for the crazed townsfolk to attack him in such an enclosed space.

However, out from the back and through a curtain appeared two robed men, dragging a struggling young woman, kicking and shouting aloud in Gentish. The crowd grumbled amongst themselves until the Dark Wizard brought a hand up, and they fell silent.

The two robed men stood before him and dropped the frightened young woman to the floor. She looked up at the Dark Wizard and her panicked breaths ceased, suddenly frozen; paralyzed by her visible fright.

"Do not fear, child. Even if it is natural to despair of the unknown, we must all face it eventually. I have many times, myself. I can tell you from experience that it is quite relaxing after your fear subsides," the Dark Wizard said with a chuckle.

The two robed men grabbed the young woman once again and then threw her onto a table that was adorned with straps. They tied her down and then swiveled the specialized table so that she was facing upright, toward all in attendance. She squinted and struggled, but the straps held tight.

"Tonight, we celebrate the rebirth of Catalina," the Dark Wizard said to the roar of the crowd.

Conrad thought back to how holding the black gold had helped relax him; to ease his pain and worries. Was that what the Dark Wizard had been referring to? He reached into his pocket to hold it once more, in the hopes that it would calm him down. He let out a gasp, however, when he came up empty-handed. Brice must have stolen it while he was unconscious, he thought.

The organ played a macabre tune as the two robed men exited back through the curtain. The Dark Wizard retrieved a bowl and a piece of black gold ore. The strategist squirmed as he felt his suspicions confirmed. The organ stopped.

"What is it that men desire so much that they are willing to turn violent?" the Dark Wizard asked the crowd. Some grumbles emerged from those in attendance, but no one answered. "Power? Yes, power…"

"But what allows them to grasp power? How do the unqualified and uninitiated gain the ability to tell others what to do?" he asked. The crowd remained silent. "*Freedom. Choice.* They do not ask; they take and do what they please. And if they obtain power, it becomes easy for them to abuse."

The crowd remained silent, but Conrad could see a few people nodding in agreement.

"But I have the cure! I can end the pain and suffering! And it comes at a small cost: liberation from your selfish choices. That is the sacrifice we must make to take the next step. We must all strive for the same righteous cause, and that is impossible with free choice impeding our path!" the Dark Wizard proclaimed as he walked over to Catalina. She cried as the robed man stroked her dark hair.

"Most men feel that freedom is a good thing. But when it brings down so many others, what good does it do? Allow me to present you all with an example," the Dark Wizard said as he held out his index finger. On the other hand, he bit his thumb hard so that it was bleeding. "Unhein cluis diabonis!"

Out of his index finger grew a long, red nail, no less than a foot in length. Before anyone could react to the supernatural feat, the Dark Wizard slashed across the woman's neck and slit it open effortlessly. Blood erupted from the open wound like a geyser as all watched on in silence. Catalina squirmed, struggled, and gurgled as Conrad clenched the back of the wooden bench before him. He wanted to intervene but knew that it was hopeless. She was going to die, and so too would he by making a move.

"I had the free choice to do whatever I wanted to this poor, helpless soul," the Dark Wizard said as he held the bowl below her neck. The blood spilled into it like a bucket pouring water. "Think of how many have abused this same power... think of all those times that other countries have attempted to invade and control you."

Catalina's struggling soon ceased as the Dark Wizard placed the black gold ore into the bowl. He then held a hand over the bowl and recited a series of chants to the deep hums of all the church-goers and the roar of the organ:

Slara teat feinum
Pleite an chroide
Resnu domin altigh
Etas tu adin thad chomivum
Teig dorchae cunabhan tu
An duino as exuan

Wind broke through the church doors and howled like the hungriest of wolves. The candles all around blew out, aside from the ones next to the Dark Wizard, which raged on in defiance. The crowd watched in awe as a dark liquid rose from the bowl and swirled around the robed man's hand.

"But if we eliminate that easily-abused freedom, and give *everyone* power..." the Dark Wizard trailed off as he directed the floating dark liquid toward the woman. "We can accomplish wonderful things."

The substance shot into the open wound on Catalina's neck, and her body contorted and twisted uncontrollably, the table straps groaning against her jerky movements. The gouge on her neck closed slowly but surely, and eventually, her spasms ended. The crowd gasped collectively as the wound turned into a few dark scabs.

"And so now..." the robed man said as he unhooked the woman from her restraints. To gasps from all, she stood without aid and the light had returned to her once dead eyes. "Catalina is reborn!"

The crowd erupted into cheers and stood in praise; all aside from Conrad, who remained planted on the bench out of pure shock. Had that been why his wounds were healing so quickly? Had it been this Dark Wizard's influence?

Catalina looked to the Dark Wizard with increasingly red eyes, then lowered to a knee and bowed before him.

"Another soul has been healed; saved from pain and suffering.

Soon, my loyal disciples, the world will come to know *our way*," the Dark Wizard said as he placed a hand on her shoulder. She then stood and scurried over to the front-most bench in the church.

"And now, for *less pleasant* proceedings…" the Dark Wizard said to some grumbles from the crowd. "Our humble town has improved so much in a short time, but there are those who still resist our ways."

Conrad was sure that this time, the robed man was referring to him. He was going to be made an example of. If only he could find a weapon, he thought.

Yet, once again, he was surprised to see the two robed men return from out of the side curtain, this time dragging a balding man along by his arms. The crowd promptly booed him with great intensity and shouted what Conrad could only assume were obscenities and insults in Old Gentish. The rabid townsfolk quieted as soon as the Dark Wizard held up his hand.

"Clement here has been warned not once, but twice, to stop using precious materials for his own selfish goals," he said as the two robed men threw the man to the ground. "Valuable items such as wood are to be used only for the benefit of *the people*. But you were using it all for *yourself*, weren't you?"

"I-I chopped the wood myself! I thought it was allowed!" the balding man pleaded. Conrad raised an eyebrow. Even if Feliz had only been Brice in disguise, what he'd told him appeared to be true: Most of the Gentish knew and were capable of speaking King's Tongue. And now that his mind was clearing, he realized that the Dark Wizard himself had been speaking the language all along, and all in attendance had followed what he was saying.

"But that wood is not *your* property, Clement. It is the property of the Bosfueran people!" the Dark Wizard boomed back to thunderous applause from the crowd. "And you don't get to decide what is done with it."

"It was only meant for a hobby…" Clement said as he hung his head.

"And what is it that you've done with the wood?"

"I was building a boat."

"A boat? Were you thinking of fleeing the country?" the Dark Wizard asked with contempt.

"N-no! It was a hobby, a project! S-something to keep me busy!" Clement said with desperation on his tongue.

"All of your efforts should be on the town, Clement. It is all about the greater good of Bosfueras…" the Dark Wizard said as the crowd hummed a prayer that Conrad couldn't understand. "But we have been over this already. I fear that you are not going to learn our ways."

The townsfolk broke out into grumbles and shouts. Their body language was beginning to reach more aggressive heights. Some looked ready to hop off the benches and attack.

"What is wrong with you all?" Clement asked aloud. The crowd simmered. "You know me! I've lived here my whole life! I never wronged or hurt anyone!"

"That's not true," the Dark Wizard replied. "You've hurt the people of this fine town with your selfish actions. We have given you all that you need, but it's not enough for you, is it? Greedy fool!"

"Y-you've taken everything away from me! Y-you can't tell me what to do…" Clement sobbed.

"That much is certain," he shot back. "I'm afraid your fate will be left up to the people. The people whom you have stolen from."

The robed man pointed out into the crowd with the same long, red nail he'd used to slice Catalina. "What say you?"

The rowdy townsfolk burst into a series of shouts and cries. In all of the rabble of Old Gentish around him, Conrad could make out a commonly used phrase that sounded much like the Gentish word for 'kill'.

"Your fate is sealed, then," the Dark Wizard said as he held his palm out. He brought the elongated nail from his index finger across and it split open. With a clenching of his fist, the blood spurted out and began dripping down his wrist.

Tears rolled down Clement's cheeks as the Dark Wizard recited a brief series of chants:

Invoim ar manha martuas
Dimoil amos as de domferis
Adun naimere threcos meos

Out of the stage floor burst a pair of large arms made of bone. Each was about as tall as the Dark Wizard himself, and they flexed their bony fingers like they hadn't had the opportunity to move in some time. The two robed men lifted Clement and then strapped him to the same table that Catalina had been on earlier. He didn't bother to struggle as they swiveled him up to look directly at the Dark Wizard and his giant bone hands.

A BLACK MASS

"Your fate is now in the grasp of my Dark Hands," the robed man said as he pointed to the arms. The two hands faced each other as if they were about to clap, and a green energy gathered between them. "Do you have any last words?"

Clement sniffled and then let out a sigh. "You have taken most things from me: my friends, my family, and my property, but there is one thing you'll *never* be able to take."

"Do tell."

"My thoughts. You'll never take my thoughts away..." Clement trailed off, then let out a few defeated chuckles. The chuckles then turned into tear-filled laughs.

"If only those thoughts had any substance to them," the Dark Wizard replied, and then pointed at the Dark Hands while chanting, "Cruinega an tium borma!"

The green energy pulsated and created a small gust of wind that stunned all in the crowd. Clement continued to laugh, however.

"Repent!"

From the Dark Hands shot out a brilliant beam of green light, and all in attendance shielded their eyes. All Conrad could hear was a loud, high-pitched noise, and then came sizzles that penetrated his skull, eliciting such discomfort that he trembled. Moments later, after the noises subsided and a distinct burning smell filled the hazy air, he looked up to see that there was a hole in the backside of the church wall. The blast had punched through several rooms, all the way to the outside.

"Unbelievable..." Conrad muttered, but then he laid eyes on the attack's true victim, and his jaw hung open.

Clement had been split in two: His entire abdomen was missing. The table holding him up had a large hole punched through it. There was no visible blood, however; as his entire body had been cauterized by the extreme heat of the blast. A slight sense of relief came to Conrad when he noticed that the defiant man had died with a smile on his face. It was a minor victory, as even in the face of such a fierce attack, he had indeed kept his thoughts; his beliefs.

The townsfolk erupted with cheers for an uncomfortably long time, and after the clapping died down, the Dark Wizard motioned for the robed men to clean up the mess. The organ started blaring, the Dark Hands retracted back into the ground without a trace, and the large cathedral doors opened up, greeted by flashes of lightning and the pounding rain outside.

"Join me again tomorrow night," the Dark Wizard said to his faithful followers. Catalina stood and left with the other townsfolk as if nothing had happened to her. Conrad, however, remained seated.

As the last of the crowd left, the robed man turned to him and said, "Well? What did you think?"

The strategist hesitated for a moment. "It was a nice sermon."

"I can tell when you're lying to me, boy," the Dark Wizard shot back. The candles all about the room flared up in reaction to his malice. "Don't think because I've kept you around for this long that I won't kill you where you sit."

"If that's the case, why go through all of this trouble?" Conrad asked.

"A fair question, but before I answer… do you agree that free choice allows others to abuse their power?" he asked.

"Perhaps…"

"You know deep down that it does. Drake wields his power and free choice like a club. What could have stopped him from enacting his plan to extract black gold from Mt. Couture?"

"Bad example," he replied with a confident smile. "After all, *you* made it happen, didn't you? Drake never has a plan without the knowledge of black gold existing. Only you could have told him."

"A means to an end. You witnessed for yourself what I could do with it."

"All I've witnessed thus far are the abominations and devilry of a *pretender*," Conrad retorted.

The Dark Wizard cackled as he descended the stage. "That's the Dark Savior in you talking."

"What is that supposed to mean?"

"He means that we conducted a lil' experiment on ye," Brice called from behind. Conrad scowled as he looked back at the big-nosed man.

"Yes… that was not why I brought you here; and believe me, you being here was by my design; but there are still some things we need to understand about black gold," the Dark Wizard said as he dropped his hood.

His face reminded Conrad of a demon trying to imitate a human. His brow formed a permanent glare to his dark eyes, ever watchful, and he had long, black hair. His goatee was his only facial hair, but it seemed unnaturally long, and his skin was pale; as if he had bathed in darkness all of his life.

"Oh… does my appearance make you uncomfortable?" he asked,

then placed a hand over his forehead. As he dragged the hand down, his facial features changed. Conrad's eyes became wide with fright when the transformation was complete.

"Utrix…" he muttered. His worst fears had been confirmed. The entire setup of the mission had been a trap laid out by the Dark Wizard. His mind raced in circles, trying to figure out why, and what it all meant.

"I think deep down you knew, but didn't care. Your curiosity overtook your caution, and even though I sent you on a suicide mission, you had to know the truth," the Dark Wizard said in Utrix's voice.

"Th-that is what a Wizard would do…"

"No. That is what a *Dark Wizard* would do," he replied with a chuckle.

"That can't be right…"

"Oh, but it is. Most Wizards, as you've come to find out, prefer sitting around and taking no action while all around them suffer. They start off with the best of intentions, but eventually, they die after years of irrelevancy. Why do you think that is, despite the existence of Anima, which could forever keep them alive? It's because their Anima depletes. They stop helping people because eventually, they no longer care," the Dark Wizard explained.

"You lie! Aldous-"

"Will soon be excommunicated or dead," the Dark Wizard interrupted. "I truly do pity him. He's one of the few Wizards willing to stick his neck out in the name of something… even if it's something of little value. The others care about little else than clinging onto their waning power. They're not like us, Conrad. They're not willing to do what has to be done."

"I'm not willing to brainwash people!" Conrad shot back. "I'm not willing to kill those who think differently from me!"

"Is that right?" Brice asked as he approached the bench with crossed arms. Conrad gasped as he transformed into Feliz once more. "What about when you ran off, despite my screams of agony at the hands of Willoughby?"

"I had a mission-"

"You had a mission," Brice said. "You didn't have second thoughts killing an 'abomination' either, did you? Or stabbing me?"

"I-I had no choice…"

"How many of the townsfolk did you kill?" the Dark Wizard jumped in.

"I don't know. I was attacked by them-"

"You trespassed onto our land uninvited, and you expect not to be attacked?" Brice added.

"How many wild animals did you kill?" the Dark Wizard asked.

"Enough!" Conrad pleaded. "I did what I had to do…"

"You certainly did. Now, look at the state of man: We have a Council of Wizards who sit back and do nothing as the Dark Savior's influence slowly destroys lives, monarchs holding people back and causing them to regress, and rampant degeneration of human societies thanks to their poor choices," the Dark Wizard said. Conrad raised an eyebrow. "Think of how far mankind could have come by now if we all had the same goals; the same vision! Man has had control of the world for thousands of years, and how much have they changed? How have they improved? They are *limited* by their freedom."

"What you're suggesting is… a hive mind?"

"Something like that. Imagine what this world would be capable of when its civilized beings are focused! Right now, the needs and wants of the many are too different from one another. And their goals are corruptible. What if we had a way to make them *incorruptible*? Loyal to the last breath? All countries and peoples united and powerful."

"But someone has to control them all. And that would be *you*, I take it?" the strategist asked while casting a suspicious eye.

"Not only me. I have deemed some worthy of sharing this power with me. Only those who understand the vision of a better world, and use their power to help that vision come true. That's where *you* come in," the Dark Wizard said. Conrad cocked his head. "I see the potential in you to become a proficient Wizard… but why be good, when you can be *exceptional*? So, I make you this offer: Align yourself with me, and I will teach you the dark arts of Wizardry. It will help you to understand and feel in the way you've been yearning for. Then, I will share with you an *inordinate power*, and by my side, we will ensure that all civilized beings progress to the next stage."

Conrad remained silent. He could understand the temptation of what the Dark Wizard was preaching, but the cost was too high. He would be stripping people of their humanity at his own whim, and what gave him the right to do that? The very freedom that the Dark Wizard spoke out against.

He darted his eyes to his hip. His rapier had been confiscated. Not that he stood much of a chance at slaying a Dark Wizard.

"Before I answer… what was your true goal in unleashing Greed from his prison? I don't understand that part of your plan," Conrad said. He was trying to buy time and think of a plan.

"The Dark Savior is the 'inordinate power' that I speak of. My goal is to progress the world past hurdles placed before it by man's foolish actions; their self-destructive liberty. It wasn't until recently that I found the best means to do that," the Dark Wizard replied while gesturing to the altar. "Look what a single ore produced by Greed can do. With my vision and the various powers that each spawn of the Savior can bestow, we can save the world."

The Dark Wizard then returned to his earlier, more demonic form. "But I can sense that you are not convinced."

"Are you going to kill me?"

"No…" he said, pointing at him.

Conrad bent over and vomited a black substance, similar to the one that had been forced into Catalina's neck wound earlier on. He tried to sit back up but felt a searing pain in his back, shoulder, legs, and neck. He felt blood dripping from the bites sustained at the hands of the mutated rabbits. The wounds from before! Somehow, they had returned.

"As Brice said, your time here has been an experiment. I had Mr. Willoughby inject you with my special blend of dark essence. It's something I concocted with dark magic and the black gold itself. Of course, I used this to create my own brand of the black gold, which keeps the townsfolk obedient and productive, but also more resistant to pain. I then armed the town archers with black-tipped arrows. It seems they hit you at least once," the Dark Wizard said with a chuckle as the liquid lifted off the floor and floated into the bowl up by the altar.

"S-so you wanted to… convert me l-like the others?" Conrad struggled to get the words out as his vision blurred. He felt hungry and tired. The pain in his shoulder, back, and legs were nearly impossible to bear.

"I only wished to give you a taste of it, actually. Wasn't it the most relaxing moment of your life when you touched my black gold?" the Dark Wizard asked.

Conrad thought back to the cabin where he had held it in his hands and time seemed to slow down. He then thought back to when Feliz had given it to him: It had been relaxing at first, but then the Savior and a blinding rage had clouded his mind.

The strategist pointed to Brice and said, "But when *he* gave it to me-"

"That was the experiment," Brice said with a chuckle. "I gave ye a piece o' black gold directly from Greed himself. It made ye so much more aggressive and angrier."

"Indeed. There were two reasons for the experiment: One was to see if the Savior's black gold influence could overwhelm mine. Sadly, that appears to be the case. But on the other hand, I wanted to show you how humane my methods are. It healed wounds that could have killed you. It made you feel better, did it not?"

Conrad remained silent until he cried out in pain once again and hunched over.

"Your prior wounds are returning because I have stripped the dark essence from your body before it could truly heal without its aid. The injuries will most likely become infected and cause you a painful death if you don't act soon," he said.

"At the cost of my humanity?"

"No. I was planning to teach you a dark magic that could heal your injuries. Like I said, I wanted you at my side, to share the *inordinate power*," the Dark Wizard replied. Conrad gasped, and for a fleeting moment, he considered the possibility. "*But...* it is important for a Dark Wizard in training to understand pain and suffering. So, I'll give you some alone-time to consider the idea."

Conrad's eyes widened. "N-no..."

"By then, you'll be begging for the dark essence," he said with a deep laugh.

"P-please, don't-"

"Take him to the dungeon," the Dark Wizard said, smiling at Brice.

Before he could turn to defend himself, Conrad felt a heavy blow at the side of his head and his ears rang as all went dark.

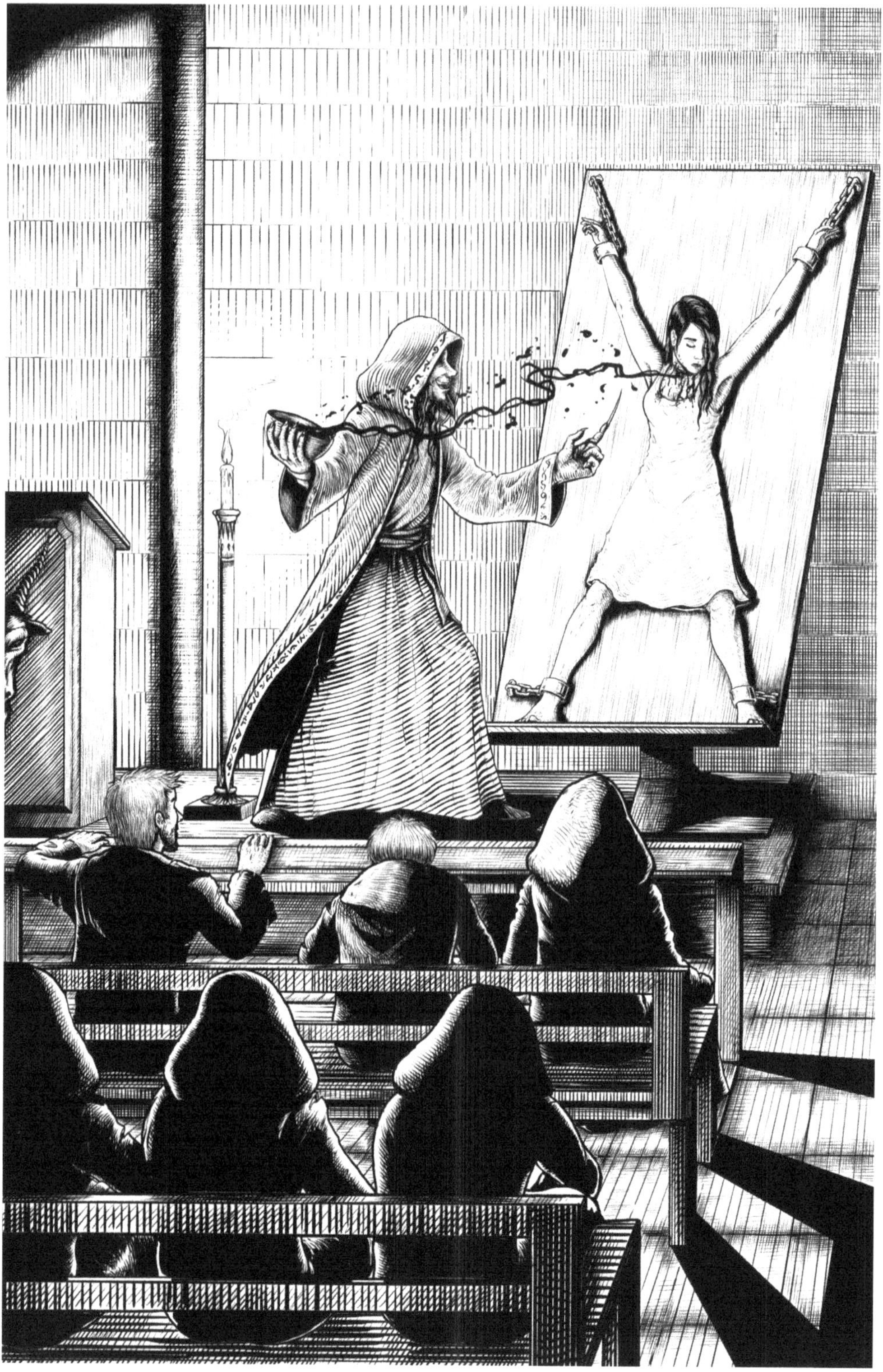

CHAPTER 13
DIPLOMATIC MISSION

Drake Danvers walked the filth-ridden streets of Endoshire with his entourage; the type of bottom-feeders that normally attached themselves to those in power. Drake himself had his golden blond hair slicked back and wore a grand red cape over his silk clothing as if he were royalty.

The city was packed with hustle and bustle, as was normally the case after noon. Merchants and performers had set up in spots open enough for them along the main road, as most side streets were tightly packed into rows of tall stone buildings where people lived and businesses thrived. Drake and the others brushed shoulders with a variety of men and women: The pale, large folk of Currencolt; the bronzed, thin people of Mithika; and the dark-skinned men of the desert countries, most of them merchants. Aside from humans, he spotted a flock of avian circling above, and some roamed the city streets, though they were well-hidden by crowds of the larger species: A few packs of trolls were easy to spot, as they were giant and green. They could be seen bothering the merchants here and there, but Drake's eyes were drawn to the centaurs. It was surprising to see the half-horse, half-men trotting along, as they were notably on poor terms with Sigraveld as a country.

Then again, maybe it wasn't so surprising, he thought. Even though they had been aggressors toward the centaurs in recent times, Sigraveld was accepted as a necessary evil. After all, there was no

DIPLOMATIC MISSION

better place in the world than Endoshire to trade, bargain, sell, or buy. This was in part thanks to the country's fantastic location: It was quite literally at the world's center, and several dozen countries surrounded it in a half-circle. While certain far-east countries like Luneria were forced to either travel around the half-circle of landmass or cut through narrow rivers, the majority of the world had an easy time reaching the city of Endoshire and trading there.

Endoshire was an enigma compared to the rest of Sigraveld. The king had decreed that it become easy for folk of all kinds to come and go, and regulations remained lax so that trading would be simple. Unlike the rest of the country, it was an easy city to immigrate to, if there was enough space. The normally heavy hand of the kingdom steering clear of Endoshire had brought it incredible riches.

Drake recalled his first time visiting. It felt cold, calculating, and unfriendly: exactly his style and preference. Faiwell, in comparison, was close-knit thanks to the Miner's Guild and its rural setting. Most there had a similar mindset and way of life. It was *comfortable*, he thought, which was why he hated it so much. However, he was already deep enough into controlling the land that he couldn't think to abandon it.

Under the guise of a diplomatic mission, he had come to Endoshire to destroy Degenerate's monolith, which was hidden in the city sewers. While waiting for his team to gather, however, he planned on making some deals that would benefit him back in Federland as well as aid him in the beginnings of his grand vision for the world. One such deal was with a slaver who posed as a shipwright to appear legitimate.

Eventually, the group neared their destination: Dock 15 of Endoshire's harbor was an entire shipyard where several vessels could be repaired at once. It was where Drake was to meet with his potential business partner, and the walk down the stretch of docks brought him past several sailors, pirates, and even Gypsies trying to tell him his fortune. His newly-enhanced bodyguards, however, pushed them away.

Drake was bewildered by the newfound strength and stature of Hector and Ned. While before, they were by no means small or weak, the two men had grown to nearly two meters tall each and just from throwing bothersome passersby around, the Village Elder could tell that they had become powerful. The only thing that had bothered him since their enhancements was that they refused to show their faces. They remained under a cloak and hood, red and blue respectively, so that they could be differentiated. They seldom spoke now, and when they did, it was a harsh whisper that sent shivers down his spine. At first, the changes had made Drake uneasy, but with time, he'd come to view them as too beneficial to worry about.

After reaching dock 15, the entourage stood before a long, rectangular building finely crafted of wood. It took up the entire dock and seemed to be the largest of the bunch, at least so far as Drake had seen. At the end of the dock and building was a wide opening, likely meant for the ships. Just above were some windows, and they lined what looked to be a second floor. He turned to his group and handed out gold coins.

"Go have yourselves a good time," he said, to their delight. After receiving their allowance, they scurried off like the cockroaches they were, but Ned and Hector stayed behind. "You two, come with me."

They entered the building and were greeted by one of the workers in a waiting room. There were papers and books stacked all around, even on the chairs and tables. No doubt meant to be records feigning their legitimacy, Drake thought with a smirk.

"Can I help ya?" the man asked.

"I'm here to see Sampson," Drake replied with a confident smile.

"Yeh? Well, lots'a piss-pots wanna see him," the man said with crossed arms. He was hairy, burly, and certainly spoke like a sailor.

"What is your point? Are you going to fetch him for me or not?"

"Look here, lil' man-" He reached out to grab Drake, but was intercepted by Hector, who grasped his wrist.

The man struggled, but couldn't remove Hector's gloved hand no matter how much he tugged.

Crack

He cried out in pain as a sweat boiled on his brow. His wrist had already turned red.

"Awright, awright! I'm sorry!"

"Are you going to fetch Sampson for me?" Drake asked in a casual tone.

"Y-yes! I will! I will!" the worker replied in desperation.

The Village Elder nodded at Hector, and he let go. Drake then walked up to the worker and gave him a couple of light taps on the cheek.

"Chop, chop! I haven't got all day."

The worker grimaced while gingerly caressing his wrist, but looking back up at Hector stilled any further aggression on his part.

"R-right away, sir…" he replied.

Soon after, the worker returned with a short and fat man wearing a fancy fur coat. He had dirty blond hair and a round, chubby face that exaggerated his mischievous smile. He reminded Drake of a slimy merchant trying to sell faulty products.

However, instead of showing repulsion, the Village Elder put forward his signature smile that had sealed so many deals in the past.

He extended his hand out and said, "Hello, Sampson. I am Drake Danvers. It's a pleasure to finally meet you, in person."

Sampson took his hand and shook it, but Drake felt the grime and had to do everything in his power to keep the smile intact.

"Ah, yes! I was wonderin' when you'd show up!" said Sampson as he pulled his hand back, then shooed his worker away. His voice was higher-pitched than expected. "From what I recall of our letters, you were lookin' fer some *fine merchandise*, yes?"

"But of course," Drake replied. "I hear you're the best around these parts."

"You heard correct, my friend. Follow me!" the fat man said, then waddled through a doorway on their right.

Drake and his bodyguards followed into an open area that split into smaller, interconnected docks where ships were being worked on. Each vessel was enclosed by the docks in a rectangular shape, but there were hinges and chains attached to pulley systems that could allow the planks to be lifted like a draw bridge. High above was a complex system of scaffolding where a few men commanded the pulley systems and some others had been lowered on platforms to work on the upper edges of the ships. Already, Drake was impressed with the operation, and this was merely *a front*, he thought with excitement building in his chest.

An overwhelming scent of salt permeated throughout, as the echoes of tide slapping against the ships underneath the wooden planks dominated Drake's ears. His eyes, however, were taken by a large, black ship on their left as they walked past.

"You like that one, eh?" Sampson asked with pride. "Sometimes, the royal navy of Sigraveld asks us for a few favors here 'n there… that's how legitimate we are."

"You grant these favors so they will look the other way?" Drake asked with a knowing smile.

"Naturally."

"I'm impressed, but I was hoping to see... the smaller pieces of the operation, shall we say?"

Sampson raised an eyebrow before letting out a shrill laugh. "Look closely, my friend! You *are* seeing the smaller parts of my operation."

Drake scanned the boat to see several men in ragged clothing scrubbing the deck, while others were performing maintenance on the mast to ensure its stability.

"You mean to say that all of these workers..."

"Are not workers at all. Or at least, most of 'em aren't," Sampson said with a devious grin. He then leaned in to whisper, "A slave is helpful around the house, sure, but what if we taught 'em important things like fixing and building ships?"

Drake was taken aback for a moment. "No one would suspect a thing because most of this 'job' is indoors, and even at first glance, they appear to be regular workers. I'm sure this makes you a fine sum of money."

"Of course! I could, perhaps, get by working as an honest shipwright, but it's my side-business that's the true moneymaker."

"If I may ask; and please don't take this the wrong way... how do you keep them from running or telling the authorities? What if I were to report you to an official or some such thing?" Drake asked.

Sampson paused for a moment. At first, he frowned, but then a smile spread across his chubby cheeks. Even for Drake, it was hard to get a read on him; the mark of a true businessman, he thought.

"There are several ways to keep my operation going," he began as they walked through a new doorway and away from the ships. "Most of the slaves are 'broken in', one way or another. But even if they did attempt to alert the authorities, they are already bought off. Nothing would be done about it."

"Fascinating..." Drake trailed off as the two men sat at a table. Drake's bodyguards flanked him, both crossing their arms and standing still as the night.

"Erm... do yer men wanna sit?" Sampson asked.

"Don't mind them. They prefer to stand," Drake replied with a chuckle. "But back on topic: Do you truly never have any issues? Even with an operation of this size?"

"We clothe, feed, and train our slaves with the promise that they'll one day be free. In a way, they are free of responsibility. They don't have to provide for themselves, or even think for themselves, really.

Especially the ones born into it; they know nothing of freedom," Sampson said.

"I see… but what if you had an angry client…"

"Let me tell ya somethin' about this city, Drake. Nobody cares for one another 'round here. You probably ain't used to such a mindset, bein' from a close-knit village, but Endoshire is a whole 'nother story. For as long as I can remember, I would see beatings in the alleyways, women n' children mistreated by thugs, and the open ownership of slaves. Y'know what people did about that?" the fat man asked with a grin. "Nothin'. Absolutely nothin'!"

Sampson burst out with laughter, but Drake remained stone-faced, and his laughs quickly tapered off.

"Sure, we had a few runners and trouble-makers here 'n there, but that's where my connections come in. As you said earlier, they tend to look the other way. And then we *take care of* those runners and trouble-makers if ya catch my drift."

"I understand doing what must be done, after all," Drake assured him, holding out a hand. "I was only curious as to how you handled the inherent problems that come with your line of work. I have a few ideas of my own."

"Anyhow, did ya wanna take a closer look at any of my 'workers'?" Sampson asked.

"Actually, I was hoping to get a look at your more… *intimate workers*, shall we say?"

"Yes, yes, of course. I had forgotten that in your letters, the ladies were your primary interest," Sampson said, clasping his hands together. "We're gonna have to visit another location to see them, though."

"That's fine with me."

"Very well," Sampson replied as he stood.

Drake and his bodyguards followed him out of the shipyard and back into the city. After walking beyond the docks and the wealthy shops, they came upon an open section filled with beautiful trees and patches of flowers along the road. It stood out as the only nature Drake had seen since arriving in Endoshire. Between a couple of oaks, Sampson finally stopped in front of a tall, wooden building. He retrieved a keyring from his fur coat pocket, but before using the key, he turned to face the trio.

"Before I let ya in, a warning…"

"Oh?" Drake asked with an amused snort.

"I don't sell *the help* to anyone from Endoshire, understand? Especially the ladies... I only work with those from other countries, in that regard," Sampson said.

"I can understand that. There's no benefit in selling good workers to your competition," Drake replied.

"Exactly. What you do in Federland don't concern me. Do whatever you please! But I don't want ya braggin' about or discussin' our dealings here today with anyone in the city. Not unless it concerns ship work."

"I understand," the Village Elder said. He had no intentions of speaking with anyone in Federland, either.

"Excellent! Come on in, my friend," Sampson said as he unlocked the door and entered.

The inside of the building was well-decorated with colorful walls and paintings hanging on them. A lovely aroma filled the air as they walked through an open area filled with furniture and papers; the smell reminded Drake of a bed of roses. He suspected that they were inside of a repurposed inn. The front desk, though empty, was a giveaway. The group eventually came to an odd iron door that stood out like a sore thumb among all of the wooden foundations.

"You can never be too careful..." Sampson said as he fiddled with his key ring. With a different key this time, he unlocked the great door and it groaned while opening.

Drake and his men walked into a dim-lit hallway with several doors on each side of them. The doors were wooden and had small openings toward the top that were blocked off by iron bars. Sampson stopped at the third door down on their right.

"Would you like to take a look?" he asked.

The Village Elder obliged and peered through the opening. The inside appeared surprisingly cozy: A canvas and painting were set atop a fine wooden desk, to go along with a padded chair. In the corner was a fluffy bed, and the walls were colorful, as the main area of the building had been. There were no windows, however, and the only source of light was a lantern on the table.

"I take it the lack of windows is on purpose?" he asked.

"Yes..." Sampson muttered. "She is one of our newest, so as a precaution, she gets a dark room. If she is obedient, we will eventually send her up to a room with windows. We can't risk her alertin' anyone... not that they'd care, but it is still a precaution worth takin'."

Drake focused on the woman through the iron bars. She had long, brown hair, doe-like eyes, and bronzed skin that looked softer than a pillow. She gazed back at him, and he could see the worry in her expression.

"Is she Mithikan?"

"It is always hard to tell with these girls, ain't it?"

"You don't know?"

"Well, we found her here in Endoshire. Much of Mithika is a hell-hole these days, so it wouldn't be surprisin' if she was from there. She insists that she is Sigrian, though. Does she look Sigrian to you?" Sampson replied with a shrug.

"No, not at all…" Drake trailed off, then squinted to study her closer. She wore a nice blue dress; or nice for a slave, anyhow; and had a trim figure, but was not skin and bones. She appeared healthy, to his eyes. But perhaps he was mistaking her health for *youth*. "How old?"

"Uhh…"

"You don't know that, either?"

"She has given us different answers. We believe that she is in her early 20s. One time, she told us that she was 56," Sampson said. Drake looked back at him, wide-eyed. "56!"

The two men laughed in unison. Drake was pleased to hear that she was feisty. Although he had told himself that he wouldn't become attached to the first slave he encountered, there was no denying her charms.

"You there, girl," he called into the room in a stern tone. She looked up and then walked over to the slit. "How old are you?"

"37," she replied. The Village Elder chuckled.

"Methinks I'll have'ta get in there and discipline her for disrespecin' ya, Mr. Danvers," Sampson said as he stepped forward.

Drake held up a hand. "That won't be necessary." He then looked back to the woman. "What is your name?"

"Rose." Her voice felt meek and defiant all at once.

"How lovely," Drake replied with amusement in his green eyes. She smiled back at him half-heartedly.

"Would you like to see more?" Sampson asked.

"Certainly, but before that, I would like to purchase her."

"So soon? Without seeing the others?"

Drake smiled and said, "My friend, let's consider Rose the first of many that I'll take off your hands."

"Oh…" A grin came to Sampson's face. "In that case, shall we talk price?"

The group of four continued down the hallway. At the end and through an open doorway was a small study area. They arrived at a table with two chairs and sat to discuss the purchase.

"I must say, you have good taste. Rose is one of our most prized workers, despite bein' new. But I tell ya what. Since you're a new customer, and I like you, I'd be willin' to part with her for… 10,000 notes," Sampson said.

"I'm afraid that just won't do," Drake said to the frown of the fat man. "I agree that she'd be a wonderful prize, but she lacks experience. We've seen first-hand that she could be difficult to control, as well. Even still, I'm willing to take the risk for 7,000 notes."

Sampson's hyena-like laugh overtook the small room. "I think you'll find that your future clients *prefer* the inexperience, Mr. Danvers."

"Is that so?"

"It is. And that wench is gonna make me a lot more than 10,000, believe me. Hell, there are few times where I use my own product, but for a beauty like her? I may have'ta make an exception," Sampson said.

Drake flexed every muscle in his face to not show how repulsed he was.

"Meet me in the middle at 8,500 notes," the Village Elder offered. After a slight frown from Sampson caught his eye, he added, "And I shall pay it all right here and now with the added bonus that I'll be a long-time customer of yours."

After a few moments stroking his chin, Sampson stuck a hand out and said, "You have a deal."

Both flashed confident smiles as they shook hands. It would be the beginning of a prosperous business partnership, Drake thought.

"Now, shall we continue to the rest of my ladies?" Sampson asked.

"Of course. But before we do that, I am obliged to ask, for my 'diplomatic mission'…" Drake trailed off. "Do you have any interest in bringing your shipwright business to Federland? No? Alright, well at least I tried!"

Both men burst out laughing, then walked to a set of stairs in a new hallway, where they could see more of the workers.

∽

Rose sat in her cell, sweating profusely. Sampson was a pig and a monster, but at least she knew what to expect from him. Being sold to someone new had her stomach in knots. Perhaps it would fall through, she thought. Or maybe the man was buying her freedom. She quickly shook those ideas out of her head, however. In the past year, she had learned that having hope in this city was destined for heartbreak.

Eventually, Drake returned to her room with Sampson, who opened the door with chains in hand to restrain her. Rose stood and held her hands out as her heart and head sank. She had been sold, after all.

"Those won't be necessary," Drake said with a cool smile.

"Are you sure? It is unlikely, but ya never know when there may be a runner on your hands," Sampson replied.

"Oh, I'm sure. My men are quite fast and skilled," he said, looking back at the two towering, cloaked figures who filled the doorway. Rose dared not to look them in their cold eyes. "There is no one they can't catch."

The fat man shrugged and said, "If ya say so."

He walked up to Rose with a grand smile on his face and said, "Ya made me a fine sum of money, today. We didn't have much time together, but I know you'll do well for Mr. Danvers over here, won't you?"

Rose didn't respond and instead kept her eyes on the floor. She braced herself for punishment: A slap or backhanded punch to the face was likely coming. However, instead, she felt a slap on her bottom, and she stumbled forward while yelping like a frightened pup.

"Off ya go!" he said pleasantly.

Before she knew it, Rose had changed hands and was now a slave to Drake; a man she knew nothing about, save his seemingly well-mannered behavior. As they walked the streets of Endoshire, on the way back to his place, he spoke to her.

"Do you know why I bought you?" he asked.

"You said that I was lovely," she replied in a near-whisper.

"That is true, but it is not the only reason."

"Then, why?"

"You appear to be about my daughter's age. I couldn't bear to see you cooped up in that tiny cell," Drake said.

Rose stared back at him, wide-eyed. She waited for him to laugh or say that he was only joking, but he wore a smooth, confident smile on that sharp face of his.

"H-how..." she muttered. Drake tilted his head. "How could you associate me with your daughter? Especially when you plan on lending me out to others like a common farming tool-"

The Village Elder held up a hand to silence her outburst, and it worked. There was something about him, she thought. He hadn't laid a finger on her, but she feared him; his every word and move made her nervous.

"Now, now. I never said that you reminded me of my daughter; only that you look about her age," Drake said, grabbing a strand of her hair and caressing it. She wanted to turn away but knew that it wouldn't end well for her. "I must confess to you that I actually hate my daughter, though. She is rotten and spoiled; never had to work a hard day in her life. Not like you. You are lovely and have been through hardship."

"Y-you don't know anything about me…" Rose mumbled.

"Not much now, true, but I have a good intuition when it comes to people. I have a feeling that you are going to suit my needs *perfectly*."

As Drake spoke, Rose eyed a side alley to her left. In her estimation, it would allow her to cut through the wealthy district and bring her to one of the main roads, where it would be crowded and difficult to track her. Was it worth the risk? Before she could think about it further, she felt a hand grip her wrist. Rose looked up in horror to see Drake's demanding green eyes locked on her. Now, she was likely to receive punishment, she thought with a shiver.

"Please, don't run," he said, letting her go. Rose cocked her head and gasped. "If you do, my men will catch you, and I worry that they will be too rough."

"I'm sorry…"

"And besides, there is no need for you to run. My dear, *you are no longer a slave*."

The words echoed in Rose's mind. She looked back up at him, once again expecting Drake to laugh or smirk; to show that he wasn't serious in some way. But she saw that confident smile once more, and this time, her eyes lit up like a shooting star in the night sky.

"You finally understand? Good. I will explain it to you in more detail when we reach my living arrangement," Drake said.

For the first time in years, Rose felt excitement, not sorrow, for her future. She had been chosen as one of the lucky few to be free; a rarity for slaves her age.

Eventually, they reached a grand building at the northeast end of the city. They entered and ascended a few flights of stairs before one of

DIPLOMATIC MISSION

his bodyguards retrieved a set of keys and opened up a large, wooden door. The room they entered was tall and expansive; covered to the brim with expensive jewelry, paintings, wine, and food. It was without question the most luxurious place Rose had ever visited. Her eyes lit up once more.

"Nice, isn't it? I thought you could use a place to stay," Drake said. She looked back at him and her lips quivered. She ran over to Drake with tears streaming down her cheeks and embraced him. Sure, she barely knew him, but he had already done so much for her. "If you think this is luxurious, wait until you see your room."

Rose ceased her sniffles and followed Drake to a big oak door across the room. He opened it to reveal what appeared to be a master bedroom. There was a balcony that overlooked the sea, with a gigantic bed to the right covered in the finest silk. Wine and grapes decorated the room, and rare paintings were hung up on the wall. Even the dresser and candle holders were the finest she'd ever seen.

More tears of joy filled her eyes as she turned back to face her savior. He flashed that same confident smile as always.

"I-I don't know what to say… this is so generous… thank you…"

"But of course, my dear. I would accept nothing less than the finest room for us," Drake said cheerfully.

"Yes, well-" She cut herself off and her eyes lost focus. "What do you mean, 'us'?"

The Village Elder let out a mocking chuckle. "Well, this is *my* room. Or should I say, 'our room', now?"

"I don't understand…" Rose muttered. Her breathing became heavier and she felt a cold sweat breaking out on her crinkled brow.

"Ah, yes. I forgot! I've yet to give you all the details," Drake said as he pulled a rolled-up piece of paper out of his pocket. "You are no longer a slave, but you *are* an indentured servant."

"Wh-wha?" was all Rose could get out of her trembling lips as Drake held the contract up for her to see.

"You are aware of what indentured servitude is, aren't you?" he asked. She couldn't find the strength to respond. "Since I bought and freed you, there is a debt owed, plus interest. You will need to make up the equivalent of between 10,000 and 12,000 notes, depending on how quickly you serve me."

Rose studied the paper carefully, and the contract was exactly as he had said. Since Sampson owned her before, he had agreed to the terms on her behalf. His signature was on the contract.

"You didn't think your freedom would be free, did you?" Drake asked with a chuckle as he unbuttoned his shirt. Rose's heart sank. She had broken her own rule. She had lulled herself into false hope in a city where hopes and dreams went to die. "Now then, how about we start working off your debt…"

With her slim hopes dashed, Rose now understood that she had escaped the confines of one monster only to be captured and imprisoned by another.

CHAPTER 14
A STARVING CITY

While crossing through the hilly border of Currencolt into Mithika, Joel marveled at just how simple of a process it had been. There had been no true barrier, and the only security had been a few guards, who merely gave cursory glances at Alistair and then waved them through.

At first, Joel had chalked it up to the countries being close allies, but while passing through the early towns and cities on the trip southward, he couldn't help but notice that they flew not a Currencolt flag along with their own, but one that bore a great, pouncing lion.

Eventually, after seeing enough of these flags, he decided to ask Aldous about them via hand signal.

"Ah, yes. That is indeed the flaggy-do of Sigraveld," the old Wizard mused. "Mithika was once the top power of the world, but like all great kingdoms and empires, they eventually collapsed. In their case, it has been a slow, painful decline. Sigraveld, of course, took their place as the wealthiest country; and to make matters more humiliating, they stepped in and offered Mithika a helping hand in their time of need…"

"Bunch'a knobs!" Alistair said, spitting outside the carriage and onto the increasingly varied landscape. They were now traveling along the rocky shores of a crystal-clear lake, and a mountainous path loomed on the horizon. It was different from back at home, though. The climate was warm and not too dry or wet.

Joel raised an eyebrow and signed some more. What was wrong with one country helping out another?

"The problem was that Sigraveld's 'help' came at a steep price: this kingdom's sovereignty. Mithika may have its own king, queen, and army, but unofficially, they are a puppet state to the Sigrians." Aldous snorted. "And I must say that such changes caused great instability within the region."

He nodded his head at Alistair, who crossed his arms and said, "It changed everythin'! Tradin' with Mithika was no longer so easy for my country, an' it was part o' the reason we fell on hard times, too! That set us up to be taken over by those waifs!"

"Indeed," the old Wizard said with a shake of his head. "It is well-known, at this point, that Sigraveld aims to become the largest empire in all of history, and the early steps were to conquer lands nearby. This recent line of Sigrian kings has taken a different, fascinating approach to their conquering, though. None of them have attempted forceful invasions. They have only used the guise of helping struggling countries as their means of takeover, and it has worked every time. The only true conflict in recent times came in relation to *the centaurs*."

A smile cracked on Joel's face. He'd never seen a centaur; half-man, half-horse, up close before. What an interesting experience it would be to speak with one, he thought.

"Aye," Alistair said. "They were *not happy* with Sigraveld, ta say tha least! But I don' remember why…"

"The centaurs have always resided in the northeast portion of Mithika, along the Sigrian channel. They once lived in peace with the humans of this country and had even fought side-by-side with them at war. But Sigraveld, if nothing else, is well-known for its strict population control… outside of Endoshire, anyhow. Their strategy has always been to displace their undesirables to other countries under their control, and when a thousand Sigrians showed up on the centaurs' shores, they did not take kindly to the gesture."

Uh-oh, Joel thought. With the battle prowess of what could best be described as cavalry, archer, and knight combined, and their anger at the unwanted invasion of their space, it likely resulted in-

"A massacre unfolded on that day," Aldous said before sighing. "A war nearly broke out, too. The Sigrian king was angry. He commanded Mithika to strike back against the centaurs. They had one bloody battle before the Mithikans relented. They could not bring themselves to fight those who had always been by their side."

"Oi! That's right! But then the centaurs became cross with Mithika, right? That's how they got their own country!" Alistair blurted out.

"Yes, Mithika's king gave in and ceded the territory; now known as Centauri. There were harsh consequences for this entire region. The centaurs lost both Sigraveld and Mithika as trading partners. And with the recent Sigrian takeover of Currencolt, they became estranged, too," Aldous said. "The effects were even worse for Mithika because while they did not appreciate Sigraveld's meddling, there was no denying that conditions were improving under their rule. That came to a sudden halt after the Mithikans disobeyed Sigrian orders to kill the centaurs."

Aldous made a grand gesture to the lake, now in their rearview. "Enjoy the sights, my friends, while they last. The beauty of the grand marble structures in the cities and the crystal-clear lakes out in the wild will soon give way to the chaos and ruin that have overtaken the bottom half of this country. Thironas, I'm afraid, is at the center of it all…"

∽

AND SO, the trio traveled along the Mithikan coast for some breathtaking views: beautiful beaches that looked to be untouched, plateaus sprouting from the land off in the distance, and advanced towns and cities that made settlements like Faiwell and Ghobmor feel simple by comparison. Buildings as large, or larger, than the Miner's Guild back home were common, and all were expertly chiseled out of marble.

One detail that Joel noticed in each city was how there would always be sections of housing and buildings built higher up than the others; whether atop a hill or even along the edges of a mountain. Aldous explained that in Mithika, the people and businesses held in the highest regard were quite literally propped up above all others. It was often believed that those at the top had 'the view of the Gods' and were therefore blessed by them.

By the fifth day of travel, the lovely views turned mediocre. They began passing through towns filled with litter, and few of its residents were outside working. Instead, they loitered around, often digging through abandoned homes for scraps. The last town before Thironas was especially bad. It was filled with raggedy-clothed, starving people, who were as dirty and downtrodden as they were desperate.

"Is this tha work of Famine?" Alistair asked as the carriage brushed by a couple of men, badgering them for food.

Aldous nodded while tossing the beggars an apple. "His influence is spreading faster than I thought. It's worse than at Mt. Couture..."

Joel made hand signals to the old Wizard.

"I am not sure the King Wizard of this area can do much. He is an Augmenting Wizard of the mind," he said.

"What does that mean?" the big redhead asked.

"Humans usually call 'em 'Psychics'."

"Ahhh, I understand, now! He can control people's minds, then?" Alistair said.

"Perhaps…" Aldous trailed off. He tapped his walking stick on the carriage floor a few times. More beggars approached as they neared the city limits, but there was only so much that they could give. "He is not equipped to deal with something like this, I know that much."

"You've met 'im?"

"Yes. His name is Zamarim. He is fiercely loyal to the Wizard's Council, but also fair in his judgment. If I can get him to read my mind, he will understand everything," Aldous said.

Joel frowned before signing back in response.

"He's got a good point! Tha Mountain King was hard ta reach. What about this Zamarim fella?" Alistair said.

"Just south of Thironas is Lake Teras. He resides on an island at the center of that lake."

"Oh, and let me guess! There's a big ol' monstah lurkin' at the bottom o' that lake, ain't there?" Alistair sneered.

"Now you're catching on," Aldous said with a chuckle. "But it should not be a problem. My command over watery things n' such will come in handy. I know what to expect with the Guardian Beast and Wizard King. Unfortunately, I know nothing about the Keeper of the Key or Wizard Scout 'round these parts."

"Now that ya mention it, no one ever explained ta me how they choose Wizard Scouts or Keeper of the Key. Should I expect folk like the two of you?" Alistair asked.

"In regards to Scouts, it is different for each monolith and its needs. Take me, for example: Not only was I familiar with the Mountain King, who had helped train me, but I could become one with lightning and travel along the clouds of any storm he might have conjured up; a quick way to communicate with him in times of emergency. But no seal and its environment are the same as the other, and so I cannot be sure that Thironas' Scout will be anything like me," he replied before smirking at Joel. "And as for Key Keepers…"

The mute narrowed his eyes at him. He had not yet told Alistair of his luxian heritage, and while he was confident that the big man would accept him with open arms, he was not so sure that he'd be capable of keeping the secret under wraps. Even Aldous had been bad about keeping secrets, lately, and now he was about to tell-

"Well, let's just say that they share much in common, but it is a long story," the old Wizard said. Joel breathed a sigh of relief. "For now, I say that we should focus on our plan."

Alistair and Joel looked at each other with raised eyebrows.

"Erm… what *is* the plan?" Alistair asked.

"Ah, right! I haven't told you," Aldous replied with a nervous laugh. "When we reach Thironas, it would be wise to visit the lord of the settlement. Lake Teras is blocked off by a great wall that stretches all the way around it, and I believe armed marksmen sit atop it to guard the place."

Joel signed back to him, looking for clarification.

"I'm afraid that I don't know who the lord is, but I believe he will be instrumental in our gaining access to the lake."

"Why is it so heavily guarded, anyway? Do they know about Famine?" Alistair asked.

"I don't believe so. The wall was built many generations ago for fear of the *Lake Watcher*. It is the Guardian Beast of this monolith, and the people of Thironas feared it would invade and destroy their city," Aldous explained.

Joel made more hand gestures as their carriage passed through the city limits. The beggars had given up on asking them for food. Most were too sluggish to keep pace with the trotting horses.

"It has been some time since I last visited Thironas, but I doubt much has changed, save further decay of the city. I could, of course, force my way through the wall… but that would cause a commotion, and likely catch the attention of the Wizard's Council."

Alistair snorted. "Them buggers are always watchin', eh?"

"Something like that. Mayhap not directly, but if chatter picks up of a Wizard forcing his way through the wall, then they will find out," Aldous replied.

"Still, this don't seem like much of a plan ta me! Why would tha lord of the land let us over tha wall? An' what about tha team that

Drake put together? Do we know who they are?" Alistair said. Joel nodded along.

"I don't think you understand," Aldous said, each word growing sterner. "This is all that I have to offer. I have limited information on Drake's team and our options are almost zero. The two of you are the only ones willing to help me, because the Council is run by a bunch of lazy fools!"

Joel and Alistair exchanged worried glances. Aldous sighed and then massaged his head. Then, he looked at the pair with tired eyes. "If another seal is broken… if Famine is unleashed… it will be the point of no return. It means all seven of the seals will be broken. The Council is already at their limit containing Greed. It will be the beginning of the end."

Joel frowned and made hand signals.

"I'm not being *dramatic*," Aldous argued back. "The end of life as we know it is at hand! And no one is worried! We have become comfortable, so much that we're about to let something in that will ensure our destruction!"

The group remained silent and allowed the trotting of the horses to overtake their ears as a solemn air came over them all.

Aldous sighed. "This is the best I can do, for now. I'm sorry if it seems to lack thought. But in our current predicament, and with so little help, it's all I have."

"Well, I suppose we gotta give 'em hell, eh lads?" Alistair said with a raised fist. Joel raised his fist in solidarity, but Aldous did not follow. He crossed his arms and eventually dozed off. All optimism had been sucked from the carriage.

∼

On the sixth day of travel, the trio reached Thironas. Much like the settlement before it, the streets were riddled with litter, and the people were starving. There were traces of a former beauty, but ruin and desperation overwhelmed Joel's senses from the moment he spotted the decay of the slums. Rather than taking the horses and carriage to a stable, Aldous elected to set up a base camp outside the city limits and in the woods.

"The people 'round here are desperate," he said. "They'll eat our supplies, and eventually, our horses."

"Ew! Eatin' horses! How barbaric!" Alistair said with crossed arms.

"Starve for long enough, and you'll be ready to eat *anything*," Aldous said as he clanked his walking stick off the ground. "With that in mind, we must be cautious around these folk. Not only because of their desperation but because we don't know the full effects, if any at all, that Famine's imprint has left on them. It may be just as bad as the Gold Fever at Mt. Couture."

The group set off into the cityscape early in the morning. The streets were nearly empty, save a few beggars. Yet, they had not the energy to walk up and ask them for anything. They instead babbled incoherently under their breaths while sitting and rocking back and forth.

"We cannot save them from this," Aldous said, holding his head high. "We can only prevent worse."

The slums were as downtrodden up close as they had seemed from afar to Joel. Worn-out shacks built closely together lined the streets; many of which were broken down and showed no signs of life within them. Abandoned food stands and markets were also common, and they appeared to have been looted some time ago. Perhaps even worse than the view was the smell. Joel was certain that it was human waste, and that was a bad sign of just how much society had degenerated around these parts.

Straight ahead, looming over the trio, was a small plateau. It had a spacious, carved-out path twisting and turning up the front. The road was in dire need of maintenance, and the statues propped up at the top of the plateau, depicting knights and their King, were falling apart.

"Thironas is no different from the other Mithikan cities in that their wealthy and influential reside higher up than the poor," Aldous said, nodding at the plateau. "It shouldn't be difficult to find the lord up there."

While the group walked up the barren path, Alistair shielded his brow with a flat hand and then looked to the sky.

"Look up thar, fellas," he said. Joel and Aldous gazed high above to see a shadowy, winged figure. "There's a buzzard circling this place, a sign o' death."

"That's no buzzard. It's too large," Aldous said, squinting. "Whatever winged-majigger it is, it is too high up to be certain."

After climbing the path for some time, the trio reached the top of the plateau and took a breather. This section of the city looked nicer than the shanties below, but still, there was a degraded quality to it.

The houses were dirty, though large, and disheveled people roamed the streets.

They continued onto Thironas' main street, following it until reaching a great circle of buildings: The city center, where a large crowd had gathered up ahead. In Joel's estimation, there were easily hundreds of people, and they were rowdy. Shouting, shoving, and throwing things.

Joel, Aldous, and Alistair did their best to walk around the circle of humanity undetected. It seemed they were in no danger of being noticed, as everyone was too entranced by the man in the middle of it all, up on a pedestal. He wore a fancy tunic, but more importantly, had food scattered all about him.

At the edge of the city center, Aldous and the others took a seat on a weathered bench. "Let's watch from afar. Mayhap we'll spot the lord of Thironas this way, or any suspicious folk that could be a part of Drake's team."

Over the hours, many starving citizens were given food. Behind the man handing out rations were a dozen knights, fully clad in armor. They each carried a flag bearing the Mithikan kingdom's symbol: A golden hydra with a green backdrop that was lined in yellow. Every so often, someone would act out of line, and the knights would rough them up. Their displays of power quelled the rowdy group for a time, before having to demonstrate their capabilities and instill fear in the crowd again.

After the last of the rations were given out, the remaining people were told to go home. This caused a minor uproar, but it was quickly silenced by the knights drawing their swords and polearms. It looked like a bloodbath was upon them, but the man in the fancy tunic called the warriors off. They obeyed his command, and then the crowd dispersed. Between the hundreds of people leaving, Joel's keen eye picked up on the knights walking to the west end of the center, toward a grand clock tower.

The mute made hand signals to his friends and then pointed at the clock tower.

"Good eye, m'boy. The man handing out food wore clothing often seen on nobles, and he was well-guarded. I say we follow 'em." Aldous stood and then stretched, his back cracking in the process.

"Aye. It ain't like we have much more ta go on," Alistair added.

The trio made their way across the city center and approached the clock tower. It was attached to a white rectangular building that stood out as the cleanliest in the center. The building had a large wooden door for an entrance, and two of the knights from earlier guarded it.

Aldous approached the pair, who each reacted by placing hands on their sword hilts. The old Wizard put his hands up and shook them.

"No need for that. We come in peace!"

"State your business," the knight on the right replied with contempt on his tongue.

"We wish to see the lord of the land," Aldous said.

"Lord Roland is busy and has no time for guests. If you wanted food, you should have been quicker to get in line. You'll have to wait until next week," said the knight on the left.

"You misunderstand, my friends. We come from Federland and Currencolt, respectively," Aldous said as he gestured toward Joel and Alistair. "As guests of this fine land, we would be honored to speak with Lord Roland, even if for but a moment."

"I won't repeat myself, old cumberground. What do you want with the lord?" The rightward knight drew his sword and held it within inches of Aldous' throat.

Alistair immediately drew his battle axe, while Joel placed a hand on the hilt of his luxmortite blade.

"Typical doaty knights! Lookin' fer an excuse ta get yer arses kicked! Well, just try it! You'll find we've gots plenty o' energy, unlike those folk you were pushin' 'round earlier!" Alistair said with a boastful smile.

"So, you were spying on us, then? Currencolt may be an ally, but how do we know you aren't a dirty traitor, siding with Federland over the Sigrian crown?" the left knight asked as he brought out his sword.

"Now, now…" Aldous chimed in, but everyone's body language grew more aggressive by the second.

"'Tha Sigrian crown?" the big man asked, spitting to his left, narrowly missing a disgusted Joel. "Where is yer pride? Or are ya truly nothin' more than Sigraveld's whippin' boys, now?" He let out an obnoxious laugh.

"Ah, so you *are* a traitor to the crown. The punishment for treason is death…" the rightward knight trailed off as they both looked at each other through their helmets. Joel imagined that they were grinning. "I suppose we'll have to carry out the sentence."

Aldous cleared his throat, then said, "There is really no need-"

"Let 'em try! It's *their* death wish!" Alistair said as he raised his axe into attacking position.

As the knights prepared to attack, Joel finally drew his sword, which stopped the leftward knight in his tracks. He then held up a hand and the other knight halted as well.

"What is it?" he asked

"That sword…" the left knight muttered, pointing at Joel's luxmortite blade. "It's blue. Is that you, Ometos?"

The trio looked at each other in confusion as the knights sheathed their swords.

"I've never seen him without the mask before. He is younger than I thought…" the right knight muttered to his cohort.

"Erm… yes, well, as you know, Ometos can be a wee bit *impatient*, at times. Please don't make him wait any longer," Aldous said as he flashed Joel a knowing glance. The mute attempted his angriest, most intense expression, but he could see the cheeks of his friends flaring out. They were holding back laughter, and he could feel himself blushing, now.

"Of course. My apologies…" the leftward knight said as he turned and opened the door. "Please, follow me."

Joel and Alistair withdrew their weapons and the trio followed the man into the building. Inside was old and worn; littered with many weathered papers and men sitting at tables trying to sift through them. The knight led the trio leftward through a door, where they could see the giant mechanism that worked the clock of the tower. With each second that passed, Joel could both hear and *feel* the ticking hand and its gears shaking the building ever so slightly. The old staircase creaked with each step as they spiraled toward the tower's top, but the group was too enamored with the grand structure of the clock's inner workings to care. Aldous' smile held hints of child-like wonder as they ascended. Even for Joel, who lived with him, it was a rare moment to see him like this.

At the top of the stairs was a platform and door that led to a small, walled-off section of the clock tower. The knight turned and signaled for the trio to wait. He entered the room and closed the door behind him.

"So… uh… who is Ometos?" Alistair asked. Joel shrugged and looked at his Wizard friend.

"A Mithikan god. As I recall, he had two faces," Aldous replied.

"Are ya tryin' ta tell me that Mithikan Gods truly walked among us all them years ago?" he replied with a potent mixture of disbelief and disgust. "Everyone knows they're only myths! It's the great Gods O' Stone that are the *real* deities, methinks."

Joel let out a snorting chuckle. The Currens believed in living, breathing, mountain-sized stone Gods, as he'd been told while making the trip across the sea. It seemed no more believable than Mithika's Gods, but he enjoyed hearing ideas of how they'd been created or why they existed, regardless.

"I can confirm that Mithika once housed powerful beings who called themselves Gods. But they haven't roamed the land for millennia, now," Aldous replied while tapping his walking stick on the wooden floor. "Some within the Council suspect that they were actually Warlocks, Dark Wizards, and Witches looking to control the masses. Another idea is that Stalmoz created them in his experiments before finally settling on the melior as his ultimate species."

Joel made hand signals in response. He wanted to get back on topic before the knight returned.

"Keep up the act, for now. Obviously, they are not talking about the real God Ometos, but a man wearing a mask to represent him. Interesting that your luxmortite sword caused the guard to mistake you for him. This 'Ometos' could be a fellow Keeper of the Key," Aldous said.

"Hold up, why do Keepers of tha Key get those powerful luxmortite blades? Surely, there must be a battle axe made of such pristine metal!" Alistair said with bawled fists and child-like excitement in his eyes.

"Well, you see-"

Just then, the door flung open, silencing the trio as the knight stepped out.

"Lord Roland will see you."

"Thank you," Aldous said while bowing graciously. He followed the knight through the doorway, and Joel and Alistair brought up the rear. Once inside, the knight left and shut the door behind him.

The room had a nice windowed view out the back of the clock tower. It overlooked the west side of the city and further, beyond the border. Before the trio sat a man sifting through papers that overflowed his desk. He had long, dark hair tied up into a ponytail; and his green, watchful eyes were easy to miss with those sizable bags underneath them. With his broad shoulders and long frame, he reminded Joel of Dalton, except that his stomach had shrunk beneath his ribcage, which poked through the fabric of his shirt. If even the lord of Thironas was feeling the effects of the famine, then the situation was likely even worse than they'd feared.

"How can I help you, gentlemen?" Lord Roland asked. His voice was commanding with hints of rasp mixed in. "Or perhaps a more pertinent question is: *Who are you*?"

Joel shot Aldous a nervous glance.

"Don't you recognize him?" Aldous said while pointing at Joel, who squirmed in his boots. "This is Ometos. He brought me here to speak with y-"

"That's not Ometos," Roland interrupted. "I know him; I have seen him without the mask. I can see a resemblance, and it is odd that you both own blue blades, but you are not him." He pointed to Joel, who had begun to sweat. He was truly out of his element, playing along with Aldous' lie.

"Erm..." Aldous mumbled. Now, it was becoming clear to Joel that he had no backup plan.

"So then, my question remains: Who are you and what do you want?" Roland asked. His voice grew more impatient with each word.

Their attempt to protect Thironas was off to a rough start.

CHAPTER 15
OMETOS

Aldous sighed and held a gentle hand upward. It did little to quell the stern glare of Roland, however. "Alright, I admit that he is not Ometos. I apologize for lying to you, but we needed to speak with you as soon as possible."

"And why do you say that? What makes you think I have time for your problems? Princess Ella is due here in three days' time, and there is much preparation required for her arrival," Roland said while rubbing his tired eyes.

"Then, I shall make this quick," he replied, his temperament falling to ice-cold levels. "Thironas is in grave danger. My name is Aldous. I am a Wizard from the west. We have traveled here to prevent the horror that lurks in Lake Teras from escaping and wreaking havoc, not only on your people but the whole world."

"You refer to the Lake Watcher monster? Perhaps you haven't noticed, but there is a *giant wall* constructed around the shores to keep the beast contained. It has been that way for thousands of years, I am told. What makes you think there is a problem now?"

"Yes… the Lake Watcher," Aldous replied. *Another lie*, Joel thought as concern welled up inside of him. It was certainly their duty to keep Famine a secret from the general populace, but lately, he couldn't tell if his Wizard cohort was fibbing out of necessity or *habit*. "A nefarious group from the west aims to set the monster free. They have already succeeded in unleashing a beast in Federland, where we are from. I want to stop them before it is too late. The lives of your people depend on it. I need access to the lake. Tell your guards atop the great wall to stand down and allow me passage. I promise to take care of the rest."

"Eloquently spoken, but I must say that something about your claims ring of mistruth, old man. I can't put my finger on it." Roland stood, hands tucked behind his back, and then walked over to his window to look over the cityscape. "But even if I wanted to help you, the guards are not under my jurisdiction. They are controlled directly by the Mithikan Kingdom… or should I say Sigraveld? Either way, it is not my call to make."

"Why wouldn't they give ya power over yer own district?" Alistair butted in.

"A fair question. One I've pondered for years, now. They made me lord of this land, but I am powerless to do anything with my title. Much like the Mithikan king, I am little more than a puppet. I imagine that soon, when the Mithikan prince and Sigrian princess marry, I'll be stripped of my title, anyway. So, what does it matter?"

"Are you saying that the guards of the wall would even fire upon *you*?" Aldous asked.

"That's how the previous lord of Thironas died," Roland replied while turning to face the trio. He was smirking, but it felt to Joel like a façade. Before him was a man trying to appear cool and collected, but in reality, he was trapped in a cycle of despair. "And I don't plan on dying based on your hunch."

"It's not a hunch, but a *fact*. If we do not act soon, disaster will come to your city," the old Wizard argued.

"Look around you. Disaster has already arrived!" he shot back. The brief flare-up of emotions seemed to exhaust him, though, and his whole body slumped as he let out a sigh. "The current famine is unprecedented; the longest in our history. All solutions that I have come up with have been turned down. It doesn't matter what I want. Powers greater than I have sealed this city's fate."

"We noticed that you were able to hand out an abundance of food to the starving people, earlier. Surely this means that conditions are improving…" Aldous said.

"The food didn't come from our own land, nor was it approved by the Mithikan Kingdom. A man in a strange mask, calling himself 'Ometos' has been helping us. Recently, he gained access to a great supply of food. I have no idea where he got it, or how, but I don't care, either. It keeps us from starving, for now."

Aldous stroked his beard. "Would it be possible for us to meet up with Ometos?"

"I am one of the few people that he's willing to communicate with; someone that he trusts. I can't just send *anyone* his way," Lord Roland said while returning to his seat.

"We ain't just anyone, boyo! Did ya not understand what he was sayin'? We're here ta help ya!" Alistair bellowed.

"I don't know anything about you," Roland replied, eyeing the papers on his table. "Now, if you'll excuse me…"

"Wait," Aldous said, nudging his head toward Joel. "Aren't you wondering why they both wield blue swords?"

"I was curious, but not enough to believe your story."

"It's because the man behind that mask is an appointed guardian of this land, meant to protect it from what lurks in the shadows," the old Wizard said, gesturing to the mute. "Joel here was similarly appointed to protect Federland. There should also be a couple of Wizards watching over the lake. Have you encountered them?"

"Now that you mention it, there was one fellow… I've seen him a few times when speaking with Ometos, but he seemed to have little interest in me or the people of Thironas. I had a difficult time believing he was a Wizard. He seemed weak, much like you, old man," Roland said. "I get the distinct impression that Wizards are but a myth spread by the desperate."

"Appearances can be deceiving," Aldous said, holding up an index finger. A small ball of lightning took form right at the tip, zapping; sizzling; just begging to escape and strike something, but the old Wizard's magic held it together. Roland gasped, trembling hands on his desk as he stood. "And Joel here can break through metal with his sword."

"Show me," Roland said. He bent over and grabbed a dusty sword off the floor, then walked over to the mute.

Joel drew his blue blade as the lord held his sword out for him to strike. He raised the luxmortite sword above his head but hesitated. A faint echo called to him from afar: They were screams of agony; of vitriol. Now, all he could think of were the innocents he had killed while training, back then; and worse, the incident that had turned him mute in the first place.

"What are you waiting for?" Lord Roland asked.

A fine question, he thought, shaking the cobwebs out. *It's only a sword*, he thought. Yet, when Joel brought the blade down, his eyes widened to see not a blade as his target, but the exposed neck of Jed Thaeon. He swiftly tried to pull up, but the result was a half-hearted swing instead of stopping. Even still, a loud *clang* rang throughout the room and sure enough, Roland's sword cracked. Once again, he gasped and then held the blade up to inspect.

"That was a steel you just cracked… and with such a weak swing…" Roland muttered with a blank stare.

"Do you understand, now? If we wished it, we could have come here by force and done what we wanted to. We ask for your help in the name of keeping peace in this land. We failed in our duty back home. Let us help you prevent the same catastrophe from happening here," Aldous said. Joel put his sword away. A mixture of disappointment and anxiety overcame him. He had summoned the strength, courage, and fighting spirit of a lion back at Mt. Couture, when it had mattered most. Why had he been so meek at a mere demonstration of his sword's abilities?

Roland tossed the sword over his shoulder, then walked to the side wall, where a mount held various other blades. He grabbed a claymore and then sheathed it.

"Let's go. It is a bit of a journey to reach Ometos, and I'd like to be back before dark," he said.

The group of four exited the clock tower with Roland leading the way. The two knights guarding the entrance stood at attention.

"You two, come with us," Roland said. Without a word, the knights followed them, their armor and weapons clanking with each step.

At the city center, they took a right and followed the road for about a quarter-hour. The nicest, largest houses of Thironas were in this section, but even they could not escape the ill effects of the famine. Many of them were built of sturdy stone, but cracks in the foundations were apparent, and even more so was the dirt and dust that often coated the houses' edges.

Eventually, they arrived at an intersection where Lord Roland led them to the left. The quality of housing began to degrade, and even the trees that lined the road seemed to wither in reaction to Thironas' depressing reality. After a half hour, the group came to a gigantic bridge that sloped downward and over the peasants below. Alistair gawked at the sight of the marble bridge propped up by enormous columns.

"Whoa! I can't believe anyone ever had tha resources ta build somethin' like that!" the big man said with wonder.

"Have you ever heard the phrase, 'history is built on the backs of giants'?" Roland asked.

"No, what does that mean?"

"It means that we could never hope to build a bridge like this now. It was created during the height of Mithikan power, and even then, it took many years to construct," he replied before stopping the group to walk toward one of the bridge's edges. He kicked at a piece of crumbling marble and it flew off the ledge. "It is only a matter of time before it falls apart, but I imagine that will be well after people leave this place."

"Don't be so quick to despair, my Lord," Aldous chimed in. "We may yet be able to save Thironas."

Roland scoffed, then returned to the front of the group. They journeyed across the grand bridge for a half hour until reaching a portion that crossed over a river.

"Does that river lead to the lake?" Aldous asked.

"It does," Roland said.

Aldous stopped, and so too did the others to look back at him. He walked to the right ledge of the bridge and then stood on the railing.

"This is where we part ways, for now, my friends."

"What do you think you're doing?" one of the knights asked, starting for him and holding out a hand for him to grab. "Get down from there, now!"

With a knowing smile, Aldous turned forward and raised his arms. Joel's ears twitched as a familiar sound reached them. It was like a waterfall, but-

Suddenly, a great jet plume of water shot up from the river, behind Aldous. The knights and Roland gasped at the sight while taking steps back and shielding their eyes from the shower that reached them. Joel and Alistair were too busy looking at each other in confusion to block the water from splashing them.

"But I thought you wished to meet Ometos?" Roland asked, raising his voice over the roar of the geyser.

"Joel and Alistair here will meet with him. I shall use this river to sneak behind the wall and find the Wizards that I suspect live beyond it," Aldous replied.

"B-but-" Alistair mumbled.

"Try to obtain as much information from him as possible, you two! Make sure he is protected. For he is important; not only to the safety of

Thironas but the whole world!" Aldous said as he hopped off the ledge and onto the water jet.

The knights gasped once more as Aldous slowly descended below the view of the bridge. The remaining group ran to the ledge just in time to see him speeding down the river atop his water jet, which hovered just above the current. Roland shot Joel and Alistair a curious gaze. He was probably suspicious of them, now; or perhaps they weren't as interesting of company as a Wizard, the mute thought. Still, he resumed leading them over the empty bridge.

"I don' get it," Alistair tried whispering to Joel. True to form, it had come out at normal volume, though. "Shouldn't he be thar ta speak with the Key Keeper fella? And what did he mean about protectin' him?"

Joel understood completely. If Drake's team somehow knew what a Key Keeper's role was, they could strike them first and steal the key. Thus, there would be no way to reseal the monolith if it was broken. Without Joel's key, the Wizard's Council still hadn't been able to close the portal containing Greed, so far as he knew. A second portal that couldn't be resealed would be disastrous.

Still, protecting the monolith was the top priority, and the odds of Drake's men knowing of the Key Keeper's location seemed low. Aldous had most likely given them the less dangerous task. With Drake's team possibly lurking around the corner, time was of the essence, and splitting up to cover more ground made the most sense.

The mute signed his thoughts back to Alistair.

"Oooo, I get it now, lad. I suppose he doesn't think I can handle me'self, then?" the big man asked, his spirits dampening.

Joel shook his head and made more hand signals.

"Don't try ta go easy on me! I know everyone thinks I'm a burden! But I'll show 'em. I've gotten much better in combat since last year!" he said with a boisterous chuckle before slapping Joel hard on the shoulder.

After some more time walking, Roland looked back at Alistair and nudged his head toward Joel. "Why is he so quiet? Is he deaf?"

"Joel is a mute. He can only talk with the Universal Sign Language."

"I see. I suppose you'll have to translate, then, if need be."

"Not a problem! I'm an expert, these days! Ain't that right, lad?" Alistair asked, then tried to give Joel a hard slap on the back, but he ducked the attempt with lightning-like speed. Alistair lost his balance and stumbled forward due to the momentum of his swing. "What'd ya do that for? I nearly ate the ground fer lunch!"

The mute let out an inaudible chuckle.

After another quarter-hour, the bridge finally declined to its end. Before the travelers was a decaying path, littered with the odd rock or boulder once every few meters. Aside from that, the land was barren. There was a visible mountain range off in the distance to the northeast, but everywhere else seemed flat and without life.

The two knights behind Joel and Alistair took their helmets off and let out a strained breath each. They hunched over with hands to knees. The heat had risen greatly as the distance from Thironas grew.

"I dunno how ya lasted this long, fellas!" Alistair said with a chuckle. "It's hotter than sin out here!"

"Yes, the heat does become difficult out on the open plains. Not as bad as a desert, but the next worst thing," Roland said as he eyed the two knights. "Those two are under orders from the kingdom to wear their helmets at all times while on duty…"

The knights frowned in unison. They both wore brown beards and one had a battle scar above his left eye. Their faces were drenched in sweat.

"But I suppose it matters little, out here," the lord said, much to the knights' visible relief. "We can take a short break, but then we'll need to get moving. There's still a journey ahead of us in those mountains." He pointed to the range in the northeast.

∾

MEANWHILE, Aldous traveled downstream, not by way of the current, but by walking. He had submerged himself and then created an air bubble that encompassed his body. This, he thought, would allow him to bypass the wall while avoiding detection. After having walked for an hour, he could finally see the structure of the wall above the water.

Aldous had suspected it wouldn't be as easy as walking in, and he was correct: The underwater section of the passage was blocked off by iron bars that were too narrow for him to fit through. He held a hand out, intent on diverting water pressure to bend a couple of the bars and grant himself entry. However, something gave him pause: Would he be risking the safety of the people? After a moment, he laughed at the thought. The Guardian Beast could break through the wall any time it wanted to. It *chose* to stay and continue its duty.

With some extra concentration and a strong gesture of his hand, the water diverted to the left and right of the two iron bars before him, outside of the bubble. Slowly but surely, the iron groaned and bent. Soon, there was a gap in the iron large enough for him to pass, and Aldous continued downstream. The riverbed began to widen, and eventually, it became vast. He had reached his destination.

In sharp contrast to the stream, which had been crystal-clear, Lake Teras was murky, and it made the old Wizard uneasy. He directed the water down and propelled himself to the surface, where he saw the shoreline to his back left and right. On the right side, he spotted a shack off in the distance.

Aldous walked with confidence along the sandy shores, in the direction of the shack. He could see armed guards all around on top of the wall to his right, but they were at least a couple hundred meters off in the distance. Without concentrating, they probably wouldn't notice him, especially since they were all facing in the direction of outside the walls for potential intruders.

After a brisk stroll, Aldous reached the shack. Just outside of it were a cluster of trees, and an old man relaxing in a rocking chair underneath them. He approached the snoring fellow, who wore raggedy clothing, donned a straw hat that was tipped downward, and had a long piece of grain in his mouth. He was clean-shaven, but had fuzzy gray eyebrows and what looked to be wily hair underneath the hat.

With a clearing of his throat, Aldous startled the old man out of his slumber, and he flung forward in the chair while gripping his knees, as if bracing for a fall.

"Hello, there," the old Wizard said with as much cheer as he could muster. "Not a busy beach, is it?"

The man in the rocking chair tipped his hat up and gazed back at him with lackadaisical eyes.

"I should imagine not. The Lake Watcher resides here," he said before cocking his head. "How did you get past the wall and armed guards?"

"Wouldn't you like to know?" Aldous asked with a chuckle.

"You know how dangerous it is 'round here, do you not? Even standing in this very spot, yer puttin' yerself at risk."

"Oho! Then, why are you here?"

"'Cause I ain't in danger. Trust me," he replied with a snort. "You, on the other hand, would be fish food if you got into the water. So, steer clear, ya hear?" The old man then tipped his hat back down.

"I'll take my chances," Aldous said as he walked up to the shoreline. He pushed his walking stick into the ground with authority and then closed his eyes.

With a sudden burst of energy, his eyes opened, and slowly but surely, the water began to part. Soon, the lakebed became visible, and a path gradually appeared, headed toward the center island, barely visible at the horizon. He had parted the water up to about 20 meters away when he heard the man stir from his chair and then his clunky, dragging footsteps in the mixture of sand and grass.

"So, yer a Wizard, huh?" he asked.

"Why, yes I am," Aldous replied without looking back.

"I'm a Wizard, too."

Aldous held an open palm out toward his watery path, halting its creation, before turning to face the man in the straw hat.

"The name's Thurick. And you are?"

"Aldous."

"Aldous, eh? I have heard of you... Scout of the Greed monolith, right?" Thurick asked.

"Indeed..." he replied in a defensive tone. It wouldn't surprise him to learn that nasty rumors were spreading among mainstays of the Council, but had even fellow monolith guardians been informed of the Mt. Couture disaster?

"It is nice to finally meet another Scout. Yer the first I ever met... but shouldn't you be guardin' yer monolith?"

Aldous let out a long breath through his nose. "So, you didn't hear the news, then?"

"The Council has a knack for keeping us in the dark," Thurick replied.

"A little over a year ago, the Greed monolith was broken, and the key was lost. The Council has been holding him off in the Cold World with the help of the Guardian Beast," he replied. "But of course, such a measure can only be temporary."

"Oh, that ain't good..." Thurick said. Aldous picked up on a certain carelessness to his words; as if they were only making small talk.

"I came here in the hopes of speaking with Zamarim. We must prevent the other seals from being broken, y'see. Does he still reside on that island?" Aldous asked as he pointed out to the middle of the lake.

"That's right. But hold up, are you tryin' to say *this* monolith is in danger of bein' broken, too?"

"Precisely. A human is working together with what I believe to be a Dark Wizard. They aim to break all seven seals and unleash the split identities of Stalmoz," Aldous said.

"Wait... wait... a human? This all sounds ridiculous!" Thurick laughed derisively.

"Please, it is important that I-"

"Well, I ain't gonna stop ya."

"R-really?" Aldous tilted his head.

"If yer worthy enough to cross the lake unharmed, then there is little I can do to stop you, anyway," Thurick explained. "Besides, Zamarim will probably set you straight."

"We'll see about that," Aldous said with a confident smile. "He needs only to read my mind, and he will understand all."

Thurick shrugged, tilted his straw hat back down, and then returned to his rocking chair. Aldous, on the other hand, regained focus on the water and pressed his walking stick into the sand. The already-parted water began to cut further into the lake. At this rate, it wouldn't be too long before his path reached the island.

∽

THERE WAS little of note on Roland, Joel, Alistair, and the knights' journey to the mountains; aside from some broken-down carriages, skeletons, and the odd rat trying to scavenge food. After two hours of travel and occasional rest, they reached the first mountain of the range. Along the base, they came across a path leading up the rocky ledges and through a system of partial caves, from what Joel could tell.

"The two of you will stay here and stand guard," Roland said to the knights. "Don't let anyone else up this path. Is that understood?" They only nodded in reply.

Lord Roland led Alistair and Joel up the trail with surprising vigor for a man who looked to be starving. After reaching a high ledge, they passed through a partial cave with beams of light poking through it. Their breaths and steps echoed off the walls, and in the quiet of the mountain, it was all they could hear. Midway through the cave, the group came to a three-pronged fork in the trail. Roland took the path to the right, which hugged the edge of the mountain and was only wide enough for a single-file line.

In and out of the partial caves they went, slowly ascending as they did. No cave ever overstayed its welcome, as whenever Joel tired of the dark, they came out to a blinding light along the mountainside. At another fork in the path, Roland took a left, and that led them to a set of stairs carved from the rock of the mountain. The stairs themselves curiously branched midway up. The lord took the right stairs, and the trio found themselves climbing for some time after that. Joel eyed Alistair, huffing and puffing just behind him. Only a year ago, he'd have needed several breaks to make it this far. His stamina had greatly improved. Now, he was curious to see how he'd improved in battle; although preferably in a practice duel and not against their unseen enemies.

"How much longer 'till we get there?" the big man asked.

"We are close," Roland replied without looking back.

At the top of the steps was a long tunnel, carved so expertly out of the rock that it looked more like a hallway. It was littered with artifacts that showed previous signs of life: old chests with broken locks, shattered tables, torn articles of clothing, and rusted weapons.

"Is this where that Ometos fella' lives?" Alistair asked.

"We're not quite there, yet. This mountain was once the home of bandits. They carved out a complicated system of paths, leading to here. Great for ambushes against their enemies or rivals. Some time ago, however, Thironas forces drove them out and killed many in the process. They were becoming a problem, I suppose…" Roland said as he took a left down a new hallway.

The area became darker and more cramped with each step they took. Alistair clumsily bumped into Joel as they took a right down a new corridor.

"Oof! Couldn't this knob have found a better place ta live? It must be a pain in the arse coming to an' from here all the time!"

"True," Roland said as he came to a sudden stop. "But perhaps privacy is worth the inconvenience. Especially if he's going to provide starving people with food. Someone desperate enough would probably try to rob him."

He began climbing what appeared to be a ladder when Joel squinted enough. After a few moments, a latch from above was opened and light shone through.

"You'll be free to ask Ometos all about his living arrangements, soon. We have arrived."

Alistair and Joel climbed up behind him and came out to find themselves in a field. There was some grass growing out of the ground, a few trees, a cascade that fell from a cliff face to the left, and a creek that went down the mountainside to their right. It truly was a bizarre piece of landscape; as if it had been carved out of the mountain just for someone to live there. At the end of the small field was a house made of stone.

The trio crossed the field and reached the house. Roland pounded on the door.

"Ometos. This is Lord Roland. I have brought some people along that I think you would be interested in meeting."

After waiting for a short time, the lord opened the door himself and walked in. Alistair and Joel followed close behind. They traveled through a small hallway and into an open room, where a cloaked man sat at a table by the window. He wore a white mask that Joel found disturbing: It had small eye slits that tilted downward, as if angry or grinning in some way. The lips too were vague; looking half like a sinister smile, half like a frown. It had a nose, as was common for a mask, but at the top was another, upside-down nose and a sad mouth to go along with it. If the mask was flipped around, it would be a sorrowful expression for sure, but no less creepy from the mute's perspective.

"Lord Roland..." a muffled voice said through the mask. Joel's ears twitched. Was he imagining things, or had he sounded *familiar*? "This is an unexpected visit. And I thought we agreed to always meet alone?"

"Yes, well, this is a glaring exception," he replied, stepping aside and gesturing at Joel. "This boy here... he wields the same kind of blade that you do. It is blue and able to cut through metal. These two requested to meet with you, specifically. They say that you are the guardian of this land and that they wish to ensure its safety alongside you."

The masked man looked at Joel, then tilted his head. He stood while turning his mysterious gaze back at the lord.

"You were right about one thing, Roland. I *am* interested," Ometos said.

"Good, 'cause we gots lots ta talk abo-" Alistair silenced himself as the masked man held up a hand. The creepy mask turned to Joel once more.

"It's been a long time, Joel..." he said. A chill shot down his spine. He had figured out why the voice sounded familiar.

CHAPTER 16
THE GRUDGE

Joel watched as Ometos ripped off his cloak and tossed it over a shoulder. It smoothly landed on a hook at the back wall. Then, he slowly removed his mask and placed it on the table. Standing before him was Pierce, the black-haired, dagger-eyed warrior he'd once considered a brother. He wore a dark tunic with a red sash and dark pants to go along with it.

"You know this fella?" Alistair asked, looking at Joel with a raised eyebrow.

"Of course he does," Pierce replied with a smirk. "I imagine it's hard to forget your victims, eh Joel?"

"'Victims'?" Alistair scoffed and then put hands to his hips. "Joel wouldn't hurt a fly!"

"*Wrong*. You stand next to an efficient killer. The only reason his body count isn't higher is a sense of guilt," he replied. Pierce drew out a dark blue dagger, but it was longer than most; not quite the length of a sword, but close. Protruding from the bottom of the blade was a gleaming, oval jewel.

"Oi! Ya both got them luxmortite swords! Where'd ya get that? Who tha hell are ya, anyway?" Alistair shouted before drawing his battle axe.

Pierce laughed and walked around the table. When he reached the pair, he lowered his dagger, and so too did Alistair lower his axe; but Joel was now sweating.

"He never told you, did he?"

"What are ya talkin' aboot? Told me what?"

"Come now, you can figure it out. Have you seen his luxmortite sword?" Pierce asked. Alistair nodded. "And who wielded such weapons? Who created them?"

"The Ancient Ones…" he muttered.

"That's right. We were called luxians back then; before most of us were wiped out by the Dark Savior."

"But how? I was led ta believe that they all died out!"

"No. Some of us were preserved in time, to be awakened later on. To guard *this*," Pierce said as he pulled a hexagonal medallion out of his pocket. It was dark blue and looked almost exactly like Joel's Greed monolith key. The only difference was in the engravings.

Alistair sharpened his eyes and focused them on Joel. "Were ya ever gonna tell me?"

The mute, having worked up a sweat without moving a muscle, could only shrug. It was difficult to look his friend in the eye, with so much of his history coming to light at once. Instead, kept focus on Pierce, for he knew what was likely on his mind.

"I suppose you're wondering why I'm here, Joel. I knew that you were scheduled to be awakened in this time period. And so, I chose the same time. I worried that I would be here for the rest of my days, trying to take care of these starving people and unable to confront you. But it seems fortune smiles upon me today," Pierce said.

"I'm lost," Roland jumped in, leaning forward in apparent disbelief. "You know him? And you're… not from this time period? An Ancient One?"

"That's right. Thousands of years before you were born, I was given this duty. But what we didn't realize back then was that we were meant to guard something that can't be contained. The result, in this land, is starving people," he replied

"You refer to the Lake Watcher?"

"No. Something *much worse*."

"Hold up. Yer complainin' about Famine, but accordin' ta Roland, yer the one who got food to tha people. How are ya gettin' that food if there's a famine goin' on?" Alistair asked.

"Because our king is worthless and spineless, we don't receive aid from Sigraveld. Even the Wizard's Council was good for little aside from sitting around and talking about it. So, I had to seek help elsewhere. Luckily, I've made a deal that will ensure the people are fed for years to come. And even better, it will end the famine that plagues this land," the dagger-eyed man said with a smile. "That's not important right now, though. Let's take this outside, gentlemen. I have business with *him*, and wouldn't want to make a mess in the house."

He pointed at Joel with his blade, and it made him squirm. He had been led to believe that Pierce wouldn't be a part of the Key Keeper program set up by his people all of those years ago.

Joel tepidly nodded and then turned to exit into the field. The others followed close behind.

~

Meanwhile, as the knights stood guard at the bottom of the mountain, a figure approached them from the left: A tall man who was covered entirely by a robe and cloak. The pair drew their weapons and awaited the intruder.

When the mystery-man reached them, the knight on the left said, "Turn back immediately. You do not have clearance to enter this passage."

He stopped but did not respond. Both knights took offensive stances with their swords.

"Last warning. We shall kill you where you stand."

The intruder took more steps forward, and as he neared, the size difference between him and the knights became apparent. Not only was the mystery-man a veritable giant over two meters tall, but he looked to have been forged out of iron.

"Stand aside. I have no quarrel with you, but I'll do what must be done for my Dark Lord," he said in monotone.

"It's two against one," the right knight said to his partner. "A sure win for us."

"Very well," the giant said as he flexed his right arm and made a fist.

After letting out a pained groan, a loud *crack* echoed off the mountain base. The giant shot his arm down, and out of his long, spacious sleeve appeared an all-white sword. He caught it in his bear paw-like hand.

"What the hell is that supposed to be? It doesn't even look like metal," the left knight jeered as they both closed in on their target.

"It's not metal… it's something far better."

The leftward knight brought his sword overhead to strike, but suddenly, like a raging bull, the giant charged in, ready to gore his prey. He lunged out with the white blade and pierced through the plated armor at the midsection like a speeding arrow through wet paper. The knight gasped aloud as he ripped the sword out of his stomach and grabbed him around his scalp. Blood emptied from the knight's plated armor like a leaky bucket as he wailed aloud in pain under the immense strain of the giant's grip.

The rightward knight charged in for an attack of his own, but he hesitated at the chilling noise of his partner's skull cracking. His pained cries turned shrill; primal. The screams penetrated his mind, and for a moment, he lost focus. The knight's eyes widened when he saw his cohort *flying at him*. In a split-second, he was struck by the other knight, and the two men shot backward, rolling and dragging against the harsh landscape.

In a daze, the knight wondered what in the world had happened. Had the intruder *thrown* his cohort at him? Like some kind of meaningless toy? After shaking out the cobwebs, the knight noticed that his partner's corpse was on top of him. He squirmed and struggled out from under the dead man and looked up in a panic. The giant was gone.

The knight let out a nervous chuckle that turned into full-on laughter. He had truly been left alone! A second chance at life! His excitement turned to hysteria, and the world around him spun. That was when he looked up and saw his own headless body collapsing to the ground in a bloody heap. The air escaped from his brain, and in his last moments, he saw the cloaked figure looming over him, gazing with contempt.

"As someone who has gotten a second chance, I don't often give them," the giant said as the white sword sucked back up into his sleeve. "Farewell."

∽

OUTSIDE OF HIS HOME, Pierce stood across from Joel and pointed his dagger at him once more, while Alistair stood by his friend's side with his axe at the ready. Roland remained on the sideline, near the creek. A light mist filled the air from the cascade at the cliff face on their left, and while wiping his face, Alistair couldn't help but notice that the mute hadn't taken up arms.

"No, no," Pierce said with a snicker. "I'm not just going to kill you. I want the satisfaction of beating you, too."

Joel shook his head and Alistair looked at him with wide eyes. He thought that his quiet friend had found the resolve to do battle back at Mt. Couture, so long as he wasn't fighting to kill. Apparently, it had only been a temporary measure. *No matter*, he thought. Today, he'd prove himself in combat, if he had to.

"It ain't no use. He don't wanna fight, lad."

Pierce scoffed. "We live in a world where only force can keep the order. Kingdoms, councils, even businesses… all kept together with the threat of violence if someone steps out of line. Do you truly believe that if criminals weren't punished for their actions, they would stop stealing and killing? That everyone is good, deep down? No. Even *you* are not that foolish. You lived through the time of the Dark Savior, after all, so you know that there are enemies who cannot be reasoned with. Your motives are far more selfish; sinister, even! For while you sit back and enjoy your so-called peace, others must fight for you to keep order!"

Joel crossed his arms and stood firm.

"But I wonder…" he trailed off before pointing his dagger in Alistair's direction. "How will you react when someone *dies* for you? Will you finally awaken from your stupor when your fat friend's blood stains the field?"

The big man's grip tightened on his battle axe. "Why you-"

"Come to think of it, you killed my parents, so it would only be fair if I killed someone that *you* care for, don't you agree?" Pierce said as he looked upward and stroked his chin. "In fact, it should be two people. So, after I kill *him*, I'll find Riza and slit her throat. How does that grab you?" A smirk came to his face.

Joel narrowed his eyes, but he didn't make any moves. Alistair's round face had turned red; he was about at his limit of patience.

"Are you surprised? I knew that the two of you were scheduled to awaken in the same time period, after all. I just don't know which monolith she holds the key to. It'll take some traveling around, but soon, I'll have plenty of time. Eventually, I will find and kill her, too… unless you stop me," Pierce said as his smirk grew to a grin.

"I'VE HEARD ABOUT ENOUGH FROM YA, LIL' WAIF!" Alistair shouted at the top of his lungs. Pierce turned his dagger-like gaze to him, unwavering. "I'm gonna give ya one chance ta back down 'cause I'm feelin' generous. Whatever problem ya got with Joel has nothin' ta do with why we're here. Yer monolith is in danger, and we're here ta help ya, ya daft knob!"

"Is that right?" he asked.

Both Joel and Alistair nodded.

"Well, I don't care," Pierce said with a chuckle. The pair returned dumbfounded stares, but Alistair's shock didn't last long. He could feel his rage reaching a boiling point. "In case you hadn't noticed, it can't get much worse around here. The spawn of Stalmoz known as Famine, even from another world, is spreading his influence into ours. It is now that we realize our solution was but a temporary one. The Dark Savior will rise once again, one way or another. We may as well enjoy what time we have left, and these people have suffered enough."

"You're saying that this monster, this 'Dark Savior' is the cause of the famine?" Lord Roland asked, his tone reflecting disbelief.

"That's right. And I've found the solution: Let the beast out of his cage."

"Don't be a fool! There ain't nothin' good about releasin' such a monster on the world!" Alistair replied.

"I'm aware of that. How could I not be? What you need to understand is that the plan to lock Stalmoz away was not well thought out. The seal between the Cold World and ours cannot hold his essence for much longer, and we're all going to face the consequences. May as well do what we want in the meantime. Today, I want to avenge my parents," he said and then pointed at Joel.

"He's clearly gone mad!" the big man said as he looked over to Roland. "Ain't ya gonna help us stop 'im? He's plannin' to unleash somethin' much worse than a single famine! I'll tell ya that much!"

"I think that I'll observe, for now. Ometos has been a savior to our people for some time. I'm not about to turn on him, but…" the lord trailed off as he eyed Pierce. "I would very much like to see this monster up close; to be sure your plan is safe."

"That can be arranged," he replied before turning back to Joel. "Right after I take care of some unfinished business."

"You'll have to go through me, first!" Alistair cried.

"I intend to," Pierce said as he inched in closer and readied his dagger. The big redhead held his axe horizontally, ready to take a swipe at any moment.

Pierce made the first move with lightning-like speed. He dashed out and swung at Alistair's head. The big man narrowly avoided

THE GRUDGE

thanks to the dagger's lack of reach and then swung the battle axe toward his opponent's chest area.

The dagger-eyed man ducked the swing, then in one swift uppercut motion, brought his blade up and jumped. Alistair gasped and hopped back, but the dagger cut into his clothes and broke skin. The rings of shredded chainmail echoed in the field as both men paused.

Alistair saw Joel breathing heavily out of the corner of his eye. He seemed pale as a ghost, so he gave the mute a quick nod to ensure him that he was alright.

"You're as clumsy as you look! This will be easy," Pierce said as he took a crouched stance.

Thanks to the chainmail, the cut on Alistair's chest was only superficial. Even still, the dagger had cut through it with relative ease. The luxmortite was clearly superior to steel. The big man knew he couldn't allow Pierce to swing that dagger again, but with his quick, acrobatic style, how could he stop his attacks? After a moment of thought, he decided the best strategy to be close, fast swings to keep him on his heels. With that in mind, he choked up on the axe grip.

"Heh! Yer not the first waif ta underestimate me! Well, I've been practicin'! And yer gonna taste a lil' piece of me axe before this fight is through!" Alistair shouted as he charged in for a surprise attack.

With a closer grip on his axe handle, the big redhead took a screaming-fast swing that Pierce narrowly bent back to avoid. Before he could respond with an attack of his own, Alistair had already begun his next swing, a vertical slash down.

Pierce rolled to his left as the grass and dirt parted before the axe head struck rock. Like a cat, he hopped to his feet and then turned while bringing his dagger around. However, well before the blade reached its destination, Alistair's big boot collided with his chest. Pierce let out a pained gasp as he tumbled onto his bottom. The dagger-eyed man looked up at Alistair as he coughed and held his chest.

"Ya like me big boot? How'd ya like one to yer *face*, next?" Alistair said before bursting out into obnoxious laughter.

That'll show 'im, he thought before looking at Joel out of the corner of his eye. His quiet cohort was smiling, and a newfound pride welled up in Alistair's chest. He'd gotten better, and he *was* cut out for battle, no matter what his family might have thought. Today, he was proving it.

Pierce stood slowly and readied his dagger once more. Alistair, not wanting to give him time to recover, was quick to resume the onslaught and swung his axe diagonal and upward.

The dagger-eyed man sidestepped and directed the axe head to his right using his blade. With that new opening, he went for a stab straight at the big man's gut. Alistair also sidestepped, however, and brought his axe around low and diagonal, aiming for the knee.

Pierce hopped over the axe head, and with that momentum came a thundering jump kick that caught Alistair in the jaw. His eyes glazed over and he stumbled back as the dagger-eyed man lunged forward for another stab. The big redhead regained his bearings just in time and maneuvered his axe head to block the blade.

The impact made an odd noise: It was like an eggshell cracking, but more straining on the ears. Pierce retreated with a grimace.

"What a shame…" he muttered. Alistair looked down to see that the axe head had cracked. It wasn't completely broken, but another impact like that would seal its fate, he thought. "I don't find it sporting to break lesser metals with luxmortite."

"Hold up," Alistair said with growing agitation. "Yer tryin' ta tell me that you were avoidin' a clash o' blades on purpose?"

"Of course," Pierce said as he twirled the dagger in his hand, casually. "You didn't think you really stood a chance, did you?"

"You an' everyone else… always treatin' me like I'm a joke, eh?" he said under his breath.

"Luxian sword techniques are superior because only our trim yet compact bodies can handle such strenuous movements. But even among humans, you are *painfully average*. Say whatever is needed to help you accept the inevitable conclusion, but the end is near for you."

Alistair gritted his teeth and lowered his hands on the axe handle until they were at the bottom. He swung his mighty axe downward and diagonal, which Pierce easily sidestepped. However, Alistair continued the momentum into another downward diagonal swing from the other side. It was once again sidestepped, but not so easily. The pattern repeated over and over as Pierce moved backward, and each swing came just a bit closer to hitting. Soon, the big man could feel vibrations in his axe from the wind of his attacks bouncing off of his foe.

With each swing, Alistair's smile grew; as it would only be a matter of time before he landed a crushing blow. Pierce, on the other hand, continued to dodge and showed no worry in his expression.

Suddenly, the dagger-eyed man stopped backing up and dug his feet in. Alistair brought his axe down and diagonal with more force and speed than ever before, and Pierce placed both hands on his dagger handle as he dropped to a knee and tilted his right shoulder back. He then held the blade out, and it collided with the battle axe's shaft. With a loud *crack*, the axe head separated from its shaft, and it flew into the ground, where it shattered on impact.

"Damn it all!" Alistair cried as he heard a gasp from Lord Roland behind him. *So close*, he thought, looking at the broken axe shaft in his hand. He'd been a mere hair's length away from striking him in the cheek or shoulder.

There was no time to lament, though, as Pierce swung his dagger upward and to the right at Alistair, who contorted his upper body leftward for a last-second dodge. However, the dagger-eyed man continued his momentum and turned the missed swing into a spinning kick. The heel of his boot smashed into the back of the big man's skull, and his vision fell to blackness. He dropped to his hands and knees, and now he could feel Pierce standing over him, ready to bring the dagger down execution-style.

Triston was right, he thought while trembling and ripping the grass with his balled fists. Alistair let despair take hold as he awaited the final blow. However, it never came. Instead, he only heard a loud *clang* overhead.

∽

JOEL HELD his luxmortite blade out, blocking the dagger, and then lifted it with all of his strength to throw Pierce and his blade back. Alistair was sprawled out on the ground, groaning.

"That's more like it," Pierce said with a smirk. Joel took a step back and held his sword out in a defensive stance. "Playing defense? Your stances used to hold far more imagination… but I suppose you're more of an empty shell, now."

The mute narrowed his eyes. Even if he could speak, nothing would dispel the hatred irradiating from Pierce. Even though the idea of fighting made him sick to his stomach right now, Alistair was obviously incapacitated, and so he had to buy some time before they could escape.

Pierce closed in with his dagger held out and ready to swipe. Joel backpedaled, but it quickly became apparent that he'd be caught, so he dug one foot in front of the other and bent both knees while holding his sword outward and slightly tilted.

As their blades met, Joel pushed the dagger leftward and forced Pierce to step back. He then returned to his guard. The dagger-eyed man tried a variety of attacks, but they always ended the same way: Joel would beat the dagger away, regardless of its angle. With each attempt, the frustration and anger in Pierce's expression became more apparent. The reach disadvantage meant that there would need to be a series of parries and blows before he could land a hit. However, with Joel never taking any risks, he left no openings.

Finally, Pierce ceased his onslaught and spit in disgust. "*Coward.* There is no satisfaction in killing you, if that's all you're going to do."

Same old Pierce, Joel thought with a smile. His frustration was blinding him. If he stayed careful, he could ward off his attacks while Alistair recovered. The big man was already starting to show signs of life.

"You leave me no choice, then, but to turn this into theatrics," Pierce said as he held his hand out. With an expression reflecting death, he slowly pulled the dagger across his palm.

Joel raised an eyebrow as the blood poured from his palm and onto the dagger. A tingle ran down his spine as his eyes fixated on the blood; the very same that he had spilled on *that dreaded day*. The blade pulsed a light blue and soon, it was encased by the odd light. He pulled the dagger to his side and then flung it at Joel, straight as an arrow. It was about the speed of an arrow, too, but the mute managed to contort himself enough so that it flew past him.

After the near miss, he closed in on the dagger-eyed man with his sword in attacking position. He had no desire to strike him but wanted to force a surrender. However, even as Joel proceeded, Pierce showed no signs of worry. The glow of the dagger must have had some sort of magical property, he thought. From behind, he heard the *whoosh* of the wind, and in that split-second, he could tell that it was something drawing nearer, not further away.

The mute threw himself to the ground and felt the wind smack his back as something zoomed over him. He looked up to see Pierce holding the dagger once more.

"Do you recognize this blade?" he asked. Joel tilted his head as he stood. "It belonged to my father. He wanted to give it to me one day… of course, he never got the chance. It was taken by me, just like his life was taken by you. My father lives on through this weapon, and so does my mother. Their blood, which is on your hands, flows through it." He held the glowing blade up triumphantly.

Joel finally understood. Pierce had *charmed* the dagger. It was a powerful magic performed by Wizards of their time that could bestow mysterious abilities onto other objects. His blood must have been the trigger for it, he thought. The mute knew charms all too well: the greater the sacrifice or emotion, the greater the power of the object. He had also charmed something in the past, although it was different in nature from Pierce's dagger.

"Incredible…" Roland muttered.

"It will always come back to me, and it listens to my every command. Depending on how much blood is put into it, of course," Pierce said as he held an open palm upward, and his blade levitated just above, pointed at the sky. "As I said before, my parents' blood flows through this dagger, and so too does mine. Since it was charmed in this way, only *true members* of my family can use it. So, even if you killed me here today, it would be but an ordinary blade for you."

With a frown, Joel resumed his defensive stance. He knew that Pierce had to be saying it out of anger. Up until *that dreaded day*, the Thaeons had treated him like family.

Pierce charged forward and threw his dagger once more. Joel deflected it with his sword, but rather than continuing off on its new expected trajectory, it remained in place and then swung in Joel's direction. It was as if an invisible man were attacking him with it.

The mute deflected the blade again, but as he did, Pierce jumped in and nailed him with an uppercut to the gut. He doubled over and let out a gasp, but quickly looked up to see Pierce pointing a finger down.

Without being able to catch his breath, Joel rolled to his right, then swung the sword to his left blindly. He heard a *clang* and felt the stinging vibration of blades clashing. Figuring that it must have pushed the charmed dagger back enough, Joel decided to turn it into an attack. He charged at a surprised Pierce and swung the blade at his neck.

A silent gasp escaped Joel's mouth as his eyes played more tricks on him, like back in the clock tower. He no longer saw Pierce with a blade to his neck, but Osanna. Blood erupted from her throat as she gurgled and screamed, and the mute held up at the last moment with trembling hands.

In a panic, Pierce ducked to avoid the blow, only to look up and see that the mute had stopped his blade short. He scoffed, then pointed a finger back at himself. Joel heard the whirs of the wind behind him, and it sounded like the dagger was coming for his head.

More alert than ever, he ducked the charmed blade, and in the split-second that he saw it pass, Joel watched a gasping Pierce put his hand up to signal a stop. It was on course to hit him right between the eyes, and in that moment, a lump came to Joel's throat in the form of his regret. However, the dagger halted, mere inches away from striking him. Both of them sighed with relief as Pierce let the blade fall into his hand.

"Are we done with the games?" he asked with a snarl. Joel shrugged. He snuck a glance in Alistair's direction to see that he'd reached a knee.

The big redhead gave him a nod. It seemed he understood the situation and knew that they should run. Joel couldn't play defense forever, and even *that* had his stomach in knots. Since when had the mere act of defending himself become so unbearable? The way the battle was shaping up, Pierce would likely capitalize on his hesitations and kill him, he thought.

"If you want to steal all satisfaction from me, then our duel no longer has meaning. Now all that matters is that you still draw breath," the dagger-eyed man said as he turned to face Roland. "Help me finish these two off, and I'll take you straight to the source of the famine. We can end this needless suffering once and for all."

Roland opened his mouth, but no words came out. After what looked to be a moment of thought, he said, "I don't like the idea of helping you carry out a personal vendetta."

Relief swept over Joel. Even if he did look to be starving and tired, he could tell that Roland had seen his fair share of battle, and with Alistair still incapacitated-

"But I'll do what I must for my people," he finished.

The situation was growing dire. Making a run for it would be dangerous with the charmed dagger in play. Especially since it was capable of changing direction in mid-flight.

"Actually, I had something different in mind," a husky, but familiar voice called from behind. It was a large, cloaked man approaching from the other side of the field.

"You're here sooner than expected," Pierce replied in a curt tone.

"Relax," the giant said as he held up a hand.

Eventually, he reached the group and pulled down the hood of his cloak. Blond, mid-length hair flowed down, with long sideburns to go along with it at an iron jawline. A familiar stone face stared down at Pierce. *Angus*, Joel thought with a gasp.

"The way I see it, there is no need to fight. Not if they're cooperative."

"I'll never work with him," Pierce said, nudging his head at Joel. "Besides, their goal is the opposite of yours."

Joel raised an eyebrow. What would Angus be doing in Thironas? Was he one of Drake's men?

"True, but I would be remiss if I didn't extend the offer. I am also here to retrieve your monolith key. I have held up my end of the bargain, after all," the giant replied.

Pierce frowned. "That was never part of our agreement. The key stays with me, and I'll help you destroy the monolith. Those were our terms."

"Yes, well, Drake feels that he has been generous enough that the key should be in his possession. I tend to agree. After all, you could close the monolith and go back on your deal at any time with it in your possession," Angus replied.

"I could just as easily say that about you lot and your food deliveries. What keeps you from stopping them after you've had your way? There needs to be an equalizer in our deal, and that happens to be this key." He retrieved the medallion from his pocket and hung it from a chain around his neck. "But if, perhaps, you think you are being treated unfairly…"

Pierce made a gesture and the floating dagger pointed to the giant. Angus smiled as much as his stone face would allow.

"Let's not forget the true goal. We are on the same side. There is no need for us to fight."

All remained silent, save the cascade at the left cliff face. Angus turned his attention to Joel and Alistair.

"That goes for the both of you, too. Whatever misguided reasons you may have for wanting to protect the monolith, you must realize that unchecked as it is, the people of this land will continue to suffer in vain. The Dark Savior is coming back, one way or another. I suggest you choose the right side," he said.

Joel shook his head, while a recovered Alistair grimaced in response.

"Oooo, great! Meat-stain is here, too!" he complained.

"Perhaps you think that I hold a grudge for our confrontation at

Mt. Couture? I can assure you, it's all water under the bridge. *The cause is far bigger than my ego.*"

Joel had suspected over the past year that the 'missing' people from Mt. Couture like Angus and Edith had survived. He had questions in regards to the missing key for Greed's monolith, so unlike Alistair, he was happy to see Angus. It did worry him, however, to see that the giant was as cool and confident as ever.

"Together, with Drake and his team, we will bring order and peace to the world, one country at a time, until all are united to the same cause," Angus said in a prideful tone. "So, what do you say? Will you join us?"

CHAPTER 17
LAKE WATCHER

Great walls of water flanked Aldous as he traversed the lakebed, headed for the center island. True to his word, Thurick had not interfered. He'd remained in his rocking chair, snoozing as Aldous parted the water.

Although he had created the path to avoid the ever-dangerous Guardian Beast roaming the lake, an attack was still possible. The old Wizard had seen the creature in action before, and when it got hold of live prey, it wasn't a pleasant sight. In his estimation, the previous Wizard Scout had probably been killed by it due to negligence. If Thurick remained as nonchalant as he had acted earlier, he was as good as dead, too.

As he walked, Aldous snuck glances at the walls, and a light sweat came to his brow. The water to his left and right was murky, as if the darkness of Famine had managed to cloud even the lake's natural beauty. He thought back to his previous time visiting: The water had been crystal blue, back then.

Then, out of the corner of his left eye, he spotted something darting through the cloudy water. Aldous gasped and readied his walking stick while turning to the threat, but then he relaxed his posture and lowered his artifact. It had only been a fish. Still, he remained on high alert, for every once in a while, he came across the skeletal remains of lake-dwellers, perfectly preserved on his lakebed path. The monster was still here, and an attack was imminent, he thought.

SEVEN SEALS

∼

A GROUP of eight men approached the great wall of Lake Teras from the northeast side. The leading man of the pack looked up at the top of the barrier to see several bloodied guards slumped over. There was a hole in the stone before them, about a meter in diameter.

"I don't believe it… he actually pulled it off!" the leader of the pack said with a laugh. He turned back to the others. "Through this hole, we'll take another step closer to unspeakable treasures, my friends."

Bartholomew Montgomery, commonly referred to as 'the Vulture' among the fearful, came from an influential family who led groups of outlaws all around the world. *The League of Bandits* was more than just a criminal enterprise, though. They were a legacy that had established dominance over hundreds of years. However, one sore spot for the family was the subject of Mithika. Many years ago, their ancestors had been killed and exiled from the mountains surrounding Thironas.

Bart wished to retake their abandoned mountain base, but much of the Montgomery family had disagreed; arguing that Thironas and Mithika as a whole were a lost cause. However, in the face of Thironas' famine, Bart had seen opportunity. He had only managed to convince nine of his fellow bandits to come along with him on the journey, and the prevailing thought among the League was that they would all be excommunicated for going against the elder members' wishes.

The group of ten never returned to find out what their punishments were to be, as there had been much to profit from in Thironas and some of the nearby cities that were suffering. At first, theft had been a simple task against the weakened wealthy class of Thironas, but soon, a new problem arose: Even the rich had lost much of their wealth. In response, Bart and his men had taken their efforts to other parts of Mithika, yet their small numbers and hardier targets proved to be a great challenge for them. One incident, that had seen more than half of the crew killed at the hands of angry villagers, convinced Bart to return to Thironas and resume his search for the abandoned mountain base of his ancestors.

After an exhaustive search, he had rediscovered the hideout in the mountains; and in doing so, had come across a strange man in a mask who called himself Ometos. To both of their surprises, they had bonded over their lament at the state of Thironas, albeit for entirely different reasons.

Such an unlikely friendship had given Bart the idea to recruit new bandits from the city. He realized that through the desperation of the poor, some would be willing to adopt the bandit lifestyle. In short order, he had managed to recruit five new members.

During that time, Ometos had introduced Bartholomew to a large, cloaked man, whom he referred to as 'the benefactor'. The giant revealed a plan to infiltrate the Lake Teras wall so that a great treasure could be obtained on the island at the lake's center. This was a well-told Mithikan legend from thousands of years ago; supposedly one of the most coveted treasure stashes in their history. In exchange for the bandits' help in finding this treasure, Ometos and the benefactor had offered to split it with them.

Naturally, Bart agreed, having not sniffed a treasure in some time, and having nowhere else to go. The plan had seemed hard to believe, however. He'd been told that a map would come to him from the sky; depicting Lake Teras, the wall, and where they could sneak through it. Even harder to believe was that a path to the island at the lake's center was supposed to reveal itself to him after bypassing the wall.

Sure enough, it had come to pass. Bart didn't understand how a map had magically dropped to them from the sky. Or how there was a hole in the wall with several dead guards that normally would have shot them long before they had a chance to enter; but it mattered little. The new objective was reaching that center island.

Bartholomew watched as his men crawled through to the other side of the wall. He looked up to see that two had stayed behind. One was a small young man, Giles. He wore torn clothes and had a face that reminded him of a baby deer. The other, Norman, was tall and thin, but he had a mischievous look in comparison. As was common in Mithika, both had dark hair and bronzed skin.

"Giles. Norman. What are you waiting for? Our treasure awaits," he said while gesturing to the hole in the wall.

∽

"Yes, sir. We'll be right there," Norman assured him as he turned back to his friend with a furrowed brow. "Hurry up, he's waiting."

"I don't think this is a good idea…" Giles muttered.

"You choose the coward's way out, now? When we're this close to a better life? It's not like you have anything to go back to," Norman replied. Giles hung his head. "Don't take it so hard… I only mean to say that you have nothing to lose. Neither of us do."

"Are you boys having second thoughts? I took you in with the understanding that you were interested in the bandit life," Bart said with crossed arms. "If you're hesitating now, with the treasure right at our fingertips, then go home. I have no time for that."

"N-no sir, we're going," Norman said before turning back to Giles with a demanding stare. "Isn't that right?"

Giles sighed. "Yes…"

The two young men crouched while passing through the hole in the wall, and Bartholomew followed soon after. As soon as he made it through, one of his subordinates said, "Boss… you gotta see this…"

Bart joined the others in their gawking. Further ahead, to the east, the lake was parting. A chuckle soon gave way to laughter.

"I don't believe it! Everything that the benefactor said has come to pass!" He walked to the front of the group. "That's our path to the island. Let's move!"

The group of eight made their way toward the source of the parting water, near a shack that stuck out like a sore thumb along the shoreline. As they approached, Bart called back, "Remember the plan! Stick to our story!"

Soon, the bandits reached an old man in a rocking chair. He jolted forward in surprise when they were within a few strides of him. He tipped his straw hat up and upon turning to see Bartholomew and the crew, his expression of shock turned to a carefree smile.

"Today just keeps getting stranger and stranger…" he muttered with a chuckle before standing and outstretching his arms in a welcoming manner. "'Ello there! How are you on this fine day?"

Bartholomew frowned. "We're starving, poor-"

"And smelly," he finished with a smirk.

"It'd be easier to bathe if there were a viable water supply nearby, but a great wall separates us from it," one of the men interjected. He sounded nasally and sick.

"That's true, but it's fer yer own good," said the straw-hatted man. "How did you get through the wall, anyhow? The guards should have killed you before you could climb it."

"The better question is: How did you cut that path in the water?" Norman asked.

"Are you a Wizard?" Giles added.

Norman scoffed at him. "Wizards ain't real!"

Giles put hands to hips and said, "Then, how do you explain the water parting?"

The other bandits nodded in agreement and Norman groaned.

"My name is Thurick. I *am* a Wizard, but it was not I who created the path," he said, turning to the split water. "Another Wizard came along and performed the feat. It seems he can control water." He shrugged.

"Look at where the path leads. The island at the center of the lake is said to house many treasures. We could make some money an' finally feed ourselves!" Bart said excitedly.

"I suppose you could follow him in there. I won't stop you, but there is a difference between a Wizard challenging the Lake Watcher, and a pack of humans trying their luck; a difference between a worthy foe and *prey*. It will be cautious against the Wizard… not so much against you, my friends," Thurick said. All except Giles returned uncaring expressions such as eye rolls or shrugs. "I see. So, the citizens of Thironas have gotten that desperate, eh? Best of luck to you, then."

The bandits ventured onto the lakebed path, and as the last in line, Giles' ears picked up on Thurick muttering something:

"Fools…"

He turned to see Thurick in his rocking chair and lowering his straw hat; probably to snooze, he thought.

"What an idiot!" Bart said with excitement when they were far enough away. "Once again, the benefactor was correct. He didn't even try to stop us. The sob-story must have worked."

"But what about the Lake Watcher?" Giles asked. "The legend says-"

"Balls ta the legend!" one of the men cried out. The others laughed.

"The legends are just that: legends. Stories to tell. The Mithikan Kingdom has kept this lake from the people for too long. And look what has happened to Thironas," Bart said with a shrug. "After we obtain our treasures and expose that nothing else is here, we'll be heroes to this city."

All except Giles cheered as they marched along the damp lakebed. He didn't know much about Wizards, but he got the impression that their advice should be heeded. He worried that they were all walking to their deaths, and now, with the treasure nearly in their grasp, he was powerless to deter his fellow bandits.

∼

Up ahead, as Aldous continued his cautious journey, he noticed a shadow cast on his path; not from the water, but from the sky. It was that odd bird again; the one that Alistair had mistaken for a buzzard. However, it was far larger than most birds, and certainly too big for an avian, he thought. Could it have been some means for the Wizard's Council to spy on him? His mind raced and so too did his heartbeat. If that were the case, his actions today would see him excommunicated for sure.

At that moment, he noticed something out of the corner of his eye once more. He tried to put it out of his mind, thinking it was only a fish; but this time, it was *big*, and the movement wasn't temporary. It continued to follow him. Aldous turned his head slowly to see a shadowy figure in the gloomy water. It was difficult to make out exactly what it was, but it followed him from a distance in the same direction he was going. It had to be the Guardian, he thought.

"Oi! Wizard!" a voice from behind called out.

Aldous turned to see a group of eight jogging toward him. He gasped, and once again, his mind raced. How had they bypassed the wall? What were the odds that a band of humans would infiltrate the lake on the same day as him? Now, there were many more factors for him to worry about.

The old Wizard stopped and turned to face the men, as one by one, they stopped and stood before him. Many appeared to be Mithikan, but Aldous could tell that some were from different lands. They wore ragged but versatile clothing: All were dressed in long boots and dull tunics, with a variety of bandanas or other small accessories. Useful for anything from a quick fight to a tough day out in the fields.

"What do you think you're doing?" Aldous asked with a scowl.

"My name is Bartholomew… I hail from the slums… and these are my friends… we tire of starving and living in destitution… so, we are here to follow you…" Bart said with apparent cheer as he caught his breath. "That island at the lake's center is said to house many treasures that would fetch a king's ransom. Up 'till now, no one has made it past the grand wall, but we found a way. They also say that it is impossible to cross this lake, but it would seem fate demands success of us on this day."

Aldous looked over the leader of the pack. He stood out as the most obvious non-Mithikan of the bunch. He had a light brown beard to go along with dark brown eyes. He adorned the nicest outfit in his group, although it still wasn't quite what rich folk would wear. Still, the long boots and versatile pants led the old Wizard to believe that he was a jack of all trades, and probably lying about his destitution.

"Fools!" Aldous shot back. All of the men, save Bartholomew, were taken aback at his suddenly overwhelming presence. "Just because I've carved out a path, doesn't mean it is a safe one. There lurks in this lake a monster that will kill you in the vilest of ways. Turn back now, while you still have meat on those bones of yours."

"No way! Not when the opportunity is *this* good. We can sell the junk on that island to get ourselves some food!" one of the men argued. Bart looked back and smiled at his cohort before nodding along.

"I find your story to be dubious at best. It is more likely that you are choosing to throw your lives away over sheer greed," the old Wizard said with a sigh. Then, he turned and resumed walking. "But I don't have time to deal with this. Do as you wish."

As he walked, Aldous' mind strained. Since when did he not care for human lives? To clear his head, he told himself that it was for the greater good; that he was simply focused on the task at hand. Yet, he couldn't help but wonder if his Anima was soon to take a hit.

The group of eight followed close behind, grumbling to themselves. Aldous looked to his left once more. The dark figure remained, but instead of swimming parallel to where *he* was, it was next to the humans, now.

"You see?" Aldous asked as he pointed the walking stick to his back left. "It has already identified you as prey."

A small young man increased his pace until he was next to Aldous. "'Scuse me, sir. My name is Giles. I understand that you are cross with us, but I truly do hail from the slums of Mithika, for what it's worth… with that said, I have a question that I hope you are willing to answer: Is the 'monster' you refer to the Lake Watcher? From the old legends?"

Aldous cast his gaze down on him like a dark spell, ready to scold him, but then he saw his boyish face. He was taken aback by the similarity to Joel. It wasn't their looks that matched up, but their demeanor. Well-mannered, meek, and quiet. He couldn't help but be a little nicer to him than the others.

"Why yes, that is correct."

"So, yer sayin' it's real, old man?" a tall, thin young man jumped in.

"Quit playing into that silly legend, Norman," Bartholomew said, waving him off. "This old fellow just wants all the treasure for himself, methinks. It'll take more than some stories to scare us off."

The old Wizard snorted. "No treasures await you on this journey. Only misery and death, if you continue. You should turn back before it's too late."

"What's it gonna do while we're on dry land?" one of the men asked as he laughed and slapped the water wall to his left. Aldous narrowed his eyes. Now, they were taunting the beast.

"This is your last warning."

"We'll do what we must to survive!" Norman shouted to the cheers of most of the others. Giles, on the other hand, remained silent.

"But you won't surviv-"

A great splash erupted from the water wall on the left, dampening most of the group and forcing them to throw arms up and shield their faces. When all settled, one of the men had disappeared.

"Amaury? Where'd he go?" one of the men cried aloud in a panic.

"I tried to tell you. The monster will pick you off one by one!" Aldous said as he slammed the bottom of his walking stick into the lakebed. The water walls splashed out a pair of boots and tattered clothing. "*This* is all that is left of him."

"Oh, God…" Giles muttered, now trembling.

"Let it come for me, then!" Bartholomew cried as he drew his sword. "No one, or no creature, shall bring harm to my crew! My brothers!"

"A useless gesture. You shouldn't have brought them along if you wanted them to live. Now, our best bet is to make a run for it," Aldous replied, beginning to jog. "Stay close to me!"

As the group ran along the path, Aldous' ears picked up on something slicing through the water. He glanced left and behind to see a cresting wave in the water wall, speeding toward them at too quickly to avoid.

"Prepare yourselves!" he said.

A panicked, pained cry from behind saw Aldous stopping in his tracks. He looked back to see one of the men being dragged into the water by a long, red, tongue-like organ. It had dug into his leg and latched on. The others grabbed hold of their friend, yet despite their combined efforts, he was slowly tugged toward the wall of water.

"It hurts!" he shouted as Aldous fixed eyes on his leg. It was shrinking, and the tongue was growing outward and into the water. Nearly all aspects of the leg; muscle, fat, nutrients; were being *sucked up*. The leg continued to shrivel like an old raisin until it lost all color, and then it was merely sagging skin and bone. After much screaming and struggle, the tortured man's skin gave way and started to tear. He wailed so loud that Aldous' ears rang as his leg snapped off and shot into the wall of water. All that remained was his upper thigh. Blood spurted out like water at a dam that had collapsed, and he became pale and tired.

"The hell was that?" Norman asked with panic on his tongue.

"The Lake Watcher," Aldous said with contempt. "I tried to warn you."

"P-please don' l-leave me," the gravely injured man said as he squirmed on the ground. The blood loss was sending him into shock.

"He doesn't have long to live. Take him back to the shore, and I'll ward off the beast," said Aldous.

Bartholomew grimaced. "But the treasure-"

"Have you not learned?" he shot back as another great splash smacked the lakebed on the path ahead. All turned to see that the beast had finally revealed itself.

Standing before the men was a dark creature with an exceptionally long snout, similar to a truncated cone with its mouth looking like a small hole. Its face was almost entirely blank, save for its two eyes, which were themselves empty and black; like the eye sockets of a skull. It had two front legs, similar to a crocodile's, complete with claws, but most of its body was slug-like and chunky toward the back. Its flailing tail was the only notable deviation. It was long, thin, and had a stinger of sorts at its end. To make matters more intimidating, the monster was about the size of an elephant and nearly took up the entire width of the exposed lakebed.

With surprising speed for its size, the monster leaped forward so that it was hovering over the gravely injured man.

"N-no! Noooo!" he cried with a sudden burst of energy. Aldous and the others rushed in, but the old Wizard already knew that it was too late. The Lake Watcher plunged its snout into his head, and the *crack* of his skull, followed shortly by the beast's grotesque slurping noises froze everyone in place.

"Get it off! Get it off!" the man shouted, but no one dared to make a move. It was already over for him.

All watched on in horror as the life drained from his face: His cheeks shriveled until collapsing into themselves, and all color faded from his face as other features such as his eyebrows and nose began to sag lower than humanly possible, like melting wax. Eventually, his cries turned to moans and then gargles as his skin became loose and gray. In seconds, the outline of his skull became apparent. There were no muscles, fluids, or organs left. The man was now slack-jawed, and his eyes had melted into little clots of blood. Finally, the monster released its snout from his empty head, but it remained hovering over the body as if deciding what to devour next.

From behind, one of the men brought a sword down upon the beast's slug-like body, but it shattered on contact, eliciting gasps from all around besides Aldous. Without looking back, the Lake Watcher flung its tail at the attacking man and nailed him in the gut with its stinger, which itself was nearly as long as a sword. The sound of flesh peeling and gulping into the tail once again took hold of, and paralyzed, all on the lakebed path. The man's dry gasps and convulsing only added to the horror. In mere seconds, his spine and bones gave way, and his upper body folded back like an accordion, all to the tune of *cricks* and *cracks* of tearing muscle and breaking bone.

"The rest of you need to run," Aldous said as he held a hand out. Water gathered around him as most of the men dashed for the island off in the distance.

Bartholomew, Giles, and one of the other bandits stayed behind, however.

"I'm not leaving him!" Bart said as he drew a pair of smaller battle axes. Giles and the other bandit readied their weapons, as well. Giles' eyes reflected a nervous determination, which once again reminded the old Wizard of Joel.

Bart threw one of the small axes at the Lake Watcher, but like the sword before, it shattered on contact like a clay bowl against the wall.

"Impossible…" he muttered as the monster's tail coiled. In his shock, he remained still as the beast went for another killing blow. The tail struck like a bolt of lightning.

However, before the stinger could reach him, one of his men dove in front. Bartholomew trembled as he watched his friend take the sharp edge to his gut.

In a panic, he grabbed hold of his friend and pulled. Giles joined in trying to free him from the stinger, but it was no use. Within seconds, the bandit's skin turned grey and all aspects of him sagged. With no muscle to hold him up, the man collapsed into an old pile of bones and skin, and Bartholomew and Giles fell back onto their bottoms, taking some weathered appendages with them.

Giles yelped like a frightened pup as he dropped the two fingers that had come along with him on his fall, but Bart's reaction was far different: Still grounded, he tossed his deceased friend's hand over his shoulder while crying out in anger and throwing his second axe at the monster. The result was the same, but it did turn the Lake Watcher's attention toward the pair. By then, Aldous had gathered enough liquid to mount an attack that could halt the beast; at least temporarily.

The Lake Watcher lunged out at Bartholomew and Giles with frightening speed, but not beyond what Aldous could track. With a wave of his hand, the old Wizard sent giant blades of water at the beast. An explosion of droplets erupted on contact, pushing the Lake Watcher back. It bellowed like a distorted trumpet, and through the haze of the attack's remains, shot its tongue at Aldous. However, he side-stepped and then whacked it away with his walking stick.

He looked over his shoulder to see that the two men who had wisely run off managed to gain considerable ground. Giles and Bart had also reached his side. With that in mind, Aldous raised both hands above his head and closed his eyes. His ears twitched as he heard the scurrying claws and slithering mass of the Lake Watcher rapidly approaching. When those noises ended, he was certain that it had lunged out at him like a cat preying on a mouse; and that impact was but a split-second away. Yet, Aldous was no ordinary mouse.

The old Wizard's eyes burst open with the ferocity of a hundred fires to see that he was now face-to-face with the Lake Watcher, in mid-pounce. He brought both hands down and the great walls of water collapsed on the beast with such force that it was washed away. The path behind Aldous remained open, so he turned and made a run for it. Giles and Bart followed him despite their pained and tired breaths.

Eventually, they caught up with the two remaining men. The pair seemed to have little energy left in their panicked bodies, and Aldous couldn't fault them for that. They had likely witnessed the most gruesome scene of their entire lives.

"W-we'll never… make it…" Giles said between breaths and stumbling strides.

"Out of energy, eh?" Aldous asked as he pointed at the water wall on his right. He then motioned toward himself and a small stream slithered underneath him and the bandits. "How about we go for a ride, then?"

The water burst to make a jet that propelled him and the others up, and then the lake below collapsed into the formerly exposed path. Aldous pointed his walking stick toward the island, and then, as if riding a wave, the group traveled along the jet stream, the high speeds of the wind blowing their hair back in a straight line and forcing them to shield their eyes.

"Why didn't ya do this sooner?" one of the men asked grumpily.

Aldous glanced up at the sky. Whatever bird-like creature had been watching over him was now gone. He sighed as the knots in his stomach tightened ever more. If it had been a Council spy, then he'd all but ensured his excommunication, just now.

"I wanted to be discrete. The Wizard Zamarim does not like to be disturbed. Do you know of him?"

"Never heard of him," Bart replied. The others shrugged.

"That is by design," Aldous said with a smile. "Zamarim is one of the world's most powerful Psychics, so mind your thoughts. Soon, we will be in his domain."

"And how do ya propose we 'mind our thoughts'?" Norman asked.

The old Wizard raised an eyebrow. "Point taken… that's why you'll stay put when I tell you to."

Behind them, Aldous could hear splashes over the near-overwhelming roar of his geyser. The monster was hot on their tail, occasionally jumping out of the water and trying to reach them. However, the water jet had propelled him and the remaining men just out of its reach.

After traveling for a short while, Aldous and the others arrived on the island. Bart and his men came crashing to the ground as the water jet hit land like a giant wave crashing into the rocks. Aldous, on the other hand, landed gracefully. He spun himself around to check for the Guardian, but there was no sign of it. Perhaps it knew not to enter the Wizard King's territory. The Nightcrawler had usually steered clear of the Mountain King back on Mt. Couture, too.

That was when the entire group became aware of an odd sensation. It was as if they'd entered a different world; the sounds were hollow, the air was thick, and there was a strange blue tint to everything that could be observed by all. Aldous knew all too well what it meant: Zamarim would have the ability to detect and affect their minds from there on.

The island itself was covered in a thick forest. The trees had once been lush and green as Aldous recalled, but they had become dull and their leaves now reminded him of bile. He could only hope that Zamarim had not succumbed to the negative effects of Famine, much like the Mountain King had fallen to Gold Fever from guarding Greed.

"Look over there! Fruit! Actual fruit!" Norman shouted gleefully as he ran over to a tree.

Aldous and the others followed him, then looked up to see odd fruits hanging from the branches. Each was dark violet and about the size of a coconut.

"Let's shake it down," Norman said with glee.

Giles put a hand on his shoulder. "But it could be poisonous-"

"So be it! I haven't had a good meal in days!"

That had put an end to any arguments. Even Aldous didn't have the heart to tell them no.

The men shook the tree with all of their remaining vigor, and soon, one of the fruits gave way and dropped into Norman's hands. He felt it out and then sniffed it before shrugging.

"This is like no fruit I've ever seen. Doesn't seem to have a smell, but it's ripe, like an apple. I hope it tastes like one. Imagine getting' ta eat a giant apple?"

"In all of my travels, I've never seen a fruit like this one, either. How odd," Bartholomew said as Aldous raised an eyebrow.

"Surely you couldn't have traveled far if you've been living here your whole life, poor and starving, right?"

Bart let out a nervous chuckle. "Right..."

Norman took a bite of the violet fruit and chewed for a moment before widening his eyes.

"What's wrong? Is it poison?" Aldous asked.

"It can't be..." Norman mumbled as he took another bite.

Concern overcame the old Wizard. Could it have been addictive, like the black gold? Was this the imprint of Famine?

"No!" he shouted before throwing the fruit against the tree. It exploded into a violet dust cloud on impact.

"What in the..." Bartholomew trailed off. "How did that happen?"

Norman sulked and then muttered, "The fruit... it dissolves in your mouth before you can swallow anything."

"That's impossible!" one of the others cried. He and Bart rushed to the same tree and shook at it until another fruit fell.

The other man took bites, and sure enough, the precious nutrients dissolved in his mouth before he could swallow.

"Let me see that," Bart said before swiping the fruit from his underling. He took a bite, and like the others, found himself in a state of shock. "How odd... you wanna try for yourself, Giles?"

"I don' think there's much point," he replied, holding a hand up and shaking it.

"You're right," Bart said as he turned and threw the fruit up against a tree. Like before, it exploded into dust on impact. "We have more important things to worry about. Like the treasure of a lifetime!"

"I see…" Aldous trailed off, a smile coming to his face. He was glad that they hadn't become ravenous over it, as tended to happen with the black gold. "This fruit seems to be the work of Famine."

"No, famine is when ya *can't* grow food, old man," Norman corrected.

"You misunderstand," Aldous said with a chuckle. "But maybe that is for the best. Now, let's go. We need to reach the island's center."

"What's there?" Bartholomew asked.

"The Psychic that I mentioned before."

According to the Wizard's Council, 'Psychics' were Augmenter Wizards that chose to power their mind. Aldous felt it was easier for the layman if he simply referred to him as a 'Psychic' and not a 'Mind Augmenter'.

The journey through the forest seemed lifeless. Aside from many of the trees bearing useless fruit, the group encountered nothing of note. Although Aldous did notice that the grass turned a dull shade of yellow as they neared the island's center. Eventually, they reached a large cliff with a cave carved into it.

"Perhaps it would be best if you waited out here," Aldous said, turning to the others.

"What? But the treasure…" Bart muttered.

"There is no treasure on this island, m'boy. Besides, even if there was, you'd never make it past a Psychic of Zamarim's stature. Even I, someone with training in resistance of the mind, could be reduced to a stupefied state by him if he wished it. Imagine what he could do to you?"

Bartholomew let out a dramatic sigh. "Fine…"

Aldous walked into the cave alone. It was dimly lit with what appeared to be torches off in the distance. He wasn't sure if it was the dark nature of where he was or perhaps the work of Zamarim, but the old Wizard couldn't help but reflect: He had been held responsible for the Mt. Couture disaster, and would almost certainly be excommunicated if the Council found out about his meeting with a Wizard King from a different monolith without special permission.

Even so, Aldous had grown tired of the Council's inaction. Their endless bureaucracy would be the death of them all, he thought. If he had to spend the rest of his days as a Warlock or even a Dark Wizard, then so be it.

"Such dark thoughts…" a voice echoed in his mind. It was calm, but harsh all at once. An odd contradiction.

"Zamarim? Is that you?" Aldous' voice bounced off the tunnel walls with more flair than he had expected, and the torches off in the distance seemed to flicker in reaction.

"What are you doing here, Aldous?" the voice echoed as he increased his pace. Now he was near a set of torches. "The Council forbids we see or speak with one another. You know that."

"Then, you must know why I am here. You've been probing my mind, have you not?"

"Not too deeply… thoughts tend to become irrational when panic has set in. I sense much *fear* in you."

Aldous finally arrived at the torches. He waved his hand to absorb some of the flame into the top of his walking stick, creating a makeshift light of his own. He held it up to see that he was in a spacious room with a couple of branching paths and a large platform at the center. It was difficult to see all of the details, however. He peered to his left, and on the rounded wall, he saw a torch holder. The old Wizard shot a fireball out of his artifact to light it up. On the right was another unlit torch. He shot the fire into that as well, and it set off a chain reaction.

Throughout the spacious cave, blue lines of light streaked along the walls until they met up on the ceiling to provide one, grand light. Aldous smiled at the brilliant display. The luxian technology still impressed him, despite having seen it plenty of times before. It felt muted under the blue tint of Zamarim's territory, however.

With a brief look around, Aldous scratched his beard in confusion. "Why does this place feel so different?"

"It's funny how a place can change when you haven't visited in a long time," the voice of Zamarim echoed. "Or is it that *you've* changed?"

"Nonsense. I am here to help you."

"Is that so? Your thoughts betray your words. I can feel it: your guilt. It is weighing heavily on your Anima; your soul."

"That's irrelevant," Aldous said.

"On the contrary, your state of mind is of the utmost importance," said Zamarim, as Aldous felt a strain on his chest. He let out a surprised grunt and fell to a knee. "Do you feel that? That is the weight of your guilt; your reckless actions; your needless lies. Is that the Aldous that I know? I think not."

"All of my recent actions have been necessary evils in the face of an impossible situation," a straining Aldous squeaked out. "For the greater good."

The weight on Aldous' chest finally ceased as he let out a relieved breath and the voice echoed, "'For the greater good'? It is a long and twisted road to ruin, but on that path, we don't often realize where we are headed."

"I didn't come here for the lecture. It is imperative that we work together to keep this monolith safe!" Aldous said.

"The only potential danger I've seen thus far is an unstable Wizard who is letting his own failure control him. And the humans that he helped reach this sacred land… it has been thousands of years since a human stepped foot here. Thousands! And you let them in. You haven't learned a thing from your failures!" Zamarim echoed angrily. The noise became like an unbearable ringing in Aldous' ears. "Wizard Scouts are forbidden from visiting other monolith locations without express permission. We shouldn't be talking right now. Give me one good reason not to report you to the Council."

"Surely you have read my mind enough to know that there is a plot to destroy your monolith…" Aldous trailed off. "I didn't come here to mince words. I came here to warn and help you! The Wizard's Council refuses to admit the danger we're all in! They won't take action!"

The angry outburst, in combination with the strain that Zamarim had placed on him earlier, saw a stubborn sweat come to Aldous' brow. Try as he might to wipe it away, more drops took their place. His breaths were heavy; flustered.

"It is truly unfortunate how the mind clouds itself," Zamarim said in a disappointed tone. "Perhaps you need some time to clear your head."

Aldous' eyes widened. "You can't mean…"

As he mumbled the words, his vision slowly turned bluer and bluer until that was all he would see.

"No! We don't have time! We don't have time for this!"

"I beg to differ," Zamarim said as he appeared out of the blue in a blinding light.

The Wizard before him was bald with a lanky yet soft build. A graying, dirty blond goatee lined his chin and upper lip, and he wore a purple robe with various glowing Rune symbols along the edges. His hands were adorned with black gloves, and they too were decorated with glowing Rune symbols.

"Shall we take a journey?" Zamarim asked. Aldous let out a sigh. He didn't have a choice in the matter.

~

Bartholomew turned to face the cave with an impatient stride in his step.

"We've waited long enough. The treasures await, and no old man will be standing in our way," he said.

Many in the group agreed, but Giles, as usual, objected. "Shouldn't we listen to the Wizard? They're supposed to help people, aren't they?"

"He *did* save us…" Bart agreed, then put hands to hips. "Then again, he may not have our best interests at heart. He doesn't care about us and would prefer it if we simply disappeared. He certainly doesn't care about *you*, and the struggling people of this land." He pointed at Giles with authority.

"Yeah! Balls to the Wizard!" Norman called out. The other bandit cheered along with him.

"Besides, we cannot let our brothers' deaths be in vain. In their memory, we have to make this count. We may never get a chance like today again," said Bartholomew.

That had been enough to convince Giles, who nodded in approval in his usual meek manner. The bandits drew their weapons and entered the cave. They could see a great blue light down the tunnel.

"What the hell is that?" Bart asked aloud as he heard one of his men crash to the ground behind him. "Hey! Are you alright?" He bent over to check on the bandit, then turned to see Giles fall unconscious. He was breathing, but his eyes were glazed over, and drool dripped from his open mouth.

Norman looked to his leader with fear in his eyes. "Wh-what do we do?"

"Retreat!" Bartholomew cried. The pair turned and ran for the exit.

Midway back, Bart felt Norman grabbing hold of his arm. He looked back to see that he was in the midst of a fall, and he had those same blank eyes that he'd seen from the others when they had fallen unconscious.

The bandit leader wriggled free and threw him to the ground.

"Sorry…" Bartholomew muttered as he returned focus to the light at the end of the tunnel. The tint of blue that he'd been experiencing since arriving on the island intensified, and soon, it was all he could see. His head became light as a feather, but that didn't stop panic from overcoming him. "N-no! No!"

A falling sensation was the last thing that Bart felt before being taken in completely. Suddenly, the inevitable impact with the ground, the Wizards, and the treasure no longer mattered. The blue void called to him, and he fully intended to answer that call.

CHAPTER 18
THE HIDDEN DUALITY

At the bottom of the mountain, a young woman approached where the Mithikan knights' corpses lay. She was small, with long, dark hair and eyes to match. Her face, though pretty, seemed tired and reflected malnourishment. She wore old peasant's clothes: a mid-length dress that was tattered at the bottom, worn-out boots, and a girdle on the outside that had loose strings.

She gazed upon the impaled knight and beheaded man with wide eyes and then knelt to say a prayer. After finishing, she turned and made her way up the mountainous path at a hurried pace.

"Could *the other* have done this?" she muttered. The wind howled as her jog turned into a sprint.

∽

"YER A KNOB!" Alistair bellowed while pointing at Angus. "As if we'd ever work with a murderin' madman like you! Besides, yer plan is daft! Only an idiot would wanna unleash a spawn of the Dark Savior onto this world!"

"Simple-minded, as always. But your complaints, in the grand scheme of it all, don't matter," Angus replied while shaking his head. "What truly matters is our plan. We don't want to bring the Dark Savior back. We wish only to control his split identities. It *can* be done. It *must* be done, to bring order."

"To try and control the Dark Savior is *worse* than playing with fire," Pierce said with crossed arms.

"A *non-believer*, eh?" Angus asked with a smirk. "If only you knew the power we have on our side. Someone capable of unthinkable feats with the dark essence…"

Joel's eyes widened. He made hand signals in front of the group. Alistair raised an eyebrow.

"What did he say?" Angus asked.

"He wants ta know if yer workin' with a Dark Wizard."

"That is correct, and he can manipulate the imprints left by the different spawns of the Savior," he replied.

"And just what is that supposed to mean?" Alistair asked with a huff.

"You are lookin' at an example of the Dark Wizard's work," Angus said before cracking as much of a smile as his stone face would allow. "Perhaps a demonstration is in order."

Angus raised his fist and then straightened his arm in Joel's direction. Suddenly, a white arrow flew at the surprised mute. He dropped to the ground, and a split-second later, he heard a *whoosh* over his head. Joel got to one knee and immediately brought his attention back to Angus, expecting a follow-up attack.

Instead, the giant let his arm dangle and clenched his fist once more. A loud *crack* echoed across the field. He then rubbed his forearm gingerly. Joel squinted and noticed that fresh blood was dripping from the arm, but there was no wound.

"Tha hell was that?" Alistair asked, leaning in.

"Just a small sample of what my Wizard friend can do."

"So, this Dark Wizard is taking essence from one of the Dark Savior's imprints, and then putting it into your body?" Pierce asked.

"There is more to it, from what I'm told, but you have the right idea," Angus confirmed.

Joel finally put it together: Angus had shot a sharp piece of *bone* out of his arm. The Dark Wizard must have imbued him with the ability to regenerate, he thought. It would make sense, too; Greed possessed that ability, and the Dark Wizard had access to Greed's imprint: black gold. He wasn't sure how the giant had been able to shoot the bone, though.

"Do you understand now? I am far beyond any of your capabilities. The only sensible choice is to join up with me and the others," said Angus.

"Don't be so sure of that," Pierce jumped in, pointing his dagger at him. "Way before your time, there was the melior, a species created by the Dark Savior. They were big and combat-efficient, just like you. But we, the luxians, were able to kill them. Care to guess how?" Pierce lifted his dagger slightly, then nodded with a confident smile.

"It matters little. We share the same cause," Angus replied in a calming tone. "So long as you provide me with the key, I will not have to harm you."

"Is that supposed to scare me?" Pierce asked with a chuckle. "It seems to me that our interests do not fully align anymore. The Dark Savior cannot be controlled. I won't be handing over my key."

"That's a shame. If we can't agree, then violence is the only answer," the giant said.

"We agree on that much," Pierce replied as he gave a quick nod to Angus' side.

The big man turned to see Lord Roland charging at him with a claymore in hand. Reflexively, he held his arm up at the last second to defend before the lord brought his blade down.

Thunk

Crack

Joel cocked his head. He'd expected to hear the familiar, gut-wrenching sound of chopped flesh, but instead, the sword strike had wrung hollow. His mouth fell agape to see that Angus' arm remained undamaged. Instead, it was Roland's claymore that had cracked like frail glass.

Upon closer inspection, the mute could see why: Angus had grown a bone shield in the second or so that he had to react to Roland's attack. It protruded out of the top of his forearm and took the shape of an oval at its top and a rectangle near the bottom.

Angus wound up for a backhanded swing, and the lord grunted before jumping back. However, it wasn't enough to evade, and a piece of the bony shield collided with Roland. He gasped aloud and flew back as if he'd been kicked by a horse, before crashing to the ground. He got to his hands and knees, but before he could get up, he began coughing blood. The fit quickly ended when he fell unconscious.

Not good, Joel thought. Angus' strength had to have been enhanced by whatever devilry the Dark Wizard had performed on him. Even a glancing blow had been enough to fell Roland, who the mute had pegged as an experienced warrior in his own right; albeit a starving one.

"You see?" Angus asked as he turned to face Pierce. The dagger-eyed man took a crouched stance with his blade at the ready. "I can't be beaten by the likes of you. Hand over the key."

"Your display earlier was telling," Pierce said as he held a palm out. He pulled the dagger across it and blood spurted onto his luxmortite weapon. It became encased by a blue aura. "You can crush the primitive weaponry of humans, but your reactions are slow."

Angus raised an eyebrow. "Just moments ago, you were on board with our plans. I give you one last chance to rethink this-"

"I was with you until finding out you had the means to control the Dark Savior's power," Pierce replied.

"We ain't joinin' ya, either! Yer plans are crazy!" Alistair shouted, then raised a fist; Joel did the same, but silently.

"I didn't *really* wanna work with you anyway, fat-head. It was the two luxians that had me interested," Angus shot back. Alistair's face turned red.

"Joke's on you! It's three against one, and we gots tha weapons to kill ya!" the big redhead retorted.

Pierce scowled and without looking back said, "I'm not on your side, and I don't need your help, either. Once I dispose of this worm, you two are next. Having a common enemy doesn't mean we're friends."

Alistair looked back at Joel. An uncharacteristic face filled with worry was all the mute could see as Angus walked toward the pair.

Pierce jumped in and pointed at him, a command to his charmed dagger that saw it shooting at the giant swiftly. Angus stood perfectly still, allowing the blade to fly straight into his gut. His eyes widened as he felt the blow, but he didn't make a sound. Instead, he reached into his abdomen and grabbed the dagger. With a snicker, he grasped it tightly and looked down upon Pierce like a parent would their child. The wound in his stomach closed up before their very eyes; soon to be a distant memory.

"So, you can regenerate, too... I'll just have to carve you up until you can't, then," the dagger-eyed man said.

He motioned with a finger for his dagger to return, but as it tried to move, Angus held on. Pierce's eyes widened as he made a stronger gesture, but even still, the big man's grip never slipped. Instead, the dagger moved slowly and pulled him along with it. Dirt pushed and dragged along his boots from the incredible resistance and strain of the struggle.

Eventually within an arm's reach, Angus smirked and let go of the dagger. It flew, full-speed, at Pierce, but he had anticipated the move: as the giant's first finger had slipped, he'd already begun ducking. The blade flew over his head, and without letting up, he directed it back at Angus. However, this time, he controlled the dagger to slash down vertically.

Angus sidestepped, then pulled his arm back for a sideswipe. As he was doing so, Pierce maneuvered the dagger around the giant's back and commanded it to slash. At a moment's notice, Angus swung his backhand, which Pierce jumped back to avoid. Joel's keen eye picked up on the intricacies of the exchange and worry overcame him, certain that Pierce had been clipped by the bone shield; partially on his stomach and chest.

The dagger-eyed man landed on his feet, then grasped his chest and shook the cobwebs out. His blade had slashed Angus' back in the exchange, but the giant showed no signs of pain and walked toward him, undeterred.

"It was only a glancing blow, and yet..." Pierce trailed off before sputtering into a series of coughs.

Angus shook his head. "It would have been a glancing blow... if you were fighting against an ordinary man. Of course, if I had hit you directly earlier, your lungs would have exploded from the impact."

"Understood," Pierce said as the charmed dagger floated back to his side.

Angus clenched his massive fists and they cracked loudly. He charged in and threw a booming jab at Pierce, but this time, he was able to completely dodge by contorting his upper body to the left.

No, Joel thought with a shudder. There was more to the attack. Bone fragments from Angus' knuckles had shot out in the process of his punch. Pierce had noticed too, as he contorted his body once more to evade a few of them, and in that sequence, directed his dagger to slice at the giant's throat. Angus put his other arm up, and the blade cut into his forearm, but not all the way through. Two of the five bone shards shot into the side of Pierce like small arrow tips. As he winced in pain, Angus prepared his next attack.

With his other hand, Angus threw a massive uppercut that sounded to Joel like a stampeding herd of buffalo. Pierce jumped back to avoid the blow, but it was too fast. The tip of his knuckle scraped the dagger-eyed man's stomach, and even such an insignificant amount of contact sent him flying back. After finally landing, Pierce rolled along the grass before settling a few meters away. Joel's fist tightened as he watched him struggling on the ground. A couple of bone fragments poked out from his torso.

Pierce coughed and spit out blood as he looked up at an approaching Angus. He swayed back and forth to gain the momentum needed to stand, and his breaths were hoarse and heavy.

"You barely touched me…" he muttered while stumbling to his feet.

"Lucky you," Angus said as he stretched one of his muscular arms out. "You've got great reaction speed. Is that a trait of the luxians?"

Pierce didn't reply and instead motioned his finger for the dagger to return to him. The blade left Angus' forearm, and the deep, bloody wound began regenerating mere moments later. After catching the dagger, its light blue glow faded, and Pierce sighed.

"Not now…"

He held out his palm once more and hovered the blade over it, ready to slice.

"Is that a good idea? You've lost some blood," Angus said, pointing at Pierce's stomach.

The dagger-eyed man looked down and gasped at all of the red pouring from his abdomen. His eyes glazing over, he promptly fell to a knee and began taking heavy breaths. Joel drew his sword as a tingle shot down his spine.

"It's a shame you didn't take my offer. We could have brought peace and order to the world together… but you had your chance," Angus said as he approached and pulled his fist back for the final blow.

"Just end it already," Pierce said between labored breaths. "I've heard all of this nonsense before. You people never learn."

"The bitter last words of a dead man!" Angus shouted as he began his monstrous punch.

Without a thought racing through his mind, Joel sprang into action with his sword at the ready. As the giant was in the midst of his punch, he plunged the blade into his leg, eliciting both a pause and a grunt. Joel dug it in as deep as he could to inflict maximum pain; hoping he would focus on him instead of Pierce.

The dagger-eyed man turned his blank gaze to Joel as he ripped the sword out of Angus' leg. The mute returned him a reassuring nod, though truthfully, he felt sick to his stomach.

Pierce shrieked with laughter between struggling coughs for breath, and Joel cocked his head. Not fear; not anger; not happiness;

but laughter? He couldn't even begin to understand, and for now, there would be no explanation, for he collapsed to the ground in a heap of exhaustion. At first, the mute shuddered at the sight, but when his body began to bob up and down with each breath, he let out a sigh of relief.

Joel refocused on Angus, whose stone face did little to ease his worries. Truthfully, the attack had probably surprised himself more than the others. But after what he had done on *that day*, he couldn't stand by and watch Pierce die. It would mean that he was responsible for the deaths of his entire family, and that took precedence, even over his vow not to harm others.

Besides, he thought, Angus could regenerate. The mute's eyes fell on his leg wound; or at least, where it *should have been*. It had already closed up, and yet, Joel could find no relief in his heart as his gaze fixed on the dripping blood of the former gouge. Why? He'd attacked for good reason, and his opponent was none the worse for wear. Why couldn't he get the gurgling blood of Jed and the cries of Osanna out of his head?

"I see it didn't take much to throw your peace-loving principles away," Angus taunted as Joel shuddered and raised his sword into a defensive position.

From under his cloak, Angus retrieved an odd weapon: It was chained to a handle and had a spiked ball at the end: a Morningstar flail, as it was called in some lands. The great difference was that every bit of it was white as if made from Angus' bone.

"Do you remember breaking my arm a year ago?" Angus asked. Joel nodded. "It's thanks to you that I can control my bones like this. Understand? The dark essence heals what ails you, to the most extreme degree. My arm was broken; therefore, the Dark Wizard has made it so that my bones are easily fixable."

"I don' remember ya bein' so talkative," Alistair taunted as he trudged forward until standing side-by-side with Joel. From out of his pocket, he drew a hunting knife. "Is it because yer not on Wolfgang's leash anymore? Yer new master's a lil' nicer to ya, is he?" The big man let out a loud laugh, and Joel couldn't help but smile. If anyone could bring him back from the depths of despair, it was Alistair.

"Wolfgang is but a memory, soon to be forgotten. And after today, the same fate will befall you…" Angus muttered as he closed in on the pair, spinning his flail.

"Sorry ta say, but I don' have much of a way to get close with this wee weapon, lad," Alistair said in an apparent attempt to whisper at Joel. As usual, he'd been louder than intended, but the whirs of the flail had kicked up a wind and grown so loud that it didn't matter. The mute nodded, then signed to him with a free hand. "Yeh, I got it."

Alistair stayed in position as Joel walked forward to meet Angus. He positioned the luxmortite blade in front of himself and upward in a defensive position. His initial thought was to get the bone chains tied up so that his friend could land a surprise blow.

However, before he could truly focus, Joel spotted the spiked bone club shooting toward his face at a high speed and ducked just in time. Angus spun around to subdue the great momentum of his flail, then directed the club at the mute once more.

This time, the speed of the club had decreased, so Joel took a more measured response: He swung his sword while leaning back in the hopes that he could hit the club. After all, luxmortite could crack steel; bone wouldn't be a problem, he thought. As expected, he heard the hollowed-out *thunk* of the collision, but there was no *crack*.

He raised an eyebrow as the club and chain flew back toward Angus, who sidestepped and smirked as the flail settled next to him.

"Surprised? I remember that you were able to break through my weapon and shield, before. Turns out my bones are stronger now, thanks to the dark essence," he said.

He started to swing his flail once more, but before he could fully get going, Joel rushed in with his blade pulled back for a decisive swing. However, as he began bringing it around, the banshee shrieks of Osanna wrung in his ears, and Joel couldn't help but pull up on his attack. Angus reacted easily to the half-hearted swing by moving his bone shield into position. Once again, the dull noise of metal bouncing off bone echoed in the field. The giant then swung at Joel with the shield, forcing him to back off.

"You still hesitate? Are you scared to hurt me?" Angus asked with a smirk.

Joel let out a frustrated sigh. Angus swung his flail once more, faster than ever; so fast that it bent the grass and kicked up dirt. It felt like an approaching twister. He closed in on the mute and unleashed the club, which Joel ducked, but the follow-up was impossible to avoid, as the giant spun, and so too did the flail. By spinning in synch with the flail, it had gained even greater momentum than before.

The mute held his blade out, and this time, the roundabout nature of the club allowed him to wrap the chain around the sword: his original plan. Joel pounced on a stunned Angus and threw his strongest kick, connecting with his ribs.

Angus, however, showed no signs of pain or determent. Instead, it was Joel who felt a surge of pain rushing up his shin as quiet gasps escaped his mouth. He limped backward to get some distance, but the giant didn't seem to be in any hurry. His shin throbbed and swelled, and even the tiniest weight on it felt unbearable. Now, he was like a wounded animal staring down a predator.

"I told you my bones were strong, didn't I? That goes for inside of my body, too," Angus said as he spun his flail once more. "You should have accepted my generous invitation."

"WILL YOU SHUT IT, ALREADY?" Alistair shouted as he charged in with heavy, rapid thuds against the grass. Angus turned his attention to the big redhead as his usual stone expression changed to one of surprise: Alistair's hunting knife flew at him, and none of his newfound abilities could make a difference. It was mere inches from him, now.

The blade pierced the side of Angus' neck. He grunted and stumbled back as blood spurted out of his wound. Using it as an opportunity, Joel tossed his luxmortite sword to Alistair, who was still charging. After catching it, he jumped and then brought the blade down upon Angus for the decisive blow.

This time, the giant blocked with his bone shield. Alistair used the bounce off of the shield as momentum and brought the blade around on an unsuspecting Angus. He grunted in a surprised pain as the sword chopped into him like a cleaver into fresh meat. The blade, with its impressive cutting efficiency, had reached nearly midway through his torso.

The giant coughed and shivered in shock as Alistair looked him in the eye with a smile. A waterfall of blood spilled from his midsection and stained the grass. However, after a few moments, Angus' stone-faced expression returned.

"You find something amusing?" he asked as Alistair looked down in horror. His skin was reforming *around the blade*. "Not as amusing as the look on your face, I'm sure."

Alistair pulled the sword from out of Angus' abdomen, but as he did so, the giant swung a backhand at him with his bone shield. He managed to block with the sword, but the impact sent him flying back, and in mid-air, the blade sputtered out of his hands before he crashed to the ground. Angus then flexed the muscles in his neck, and the knife popped out.

"You did well. Better than expected, actually. But in the end, you're only human."

Joel hobbled over to the sword and picked it up. Angus stood before him and wound up his flail once more.

However, before he could attack, Angus stumbled forward and fell to a knee. Pierce's dagger had lodged into his spine. Angus looked over his shoulder to see the dagger-eyed man, who was grinning at him. Now was the time to strike, Joel thought. He pushed the pain out of mind and brought his sword down on the bone shield. The mute could not bring himself to deal the finishing blow, but he could *at least* provide a distraction. The tactic worked, as the giant's angry eyes turned to face him once more.

"Those were cheap sho-" Angus was cut off by a blade suddenly stabbing through his neck.

He turned to Roland, who wielded a dagger. Angus gagged and struggled briefly as the blood leaked out of him in buckets. He attempted to speak, but all that could be heard were gurgles.

After a few moments of flailing around, the giant tumbled over like a falling tree. Roland simultaneously pulled the blade from his neck and fell to a knee. The glancing blow from earlier had greatly damaged him.

Joel hobbled over to Angus and began to tremble. He wasn't moving, and in brief moments, he saw not the giant villain of the Mt. Couture disaster, but Jed Thaeon, after he'd stabbed him back on *that day*. In fact, Roland had stabbed him in the same spot, and the mute couldn't help but stare with blank eyes.

"I don't know what's more pitiful," Pierce said as he knelt and rolled the giant slightly to retrieve his blade. He ripped it out of Angus' back, and more blood leaked out. It had a dark quality to it that Joel hadn't noticed before, and it snapped him out of his stupor. "Having to work with you to kill this oaf or your reaction to his death. Have some dignity."

"Oi! Go easy on 'im!" Alistair shouted.

"I'll do no such thing," the dagger-eyed man replied with a snarl. "In fact, we still have a score to settle. Prepare yourself for another round."

"We have our own business to settle," Angus said as he sat up and swiped at Pierce's neck.

The dagger-eyed man hopped back and took a crouched stance before raising an eyebrow and patting his chest.

"The key…"

Pierce and the others looked on in horror to see Angus stand, holding the dark blue medallion in hand. His wounds had healed, and there was no evidence of injury to begin with, save for the fresh blood.

"Now you won't be able to close the portal when I open it," Angus said.

"Give it back!" Pierce cried as he charged in with his dagger pulled back for a stab.

"Catch!" the giant said, then threw the medallion high into the air between the cliffs. Joel's mouth hung open as he lost sight of the key. It seemed to reach the clouds.

"You think this is funny?" the dagger-eyed man asked through gritting teeth.

"I wasn't talking to you," Angus said, nodding upward. A large bird swooped down from the clouds and caught the medallion.

"Oi! It's tha buzzard!" Alistair called out.

Angus let out a low-pitched chuckle. "Now, *that's* funny. I'll have to tell her that one."

He looked down at Joel, then cracked a smirk as he tucked the flail back into the confines of his cloak. At the same time, the bone shield retracted into his forearm.

"I suppose that's *another key* you failed to protect, eh?"

Joel's eyes twitched. Angus had all but confirmed that he'd been the one to steal his key one year ago. Now, he'd stolen another, and this time before his very eyes; and he was helpless to stop him.

"Mur'del!" Angus called out. The winged creature from the sky swooped down and roared past the crowd at nearly imperceptible speeds, but a black blur to Joel's eyes. When the wind and dirt settled, Angus was gone.

"What the hell was that?" Pierce asked with a mixture of panic and anger in his voice. He looked to Joel and Alistair, but neither had an answer for him.

The dagger-eyed man growled like an angry bear as he stomped toward Joel, but Alistair jumped between them.

"Leave 'im alone! How could ya try ta kill a man who saved yer sorry arse?"

"You misunderstand," he replied before stopping in front of the duo. He tossed the dagger over Alistair's shoulder, and Joel bobbled it in his hands. Pierce then turned his back to him and crossed his arms before lowering his head. The mute's state of mind was in complete disarray as it was. He couldn't even begin to imagine what he was playing at.

"Well? What are you waiting for?" Pierce asked as he looked over his shoulder. "I have failed; I have nothing to live for. You've already taken my parents. Wouldn't it be fitting if you finished the job? I'd prefer that over tolerating your presence any further…"

Joel sulked. It felt like all of his failures were assaulting him at once. To think that his former best friend, his brother, would rather be dead than be in his presence was unbearable. No matter how he tried to run or hide, it seemed that his past would always find him.

"Nothing to live for?" a woman's voice called from behind the group.

Pierce turned and then fell to his knees when he saw who it was.

"Greta…"

All in the field looked on in confusion as Pierce buried his face in a hand and grunted. After a few deep breaths, his tense posture relaxed, and he let out a sigh of relief. He rose, not with the burning fire of hatred in his eyes that Joel had become accustomed to, but peace; happiness, even. He approached the mute and held out a hand.

"Hello, brother," he said. The words rang in Joel's ears and left him breathless. "Sorry for giving you trouble, back there. I'll take my dagger back if you don't mind."

In a state of pure bewilderment, he handed the luxmortite dagger to Pierce, but somehow felt good about it. He couldn't put his finger on why.

The dagger-eyed man then walked toward Greta, who ran at him and jumped into his arms. He twirled her around in the air and they kissed. After that, they embraced and said some inaudible words to the rest of the group. Joel looked on, and his confusion subsided. Instead, he felt happiness for his friend.

"THA HELL IS GOIN' ON?" Alistair shouted.

Pierce and Greta looked back, each with amusement in their expressions.

"I suppose an explanation is owed," Pierce said as he looked down at Greta and flashed her a knowing smile. "But let's go inside, first."

The group hobbled their way into Pierce's home, where Greta got right to bandaging the men up in the best way she could. Pierce had received the worst damage of the bunch, but all needed rest and healing. They sat at a table, drinking tea as if it were a group of friends having a chat. A truly bizarre shift from earlier, Joel thought.

"I don't understand. I thought you hated these two? You wanted to kill *him* especially," Roland said, pointing at the mute.

"Me, personally? I have no quarrel with the big guy. And Joel? Well, he has saved my life multiple times, now," Pierce said with a chuckle.

"Then, why? Why'd ya say all them horrible things? Why'd ya work with a lowlife like Angus? Why'd ya try ta kill us?" Alistair demanded as he smashed a hand on the table.

"Hey! Cut that out! Yer gonna spill the tea!" Greta bellowed.

Pierce held up a hand. "It's alright. I can understand his anger."

Alistair frowned, but ultimately bit his tongue and drank some tea to keep quiet.

"The truth is… that wasn't me."

"I'm positive that it was," Lord Roland replied. "You're the same Ometos I've always known."

"Am I, though? We have spoken before, Roland, but typically… you've been talking to *the other*, as I like to call him," Pierce said.

"What's that supposed ta mean? Ya got a twin brother or somethin'?" Alistair asked.

Roland's eyes widened. "Multiple personalities…"

"Wha?" Alistair blurted out. Pierce smiled and nodded.

"It all makes sense now. The shifts in mood, the changes in plan… Ometos is the Mithikan God of duality. I see you took the name as a literal way to describe yourself," the lord said.

"Besides the 'God' part," Pierce added with a chuckle.

"What kinda boggin talk is this? I never heard of nothin' like 'multiple personalities', before!" the big redhead said.

"Mind yer manners! Show some respect, or I'll give ya somethin' to whine about!" Greta yelled back. Alistair looked personally offended, but everyone else in the room laughed.

"It's true, though. There are two people in this one body of mine," Pierce said as he turned to Joel. "All of those years ago, when my- I mean, *our* parents were infected by the black gold; and you did what you had to do to save us, I was crushed by the weight of what happened."

Joel sulked and looked down. Once again, he thought of Jed's blood-filled gurgles and Osanna's horrible screeching as she had attacked him. The time after had been difficult, too. He had lost the will to fight or talk and became a pariah. Only Riza had been there to comfort him.

"Back then, I was conflicted. I was angry at you for taking my mother and father away, but then, how could I be? You also saved me. There was nothing else that could have been done in that situation. We luxians had little to no resistance to the black gold. It was them, or us."

"So, it's true?" Alistair asked Joel, leaning in and wide-eyed. "I never thought ya had it in ya, lad."

"We were trained to kill, back then. It was a time of war, and we were about to become a part of it," Pierce said, sighing. "Anyhow, I thought about killing myself back then, after the incident. Instead, I decided to use my pain and anguish to charm the dagger that my father was about to kill me with. I used blood from both of my parents, and that helped to power the blade you see before you." He held it up and then placed it on the table.

"What *is* 'charming', anyway?" Roland asked. "In all of my years of combat experience, I've never seen anything like the sorcery your dagger performed out there."

"It is something unique to luxians like Joel and I. There are a few things that separate us from humans, and charming happens to be one of them. In the simplest terms, a charm can imbue an object with special abilities by using the emotions of a luxian. The greater the sacrifice or feeling, the stronger the charm. A Wizard needed to perform the charm, too. We couldn't do it by ourselves," said Pierce.

"I see… but what about your second personality? Does that have anything to do with the charm?" Lord Roland asked.

"Yes, I believe that the charm was how it happened. My mind was split in two to begin with: On one hand, I was bitter and hateful for the death of my parents; but on the other hand, I was thankful that Joel and I were still alive. Normally, with time, I would have settled my mind and come to a conclusion, but the charm, it seems, split me in a more literal sense. It froze my thoughts on the matter and created two entities within this one body to handle the contradiction."

"Wow! Ya can't make this stuff up!" the big man chimed in.

"The angrier, aggressive side took over more and more as time went on. In more turbulent times such as these, he tends to take the stage," the dagger-eyed man said.

"Then, why did you come out just now?" Roland asked.

"Greta," he replied, smiling back at her. She returned a warm smile.

"In peaceful times, and when in her presence, I can free myself. But just so you all know: You can tell which side of me is out by the mask."

He held up the angrier side of his mask, then flipped it over to the sad, peaceful side and put it on.

"I see…" Lord Roland muttered before sipping his tea. "And are you able to see what is happening when you're not out?"

"Yes. In some ways, it is like being trapped in a cell. Able to observe, but not interact."

"Good. Then, you must know that we have a dire situation on our hands," Roland said as the group simultaneously sulked.

Even though the battles had resolved peacefully, a major threat loomed: Angus was headed for Lake Teras to destroy the Famine monolith, and he held the only key that could repair it.

CHAPTER 19
DARK DREAMS

Angus held onto the talon of a dark avian soaring over Thironas so quickly that his eyes watered.

"I'm amazed at how fast you can fly," he said over the roar of the wind.

"That's one upside to becoming a monstrosity," said Mur'del.

"Oh? Not satisfied?"

"Satisfied with my new abilities? Yes. But now, all other avian look like children next to me," she said before tweeting. As Angus understood, it was the avian way to laugh.

What she had said was true: Most avian were about the size of a 10-year-old human, while even he was a full head shorter than her. The true scope of Mur'del's size showed with each flap of her wings; so long and powerful that even while carrying him, she could glide for a while before needing to flap again.

Angus looked up to see the dark, fine strands of her ponytail straightened into perfect lines against the wind, and that same wind did little to hinder her thanks to a beak-like nose lowering her resistance to it. She wore old, raggedy clothes that looked long outgrown, and dirty. Underneath the feathers of her wings were hands with sharp claws; one of which was holding the Famine key.

"The way I see it, you have merely taken the optimal form to reach such high speeds…"

"Speaking of which, we'll be arriving at the island shortly," she said.

"Excellent," Angus replied as he gazed over the landscape. He could see the big lake, and not far from it, the browning fields where crops were normally grown. "Do you think we're doing the people of Thironas a service by releasing Famine?"

"I don't care, to be honest. You know that I don't like humans," Mur'del replied.

"I won't take that personally. After all, we have transcended our respective species. I don't consider myself human any longer," said the giant.

"You humans are so quick to sell each other out and talk badly about one other," the avian replied in a condescending tone. "I am still avian; one who has mutated into a monster to get the job done."

"Interesting that you use the phrase, 'sell out'. You seem to be under the impression that Drake and the Dark Wizard's plans won't affect the avian. They will be stripped of their freedom, just like the humans, and if you make it to the end, you may even rule over them," he said.

"I hold you in higher regard than most, Angus, but in this case, you are surprisingly short-sighted." Mur'del snickered.

"Do tell."

"What Drake and the Dark Wizard are proposing is nothing short of a *revolution*. And on a worldwide scale. Do you know what usually happens to revolutionaries? When the cause is one of power and order? They are assassinated. Not by the enemy, but by their allies. No one trusts them, because they themselves were dirty snakes to begin with," she said.

"An interesting thought. You believe that someone else will rise up and change their plans, then? I can foresee it happening to Drake, but the Dark Wizard is another story. We cannot thrive without him. But either way, you know that my motivations are not in their ideas…"

"I cannot begin to fathom what you see in that *bratty woman*, but do what you must."

Angus only grunted in response. Now, it was Mur'del who was short-sighted, he thought.

At Pierce's home on the mountain, Joel made hand signals for Alistair to translate for the rest of the group, who remained seated around the table.

Alistair eyed Pierce. "He wants ta know what the other guy's full plans were… ya know, that other knob livin' in yer head."

"I'm sorry to say, but *the other* and I agreed, at first. The famine needed to end, one way or another. If not for the people of Thironas, then at least for Greta. What he said earlier about sealing away the Dark Savior is something that I would have said, too. Our plans back then had faults, and these effects on innocent people are one of them," he replied.

"Well, it beats lettin' Famine out on the entire world, methinks!" said Alistair.

"True, but that's where the Wizard's Council would come into play. Make no mistake, this plan was our last resort. I begged…" he trailed off with frustration on his face. "I begged the Council to take action, but they refused. The Mithikan Kingdom is in no position to do anything about it, either. So it came to this: If Famine were released onto the world, the Wizards would have no choice but to act."

Joel responded in sign language.

"He says that only tha strongest Wizards would stand a chance against a spawn of the Savior, and that's only from the weakness of bein' trapped away in tha Cold World fer all of this time. If Famine found a way to recover, no one could stop 'im," the big man translated.

"He's right about that. No *one* could stop him. But all of the might of the Wizard's Council? Thousands of powerful sorcerers at once? They would find a way to win against Famine's weakened state. The idea was to force the Council into coming up with a real solution."

Lord Roland took a hard gulp of his tea. "All Wizards of the world, to take on *one creature*?"

"And there are six more of 'em, too!" Alistair added with a snort.

"The point is that we can't sit back and allow this disaster to continue. The other and I agreed on that much," Pierce said. "With that said, I wasn't on board with the rest of his plan. I didn't trust that big fellow or his methods from the start."

"The two of you seemed to know him," Roland said, eyeing Joel and Alistair. "I take it you have clashed in the past?"

"Remember how Aldous told ya aboot tha disaster in Federland?" Alistair asked. The lord nodded, but Joel also nudged the big man and flashed some signals to him. "Oh, right… sorry, but our Wizard friend lied to ya. It's not tha Lake Watcher ya gotta worry aboot. That's a Guardian Beast. They're trained ta kill anyone or thing that comes near the seal which keeps the Dark Savior trapped."

"This is all a lot to take in, and hard to believe…" Roland muttered while glancing at Pierce, who returned a nod. "But that explains why he lied, I suppose."

"Anyhow, that big ol' meat-stain Angus was one o' the doaty people who tried and succeeded in destroyin' the Greed monolith back in Federland. He was on the same journey as us to Mt. Couture, where the monstah was contained. None of us knew it besides Joel, back then. He tried ta warn us of all tha dangers, but we didn't listen 'till it was too late."

"You knew about all of this from the beginning, eh?" Lord Roland asked Joel and Pierce with a smile. "But that is another oddity of your story: If you two are Ancient Ones, or, erm… luxians, then how did you get here? I was led to believe that your people died out, long ago."

Pierce cleared his throat. "I'll try to sum it up quickly: Thousands of years ago, a powerful being called 'the Dark Savior' waged war on our people by using humans as his puppets. Eventually, a species of his creation called the melior joined up with men and put us on the defensive. With the help of Wizards, we badly poisoned him to the point where he was captured by humans who wanted the war to end. To escape, he split himself into seven separate beings. We managed to capture them all, but they were impossible to kill and grew in strength by the day. Wizards then discovered another realm, which we called 'the Cold World'. It's a place that slowly drains the life force of most living beings away. This included the different spawns of the Savior, so that's where we sent him. It acted as the perfect counter-balance to his growing strength and regenerative abilities."

"Sounds to me like you solved the problem, then," Greta said, scratching her chin.

"I'm afraid not, dear. When a portal of that magnitude is open to another world, it's even harder to close than it was to open. Let me put it to you this way: It would be easier to transport everyone in this world at once than to transport the Dark Savior. Hundreds of Wizards were killed in the process. We didn't have the power to shut it permanently, so instead, we built monoliths that acted as seals. It's much like how a door works. You can lock it, but someone could break it down or unlock it if they wanted to. Just as well, we could rebuild the door… with the correct tools. To ensure that the monoliths would always be protected with the best of interests in mind, luxians volunteered to be frozen in time, set to be awakened every hundred years or so to replace the previous Keeper of the Key," Pierce said.

"I assume that the 'correct tool' in this case would be the medallion that was stolen from around your neck?" Roland asked.

"Correct," he replied while standing in a wobbly fashion. Greta sprang into action to hold him upright. "There is a powerful Wizard who guards the Famine monolith named Zamarim. Normally, I would have full confidence in him defending his post, but when *the other* and Angus thought up their plan, he said that he would be able to down the Wizard with what lies in his mind. He never disclosed what that meant, but he had no reason to lie. We must find a way to reach Lake Teras and stop Angus."

"In yer conditions?" Greta asked with narrowed eyes. "You can hardly move, let alone fight. You need rest."

"Right ya may be, lass. But there ain't no time ta sit 'round. Yer city, and mayhap the whole world, is at stake!" Alistair said with bluster as he stood and slammed his fist into the table. Joel could see that the sudden movement had made him light-headed, however, and he plopped back onto his seat. The heavy impact obliterated his chair, and all in the room laughed as he lay out on the floor.

"Hey! Those chairs ain't free, ye know!" Greta said with a shaking fist, but Pierce held a hand up to signal that it was fine.

"Erm… sorry…" Alistair muttered. Joel lent him a hand in standing, though it was an arduous process as he leaned from his chair while doing so.

"I see that some of those shots from the other me knocked you for a loop. My apologies. He often goes too far," Pierce said with a chuckle that turned into coughs.

Joel looked around. Greta had a good point. His shin throbbed even while sitting, and now standing at all felt out of the question. Alistair likely needed bed rest from the blows he'd taken to the head, Roland appeared to have internal injuries, and Pierce had almost certainly taken the most damage of the bunch.

"Even if we tried, I don't think we could reach the lake," Lord Roland said with a sigh. "Angus had that large flying creature to take him there… we'd have to contend with the grand wall and its guards, who will riddle us with arrows if we get too close."

"That was another issue that Angus and *the other* had planned for, believe it or not," Pierce said. "Before Angus arrived, he wanted there to be some sort of distraction or ruckus. So, we came into contact with a small group of bandits. Angus should have made a hole in the grand wall for them and killed the guards watching over it. If we're quick enough, maybe we can sneak through…"

"So, what are we waitin' for? Let's go!" Alistair shouted with excitement as he turned to leave, but dizziness overtook him and he lost his balance. Unfortunately for Joel, the redhead fell in his direction, knocking him from the chair and blotting out all light from his world.

"Sorry, lad…" the big man muttered as he pushed himself off, and Joel let out a sigh of relief.

Greta looked around, then put hands to her hips. "It seems that I'm the only healthy person in the room. I'm coming along."

"Absolutely not," said Pierce.

"I've survived on the streets all of my life. I can protect myself," she replied.

Before the dagger-eyed man could argue back, Roland jumped in and said, "With respect, I don't think you even weigh as much as my broken claymore."

"I could never risk losing you," Pierce added. "Without you, I wouldn't exist…"

"A wee bit dramatic, don'tcha think?" Alistair asked with a raised eyebrow.

"Not at all. Without her, the other side of me would take complete control. I would forever be a spectator."

Joel thought for a moment, then made hand signals to the big man. "He says that if she needs ta be around ta keep you in control, then she has to come ta the lake with us, or tha other guy will come out."

Pierce's eyes widened. Greta crossed her arms and smiled.

"A fair point," Roland said.

The dagger-eyed man let out a defeated sigh. "Very well…"

"Before we approach the lake, I suggest we stop back in the upper district of Thironas. I'm short on supplies, and we'll need to grab weapons for those of us without the brilliant blue blades," the lord said in a sarcastic tone.

All in the group agreed, and with that, they made preparations for their journey back to the starving city.

MEANWHILE, in the cave at the center island of Lake Teras, Aldous remained trapped in a dream world that had been created by Zamarim. Prominent memories of his life had been used as material for the visions.

In this particular vision, Aldous was being attacked by a group of men, and he was experiencing it once more as if it were happening for the first time. He looked up to see a flurry of kicks and punches striking his grounded body.

"We don't want yer kind here!"

"Leave this place!"

Yet, struggle as he might, they wouldn't allow him to go. The senseless attack continued, until finally, one man with a hammer approached, while others held Aldous down by his wrists and ankles. The man brought the hammer down on his knee, and the old Wizard cried out in immense pain as the vision faded to a dark blue. Zamarim appeared out of the void and stood over him as the unbearable pain in his knee began to dull.

"Do you remember *now* how dangerous humans can be?"

"But they aren't all like that..." Aldous said with grinding teeth as he returned to his feet.

"Your judgment must be absolute," the Wizard King said with obvious contempt. "Your inability to see man's true nature has brought upon you many failures. Why do you think they need protection in the first place? They are reckless... power hungry... but luckily, nature provides a self-correcting measure: death."

"You would have me kill them? For making mistakes? We were human at one time! I think you have forgotten how you ascended to a Wizard in the first place. Your Anima must be taking quite a hit while you allow the men and women of Thironas to suffer."

"When it was at the detriment of your duty, you saved them anyway!" Zamarim shot back. "Had you let the humans enter Mt. Couture on their own, they would have died there, and the Greed monolith would have remained intact."

"Ah, right. We're back to blaming me, even when a Dark Wizard is behind it all. Even when the Mountain King was corrupted by the black gold. Even when the famine coming from this seal has spread to the settlements surrounding Thironas! You see a problem in my judgment, but what about *yours*? What about the Council's lack of action?" Aldous asked.

"You make claims that someone is coming to destroy my monolith, and yet, who are the only intruders I've encountered thus far? The only ones in thousands of years, no less? A Wizard who has been blinded by his guilt and treacherous men that normally would have been slain by the Lake Watcher!" he replied. "Funny you should bring up a Dark Wizard... I wish to remind you of why the Council is slower to act; why it is unwise to jump to conclusions so quickly."

The dream turned darker, and new scenery began to take shape.

"You can't mean..."

"Yes, Aldous. It's time for you to remember how rash calls to action can result in the rise of oppression and tyranny," Zamarim said as he faded away.

The old Wizard's surroundings turned into a cliff that he stood upon. Off in the distance and below, he spotted a town that was being ravaged by a great battle. Fireballs flew, thunder erupted, lightning struck, humans clashed in hordes, and great beasts scrapped in the streets. The most noticeable detail of all was a gigantic pair of skeletal arms protruding from the ground at one end of the town.

Aldous knew the dark magic all too well: They were the *Dark Hands*, a trademark spell of Wilhelm the Oppressor. Although more than one Dark Wizard in history had gained the ability to use them, Wilhelm's were unique in that they could reach the size of large man-made towers. They loomed over the town, with each giant finger wiggling in anticipation.

A sizable cavalry charged at a figure in between the Dark Hands, but were dispatched by other armed men fighting on Wilhelm's side. Aldous then spotted a Wizard riding a pegasus through the sky. There were dust-filled sparkles shooting out from its trotting hooves, leaving a beautiful rainbow trail in its wake. The white-winged steed shot a great beam of light out of its mouth, but the blast exploded upon hitting a green barrier that protected the Dark Wizard.

Next, a tornado touched down near another Wizard, who held his hands out before the growing destructive force. Buildings were ripped apart as it expanded, and then another Wizard approached and shot a stream of fire into the vortex. The tornado roared and annihilated all in its path as the sky turned red with fiery wrath, and it slowly made its way toward the Dark Hands.

In response, the Dark Hands faced each other, as if about to clap. A blinding, green energy gathered between the palms until it grew into a great ball. *Wayward soul energy,* Aldous thought. The Mountain King had used a similar spell against him, albeit, much smaller. To have gathered so many souls at once was something that he couldn't help but admire, despite knowing what was to come of it.

After some charge-time and with the fire tornado in range, the Dark Hands fired a gargantuan blast that blinded Aldous and made his ears ring. As the cliff rumbled and he fell to his knees, all of his senses dulled, save smell. The unmistakable stench of blood and smoldering rock overcame him to such a degree that he started coughing, and those coughs soon turned to gagging. When his sight started coming back, he understood why: A cloud of vaporized rock and man was passing him by. When the wind mercifully blew it away, the full view of town took Aldous' remaining breath away. The tornado was gone, and so too were many of the combatants. A dragging crater, lined with remnants of buildings and bodies, cut through the town. It looked as if the battlefield had been victim to a skidding comet.

To the old Wizard's relief, there were survivors. They gathered from corners of the town that hadn't been decimated by the blast and began a new onslaught. Wilhelm fired bolts of black lightning at clumps of attackers, which sent dozens of lifeless bodies soaring through the air like flies that had been swatted away. A fiery rain descended from the sky: an aftermath of the flame tornado.

"I remember, now…" Aldous muttered as the raindrops stung him with their contact. Rain was the signal for him to begin his attack.

The pegasus-mounted Wizard flew up to him and called out to hop on. Aldous obeyed, and they flew at blazing speeds toward the mighty Oppressor at the town's end. Nearing their target, Aldous gathered scalding-hot water into his hands and shot it as a stream at high pressure into the green barrier surrounding the Dark Wizard. However, the water merely bounced off without inflicting any perceivable damage.

That was when Aldous remembered what a long, bloody battle it was going to be. He sighed and gathered more water from the falling rain as he and the pegasus circled town, seeking another opportunity to strike.

∽

Bartholomew Montgomery shivered in the blue void. The latest round of torturous memories had just ended, and now the mysterious bald Wizard approached.

"You again? Wh-why are you showing me these things?" he asked.

"Silence, invader! I will do what I wish with you. These visions are but reminders of the terrible things you've done in the name of your so-called 'family'," he replied.

"That's why I'm here! To make my own legacy! To escape my family!" Bart pleaded. "But I understand, now. I'll leave. Just let me out, please!"

"I don't think you fully understand. You claim that all of your bandit underlings are 'family'. But from what I have seen, it's a questionable notion at best."

"But they are! I treat them all as my own!"

"It seems to me that another vision is in order. You are just as ruthless as the other Montgomerys, but unlike them, you try to cover up your inadequacies with fanciful and romantic talk of brotherhood," Zamarim said as he began fading away and the environment morphed around him. "How did you react when one of your brothers needed you most? Let's see…"

Soon, Bart found himself in a throne room constructed of stone. In the shadows, many members of his family sat alongside him, watching as a man was held down. His arm was pinned down over a cutting board, and a man wielding a great axe stood over him.

Brother, Bartholomew thought. It just *had* to be this wretched memory.

"Do you have anything further to say for yourself?" a hoarse, commanding voice echoed. Bartholomew involuntarily moved, as he had in his other memories, and looked to see his father, king of bandits, scowling from the shadows.

"No." His brother did not look up.

"And the rest of you? Anything further on the matter? If I find out later that any of you aided him, you'll lose far more than an arm."

The family remained quiet. The man at the chopping block looked up to them, and Bart turned his gaze away. He couldn't look him in the eyes back then, and he likely couldn't now even if the vision allowed it.

"Very well," said his father. "Commence the punishment!"

Bart's eyes forced themselves shut as chopping flesh and a blood-curdling scream dominated his senses.

∽

Giles had been floating in the blue void since passing out in the cave. He could feel his mind slowly cracking from looking at the same blue nothingness for such a long period. It was maddening.

As he began to give up hope, a bald man in a robe appeared before him, and his heart began racing with excitement. He didn't care who it was. Simply laying eyes on *anyone* was a treat.

"Who are you? Where am I? Why am I here?" His mouth kept moving, but his voice had gone silent when the bald man held out a hand. Magic? Was this the Psychic that Aldous had mentioned?

"My name is Zamarim, and you are an intruder on sacred land. I have ensured that you cannot bring harm to my domain by putting you in an indefinite sleep," he said.

"Won't I need food or drink? Will I die like this?" Giles asked sheepishly.

"Since your body has effectively shut down, it can last a bit longer than normal without nourishment. As for whether I can allow you to live… it is difficult to be sure. Though, I must say that compared to the others, I cannot find much in the way of unnecessary wrongdoing in your history," Zamarim said.

"Well… thank you," Giles said with a blush.

"However, my primary concern is not with what you've done, but what you will eventually become on your current trajectory. I sense within you a great resentment. One that stems from your helplessness; your weakness. You have not committed any atrocities… yet. But you have already started down that path by joining up with this bandit scum. And you use your prior helplessness as an excuse. I think that if you relive some of your most painful moments, it will illuminate-" Suddenly, Zamarim closed his eyes so hard that his eyelids were trembling.

"Something wrong?"

"It's nothing," Zamarim replied as he faded and the scenery changed. "I want you to remember the justification used by those who've hurt you in the past. I'll be back…"

With that, the Wizard disappeared, and Giles' vision of a memory began to play out in his mind. He found himself in bed, hearing a loud crash in his home late at night. Oh, it was *this one*, he thought. The night that his mother had been killed by burglars. He cowered under his blanket as her hollowed scream struck his door.

Now at the island's center, Mur'del tilted upright and flapped her powerful wings every second or two to slow her and Angus' fall.

"I appreciate the ride," he said over the roaring wind from the avian's most recent flap.

"Think nothing of it. It was part of the mission, after all," she replied. "I'll be hovering above. Call for me when you're finished."

"That won't be necessary."

"Oh? Why not?"

"It is more important that the key remain in our hands. I am going up against one of the most powerful Wizards in the world. Our plans may not succeed, and in that event, they could retrieve the key," Angus explained as he touched down on the grass. He looked up to her while stretching his body to the tune of loudly cracking bones. "Instead, it would be best if you returned to Endoshire, now. That way, we guarantee at least some form of success."

Mur'del let out a tweet and said, "Very well. I will take the key back to Drake."

Without another word, she took off with such force that the wind nearly ripped Angus' cloak off. After she was out of sight, he dusted himself off and turned toward the cave. He walked in, fearless as ever, and quickly felt the effects of Zamarim's mind augmentation.

Angus' vision turned blue, and he became light-headed. After a few moments of struggling, he fell to a knee, and then fully onto the ground. His ears rang unbearably and all around him faded. Suddenly, he found himself standing in a blue void, but the shock of it all didn't last long. He crossed his massive arms and awaited his captor.

After a while, Zamarim finally phased in from the void. Angus' stone face struggled into a frown as the Wizard King floated toward him.

"What took you so long?"

Zamarim cocked his head. "You were expecting me?"

"But of course. You have to defend your island, after all," Angus said as the Wizard King gestured in his direction with an open palm. Nothing happened. He seemed taken aback, and then tried again, to the same lack of result. The giant couldn't help but crack a smirk at his obvious confusion.

"What's wrong? I thought you were a powerful Psychic. Can't you read my thoughts?"

"Some are more difficult to read than others," Zamarim said.

"I see. Then, how will you proceed?"

Zamarim floated closer, and as Angus tried to move, his limbs refused to obey. He'd become completely paralyzed.

"A more direct approach may be necessary," he said while pressing a palm up to his forehead.

As it seemed like Zamarim was about to take control, however, two dark entities popped out of each side of the giant and screeched. The Wizard King gasped as he stumbled back and fell to the imperceptible ground of the void. Angus remained perfectly still as he raised himself and began to hover once more.

"Those sets of eyes… one yellow, and the other red," said Zamarim, near breathless. "You have been tainted. Partially by the Dark Savior, but that other entity, I cannot be sure of what it is. The only certainty is that you are not fully human; not anymore."

"As expected, you catch on quickly," Angus replied with a confident smile. "But surely you can do better?"

An intense concentration came to Zamarim's face as he pressed a palm up to the giant's forehead once more. This time, the blue void faded and Angus found himself in a new setting: He now stood next to his old partner in crime, Wolfgang.

The brute was smaller than Angus, but he managed to command a more imposing presence. He wore dirtied pants and boots to go along with a ripped-up shirt. He tightly gripped a sword that audibly strained against his skin, and behind a soot-filled face were mischievous blue eyes that reflected the light of the moon. Angus, too, was armed. Out behind a weathered, wooden building late at night, they stood before Drake Danvers. He wore a fancy tunic, as usual, and held both hands behind his back. In the background, two chairs had been covered by sheets, and Angus picked up on the wriggling movement that came from underneath them.

"The two of you have done great work for me, lately," Drake said.

"Thank ye, Mr. Danvers. It's been our pleasure," Wolfgang replied with a smirk.

"I have decided that you are both worthy of serving under me as my left and right hands…"

Angus and Wolfgang looked at each other with glee.

"That is, of course, if you can do one last thing for me," Drake said as he turned and lifted sheets off of the two chairs to reveal a man and a woman. Each was tied up and gagged. They struggled against their restraints to no avail. "You must kill them if you wish to serve under me."

"Why?" Angus asked.

"Does it matter? Do you not trust me?" Drake asked in a sour tone.

"Ye idiot!" Wolfgang shouted as he elbowed the giant in his ribs. Angus let out a few coughs, but he didn't respond any further. It wouldn't be until the death of Bronrar that he could bring himself to fight back against him. Wolfgang then looked back to Drake. "Of course we trust ye, sir."

"These two are traitors to Faiwell. That is all you need to know. Kill them, and take your next steps toward unimaginable power, gentlemen."

Wolfgang stepped forward, and with no hesitation, stabbed the man in his stomach and twisted the blade. He struggled and let out muffled screams of pain, but as the red stain in his shirt grew, his consciousness faded, and soon, the man slumped over.

Angus approached the black-haired woman. She was crying and trying to speak through her gag. Most likely begging for her life, he thought. He currently wanted to stab and kill her, but his body wouldn't allow it, for it was not true to the memory. Back then, he had hesitated, and he clearly recalled the questions that had been on his mind: Would it be wise to blindly follow orders? How did he know she was truly a traitor? Such a quaint memory. They were happier, more naïve times for him.

"Why do you hesitate?" Drake asked. "Kill her. *Now*."

The giant waited another moment too long before Wolfgang shoved him and said, "Ye big oaf! I'll take care of this!"

The brute pulled his sword back, but before he could make the stab, Angus pushed him so hard that he fell to the ground.

Wolfgang growled like a feral beast. "Ye bastar-"

He fell silent, and his mouth remained agape as Angus stood over him with the woman's neck in the grasp of his massive hands. She had been lifted, chair and all, so that her feet dangled at the same level of his chest. He wrung the woman like a rag, and in those few unpleasant moments, she squirmed, flailed, and let out miserable choking noises through the gag. Then, in even less time than Wolfgang's victim, she fell limp.

Angus threw the woman to the ground and the chair shattered on impact, causing her corpse to roll a few strides away. The giant turned to face Drake with aggression in his eyes.

"Well done…" he said as the vision faded away.

Back in the blue subspace, Zamarim breathed heavily as Angus looked back at him with his usual stone face.

"It would seem that this is going to take some effort," the Wizard King said while a smile took shape on his face. "But your mind is still vulnerable. Shall we continue?"

"Proceed."

∼

MEANWHILE, Joel and the group had spent some time traveling back to the city center, grabbing supplies, and then trudging to the grand wall surrounding Lake Teras. Pierce led them to the spot where Angus was supposed to kill the guards and make a hole in the wall.

"Uh-oh…" Alistair said as they approached.

The group stopped to see a swarm of guards surrounding the hole. It appeared that they were already beginning to fix it.

"Let's return to the city and make a new plan," Lord Roland said.

Joel felt a pit in his stomach as he and the group made their return trip. With Aldous' increasingly unpredictable behavior and Angus in possession of the key, he worried that history might be repeating itself.

CHAPTER 20
IN DEMAND

At the crack of dawn, Drake sat up in his bed and gazed upon Rose. She slept peacefully and let out a light snore every once in a while. He smiled at the thought of her innocence. Not because of who she was now, but who he planned to turn her into.

The Village Elder slicked his hair back and left the room while in his robe. He put some tea on over a fireplace and waited patiently by the table. His two guards, Hector and Ned, stood in the corner of the room, observing in their heavily cloaked forms.

"Don't you two ever sleep?" Drake asked with a chuckle. They only nodded in return.

Eventually, the tea was ready, and he took it off the fire to pour for himself and Rose. As he walked toward his bedroom, he looked to his guards and said, "Feel free to help yourselves."

After entering the room, he peered to his right to see that Rose wasn't in bed. He looked around frantically for a few moments before realizing that she was standing on the balcony, admiring the view in her nightgown. Before her was a perfect skyline of the ocean and city. Seagulls flocked around and a few ships were going in and out of the port, wavering the orange of the sun-reflecting water.

"Beautiful, isn't it?" She turned around and Drake offered her tea.

She accepted the cup and said, "Thank you."

"I was worried for a moment. I thought you had run off," Drake said before taking a sip of his drink.

Rose turned back to the balcony view. "I cannot foresee that ending well for me."

"Smart…" he muttered before joining her at the railing.

"I still don't understand," she said before taking an inelegant gulp of her drink. Drake raised an eyebrow. He'd have to teach her proper manners. "Why did you make me an indentured servant? Does a slave not suit your needs?"

"My reasons will become clear to you soon enough. For now, I trust that you will stay put and enjoy living like royalty," Drake replied.

"Or you'll kill me?"

The Village Elder chuckled. "I wonder if you'll feel the same way by the end of today."

Before Rose could respond, a great shadow loomed over them, and she took notice with nervous eyes. They both looked up to see a dark, winged creature soar above, flip over in the midst of an alleyway, and then fly toward them. Rose squeaked like a frightened mouse and ducked for cover.

A blast of wind hit the balcony while Drake chuckled and a gigantic avian pulled up to perch on the railing. As Rose cowered on the floor, he cleared his throat, and then she looked up at him to see that all was well. He held his hand out for her to take, and though her knees had become wobbly with fear from the landing, the Village Elder held firm, and she regained footing once more.

"Excellent timing, Mur'del," Drake said as he placed the teacup to his left, on the railing. "How did the mission go?"

She smirked in return and then dropped a dark blue medallion into his hand. "I know that half of the mission went well."

"And what does that mean? Where is Angus?"

"He told me to drop him off at that island in the middle of Lake Teras, and then take the key back to you. Just in case he failed to destroy the monolith and died, he wanted to be sure the medallion was out of enemy hands."

"I see…" Drake trailed off as he played with the Famine key in his hand. "A wise move. Perhaps he will make for a fine leader of the team if he survives."

"I can agree with that," Mur'del said. "Shall I go back to see if he's alive? To pick him up? It has been two days. By now, I'm sure he has either failed or completed the mission."

"There is no need. If he can return to us, having completed his mission in one piece, then he will be the leader of the team. If not, then it simply wasn't meant to be," Drake said with a shrug. "We've prepared a nest for you at the top of the building. I'm sure you're tired from the long trip. Get some rest."

The avian nodded before hopping off the railing and spinning in mid-air. She flapped her massive wings, creating a gust of wind that made Rose shield her eyes. Mur'del then ascended past the pair and a great *thud* from atop of the building signaled her landing at the nest.

"Wh-who was that? *What* was that?" Rose asked.

Drake smiled and said, "That was Mur'del. She is a part of the team I've been putting together. Did she frighten you?"

"Well, she is an avian, isn't she? Aren't they supposed to be small?"

"Yes, but Mur'del is a special case. Much like my guards, Hector and Ned, she has transcended her species. I'd hesitate to call her avian anymore."

"You say that you are gathering a team? I thought that your focus was on bringing indentured servitude to Federland? Are they all meant to be bodyguards?" Rose asked.

"They're meant to be far more than that," Drake replied as he grabbed his teacup and took a sip. He then leaned back-first against the balcony railing. "They shall help me change the world; mold it into my vision. Indentured servants are only a small part of my plan, and a necessary step in building relationships."

"Business relationships?"

"Exactly. That is how things get done, and how I'll plant the seeds needed to change the world to my liking," Drake said.

"I still don't understand," she said.

"Today, you will experience an example first-hand," the Village Elder said as he grabbed a few strands of her hair and then stroked them. She flinched at first, but then stayed perfectly still, her eyes becoming blank. "I'm going to take you along for one of my business transactions. You'll need to wear something nice, so I suppose we can visit a shop, first."

"I have plenty of dresses here that I could wear," Rose offered.

"Nonsense. When you're with me, there's an expectation that you look your best. Understood?" Drake asked. She nodded in return. "We'll depart after we have eaten and dressed."

∽

After a morning of feasting, Rose, Drake, Ned, and Hector left the luxurious quarters and departed for the northeast end of the city, where they could find shops for fine clothing. Much like before, Rose encountered all kinds of folk: Men and women from the far-east, island natives, avian, centaurs, and trolls roamed the streets. Her eyes wandered down the alleyways to see shady transactions taking place, and even up in the windows of those tall stone buildings there seemed to be deals being made. Some buildings were connected by miniature bridges, and like everywhere else she could look, deals were being struck atop them.

By the time they reached the northeast portion of Endoshire, the streets became populated with the rich. Knights walked in half-plated armor with shields at their backs and swords at their hips. Some rode gorgeous steeds, commanding a presence and power that reminded Rose of Drake. Gussied-up women in expensive dresses walked alongside nobles and wealthy merchants, and sometimes they would shoot her a sharp eye or a snort. They could tell that Rose didn't come from money, and she began to wonder if any amount of dressing up could hide that fact.

Eventually, Drake led her and the others into a shop that displayed dresses outside. They looked incredibly expensive to Rose's eyes, and usually dresses shown outdoors were the cheaper ones.

"How about this one?" Drake asked as he held up a red dress and matching girdle. She forced a smile, yet couldn't help but let her eye wander to a different one. It was a blue silk dress with frilly sleeves and white patterns at the ends. An underdress came along with it that had a lovely gray pattern and a low-cut top. She envisioned herself wearing such a splendid dress. No other woman would dare sneer or eye her with ill-meaning if she were to adorn herself in such regality. "Ah, I see you've taken an interest in that one. Why don't you try it on?"

Rose snapped back to reality and flashed him a look of bewilderment. "Are you sure?"

"Of course. I want to see how you look in it."

The indentured servant took the dress and entered behind a changing curtain. After a short time of fitting herself into the dress, she exited to the lit-up faces of Drake and the tailor. It filled her with such excitement that she couldn't help but crack a smile.

"Gorgeous," the Village Elder said.

"Ah, it seems the dress is a bit loose in the waist and bust area, sir," the tailor said to Drake.

Rose gazed down and tugged at some of the loose silk near her waist. Then, she looked to Drake with worry and anxiety built up in her gut. *This was the one*, she thought.

"It's quite alright," Drake said with a sly smile.

"Are you sure, sir? It would only take a few days to make the adjustments."

"A reasonable time frame, my friend. But I'm afraid we're in a hurry. She needs the dress today, you see. I'm sure that she'll grow into it in time, anyway."

"You could always take it back here to have it adjusted if you wish…" the tailor suggested.

Drake let out a chuckle. "Right, of course."

"Very well. That dress will be 8,000 notes, sir."

Rose's eyes widened to the size of gold coins and she let out a gasp. That was nearly as much as he'd paid for her freedom! More money than she'd made in her entire life, and Drake was about to spend it on one dress, just for her.

After making the purchase, Rose changed into the beautiful dress. They exited the store, and Drake began looking for a jewelry shop. It wasn't long before they happened upon expensive displays outside, and went inside to see the finer items for sale.

The indentured servant was immediately drawn to a silver set that included bangles for each wrist, an extravagant necklace that sparkled brighter than any jewelry she'd ever seen before, and long earrings that she couldn't take her eyes off of.

"It would seem you've already made a decision," Drake said as he massaged her shoulders and looked on from behind with glee. "Excuse me? How much for this set?"

A merchant approached. "Ah! A fine choice. The full set is 15,000 notes."

Rose let out a sigh. "Oh, I'm sure that's too mu-"

"I'll take it."

She couldn't believe her ears. After putting all of the jewelry on, she dazzled and glowed as if she were royalty. Drake couldn't wipe the smile off of his face. It was the first feeling of true joy Rose had felt since being told of her freedom; even if there *were* catches to it.

As they exited the shop, she approached Drake with tears in her eyes and then embraced him. "Thank you."

"Of course, dear. Think nothing of it."

"But… why are you doing all of this for me? You could find any woman to lay with for less than you've just spent on me."

"As I said, when you're with me, there are certain expectations. A fine lady who comes along with me for an important deal such as this must be elegant and sightly. And believe me when I say that you are," Drake said.

Pleasing as his words were, they didn't quite add up. There was something that he wasn't telling her.

The group of four next made their way to the eastern outskirts of the city, where many fields flowed and farm work was done. They passed dozens of field workers who were in the midst of backbreaking labor. Rose felt a twinge of guilt as she tugged at the fine fabric of her new garments. She began to realize that even as an indentured servant, she wasn't living a *peasant's life*.

Toward the end of the fields, they reached a series of huts. Great *clangs* rang out, and the overpowering smell of burning metal swirled through the air. Drake and his crew entered one of the huts at the end of the row. A scruffy man clad in armor greeted them.

"Ah! Sir Drake. 'Tis a pleasure to see ye again."

"Greetings, my friend. Are the coins ready?" he replied.

"As scheduled, they are ready for ye, now. Do ye have the payment?" the armor-clad man asked.

"Naturally," he replied with a sly smile. He raised a hand, palm up, over his shoulder, and Hector handed him several notes. Next, he passed the notes over to the smith. "I believe that will more than cover the costs, correct?"

"Y-yes sir!" said the smith with breathless excitement. "Let me get the product for ye."

He left through a back exit to the outside, and then moments later, returned with a couple of sacks. Each jingled loudly with every step he took. Drake retrieved both, handed one back to Ned, and then opened the remaining bag to have a look for himself.

"Excellent. And did you follow my instructions?"

"Yes sir, I did. As odd a request as it may have been, I can respect ye wantin' it in immaculate condition. I was sure to handle it with gloves at all times."

"I couldn't have asked for better. You've earned a business partner," Drake said as the smith clapped his gloved hands together with glee. "In the near-future, I shall return, and with far more coin to be made."

"I look forward to it, Sir Drake!" he replied as the Village Elder and his entourage left the hut.

While the group walked back through the fields toward the cityscape, Rose became more confused than ever before.

"You brought me along for that? It seemed like a standard deal to me," Rose said before biting her tongue. Drake gazed back at her with those unreadable green eyes, eliciting a tingle of terror to run up her spine. She'd said too much, and now he was going to hurt her, she thought.

Instead, to her surprise, the Village Elder chuckled. "No, no. That wasn't the deal. That was to obtain what we need to make the deal."

"But I've seen piles of gold lying around our room. Surely you already had more than enough…"

Drake held up the bag and shook it in front of Rose's face. The jingling called to her like an angelic choir. "This? This isn't simply gold. Would you like to see what it is?"

After fidgeting her mouth in hesitation, Rose nodded. Drake opened the bag and held it in front of her. She peered in to see many coins bouncing with his steps, but true to the Village Elder's word, they were not golden. Instead, a shining yet dark coin glistened back at her like a twinkling star in the night sky. *Such beauty*, she thought. More beautiful than the silver she was wearing, even. She had to hold it in her hand. Surely Drake wouldn't reprimand her for taking one mere piece, would he?

A thoughtless smile spreading across her face, Rose reached for the bag, but Drake closed it and then pulled it away with lightning-like speed. A sudden anger welled up in her stomach and then boiled up to a lump in her throat. It was a childish rage; as if her favorite toy had been taken away without her ever having played with the 'toy' before. Such powerful feelings over a coin left her more bewildered than ever.

"You mustn't touch them with your bare hands, darling," Drake said.

"Why not? Come to think of it, you forced the smith to handle it with gloves, too. Is it poisonous?" Rose asked.

"In a manner of speaking? Yes. But it can also be wielded with great power," he replied.

"Why not use the power for yourself?"

"Oh, but I am! You see, part of the black gold's power is its ability to take advantage of the unsuspecting; to prey on the natural greed of mankind."

"I see... so this black gold... you are giving it to an enemy?" Rose asked.

"Not exactly. There are certain nations and settlements that we have decided to target. We will gift and trade black gold to the most influential and wealthy folk of those places," Drake explained.

"I can see that you have many plans going at once, but how does it all play into your desire to shape the world as you see fit? Slaves and the greedy alone won't allow you to rule the world…"

"There is much to explain, but we're almost at the site of the deal. Be sure to play along while we're there. Perhaps you will begin to understand."

Drake's group arrived at a small stone building, where two guards stood at the entrance. They glanced at the entourage and immediately permitted them to enter.

Inside looked to be a tavern that had been abandoned. Now, only the remnants remained, like wooden tables, stools, and the bar top. It was dark inside, but one lit-up table made it obvious where to go. Over a dozen more armed guards surrounded a well-dressed man who sat with folded hands. His beard, cut expertly into a design that left a triangular patch at the chin, drew Rose's eye. So too did his fancy golden tunic, which had white frills at the shoulders and a matching cape that hung from them. He flashed the group a slick smile as they approached.

"Ah, Drake. I've been expecting you," he said before standing and extending a hand. Rose was taken aback by how slowly he spoke, but she couldn't quite place where the accent was from.

"Nicholas, it's good to see you again," Drake said as he leaned over the table and shook his hand.

"Please, have a seat."

Drake sat and Rose took a seat next to him. Hector and Ned, however, chose to stand. Nicholas flashed the pair a curious glance.

"Don't mind them. They prefer to stand, for one reason or another," the Village Elder said with a chuckle.

"That's quite alright. My eyes weren't drawn to them, anyway," Nicholas said as he smiled smoothly at Rose. He held his palm out and she looked at Drake out of the corner of her eye. He gave her a nod, and so she placed her hand on his, and he pulled it up to kiss it gently.

IN DEMAND

"My name is Nicholas Mantel. I am a noble of Turnersia. And you are?"

"It's a pleasure to meet you," she replied in a meek tone. "My name is Rose."

"Ah, a lovely name," Nicholas said before returning his focus to Drake. "I didn't know you had courted Mithikan royalty? Consider me impressed."

"She's quite a beauty, isn't she? Not Mithikan royalty, but soon to be the closest thing that Federland has to a queen," Drake said, looking at her with pride. Rose did her best not to outwardly express shock. Instead, she gracefully smiled back at him.

"Still trying to rule over that untamable land, eh?" Nicholas asked, leaning back in his chair. "I tell you this: You could take your dealings to Turnersia at any time and you'd be a noble, as I am, with land to oversee. The king is quite fond of you; a most impressive feat, given our respective country histories."

"Yes, well, where most see enemies, I see opportunity. So, how about we get down to business?"

"Ah, right. That new precious metal you were talking about. I've been curious to see it in coin form. Is it truly as alluring as you claim? It couldn't possibly match Rose's beauty, I'm sure. Show me…"

"See for yourself," Drake replied with a confident smile. He slid one of the black gold bags over to the Turnersian noble.

Nicholas opened the bag and Rose noted the sparkles that reflected off of his cheeks. He reached in and grabbed one of the coins, then felt it with his thumb. Rose's eyes glazed over and she could almost feel herself drooling as she fixated on the splendor of the black gold.

"My, my, this is quite the piece of metal," he said before holding the coin up for some of his entourage to see. It seemed that with each sparkle, the men let out oh's and ah's in response. "What do you call it?"

"Black gold."

"Interesting. I'd love to have some. What do you want in exchange?"

"We do not know its true value, yet. So, I thought I'd start it out at half the value of gold. You are the first person to have access to these coins and one of the lucky few who will receive such a discount. I am confident that the value will surpass standard gold, in due time," Drake said.

"Consider it a deal," Nicholas said as he extended a hand. The

Village Elder shook it firmly. "I can foresee such beautiful coin becoming a legitimate currency in Turnersia, so my next question is, *when can I have more?*"

A knowing smile grew on Drake's face. "We have some aspects to work out, but you will be the first that I contact when the next batch is ready. After all, you're one of my most valued trading partners. I trust you'll let me know how the good people of Turnersia react to it?"

"Yes, yes, of course…" the noble trailed off as he gazed lovingly at the coin in his hand. Rose watched on in wonder as the man before him stupefied and appeared to lose all concept of his surroundings. He began mumbling to himself.

After a few uncomfortable moments, some of the nearby guards shook Nicholas by his shoulder. He shot a glare back up at them, to their visible surprise, and then returned to a relaxed posture.

"Well then, why don't we get your gold?" he said before snapping his fingers. One of his men brought over a bag.

The two parties counted out the different sets of gold and made their deal over the next hour. Drake and his group stayed for a few drinks after business was done. Rose couldn't wait for it to be over. Not because she wasn't enjoying herself, but because she had many questions for the Village Elder.

After finally leaving, Rose waited until they were in the busy streets to start talking. She grabbed his hand and held it as if they were a real couple. Drake raised an eyebrow at first, but then he returned to his cool demeanor that rarely seemed to waver.

"You could have sold that black gold for far more than he paid," she said.

"That is certainly true, but making a profit wasn't the point. It's all about the long-game. This is to *create a demand* for the black gold. And believe me, there will be *much* demand for it, soon enough," Drake said with a smirk. "Did you notice anything throughout that deal?"

"Yes… Nicholas' behavior changed. At first, he was obsessed with me. I daresay he wanted to take me as his own," Rose said as she looked up to see Drake nod in approval. "After touching that coin, he rarely paid me any mind. He became so distracted that we hardly got the deal done."

"Right again."

"When you told me that the black gold preys on man's greed, I thought you meant it in the same way that money and power possess others. But this is different, isn't it?"

Drake only smiled in response.

"And bringing me along was to test him, wasn't it? To see if the black gold would take the attention away from me. That bit about me being your queen was to make him desire me more, out of jealousy," Rose continued.

"Your observations impress me, but you give yourself too little credit. I meant what I said about you as my queen," Drake assured her with a prideful smile. "Your presence today wasn't only to test Nicholas, but you, as well."

Rose leaned in, waiting, as she had before, for him to laugh or tell her it that was all a cruel joke, but he never wavered. "M-me? But I'm just a slave…"

"Not anymore, you're not," he replied, raising an index finger. "I could see early on that you were something more than a sex slave. It was only a hunch back then, but over the past week, you have shown me that you are smart; observant. I knew from your prior hardships that you'd be resilient. These are the qualities that I've been looking for."

"Just like that? You'd make me a queen? Instead of your indentured servant? I don't understand…"

"You may recall that I have a daughter. I'm sure that I've mentioned her to you in passing. She is the exact opposite of you: reckless, foolish, spoiled… she is not a fitting heiress. But you? You could bear a new child for me, and you'd be the perfect mother for them," Drake said.

Rose's mind swam in an ocean of thoughts that she couldn't hope to make sense of. "This is so much for me to take in…"

"Yes, there is much for you to learn if you are to take your place at my side as queen," Drake said before stopping in the middle of the road and grabbing both of her hands. He pressed them up to his chest and looked down upon her with passion. The sea of people walking the streets parted around them, as if even they understood the importance of who stood before them. "But it's *your* choice. You can accept my proposal, and I will take your hand in marriage. You would get to see all of the world, and no object would be out of your reach. By my side, as queen of many countries, you will help me to wield power over our subjects. Or, you can go on living a normal life. If you choose this, I will let you go and never bother you again."

Rose's eyes widened and so too did her mouth; but it was difficult to form words. She was breathless. "I-I…"

"Regardless of your answer, I will be tearing up the indentured servant contract when we return to our quarters. But then you will have to choose. You can become my wife; my queen, and I will show you a world you never knew existed. Or you can choose a life of normalcy, and leave."

The indentured servant looked down at the filthy street. She thought back to her childhood, young adulthood, and her experience as a slave. Then, she thought of today, one of the greatest days of her sad life.

"Let's get to work," Rose said as she looked up and stood on her tip toes. She planted a kiss on Drake and they shared a long embrace in the middle of the street.

Drake and Rose smiled at each other as they walked down the street blissfully to their home on the north side of the city. From the black gold to his business connections, to their upcoming marriage: He was truly an expert at creating demand. Soon, she thought, it would pay off in dividends.

CHAPTER 21
A WARM BOSFUERAS WELCOME

Lucia awoke in her private quarters. The ever-present sway of the boat on the water drew out a sigh from her lips. She and Dalton had been at sea for over a month. Impatience had set in back on day 20. The fact of the matter was that there wasn't much for them to do on the trip. Practice duels with Dalton had quickly revealed themselves to be folly, for she was tired of losing. The captain and crew had kept to themselves, as Lucia had found out when attempting to make small talk with them about Luneria. The fact that there were only three crew members didn't help, though it wasn't a surprise: Journeying to Gentorgul was not a popular idea amongst sailors.

As she dressed, the burns on her torso became irritated. Another annoyance of the trip was that there were no herbs or bath water to help manage the irritation. It was a constant reminder of her blunder against Wolfgang one year ago. Had she not stopped to taunt him, she could have finished him off before he reached for the torch and burned her. That wouldn't have happened to Dalton, she thought. He would have taunted Wolfgang and *still* won.

With her outfit complete, Lucia walked through the cabin and out onto the main deck where she saw Dalton sitting on a railing.

"Ready to go for a swim?" she asked, slapping him hard off the shoulder.

"Maybe I can swim there faster," he replied with a shrug. She sat next to him on the railing.

"It should be any day, now. The estimate was 40 days, after all," the student said.

"In the meantime, what do you say we have a practice duel?"

She shook her head firmly. "I'd rather let my skills dull than lose yet another match."

"Ah, that's a shame. Then again, perhaps it would be wise to rest for the remainder of the trip," Dalton said, cracking a smirk. "I have a feeling we're about to walk into a swarming hive of hornets."

"It'll be worth it," Lucia said.

"I know…" he trailed off. "So then, you admit-"

"No."

"But you didn't let me finish."

"I know what you were going to say," Lucia said with a roll of her eyes. "Let's change the subject."

"Alright, alright," Dalton replied with a chuckle. "But I have my suspicions, is all I'm sayin'. Who knows you better than me?"

The student narrowed her eyes at him before easing up and sighing. "No one."

"Exactly! I'm only looking out for you. Your parents would have wanted you to settle down and be happy," Dalton said.

"You've been bringing up my parents often of late, but that appeal hasn't worked for you in years. Unless you want to tell me more about them…" she trailed off with a sly smile.

"Fine, what do you want to know?" he asked.

"Really?"

"Yeh, we've run out of things to talk about. Might as well."

"Why don't you ever talk about them?" she asked, tilting her head.

"Your father was a great leader. Out at war, he helped keep many of us alive with his skill, tact, and principles. To raise our morale and fighting spirit, he had sayings and mantras that he'd call upon," Dalton said before smiling and letting out a snorting chuckle. "The one that always stood out to me most was: 'Life is a bloody struggle, and then you win.'"

Lucia cocked her head. "I've heard that mantra before… or half of it, anyhow. You changed it around?"

He nodded solemnly. "Yes… life is a bloody struggle, and then *you die*. After your father died, on the final day of war no less, I was crushed. Then, your mother passed, and my amendment to that saying was born. Neither of them deserved their fates, and thinking about it only angers or saddens me, depending on the day."

"It's understandable that the memories would be painful to you... but still, I wish I had more of them," Lucia said. "I still remember my mother, but everything involving my father is hazy at best. What was he like?"

"He was my mentor, as I am to you. But I must admit that he was a far better teacher than I could ever hope to be," Dalton said.

"I could have told you that," Lucia chimed in with a chuckle.

"Shadap!" he snapped back half-heartedly. "Anyway, your father taught me nearly everything I know. He was a master swordsman who seemed able to counter anything. Not even once did I witness him lose a duel, whether on the battlefield or at practice. We all felt invincible while fighting by his side. Most importantly, he was an invaluable friend, a brother."

There was a long silence as the student and teacher looked out to the calm sea.

"How did he die?" Lucia asked.

Dalton shuddered. He continued staring off into the distance.

"He fell to his death... as I mentioned before, it was on the final day of war before we signed a peace treaty with the avian."

"And my mom?"

A long silence followed. Still, his eyes remained forward and out at sea. Perhaps she had asked too much?

"After the war, I did my best to ensure that the two of you lived happy, peaceful lives. But then, Anora became ill, and we worried that it might get passed on to you. You were sent away to live with your grandparents, and in that time, the sickness ended up killing her," Dalton said, sulking. "With my war spoils, I could afford the greatest medical care available for her. But it made no difference. No amount of wealth or battle prowess can change the fact that life ain't fair, oftentimes."

Lucia felt a twinge of guilt from deep within. She had come to terms with her parents' deaths long ago. It seemed like Dalton felt worse than she did. Now, it was becoming apparent why he hadn't often spoken about them. Those old wounds hadn't healed. Perhaps she could draw happier memories from him.

"I suppose you're right. Why don't you tell me more about what they were like, then?"

"Your father was one of the most admired in the army. Not only for his swordsmanship, or his leadership, but his dependability. Not once did he ever let us down. Every promise made was kept," he said, tapping his heels off the side of the boat. "But y'see, the best thing about Adrian was that I *hated* training under him."

Adrian, she thought while tilting her head back. She had nearly forgotten his name. "What do you mean?"

"The regiment that he put me through was hell, and it never seemed to pay off. No matter how hard I worked, he demanded more of me; and when I gave him more, it still wasn't enough. Not enough to satisfy him, and damn sure not enough to defeat him in a practice duel," Dalton said with a groan while rubbing his wrist. "I think that I can still feel the aches and pains, even today."

"Funny," Lucia said with a snort. "That's how I feel. Any strides I make in swordsmanship seem to make no difference against you."

"That's my point," said the warrior as he held up a finger. "It *does* make a difference. Back then, I hadn't realized it, but by pushing me past my limits, your father was bringing me up to his level. I don't know all the details of what you went through after running away, but I'd say you have already reached your peak physical condition."

"I had help with that," she replied, looking up with a smile. The water below reminded her of the days when she'd swim against the current of the river, and the very wooden railing she sat on called to mind her time strength training in the wilderness, just outside of Luneria's capital, Zirka.

"Since resuming our training together, all you've had to do is maintain your strength and speed. I was not so fortunate. Adrian would have me running and lifting things for hours… and then he'd take me out to the field and beat my arse so badly in a practice duel that there'd be welts and bruises all over me. I think you would've gotten a laugh out of it!"

"Almost certainly."

"But when it came time to battle others, I was shocked to find that few, if any, could stand up to my onslaughts. It was not I who was mediocre, but your father who was great. I think that when the time comes, and that time is likely to be soon, you will realize the very same thing that I did, back then."

"Somehow, you managed to turn your motivational speech into a brag for yourself," Lucia replied with an eye roll. "And how about my mother? I can remember some things about her, but I was still young when she died."

Dalton smiled. "Your mother was the only reason I ever had a home before I joined the army. She gave me a place to stay when I was without a single gold coin to my name. And I must admit that as a young lad, I was not easy to live with, at first. Both of your parents had their own way of setting me down a better path. While your father ground down my pride and instilled gratitude through a hellish training regimen-"

For a moment, Lucia lost focus. She was reminded of her early days in Luneria once more. Her experience had been similar to Dalton's: Intense training sessions had broken down her arrogance and made her better.

"-while Anora led by example. Through her, I learned patience and the value of giving to others. We would often cook and bring food to struggling neighbors, though some were more appreciative than others." He shot her an icy glare.

"My apologies, but your idea of 'cooking' leaves much to be desired. I think that it will be me who continues making us meals for the foreseeable future."

"When you insult my cooking, you insult Anora, y'know," Dalton replied as he looked off into the distance once more. He gasped aloud, then nudged Lucia with his elbow. "Look! It's land!"

Far off in the foggy distance, she could see patches of green and what appeared to be a harbor of sorts, cradled by a crescent-shaped beach.

"Finally..." Lucia hopped down from the railing and walked toward her quarters to prepare.

"I dunno what ye lot are so excited about. We ain't stoppin' thar!" the captain called back from his ship's wheel.

"What? Why not?" Dalton asked while also hopping down.

"That thar is the port of Bosfueras," the captain replied.

"And that's exactly where we want to go," Lucia insisted.

"Maybe it's where *ye* wanna go, but it ain't where *I'm* goin'. Do ye know how many of our ships disappeared goin' into that harbor in the past six months? Five. Five ships gone! The King may be a good friend of yers, but I have direct orders not to go thar. We'll drop ye off at the next port," he said.

"Pft, does he think we're giving him a choice?" Lucia asked, looking over to Dalton. They exchanged knowing smiles.

She walked up to the captain and drew her long sword. In one swift motion, the blade pressed up against his throat. She held it there firmly, so much that she could feel his nervous *gulp*.

"That doesn't work for us," Lucia said with fake cheer. "The other port is too far away, and a life depends on us reaching Bosfueras as soon as possible."

"Oh yeah? Whose life could be so important that it's worth putting me'self and the crew at risk?" the captain shot back.

"Yours," she replied, then pressed the blade against his neck a little harder.

The captain sighed. "This is suicide."

"Well then, you can die now, or die later," Lucia said.

"Oi! What's goin' on here? Leave Captain Auber alone!" a chubby, brown-haired man said from behind. He drew a short sword, but before he could even point it in Lucia's direction, Dalton had his blade tip pressed up gently against his back, freezing him in place.

"Now, now. Your captain will be fine if he cooperates, and so will you. We're not asking you to do anything crazy. Just drop us off," Dalton said.

"That *is* crazy." The captain groaned.

"What's going on out here?" another man asked from behind. He was holding a map. From brief chatter over the past month, Lucia had gathered that he was their navigator.

"We were having a little disagreement," Dalton replied with a nod. "But now the matter is settled. Isn't that right, captain?"

"Fine. We're settin' course fer Bosfueras harbor," he replied through gritting teeth.

"Wh-what? We can't!" the navigator said in a panic.

"That's right! You remember what happened last time, don'tcha?" the chubby man added. The captain darted his eyes at him and he reacted by hanging his head in shame. "Oh, right…"

Lucia withdrew her blade. "Something odd is going on. Explain yourselves."

"There ain't nothin' goin' on here 'cept yer crazy ideas that are gonna get us all killed!" Captain Auber shot back.

Dalton lowered his sword from the chubby man's back and circled around to face him. "You've been here before, haven't you? What did you witness?"

"Erm… nothin'! Nothin' at all!"

"We may as well tell them," the navigator said, rolling up his map. "Then, they will understand what they're getting into."

"Speak up," said Lucia, raising her blade once more.

"Alright, alright! Just get that sword outta me face!" the captain pleaded. Lucia obeyed. "The truth of the matter is, we ain't official sailors of the Lunerian Kingdom."

"Excuse me?" Both of Lucia's eyebrows shot up and her mouth hung open.

"Who are you, then?" Dalton added.

"Well… erm… we're pirates," he squeaked out.

The student and teacher looked at each other, and their shocked demeanor quickly turned to hysterical laughter.

"What's so funny?" the captain asked in a sour tone.

"You don't look much like pirates," Lucia said. She looked the captain over: He was a short, thin man in baggy clothes. He had the scruffy brown beard of a pirate, although even *it* looked unimpressive; bushy at the sides, but thin in the front. He wore typical sailor garb: A big, silly hat and uniform often seen in the Lunerian navy, complete with uncomfortable stockings and pants.

Dalton shook his head as the laughs finally tapered off. "You're pirates. You can do and wear whatever you want, yet you choose to dress as official sailors on behalf of Lunia-"

"Luneria," Lucia and the captain corrected in unison.

"Right, right…" he muttered with rolling eyes. "My point is, why dress like drones of the monarchy when you can adorn yourselves in clothing and weapons that might strike fear into the people you intend to thieve from? Even this ship is hardly befitting of pirates!"

"I was gettin' to that until you disrespectful whelps got to insultin' me and mah crew-" the captain cut himself off as Lucia's sword neared his neck once more. He put his hands up and then returned a nervous nod to show compliance. "See here, we simply *stumbled into* this situation, alright?"

"What do you mean?" Lucia asked.

"He means that none of us are particularly intimidating," the navigator said.

"Well, I wouldn't say that…" the captain added.

"But we are still pirates. We stowed away on this ship a while back in the hopes that we could steal some supplies here and there while pretending to be part of the crew. The Lunerian sailors were a bunch of idiots, so it worked. We were satisfied with that much, but then…" he trailed off.

"Then, you came here?" Dalton asked.

"That's right. They stopped here to complete a shipment, and most of the sailors left the ship for food and drink. They had no reason to believe anything was wrong. But then we heard the screams, and we saw the massacre unfold from this very ship. There was nothing we could do besides run," the navigator said.

"Why weren't you on the mainland with them?" Lucia asked.

"Do you want to tell them? Or should I?" The navigator eyed his blushing captain with a smirk. "Captain Auber was seasick, so we stayed back to ensure his recovery."

"A pirate captain? Seasick?" Dalton howled with laughter.

"What? I have a weak stomach!" the captain shot back, crossing his arms. "Anyway, we ended up gettin' this ship by the lucky grace o' God! So, we put it to good use. We continued to receive and send shipments from the Lunerian Kingdom to other nations, taking bits and pieces here 'n there. They haven't noticed a thing!"

"Not a bad deal for you," Dalton said as he finally put his blade away. "And we won't tell a soul as long as you drop us off. Everyone can have their way."

"No," Lucia said, frowning. "King Cedomir II is a good friend of mine. I cannot allow you three scoundrels to continue stealing from the kingdom."

"Bah! Ye see now, Franco? This is why we were supposed ta stick to the lie!" the captain complained, looking to his navigator with a judgmental eye. He wore a white pair of pants and traditional stockings but was missing the silly hat that his captain wore. It was odd to see a man like him out at sea; for he carried himself like nobility: trim, proper, and well-kept.

"My apologies, sir," Franco said with a hint of sarcasm.

Dalton eyed Lucia and whispered, "We may be close, but we still need them. Let them off the hook, for now. Conrad is more important than some far-away kingdom, isn't he?"

She let out a long breath through her nose. "In exchange for dropping us off, I suppose it could slip my mind."

"It's settled, then," the captain said as he spun his ship wheel to point in the direction of the harbor.

"We're likely to reach the port within an hour or so," Franco said. "I suggest you prepare yourselves."

"There ain't no preparin' fer what they're about to step into. Y'know, it's not too late to join me crew and forget about all of this. We could use a couple'a fightin' types! None of us are skilled at it," Auber said.

"Oi! What about me, captain?" the chubby man asked.

"Erm… I meant nothin' by it, Ebbie; just that they seem like professionals, is all."

"We don't need 'em! I can take on anyone who dares challenge us!" Ebbie said with clenched fists and a wide smile.

"Oh, really?" Dalton asked, raising an eyebrow.

"Don't mind me first mate, here. He gets a lil' *too excited*, sometimes," said Auber.

~

AFTER NEARLY AN HOUR OF PREPARATION, Lucia and Dalton exited their quarters, fully armed and armored: Both carried blades at the left hip, strapped bows to the right, mounted shields upon their backs, and carried small packs of essentials. Most of their time had been spent fitting the chainmail and a nearly full set of plated armor on each other. Only their heads remained unprotected. Lucia had also insisted on adorning a skirt over the leg plates, a difficult process that took a quarter-hour, much to Dalton's annoyance.

"The two of you look like you're ready for war," Franco said with a hint of surprise.

"We're here to rescue a friend of ours," Lucia replied.

"I'm tellin' ya, ye'll be walkin' straight to yer deaths," Captain Auber said.

"We'll see about that. Back in Faiwell, we dealt with crazed men similar to these folk, and we weren't well-armed, like this time," said Dalton. "If we've gotta chop down a few loons to get our friend back, then so be it."

"Erm… captain?" Ebbie called out. He sat atop the crow's nest of the ship with eyes fixed on the harbor.

"What is it?"

The first mate blinked and then squinted. "Catapults…"

"What was that?" the captain asked. "Me hearin' ain't no good. I coulda sworn ye said 'catapults'." He let out a nervous chuckle.

"Catapults!" Ebbie shouted. Everyone ran to the front deck, and through the clearing mist, Dalton got a good view of the harbor.

In the shallow waters, bows and masts of shipwrecks stuck out amongst the small waves. There was also a ship docked to the left, but the sails appeared to have taken damage. Next, he picked up on a watch tower at the beach's center, and then the aforementioned catapults: There were several stationed on the sandy shore ahead, and they were all armed with big stone blocks or rocks. Auber whimpered like a frightened pup as one of them launched and sent a large rock soaring in their direction.

To the left of the ship, a massive splash erupted and shot water up onto the deck. The sting of the salt in Dalton's eyes did not stop him from watching helplessly as a barrage of rock and stone rained down on their general area. None struck them, but many had come close, as evidenced by the soaked deck at their feet. How could they have been so accurate with siege weapons? A moving target such as a ship should have been near-impossible to hit.

"Oh, come on!" the captain complained sheepishly. "We've gotta turn tail 'n run!"

"No! Stay the course," Lucia said.

"Are ye mad? Did ye see how close they came to hittin' us?"

"*Stay the course.*" Lucia's icy glare silenced Auber, and Dalton let out a snorting chuckle.

"They're loadin' up some more, captain!" Ebbie called down, to which Auber groaned.

As the men on the beach scrambled to reload, Dalton's eyes wandered, and then they widened. *Of course*, he thought with a gasp. The shipwrecks had been more than a warning; they were both *obstacles and markers*. Any captain approaching the harbor would be veering left to avoid the wreckage and reach the dock, and such a ship would be taking a narrow path. The catapults must have been set to fire in this general area at all times, he thought. With so many shooting at once, they were bound to land hits and produce more wreckage, thus creating more obstacles and markers; a brilliant strategy for warding off-

Another splash jetted onto the deck, interrupting Dalton's thoughts. That one had been closer than any before, and with more rock and stone hurdling their way, it was only a matter of time before they'd be struck.

"I hope you lot are good swimmers," he said, smirking.

"I-I... don' know how to swim..." Captain Auber muttered.

Lucia burst out laughing. "A pirate who doesn't know how to swim! I'll bet-"

Just then, an explosion of water hit all on deck, and Dalton shielded his eyes as the sounds of splintered wood and rushing water filled his ears. With water beginning to fill his boots, too, the warrior lowered his arm and surveyed the area. He breathed a sigh of relief to see that Lucia was alright, and so were the pirates.

The same could not be said for the ship, however. It had become riddled with holes, some upward of a full meter around. He could feel himself sinking, and looking up at the sagging, snapping mast did little to calm his nerves.

"We must abandon ship!" he cried to the others. "Before the next volley of stones!"

Auber had panic written all over his face. "But we can't–"

A geyser of water shot out of the deck as another large rock struck the ship. Ebbie cried out as a final strike to the mast finished it off, and the crow's nest, along with him, barreled down and into the waters below.

"Ah, shit..." Dalton muttered as the final nail in the coffin, a large chunk of stone, struck wood a mere arm's length away. Now, all he could see were blurry shades of blue and brown. The ship had capsized, and this was to be its final voyage.

Sometime later, after the rain of stone and rock settled and most of the men had left the beach, Dalton, Lucia, and the pirate crew surfaced underneath the shipping dock to the left. They were hanging onto a stray piece of the boat.

"Good thing you found a wooden board for us, cap. You would have drowned for sure," Franco said with a chuckle. Auber only groaned in response.

"It was a good thing for us, too," Dalton said. "I suppose we didn't think things through. With all of these supplies and armor, we would've been too weighed down to swim for long."

"Well, I hope yer happy!" the captain whined as he slammed a fist into the wooden board. "Now, we're without a vessel, and trapped here with these ruffians!"

"As a matter of fact, I *am* happy," Lucia replied with a devious smile. "They think we're dead, so we have the element of surprise... the hunt is on, boys."

CHAPTER 22
THE HUNT IS ON

"What is thar to be excited about?" Captain Auber asked. "We're trapped!"

"Are we, though?" Dalton asked, then pointed to the vessel floating on the other side of the dock. "What about *that* ship?"

"The sails are heavily damaged," said Franco.

Auber groaned and his face contorted into what Dalton could only assume was his largest possible frown. "Hopeless… hopeless!"

"Any town with a port or dock must have some sort of shipyard," Dalton replied. "I think I saw one on the other side of the beach."

"Them crazed townsfolk will kill us before we can get thar," the captain said.

"I saw most of them leaving as our ship went down. I believe only one remains up in the watchtower at the beach's center," Lucia said with an assuring nod. "If the three of you make a run for it at once, I'm sure only one or two of you will die. The survivor can adorn the ship with its new sails."

"I-is she bein' serious?" Auber asked, looking at Dalton with frightful eyes and quivering lips. The warrior's cheeks flared out as he did his best to hold in a laugh. "I didn't even wanna come here! You lot should have'ta retrieve the new sails!"

"We don't have time to be searching around for sails," she replied while nudging him enough that he nearly fell off the makeshift raft. "*You* do."

"Watch it!" he squealed while scrambling to stay afloat.

"She's right," Dalton said, nodding toward his student. "We have business to attend to further inland. But here's what I can offer: We'll take care of the man on the watchtower, and then it will be up to you lot to make a supply run. For now, wait on the ship, where nobody can see you. We'll give you the signal when it's all clear."

The pirates remained silent at first. Only the waves gently clapping against the dock could be heard.

"Sounds like it could work, cap," Ebbie finally chimed in.

Auber sulked like a child who'd just lost an argument. "Thar ain't no other choice, now, is there?"

"It's settled, then: While we're rescuing our friend, you will fix up the ship," Lucia said. All nodded in agreement. "But it may take us some time to complete our mission. If we are not back by the time you've repaired the sails, I fully expect you to wait for us."

"Are ye crazy? We're lucky ta be alive as it is!"

"I can make it worth your while," Dalton said. "I have friends in Sigraveld that will pay big money for pirated supplies."

"That ain't good enough," Ebbie argued while looking at his captain. "We don' know these people well enough ta just take their word for it."

"Fair enough," Dalton said as he reached a hand into his submerged boot. "Will this do for an advance?" He plopped several gold coins out onto the makeshift float, and they glistened under the drops of water that had dampened them. Even brighter than the gold, though, were the pirates' eyes.

"Aye, that'll do," Auber said. His thoughtless smile brought a snorting chuckle out of the warrior. It almost looked like he was drunk. Had he ever even *seen* this much gold at once before?

"Are you sure about this?" Lucia whispered. "How do you know that *we* can trust *them*?"

"If they're not completely incompetent, they'll know to wait, because there's more where that came from," he replied with a confident smile. His gaze turned back to the pirates. "So, do we have a deal? You'll wait for us, yeah? If we manage to escape, I'll set you up with a secure financial partner in Sigraveld."

"We'll wait… within reason," Auber said.

"And what is that supposed to mean?" Lucia asked with a grimace.

"He means that we need to leave during the night. Because of the ship wreckage, our path of escape is narrow, and all of the catapults are aimed at that area of the harbor. Evading detection is our only hope, and that can only be accomplished under the veil of night. If you aren't back by then, it'll be safe to assume that you're all dead, anyway," Franco said.

The two warriors looked at each other with doubt in their eyes. It was sound reasoning, but the time frame was short. They had agreed ahead of time to be stealthy, as it was their best chance to take on an entire town that was known to become violent. The problem, however, was that their strategy would be slow compared to a reckless and direct approach.

"Well, I like a good challenge…" Dalton shrugged.

"That watchtower on the beach is perfectly placed. They'll see us immediately, especially with all of this shiny and bulky armor on. I'm sure they have a way of alerting people," Lucia said.

"I have an idea," Dalton said before jerking his head toward the pirates and smiling at them. "But I'll need you fellas to give up this board."

The trio groaned but obeyed. They clung onto the dock's ladder as Lucia and Dalton paddled off.

"The bay is in the shape of a crescent…" Dalton muttered as they kicked the water together. "If we can get around the edge undetected, we'll have a clear shot at the watchtower."

"That makes sense, provided they don't happen to turn around," Lucia said. "The guard is probably watching the bay for ships. If we're lucky, he won't see us coming."

~

As the two warriors slowly made their way around the edge of the bay, the pirates climbed up the dock ladder. At the top, they breathed sighs of relief to see that the ship was blocking their view of the beach. It had to mean that no one could see them from the watchtower.

Upon boarding the ship, Captain Auber looked at Ebbie, who was inspecting the ripped sails.

"We're gonna need three new sails to reach top speed, captain," he said.

Auber grit his teeth. "The worst possible damage. Damn it all… and even if we manage to find replacements, we're gonna have'ta wait for them two warriors. This is unreasonably dangerous."

"We could leave 'em behind," said Ebbie.

"That wouldn't work," Franco interjected. "Think of how easily they saw and struck us before, when our ship was further away. We cannot escape until nightfall when we stand at least a slight chance of leaving without their noticing."

"Aye… the way I look at it, if we're lucky enough, we'll get outta here with some valuable allies, a new ship, and someone ta sell our spoils to," Auber said as he proudly put hands to his hips. "We're gonna make out like bandits, just as planned!"

"That's our captain for ya!" Ebbie said, slapping him off the shoulder.

Franco cleared his throat. "There's one problem."

"Oh? And what's that?" the captain asked with a raised eyebrow.

"This ship isn't Lunerian. We won't be able to fool the kingdom anymore…"

Auber gasped and let his mouth hang open for a few moments. "That means…"

"That means we're gonna have to do some *real* piratin' after this!" Ebbie said with clenched fists and a wide smile.

"Er… right…" Auber muttered. Franco flashed him a knowing smile. "Let's focus on survivin' this mess first, though. Inspect and prep the ship, men!"

"Yes, sir!"

MEANWHILE, Lucia and Dalton rounded the smaller edge of the crescent-shaped bay. As the water became shallower, they felt confident enough to abandon the wooden debris and crept through the gentle tide on foot.

"We only get one shot at this," Dalton said as he grabbed the bow from his hip. "The watcher likely has a horn to alert the townsfolk. If we miss, this could turn ugly, fast."

"It's your shot to miss," Lucia said. She had not drawn her bow.

"I think that we should both shoot, to increase our odds."

She shrugged. "I know that you and my father lived and died by your archery against the avian. Meanwhile, I've only been focusing on swordplay, of late. You'll hit the target, and I will miss. Why bother?"

"I don't like this new attitude of yours. First, you gave up on our practice duels, and now, you won't even take a simple shot with the bow? I understand that you are worried about Conrad, but now is not the time to lose focus."

"You misunderstand…" Lucia muttered, looking down. "Just take the shot. Your aim will be true."

The pair snuck onto the beach, and as they walked, Dalton placed the arrow against the dark bow's string and drew it back. The tension of the string creaked and groaned, but there was no stirring from atop the watchtower as the warrior aimed up there. As they had suspected, a man was sitting at the top, looking out over the bay.

Dalton closed one eye and concentrated on his target. After a deep breath, he let the arrow go and it soared through the air. The pair watched on with bated breath as the arrow came between the roof and wall of the watch tower, and then struck the guard in his neck. Lucia heard a gasp for air and then watched as he fell from high up. Blood pooled in the sand around the corpse.

The two warriors dashed over to the body as fast as their bulky armor would allow. Dalton knelt to inspect the dead man while smiling.

"That's one for me, zero for you," he said.

Lucia raised an eyebrow. "You don't think I'm going to play along with this, do you?"

"Why not?"

"They may be our enemies, and we may have to kill them to rescue Conrad, but… to make a game out of it? That's vile," she replied.

"As the fieriest woman I've ever met, I never thought that this day would come, but it is clear to me that you are lacking motivation," Dalton said with sharp eyes. She felt a knot twist in her stomach, and it seemed to tighten with every passing moment. "Don't think I haven't noticed your evasion of competition, lately. Refocus yourself, or you will lose to me. *Again*."

Now, she was grimacing. He'd read her disheartenment well, yet somehow, his pointing it out had made her feel even worse. "I'm not interested in your games. We're here for Conrad."

"Suit yourself, but I'm still keeping score," he replied with a smirk before turning back to the corpse. "I suppose they won't be needing *this* any time soon."

The warrior stomped down on the dead watchman's horn and it shattered with a loud *crack*. The pair then looked over to the ship at the dock and waved. One of the pirates' heads popped up from the vessel, and then the three of them appeared and waved back.

"Let's hope they're not as bumbling as they seem," Lucia said.

"I have a good feeling about them," Dalton replied.

They dragged the body over to sea and let it float in the water. The beach was open and lacking in hiding spots, so it was their best option to make it less visible. Dalton pointed across the sandy landscape, to the east, where it was thickest. There, a boardwalk could take them from the beach and to a bridge that appeared to cross a river. Just before that wooden walkway, they could see a large building; what appeared to be a shipyard.

"Let's be quick," he said as the duo began walking east. "We cannot be sure if, or when, those men who manned the catapults will return."

"Right." Lucia nodded. "And we'll make haste for Conrad's sake."

"Of course," Dalton replied. "Then again, we have no idea where Conrad is at the moment. For all we know, he made it out of here, or…"

Lucia narrowed her eyes at him. She knew what he was thinking. Even if the odds had been stacked against him, Conrad was crafty and would find a way to survive. She was sure of that much.

As they reached the sandy boardwalk and neared the bridge, their worst fears came to pass. They could see some men off in the distance, trotting downhill. They looked at each other in worry. There was no cover for them to take, save jumping into the river. The men started shouting and then three of them ran forward. Another turned and started running back up the hill.

Lucia drew her bow and her heart began racing. It was her first true battle since Mt. Couture; since receiving the burns.

Dalton charged ahead with his long sword drawn and near his waist. Lucia's eyes widened. *A signal*, she thought. He was running in her line of sight on purpose to distract one of the targets. She grabbed an arrow and quickly drew it back into the bow's string. Over Dalton's bobbing shoulder and beyond, she spotted the overalls and dirty shirt of the farmer running at him. Without thinking, she loosed the arrow and it shot past the warrior, just over his shoulder, before piercing the deranged man's chest. He stumbled before falling face-first to the ground. Lucia let out a long, relieved breath. She had only been confident in the shot because Dalton was wearing plated armor.

She shook the cobwebs out and trudged ahead as Dalton engaged one of the men, who was in the process of lunging out at him with a pitchfork. However, the attack was clumsy and he easily sidestepped. He followed up with a vicious diagonal slash into the man's midsection, and he grunted as blood pooled in his shirt. The warrior pulled his bloody blade out and turned to face his other attacker, but Lucia, who was close now, saw that it was too soon to shift focus.

"Behind you!" she cried.

It was too late. He gasped as the bloodied man gripped his sword-wielding arm, and before he could pry himself away, the other man tackled him to the ground. Lucia put her head down and sprinted with all of her might. With armor on, her mentor had some leeway, but on the ground and swarmed, he'd be helpless, and they would find the gaps necessary to harm him.

To her surprise, though, Dalton called out, "Get the runner!"

Lucia dashed past him while reloading an arrow into the bow string. Despite the added weight of the armor, she was catching up to the runner, but she couldn't help but check over her shoulder to see if Dalton was alright.

As if reading her mind and quelling her worries, Dalton monkey-flipped the man who had tackled him, and with a free hand, drew his sidearm: a dagger. The other man was charging at him with a sword, but before he could get within range, the warrior threw his blade, striking him in the eye.

That was all Lucia had needed to see. She returned her focus forward and could tell that she was now within easy striking range of her target. The student stopped and took aim with her bow. Her tense arms bobbed with the heavy breaths that had come with the long run, and stinging sweat crept into her eyes as she unleashed the arrow. It flew straight into the running man's spine with such force that he stumbled and fell flat on his face. She smiled at the minor victory, but it was short-lived. The man began crawling.

"Persistent…" she muttered under a deep breath. She heard the clanking footsteps of Dalton coming from behind as she trudged up the incline in pursuit of the crawling man.

Eventually, the warriors were in stride with each other, and then they stopped next to the crawling man, who seemed to pay them no mind. It was as if his one and only focus was reaching the top of the hill.

"They seem possessed… like the Gold Fever-infected a year ago… but there's something different about 'em…" Dalton said between huffs and puffs.

"True… they don't react to pain… as much as a person should…" Lucia said. She then drew her long sword and plunged it into the crawling man's back. After struggling for a few moments, he ceased all movement.

"Well then, that makes four kills for me, and one for you," Dalton said.

"I already told you: I'm not playing your ga-" She raised an eyebrow in realization, then shot him an icy glare. "I should have two. So, it's three for you, two for me."

"I thought you didn't want to play?" he asked with a sly smile.

"Just because I don't want to make a game of it, doesn't mean you get to cheat."

"The first fella you shot wasn't dead. I had to finish him off myself."

"How odd. Their resiliency cannot be a coincidence… it seems to me that if we don't hit them in a vital spot right away, we need to hit them with a critical follow-up blow," Lucia said, rubbing her chin.

"Right. We aim for the head, neck, or heart. I landed a body shot earlier that would have stopped any normal man in their tracks, but it wasn't enough to put him down…" Dalton trailed off.

After rolling the bodies over the left ledge and into the ocean, the duo continued their stroll up the hill path. Eventually, they reached the top, where the woods began and the path made a sharp turn right. They stayed on the trail, which led them to a large cliff overlooking Bosfueras. However, since the overlook was out in the open, they opted to take refuge in some bushes at the beginning of the woods. From there, they could watch over the town while avoiding detection.

The town below seemed surprisingly normal, to Lucia's eyes. She had expected it to be in complete disarray. How else could a town full of ravenous, angry people live? The streets below were fairly busy, mostly with farmers carrying supplies or walking their livestock. Mixed in with the farms were cozy shacks with small, fenced-in front yards. Each yard was fitted with posts that held one or more lanterns, and again Lucia found herself surprised. These people were not as savage as previously described to her. She had thought that Conrad could outsmart them, but all signs pointed to their competence, and worry began building up in her chest.

"I can't stop thinking about what you said earlier," Lucia whispered. "How do we know Conrad is here? What if he escaped?"

"Then all of this trouble was for nothing…" Dalton muttered with a chuckle. Lucia narrowed her eyes at him. "He may not be here… he could be anywhere. The woods, that river under the bridge, one of these buildings… anywhere."

"When you put it that way, we didn't have much of a plan, did we?"

"We can only use what we're given. For instance…" He pointed to the grand cathedral atop a rocky hill within the town's citadel. Several armored guards patrolled near the stairs and entrance, respectively. "That church must be important for so many to be guarding it."

"You think he's in there?"

"Maybe, but if Conrad has been captured, why hold him in such a place? I'd be looking for *a dungeon*, instead."

"But there's no castle here. Where else would they build one?" Lucia asked.

"If I had to guess," Dalton said as he pointed to a rectangular stone building just outside of the citadel, off of a main road. "My bet would be on *that* building being a dungeon."

Lucia remained quiet as her eyes wandered about the town. Many guards were watching over that stone building, though not as many as at the cathedral. "So, that stone building is our first target, then?"

"Yeh, but the question is: How can we sneak in? It would be unwise to try and take on so many armored guards at once."

The student thought back to their encounter with the crazed men, earlier. They had seemed single-minded, so much so that the mortally wounded man continued to crawl without even paying attention to her or Dalton. He had only been focused on reaching the top when most others would have been too busy begging for their lives.

"I have an idea," she said while standing. "I saw something that could help us, but we'll need to sneak into town."

"There's a chance that we'll be seen, but there is just as good a chance that it'll be from afar. The townsfolk may mistake us for some of their guards thanks to our armor.

The pair trudged down the steep, rocky path. To their relief, they hadn't grabbed anyone's attention by the time they reached the bottom. Now, they were next to a couple of farms. To her left, Lucia saw a lantern hanging from a wooden post. She walked over to retrieve it but found herself repulsed by a strong smell. Her eyes wandered toward a nearby farm stand, and then they widened upon catching the source of the smell: a rotting cow carcass accompanied by a swarm of flies.

THE HUNT IS ON

"What could have done that to a cow?" Lucia asked as she grabbed the lantern with one hand and shielded her nose with the other.

"Let's hope it was just one of the townsfolk," Dalton said.

"I've had to butcher animals before... this is not how it was done. It looks to me like something ate this poor cow raw and alive. There are signs of a struggle and bite marks," she replied.

"Something tells me this is the type of place to have big ol' monsters wandering around," he said with a chuckle. "I suppose we'll have to rely on this plan of yours working if we don't wanna face them. What did you have in mind?"

"A little distraction," Lucia said with a devious smile as she held the lantern up.

※

IN THE DARK, dank dungeon, Conrad sat on the unforgiving and cold stone floor. Only the grimy wall at his back kept him from toppling over. Every movement and breath had become painful. Staying in the filthy cell for days had further infected his injuries, and to make matters worse, they had only fed him one time since being captured. Water came once in a while, but it was always dirty. Everything seemed to be a calculated measure in making him sicker.

But nothing was worse than Mr. Willoughby's shrill, stuttered breaths. In the cell next to his stood the monstrosity, ever watching with its red dots for eyes in a sea of black. Its pained breaths penetrated Conrad's ears every couple of seconds, often eliciting flinches that sent ripples of pain through his infected wounds. Adding to his torture was the creeping dread that at any moment it wished, the monster could break through the iron bars that separated them. Instead, it only chose to stare at him.

Early on, the strategist had taunted Willoughby; inviting it to break through its cell and attack him in the hopes that he could somehow escape. However, it quickly became apparent that it did not react to his words or actions. He had come to suspect that the Dark Wizard had direct control of its mind, or that it only obeyed certain leaders of the town, like Brice. It mattered little now, anyway. At present, if Willoughby were to break through, Conrad would be too weak to defend himself or even evade.

The last embers of the nearby torches had just gone out, leaving him in complete darkness, save the red glow of Willoughby's eyes. But he couldn't bear to look, even if it did provide light. Instead, he closed his eyes and focused on the powerful fumes of smoke that had been left in the wake of the torches. Though normally it would have bothered him and brought out many coughing fits, the smoke had been good for blocking the putrid stench of death and decay that had normally filled the enclosed dungeon. In the fleeting moments of light flooding this cursed space, he could see that the walls and floors were painted with dry blood and filth.

As he felt himself dozing off, Conrad's ears twitched at the groaning of the large metal door from upstairs. A great beam of light shot into the top of the room, but whatever hope it had filled him with was quickly snuffed out when the door slammed shut, and dark overtook him again. Yet, it was not complete darkness; not anymore. He watched with straining eyes as a couple of lanterns bobbed up and down while descending the tall stone steps before him.

Two hooded men approached the cell, and at the bars, they leaned in. Conrad felt himself bathing in light for the first time in more than a day. It had become blinding to his eyes, but underneath his shielding, rickety arm, he could see that the duo had brought down their hoods. He squinted, trying to make out the details of their faces.

"Eyes adjustin' to the dark yet?"

"Brice…" Conrad trailed off. Somehow, underneath all of the strain, he had managed to pepper his response with disdain. "H-how long have I been down here?"

Simply speaking or moving had begun eliciting painful, uncontrollable shivers a day or two ago. He figured it to be a symptom of the infected wounds, slowly killing him.

"Yer already fallin' apart, and it's only been a couple of days!" Brice snickered.

"I know that's not true…"

"This worm hardly draws breath, and has little of interest to say. Why are we keeping him alive?" the other man asked Brice. Conrad recognized his voice, too. It was one of the hooligans, but with his mind in such a haze, he couldn't remember his name.

"Orders from the Dark Wizard," Brice replied.

"Balls ta his orders!" the other man shot back. There was an odd mutation to his voice. It almost sounded like there was food caught in his throat. "Let me in there, and I'll ensure that nothing remains of him save stains of blood… we can say Willoughby did it."

"We'll leave him be, Barret, and that's the end of it!" Brice said with authority.

Barret, he thought. How could he have forgotten? Now, he could picture his long, built posture and curly brown hair. Back at Mt. Couture, he'd always worn a mischievous smirk that suited Brice and his underlings well. Yet, it was his bulging brown eyes that had made him difficult to be around, back then. Looking him in the eye brought to mind some pale, frightening imitation of a human.

"Just give me a few moments with the little maggot. I'll rip him apart and we'll never have to worry about 'im again!" Barret shouted as he smashed a hand into the cell bars. The entire cage rattled, and though the flinching pain surged through Conrad once more, a fire had been lit in his gut.

"Bug-eyed freak," he shot back. Brice chuckled while Barret hissed back at him like an aggressive snake.

"Ye wouldn't be so quick to talk back if I left 'im alone in there with ye!" Brice said with amusement on his tongue.

"Would you disobey your new master like that?" Conrad asked before he began panting. Since the return of his injuries, it had become difficult to speak in long sentences without needing a breather.

"Ye still don' get it. He ain't my master... he has chosen us as partners for his vision of a new world," Brice replied.

"What nonsense…"

"I see yer still not convinced. Maybe a few more days'll smarten ye up!" Brice taunted as he and Barret turned to leave.

"Wait!" Conrad cried out with the last of his energy.

Brice scoffed. "I don' take orders from ye!"

"Let me at him!" Barret said. Through the dim light of the lanterns, Conrad could see the dark outlines of his cloaked form shaking with intensity. "He will provide me with great *nutrients*."

"Ye think I'm gonna let ye in there with him?" the big-nosed man asked while shaking his head. "If anythin', *I'll* be the one to go in there and kill 'im."

"A-and what good will that do you? Th-the Dark Wizard will k-kill you for disobeying him." Conrad was shivering too much to get the words out cleanly. Brice snorted before walking back up to the cell and eyeing him with amusement.

"Did ye know that Feliz was a real person?" he asked. Conrad tilted his head. "I can't take the form of whoever I want, like the Lord of Darkness can. I have to work for it a wee bit more. Feliz was one of the resistant townsfolk. He was too stupid to understand and accept our plan to bring order. Instead of tryin' to change him, I was given an opportunity to test out my new abilities, courtesy of the dark essence."

"Your intimidation tactics need work," Conrad said in defiance. The words had barely left his mouth.

"Shut yer mouth fer once!" Brice boomed back. "Ye *do* wanna know how I took his form, don't ye?"

Conrad sighed and spoke no further. His head sank, but not voluntarily. He could feel his body shutting down on him.

"As I was sayin', the Dark Wizard turned me loose on poor Feliz, and I don' know how or why, but after I ripped 'im to bloody pieces, I got these urges, y'see… so, I tore his head open and feasted on his brain," Brice said to the utter disgust of the strategist. "Oh yes, ye haven't lived until ye've had a lil' taste of another man's mind!"

"You've obviously lost *yours*," Conrad replied. Brice cocked his head before descending into an uncontrollable series of cackles.

"Have I?" he asked as his laughs tapered off into chuckles. "I found out that there was a method to my madness… if I eat someone's brains, not only can I take their form, but I assume their identity as well!"

"So, all of those things you told me…"

"They were the true memories of Feliz. He did live in the drainage system for a while, but then we caught 'im, and, well…" Brice trailed off with a sick smile. "And I must be honest… it would be *real* helpful to assume yer identity and find out more about those friends of yers."

Conrad shuddered. Could he have meant Lucia and the others? They might have been coming for him, after all. They had likely read his letter by now.

"You wouldn't gain anything useful."

"Then, let me kill him!" Barret shouted as he ran up and slammed into the cage, rattling the iron and bending it slightly inward.

Ignoring the surge of pain that coursed through him, Conrad took notice of Barret's face in the dim light of his swaying lantern. Somehow, he seemed different. Although he still possessed the same bulged-out eyes, his face was covered in a light sludge and some sort of dark green grime protruded from his cheeks. Underneath his eyes were large bags, as if he'd not slept in months, and even worse were his teeth, which had all become jagged and yellow.

"What happened to you, Barret?" Conrad asked. "It looks like someone beat you with an ugly stick." He tried to force out a laugh, but they turned into painful coughs instead. Brice got a chuckle out of it, at least.

"The only one gettin' beaten is you!" he shouted back, then wrapped his hands around two of the cell bars and pulled at them horizontally. The iron groaned and bent under the strain of his apparent strength, and Conrad felt a pit come to his stomach. Would this be the end?

"Wait! We have orders," Brice said.

"To hell with the orders! I'm gonna rip 'im to pieces and absorb his nutrients!" Barret replied.

"Barret! Listen to yerself! Yer startin' to sound just like-"

"Willoughby?" Conrad interrupted. At that moment, for some reason, he had remembered that *Gus Willoughby* was the name of one of the hooligans. "So, you've all been mutated into monstrosities like him, then?"

"No, he was given too much dark essence, and he slowly went mad until..." Brice trailed off, eyeing Barret, who was practically frothing at the mouth.

"What?" he asked.

"Look well, gentlemen," the strategist said as he used what little strength he had left to point at Mr. Willoughby. "*That* is your future."

"Ye truly are brainless, ye know that? I just told ye that it has to do with how much dark essence is taken in. First, Gilbert was given such a large dose that it killed him. Then, Gus was given too much, so it turned him into a single-minded monster. The rest of us turned out fine."

"Who says that you all aren't turning into crazed monsters, anyway?" Conrad asked.

"Yer really askin' for it, scum," Brice said while clenching his free fist. "I'll have ye know that the Dark Wizard is out on business fer the day, so we can make up any ol' thing we want as an excuse fer why ye were torn limb from bloody limb."

Hope crept into Conrad's mind. He had monsters to deal with, but if the Dark Wizard wasn't around, perhaps an opportunity to escape would present itself.

As the idea occurred to him, the door from upstairs burst open and light shone into the dungeon once more. The three men shielded their eyes in response.

"Brice!" a voice called.

"The hell do ye want, Powell?" he replied in an annoyed tone.

"A fire has broken out at the north end of town! We need yer help!" Powell said.

"I'm busy!"

"Quit playin' with yer food and get yer ass up here! We need you!"

Brice sighed before turning to Barret. "Come with me."

"Of course," he replied militantly.

Brice and Barret ran upstairs and the great iron door slammed behind them. As the darkness enveloped them once more, Powell walked down the stairs and approached Conrad's cell. The strategist thought that his eyes were deceiving him, but he could have sworn that Powell was fumbling through a key ring, about to release him.

CHAPTER 23
THE WAITING GAME

Brice and Barret stormed toward the northeast end of Bosfueras with several of the townsfolk in tow. True to the efficiency that the Dark Wizard had envisioned, they already had buckets of water in hand and ready to use. As they neared the smoke plume, the jog turned into a dash.

A crowd had gathered around the burnt-down shack. Only embers and smoke remained from the fire. The townsfolk led by Brice and Barret went forth and doused the final remnants with many buckets of water.

"This fire was intentionally set," Brice said.

"How can you be sure?" Barret asked.

He pointed to the left corner of the wreckage, where a farmer's corpse lay. "He wasn't killed by the fire."

Barret narrowed his large eyes at the body. The man's neck had previously been sliced open, although it was well-hidden by the burns he had suffered.

"Another dissenter amongst our ranks, perhaps?" Barret asked.

"I'm leanin' more toward Conrad's lil' friends comin' to rescue him."

"How could they have infiltrated the town without us knowing?"

"I keep thinkin' of that ship the men sunk earlier. What if there were survivors? Even if it ain't Conrad's friends, survivors of that wreckage could cause a problem," Brice said.

"What's our next course of action, then?"

"Send five of the dungeon guards to the beach. Have them check everything from the shipyard to the dock."

Barret nodded and began a stroll back in the direction of the dungeon. Brice stayed behind and oversaw the cleanup of the shack. Everything had to go smoothly while the Lord of Darkness was away, or there would be hell to pay.

∼

POWELL TURNED the key until a loud click echoed in the dungeon over the sound of Willoughby's horrid breaths. The cell door creaked open. From the nasty floor, Conrad gazed up at him in bewilderment as he extended his gloved hand, offering a much-needed boost.

"You're helping me?"

"I'm helping *us*," he corrected.

In the poor lighting of Powell's lantern, Conrad could see that he was a big fellow, probably the same height as Lucia or Alistair. The skin on his face pulsated red, even in the darkness, and his body was covered in many layers of clothing, including a bulky, gray poncho. His previously long, flowing hair had become patchy since the Mt. Couture disaster. Strangest of all, up close, he smelled heavily of burnt leather.

"Can you walk on your own?" Powell asked as the strategist stumbled. He gained balance by grabbing onto one of the bent iron bars in his cell. Despite all of his aches and pains, he couldn't help but shudder. If Barret had gotten a hold of him earlier, he'd have been ripped limb from limb.

"I'll manage…" Conrad replied as the red man walked through the cell exit and beckoned him.

"Follow me. If we go through the normal passage, we will be caught. But I know of a secret exit," Powell said as he pointed to the left of Conrad's cell. It led to a long, dark hallway.

As Conrad left his cage for the first time in what felt like an eternity, he glanced at Mr. Willoughby. The monster did nothing save stare back at him. He hoped it would be the last he saw of it.

"I take it you want out of here, too?" he asked while hobbling behind the red man through the hallway. To his amazement, it smelled even worse in the hall than in his cell. He felt ready to dry-heave.

"That's right. I've had enough of this stinking hellhole," Powell replied without looking back.

The pair entered a part of the hallway that had several openings on the right and left. They all led to dead-ends with rusty chains hanging from the wall. Some passages contained old, rusty spikes on the walls and even a hole in the ceiling where a noose hung down. It had to be a torture chamber, Conrad thought.

"Then, I must ask the obvious question: Why are you not like the others? They have all been brainwashed."

"I don' know, but I don' wanna stick around to find out if they're gonna brainwash me, either," Powell replied as they took a left down a new corridor. "I didn't like you so much back when you led us on the Mt. Couture expedition, but I realize now that Brice ain't of sound mind. I just wanna go back to my old life in Faiwell. You were right not to trust him, back then."

"He may not have been kind, but he wasn't *this bad* one year ago…" the strategist trailed off. "That's why I figured the dark essence would have altered your minds. I can see that your appearance has changed. Yet you have not experienced a personality change? It's strange…"

"That's right. They experimented on us; turned us into monstrosities. I can't go a day without burnin' through my clothing… and I can't touch anyone skin-to-skin, anymore. They've already taken most of my humanity away. But not my mind. That's why I gotta get out of here. Will you help me?" Powell said as the pair came to the end of the hallway. They could either take a left or right. The red man chose right.

"I don't think there's much I can do…" Conrad muttered as he heard pitter-patter behind him. He jerked his neck and looked back, but it only revealed an immense pain in his shoulder. Nothing was there.

"Somethin' wrong? Is there anyone followin' us?"

"I thought that I heard something, but no one's there," he replied while gingerly turning his head to face forward once more. "I did notice that the river dumps out into an ocean. Does Bosfueras have a port where we could perhaps commandeer a ship?"

"Most of the ships were destroyed when the Dark Wizard took over," Powell said as he took a right down another corridor. Conrad heard more pitter-patter from behind and turned his head back in slow motion. Once again, nothing was there. "However, as tribute, the people of Bosfueras have been constructing a great ship in the Dark

Wizard's honor. It is, without a doubt, the largest vessel I've ever seen. But I'm not sure if it is complete…"

"Let's hope that it's finished," Conrad said. "It is likely our best option."

"So, you truly came here alone? You have no backup? No one to help us?"

"I'm afraid not…"

"That's surprisin'. I remember back at the mountain, you were all about making plans. Why did your infiltration of Bosfueras have such little thought put into it?" Powell asked.

"I wasn't given much choice," the strategist said with a chuckle that immediately turned into painful coughs.

"What about yer friends?" the red man asked as he took another right down the corridor.

"What about them?" Conrad replied. The fact that they had taken three rights in a row wasn't lost on him. One more would mean that they were going in circles.

"Wouldn't they come an' try to rescue you? Do they know you're here?"

"I had no opportunity to tell them. The Dark Wizard disguised himself as a Wizard from the Council and said that infiltrating Bosfueras was a secret mission. I wasn't allowed to tell anyone," Conrad said; a half-truth. He had decided not to say anything about his letter to Lucia.

"I see…" Powell trailed off as he took another right down the hallway.

"That makes four right-hand turns we've taken, now. Are you sure you know where we're going?"

"Oh, I know where we're going," the red man replied before taking a left at the end of the corridor. Conrad felt relief sweep over him. "Did anyone notice that we were gone, back in Faiwell?"

"I did," he replied with a sigh. He then stopped in the middle of the corridor and rested against the wall. It felt like his skin was deteriorating. Powell halted and turned back to face him. "Are we almost there? I don't think I can last much longer. My wounds are festering…"

"We are close," Powell assured him, then turned and resumed his walk down the corridor.

Conrad hobbled along, often hearing things behind him like the jingling of chains or the slaps of bare feet against the floor. He no longer had the strength of body or mind to look back. After walking straight down the corridor for some time, Powell took a right, which led them to a hallway that was glowing a slight tint of purple. The apparent source was coming from the end of the corridor.

"What is that odd light?" Conrad asked.

"You'll see."

"If you wish for me to trust you, then you're going to have to be forthcoming." He once again stopped and leaned against the wall.

The red man paused and then turned to face him. "We've already come this far. If I was going to hurt you, then surely I would have done it by now. Don't turn back now when you're *this close*."

And there it was, Conrad thought. The beckoning he could never seem to resist. Anytime he felt 'close' to the conclusion, it was nothing more than an illusion; a trap set to punish him more. Would this time be the same? Something felt wrong to him, but Powell's logic was sound. If he wished it, he could have killed him at any time. What would be the point of bringing him all this way?

"Very well…" Conrad sighed. He pushed off the wall and stumbled before catching himself on the parallel wall. Every motion had become an immense effort, and his eyes felt heavier than lead.

"Come. Let's escape this wretched place," Powell said with excitement on his tongue.

After a long, slow walk down the corridor, the pair entered through an archway that glowed purple from within. Conrad scanned the circular room, looking for the odd light source. Along the walls were rusty chains with cuffs at the end. Directly across, he spotted a set of stone stairs that hugged the wall and led to a big, metal door. In the middle-left section of the room, his eyes picked up on a well that was filled to nearly the top with a dark purple liquid, mysteriously bubbling and pulsating; as if it were alive.

"Is that the dark essence?" Conrad asked, leaning up against the rounded wall for rest.

"A more concentrated dose, yes," Powell replied. He walked over to the well and gazed into the odd liquid. "This is what the Dark Wizard gave us to change our bodies. The residents of the town got a lesser form of the essence. They are resistant to pain but obedient to the death. *This* dark essence strengthened my body, but I am in control of my mind."

"Or so the Dark Wizard would have you believe…" Conrad said, slumping. His legs had become wobbly and now his vision was blurring.

"Are you alright, over there?" he asked, walking up to him with narrowed eyes. "Oh, your wounds are worse than expected. There's no way you'll make it out, in this condition."

"I'll find a way."

"There is a way that we could both get out of this mess alive."

"How?"

"I think the reason I am not as crazed as the others is because I was given *less* of the dark essence than what they received. If you were to take in the dark essence, it would heal all of your wounds and make you powerful. That way, you'd be healthy, and we could fight our way outta here together," Powell said.

"I don't like that idea," Conrad replied, then took a deep breath and stood under his own power. "Look at what it did to your skin."

"That's because the dark essence tries to correct any weakness you have at the time of acceptin' it. For some reason, up 'till recently, I would get cold all the time…" Powell trailed off.

"So, it took that as a weakness and made you warm all the time?"

"Exactly. Your weakness is the infection from your wounds. What ill could possibly come of that? The dark essence will probably imbue you with strong regenerative abilities," the red man said. "All you have to do is drink a little, and we can be on our way."

The strategist's eyes wandered over to the well. Once again, Powell's logic was sound. It would be like taking and using one of the enemy's weapons, he thought. However, something scratched at the back of his mind, telling him not to do it. This time, he decided to trust his instincts.

"No… I don't think I will," said Conrad. The red man returned a puzzled stare. "If I slow you down, you can always leave me behind."

"You should reconsider. This could be the difference between life and death," Powell said.

"I realize that. But at the expense of my body? Or perhaps my humanity? It's not worth it."

"But I-"

"We should get moving," Conrad said.

Powell snorted. "Very well…"

With his first step taken across the room, Conrad spotted something out of the corner of his eye: two red dots, slowly growing larger as they approached. A pair of eyes. Was it Willoughby? *No*, he thought, it couldn't be. The monster's horrid breaths were absent. This was someone else, but he didn't wish to find out who. Conrad pointed across the room, to the door atop the small stone staircase.

"Is that the exit?" he asked in a panicked tone.

"Yes, it is," Powell replied while adjusting his gloves.

"There's no time to waste, then."

Conrad walked past the red man with as much haste as his body would allow and painstakingly climbed the stairs. Midway up, however, he felt a warming in his ankle, and in a split-second, it became a searing pain. It was as if red-hot iron cuffs had been fastened on him. Could the infection have spread down to his legs?

He looked down to see a red, steaming hand gripping his ankle through a melted hole in his boot. His skin, in but a few seconds, had burned down a couple of layers. He looked over his shoulder with wide eyes to see that it was a de-gloved Powell who had grabbed hold of him.

The full scope of the pain finally dawned on him, and Conrad let out a weak cry as he collapsed. Powell stepped aside as he tumbled down the stairs and landed on the unforgiving stone floor with a *thud*. The red man stood over him with a devious grin.

"Why? What... was the... point?" Conrad asked between labored breaths.

"Information, my naïve friend," he replied with a vain laugh. "Now, we know that no one's coming for your sorry hide. We can mess about with you all we like."

"And... the dark essence?"

"That would have made your life easier, to say the least. You would have broken the shackles of your pitiful humanity and achieved power beyond your wildest dreams."

A scoff escaped Conrad's trembling lips as his consciousness faded. "If obtaining power... means looking like... you or Barret... then I'd rather be weak..."

All went black as the haunting laughs of Powell filled his ears.

∽

ATOP THE STEEP cliff that overlooked Bosfueras, Lucia and Dalton struggled to catch their breaths as they hid in some thick bushes. After setting a shack ablaze and killing a man who had tried to interfere, dozens and dozens of townsfolk had descended on the fire with buckets and pans of water in hand. Dalton had made the call to retreat just before their arrival.

"Do you think they saw us?" Lucia asked.

"Maybe… but maybe we blended in with those armored guards, too. No one has chased us up here," Dalton said as he parted the bushes and peered down into town. There were still trails of smoke coming from the fire they had started, but the blaze itself had been put out. "They're an efficient lot, aren't they?"

"In Faiwell, that fire would have spread to at least a few other shacks before being put out," she said.

Dalton smirked. "By the way, I got another kill back there, so that makes it five-to-one. You better focus, or-"

"There's hardly any point in this game of yours, since the result is obvious: You win in all of our contests," Lucia said.

"What happened to your competitive spirit?"

"It died out, months ago," she replied with a frown. "Make no mistake: You're the anchor of this mission; you give us the best odds of success. I'm not here to prove myself, like at Mt. Couture."

"Your lack of confidence is troubling," Dalton replied. "What leads you to believe that you are merely a passenger and not a valued ally?"

"My time in Luneria forced me to become strong; to be my own woman…" she trailed off, looking down. "But since returning to you one year ago, it feels like everything is slipping back to how it once was. I felt unbeatable back when I was a mercenary. Yet now, when I am no longer fighting 'unskilled opponents', as you once put it, my limitations have become apparent."

"I said what I had to say for you to drop that unwieldy claymore and start wiping the floor with your opponent's blood," Dalton replied with a few chuckles.

"Is that what happened, though?" Lucia asked, twitching her nose. "I lost the battles when they were most important at Mt. Couture. The irritation of my burns and aching shoulder are constant reminders. I thought that if I worked harder and improved my technique, that I could reach your level; become unparalleled and untouchable in combat… but what if *this* is my ceiling?"

Dalton laughed. "Quit feelin' sorry for yourself, foolish student."

Lucia's eyes widened, which made the red crescent-shaped tattoo around her eye stretch. He couldn't help but laugh even harder.

"Your father used to say somethin' like that whenever I was whining, as you are now. If you lose on the battlefield while clinging to life, then it is not truly a loss. It's experience. Your aches, pains, and scars are but reminders not to repeat your mistakes," Dalton said as he pressed his back against a tree and sat. "Be thankful for what you have. What you gained at Mt. Couture was far more valuable than what you lost. That's why we're here, isn't it?"

She returned a weak smile. "True…"

"In most countries, a squire reaches the title of knight by the age of 21. Obviously, that ain't how we do things in Faiwell, but the way I see it, you still have another year left of training under me. I don't believe you've reached your ceiling yet, and even still, you are already the best student I've ever had," the warrior said. Lucia continued to look down as if contemplating.

Dalton smiled while looking at her. He'd been in a similar situation when comparing himself to her father back when he studied swordplay under him. Adrian had always bested him in their practice duels and shined brighter than all while in true combat. Like all good mentors, he had identified Dalton's desire to surpass him and used it to help him develop skills that otherwise would have gone untapped.

However, while Dalton had been trying to draw out Lucia's potential in the same way, he was beginning to realize how different her motivations were in the pursuit of greatness. After all, she had spent most of her life being shown or told that she was a burden; that she wasn't good enough. As a result, she always had something to prove; so much that she'd run away and lived on her own for five years to show her quality. She had carried around an oversized weapon that had no place on the battlefield to intimidate potential opponents and prove her strength. Now that she had proven most of her naysayers wrong, though, there was one more who she had to overcome: herself. Deeply embedded in her mind was a self-doubt that couldn't be undone with talking or training. The only cure was for her to see the results of her training while in a true battle to the death.

Now, there's an idea, Dalton thought with a knowing smile. "It seems to me that we should strike at night when most of these people are asleep. For now, we must play the waiting game. Agreed?"

Lucia nodded. "We'll have to pray that the pirates wait for us, but I agree."

Her words felt tired and lacking in inspiration. Yet, Dalton was sure that he could bring out her fighting spirit. All she needed was a little push.

SEVEN SEALS

∽

BACK AT THE CRESCENT-SHAPED BEACH, Captain Auber and Ebbie jogged in the direction of the shipyard. As the most all-around-skilled of the Pirates, Franco had remained behind to patch up any problems with their ship that weren't related to the sails. At the northern shore was a ramp that led up to a large, wooden building.

As the pair approached the ramp, something glistened out of the corner of Auber's right eye. He turned to see five armored guards marching across the bridge, over the river to the east. In a panic, he put his hands on Ebbie's back and pushed while sprinting for the shipyard door.

"Oi! What're ye doin' cap?"

As they stumbled through the entrance, Auber grabbed Ebbie's wrist and pulled him to the left, pushing his back up against the wall and looking through the sharpest of angles to the outside.

"What is it?" the first mate asked, to which he was shushed.

The pair looked outside for a short while before the shine of the armor reflected into Auber's eyes once more. "Ahh... can our luck be *any worse*?"

The five guards split up to search the area, and one was headed for the shipyard.

"Damn it all..."

"We can take 'im together, captain," Ebbie said with a brazen smile.

"Are ye mad? He's well-armed and wearing plated armor! We don't gots a ghost of a chance," the captain said as he looked around the inside of the shipyard. "Gotta find a place to hide..."

As his eyes adjusted to the darkness, Auber finally saw what was living in it: A massive, black ship with several decks stacking both back and upward. A whopping eight sales draped down from its impossibly high masts. The captain estimated that it was close to 100 meters long; the biggest ship he'd ever seen.

"Blimey, cap! Look at that behemoth! We should just use *that ship*." Ebbie pointed to it with child-like wonder and excitement.

"It be too risky to go back and forth across the beach," Auber said as he ran to the ship's side in search of a ramp to enter. "Our crew ain't big enough to handle somethin' like this, anyhow. That said, it'll make fer a good hidin' spot."

In the darkness, Auber finally found the ramp by crunching his toe against it. He wanted more than anything to curse out the wretched thing but knew that it might mean his death, with the guard nearby. Up the steep and long ramp the duo ran, until their legs burned and their breaths became heavy. Upon reaching the deck, the captain and his first mate took a moment to wipe the sweat from their collective brows. After the quick breather, Auber motioned toward the railing at the other side, straight ahead. With a brisk walk, they reached the railing and peered over it, on the lookout for their enemy.

It wasn't long before the glint from the guard's armor hit their eyes once again. The man stood in the entrance doorway, motionless, except for his helmet turning back and forth. He appeared to be surveying the area.

"What's he doin'?" Ebbie asked.

"Dunno, but keep it down over thar. We don' wanna get caught."

"Yes, captain."

∽

Franco watched over the beach from his hiding spot in the crow's nest of the ship. One of the armored guards approached the watchtower and knelt before picking up a clump of sand and sifting through it with his thumb. Another guard dragged the body of the watchman out of the water. He called out in another language to his cohorts, and then, with the help of a couple of others, brought the corpse over toward the middle of the beach, next to the watchtower.

"Not good…" he muttered.

In the meantime, the last of the guards walked along the dock and boarded the damaged ship. Franco ducked for cover within the nest, and for a little while, he heard the heavy thuds of the man's steps, his rummaging, and his slamming of doors. As he had first suspected, though, with so much armor on, he was not willing to climb up to check one small space. The navigator breathed a sigh of relief as he heard the clunky steps going off of the exit ramp.

After waiting some time for the coast to clear, Franco spied over the edge of the crow's nest once more. He let out a snorting chuckle to see that the guards had all convened right at the shipyard entrance.

"The captain's not going to like this. Not one bit," Franco said to himself in an amused tone.

∽

"Oh, come on…" Auber lamented under his breath as he made shooing motions toward the guards, who nearly blotted out all light from the outside.

However, after a short time, all but one of them left. As relieved as he was to see only one remaining, why the hell had he stayed behind at all? Had they discovered the body of the watchman?

"I say we fight," Ebbie suggested.

"'Course ye do. But we ain't doin' that. Our best chance is ta sneak around. And we still need to find some sails that fit our boat. The ones on this vessel are too big."

"How are we supposed to sneak around or do anythin' with this feller watchin'?"

Auber scratched at his patchy beard. "Erm… I suppose we'll have'ta wait…"

CHAPTER 24
A FEAR OF THE DARK

Auber and Ebbie sulked as they watched the light of day begin to dim outside the shipyard building. The guard blocking their only exit hadn't moved a muscle, and in searching the ship, they were unable to find a sail that would fit their own vessel.

"I think there are some supply rooms in the building," Ebbie whispered. He pointed to the back-left corner of the structure, and since his eyes had adjusted to the dark, Auber was sure that he could see some small rooms.

"But we can't risk gettin' caught… that damned guard… if only he'd leave…" Auber muttered in frustration. He then turned to the guard from his railing and his face contorted something bitter; as if he'd been sucking on a lemon. "Go on, git!" he hissed under his breath.

"We can't keep waitin' around, cap. We gotta do somethin'. 'Tis already dusk," Ebbie said.

"I know, I know," Auber replied, shooing him away with a hand motion.

"Why don' we lay out a trap for him?"

"Oh? What kinda trap?" the captain asked, his eyes suddenly alight.

∼

From the ship's deck, Ebbie picked up a barrel and threw it against one of the cabin walls with all of his might, splintering it to pieces on contact. He dashed to the railing, his heart beating faster than his steps, and grinned to see that the guard had stirred. With his poleaxe at the ready, he was marching around the vessel. The first mate's excitement reached a boiling point when he heard the guard's plodding steps coming up the ramp. He drew his short sword and awaited his opponent at the center of the main deck.

The armored man tilted his head when he reached the top, but showed no true hesitation and continued his strides forward. With his posture crouched and his vented breaths eerily echoing through the helmet, Ebbie was beginning to feel like prey. Somehow, it only excited him more.

"Come and face me, if ye have the bluster!" he cried.

The guard let out a low-pitched laugh and approached with his poleaxe extended outward. In addition to the obvious dangers of the axe head's chopping capabilities, it had a spike at the top that was sure to fatally wound if a stab were landed. Ebbie could tell he was at a massive reach disadvantage, too. Sweat dribbled down from his forehead and into his eyes. Though still excited to engage in combat, he couldn't help but admit to himself that it was a *nervous excitement*.

With but a moment's notice, the guard took a swing from far away, to which Ebbie hopped back and avoided. The armored man then transitioned his swipe into a lunging stab, and yet again the first mate evaded by backpedaling. With each swing and stab of the axe, Ebbie stepped backward, further and further, until he felt his back touch the ship railing.

Ebbie's eyes widened as the guard raised his poleaxe overhead for a final strike. There was nowhere left to run.

"Captain! Now!" he called out.

Auber jumped out from behind a crate on the deck and dashed toward the armored guard at a speed that caught Ebbie off-guard. He plowed into the man's back and let out a cry that rang both ferocious and desperate. The guard stumbled forward and dropped his poleaxe in response, and Ebbie bent down before lifting with his back to send the armored man flying over the railing.

"Gah!" Ebbie cried as a surge of pain shot up his spine. Still, the sound of splashing and thrashing in the water below brought him too much joy for some mere aches to ruin his mood.

He and Captain Auber approached the railing while rubbing their back and shoulder, respectively.

"We should leave before he escapes the water. He'll probably be mad!" The captain turned to leave.

"Wait!" said Ebbie. Auber froze and then returned to the railing for closer inspection. "I don' think this feller can swim…"

"Oh?" the captain muttered as he leaned over the railing with interest. The armored man was thrashing about in the water and shouting what sounded like obscenities in a different language, but he wasn't moving anywhere. He dunked underwater more and more until it became common. Auber grinned with pride. "Hah! Serves ye right! Messin' about with the great Captain Auber will often get ye killed!"

"Well… should we save 'im?" Ebbie asked. The captain returned an expression of pure bewilderment: Both eyebrows shot up and his jaw hung open. "What? All I'm sayin' is that it ain't sportin' to win like that."

"We're pirates, Ebbie! We don' do this fer sport! Let the bastard drown!"

"Yes, sir!"

The pair walked off the ship ramp and eventually, the splashing and shouting ceased. They made their way to the back corner of the building to find several supply rooms, where they sifted through the inventory as fast as possible. Over time, the duo came across a wide variety of sails.

"Which ones do we take, cap?" Ebbie asked.

"All of 'em."

"But there's gotta be at least ten in here."

"Well, we don' have time to sit around measuring 'em, now do we? We'll have to take all the sails and hope that some fit," the captain said as he handed a wrapped-up sail to his first mate. "You'll have to take most of 'em. I really hurt my shoulder back there, savin' ye from the guard an' all…"

"Y-yes sir…" Ebbie muttered as the weight of all the sails nearly crushed him.

∼

It was a funny sight for Franco to see Auber running toward the ship with two sails over his shoulder, while Ebbie fell far behind, struggling to carry eight at once.

The navigator descended from the crow's nest and awaited his cohorts. When they finally arrived, both were panting, but Ebbie especially. His face had turned beet-red, and he'd been drenched in sweat.

"How did you manage to evade the guard?" Franco asked.

"Oh, we didn't… evade 'im at all!" Ebbie replied between his heavy breaths. He dropped the sails at Franco's feet.

"That's right! I had to get a lil' rough with 'im, and then he was killed. But that's what happens when ye challenge the mighty Captain Auber to a duel!" Auber added with a raised fist.

Ebbie panted like a dog, and the frustration in his eyes was obvious. "B-but… I…"

"And a mighty duel it was! He nearly killed me, but in the end, I pulled through with but a minor shoulder injury!" Auber said with pride.

"Ebbie didn't help you at all?" Franco asked.

"Well… maybe a little," the captain replied before turning to his first mate. "Well done, Ebbie! Yer a credit to the Auber Pirates."

"Thank you, sir!" Ebbie said with splendor.

Auber put hands to his hips and then nodded at his crew. "Now then, let's get those new sails up."

"Yes, I can see you obtained a variety. Let's hope they fit," Franco said as he grabbed one of the wrapped-up sheets. "And what of the two warriors? It seems the guards are onto us. I saw them headed back into town, perhaps to gather reinforcements. They found the body of the watchman."

"We can give 'em some time," Auber said. "But if they ain't back before dawn, we gotta go. I suppose the rest is up to them. We stand to gain much from those two, but if it seems like we're at risk, we're leavin', and that's the end of it."

The crew nodded in agreement and got to work on fitting the sails.

⁓

Conrad was thrown back into his cell by Powell like a ragdoll. Still unconscious, his head bounced off the back wall after skidding across the grimy floor. The red man snickered as he watched the stream of blood flow down the side of his neck.

"Pitiful! Was I so fragile before the transformation?" he asked aloud, a smirk coming to his face.

"I was wonderin' where you went off to," Barret's distorted voice called from behind. There was an unmistakable buzz coming from the deepest part of his throat, and it also sounded like there was food in his mouth. Powell looked back to see him sitting on the stairs. "Takin' him out of the cell like that was reckless."

"He's too weak to run away, now. I was just gettin' some information outta him," Powell replied with a shrug.

"And what did you learn?"

"His friends have no idea that he's here. So, we won't have any Wizards to deal with."

"Anything else?" Barret asked.

"Not much. He's clueless. He came all the way here not knowin' what he was gettin' into or even knowin' how to escape," Powell said, holding back a few chuckles. "For my own jollies, I took him to the chamber to see if he would accept the dark essence and become one of us. The fool turned it down!"

The hooligans laughed in unison.

"I'm surprised you didn't leave him trapped in that maze; let Daniel have his way with 'im," the bug-eyed man said.

"If I did that, there wouldn't be anythin' left of that little vermin. We gotta keep him alive for the Dark Wizard, for some reason," the red man replied.

"I still don't understand," Barret said as he made his way down the stairs and stopped in front of Conrad's cell. "What does the Lord of Darkness see in him? He is weak! Naïve! Little more than fodder! Nutrients!"

"You sure have been talkin' a great deal about 'nutrients', of late," Powell said, raising a thin eyebrow. "You ain't thinkin' of *eating him whole*, are you? That's how it all started with Willoughby, and-"

"Don't be ridiculous. I'm fine. All I'm sayin' is that he's a waste of space," the bug-eyed man said as the iron door atop the stairs opened.

Powell smirked. "We should kill him now and say that Willoughby did it…"

"You'll do no such thing." Brice's authoritative tone echoed from the stairs. His subordinates looked to him, each frowning, as he descended. "The Dark Wizard left me in charge, and I'll see to it that everything is as he left it. That includes keeping Conrad alive."

"He can't blame us if he thinks it was Willoughby," Powell said.

"Ye are not to lay another finger on him. Understood?" said Brice in a curt tone.

"You've been barking orders at us for a long time. But now that I think of it, why should I listen to you? The Dark Wizard is the only one powerful enough to give me orders," Powell replied with a defiant grin. He looked back to Barret for support, but he had already backed down like the frightened servant he was.

"Do ye need a reminder of the pecking order 'round here?" Brice asked as he held his arm out in Powell's direction. His fingers began to turn black, and he could only see their outlines in the dim light of the lantern that had been placed on the bottom stone step.

"Yer threatenin' me? Mayhap I should melt that big ol' nose of yours down to size, so you'll shut yer mouth!" Powell retorted.

Black tendrils shot out of Brice's hand where the fingers once were, and they curved and twisted around in an unpredictable pattern at high speeds; too fast for Powell to react. The red man gasped as the tendrils came to a sudden stop within inches of his body: one near his eye, another at his temple, a third one at his neck, a fourth at his heart, and a fifth at his stomach. All in the dungeon fell silent.

"Any further questions?" Brice asked.

Powell sighed and looked down with shame. In the dark, where those damned tendrils blended in, he didn't stand a chance. "No, sir…"

"Good," the big-nosed man said as the tendrils retracted and reformed into the fingers on his hand. "Someone set fire to a shack, up there. The guards have reported that someone killed the watchman on the beach, as well. I believe the culprits were *his* friends." He motioned to Conrad.

"But I questioned him. He said that no one knows of his presence here," Powell said.

"And what makes ye think that he would tell ye *anythin'*?"

"I tricked him into thinkin' I was gonna help him escape."

"Do you truly believe he'd fall for that?" Brice asked with some chuckles. Powell sneered at him in return. His leadership was becoming difficult to tolerate. "It's obvious to me that ye ain't fit to watch over the prisoner. Instead, yer gonna come up and patrol the town with me."

"But I…"

"Barret, I'm counting on you. Keep your hands off of him, and make sure he stays put. Soon, if the Lord of Darkness sees fit, he will be one of us," Brice said before motioning for Powell to follow him up the stairs.

"Yes… of course…" the bug-eyed man replied.

CONRAD AWOKE to blurred vision and a pounding headache. Even worse was the crushing reality of Mr. Willoughby's shrill breaths; and worse still was the sight of Barret, mindlessly staring at him through the cell bars. He reached to the back of his head and felt the blood stain his fingers. The wound was sensitive; fresh.

With a weak sigh, the strategist looked to Barret. "Shall we have a chat?"

Barret scowled as his bulging eyes somehow seemed to widen more. He didn't speak, but his expression told all: He was ready to break into the cell and attack him. All it would take was a little push.

"I wonder what's going on out there..." Conrad muttered.

"What is that supposed to mean?" the bug-eyed man asked with contempt on his tongue.

"Oh, it's nothing... I just told some friends of mine that I would be here. In case the mission went wrong."

Barret raised an eyebrow, and in the dim light, Conrad gasped to see that the brow was falling apart: Only a few hairs remained.

A vain yet distorted laugh escaped Barret's lips. "Are you talking about those outcasts from the minin' expedition?"

"Those 'outcasts' stayed at the mountain and fought alongside me while you ran away. They are far more capable than yo-"

Barret slammed his fist into one of the cell's iron bars, and it groaned and bent enough that Conrad's shoulders shot up to his ears.

"We had no choice but to leave, and you know it!" he shouted.

Conrad knew that he was playing a dangerous game, and even more, his jittery body knew it, too. He took in a deep breath to regain his calm.

"I question both your strength *and* courage..." Conrad trailed off, panting. Every action, even talking, was an exhaustive process. "It is little more than bluster. You're nothing without Brice... just like the other hooligans..."

Barret hissed and let out a throaty buzz that almost sounded like a burp and cough combined. Just what was he turning into? Powell had said that the dark essence 'corrected' one's ailments at the time of accepting it into their body. What could Barret's ailment have been?

"What's your end-game?" he asked. Much to Conrad's surprise, he had regained his composure. "It should be obvious by now just how easily I could kill you... do you have something planned? A trick that could fell me, should I break into the cell and attempt to end your wretched life?"

Conrad couldn't help but smirk, even if only for a brief moment. Barret had given him a little too much credit. What he had in mind could hardly be called a 'plan'. It was merely a desperation move, for despite the obvious gulf in their physical abilities, especially in his current pitiful state, there was certainly no happy ending in sight if he stayed and waited in his cell. His best hope, though not a good one, was for Barret to break into the cell and for Conrad to somehow evade him and escape.

"I can no longer stand this horrible place…" Conrad mumbled. "So, finish me off. You said I'd be good nutrients, didn't you?"

"Nutrients…"

"That's right… kill me while you still can and get your nutrients."

"I need… nutrients…" Barret said, entranced.

Conrad fought against his stiff legs and throbbing ankle to stand while Barret felt the iron bars that separated them. He slammed his fist into the metal, and a piece of it flew off. He repeated the process to a different part of the bar, and more of it broke off.

With each piece of metal *clanging* off the ground, Conrad found himself flinching. It would be the end of his torment, one way or another. Yet the idea that he could be ripped apart like a small bug horrified him. He remembered back to Greed tearing Wolfgang's corpse to shreds like soft meat on a stick, and Mr. Willoughby devouring the cow with relative ease. Had he invited himself to be killed in the most horrific of ways?

Now, Barret had made a hole in the cell four bars wide, bent enough to perhaps make it through. Despite the imminent danger, Conrad's thoughts wandered back to the black gold. It was like a distant, happy memory. He recalled the eased state of mind it had imparted on him. What a shame that he didn't have any on his person right now.

Barret stuck his grotesque head between the bars, which rattled and bent as he started to force himself into the cell. As the strategist made peace with the likely outcome, something unexpected happened: Barret hissed and then fell into a coughing fit. Each cough grew hoarser and more distorted, until finally, he huddled over and vomited a white liquid. In a panic, he pushed himself out from between the cell bars and retreated to the corner of the room, where his repeated heaving echoed off the walls.

Conrad lumbered over to the broken iron bars and inspected the white substance. It was gooey and sticky; clearly not vomit.

"What the hell…" he muttered before returning his eyes to Barret, who remained in the corner.

A distorted, buzzing cry filled the dungeon as Barret's body contorted and shifted in directions that Conrad thought were not possible. Even louder than his screams were the *cracks* and *crunches* of the very bone under his writhing skin. Like a startled beast, Barret turned to face the strategist, and in the dim light of the torches, he saw the same white substance from before, dripping from his mouth.

On his last reserve of energy, Conrad contorted his body to fit through the fresh opening in his cell and then slipped out. On his way through, however, he felt the sharpness of a broken iron bar cut into his stomach and rip through.

Conrad stumbled and fell to the grimy floor, grabbing his sliced abdomen on the way down. He squirmed in pain for a few moments, but there was no time for that. He clawed himself up to his feet and hobbled to the stairs. At the first step, however, he came to a sudden stop. The dungeon exit required a key. Barret would almost certainly have one, he thought, but would it be worth the risk of approaching him?

In a split-second decision, the strategist instead headed for the maze that Powell had taken him through earlier. While it was true that the red man had lied to him about his intentions back then, all good lies were told in partial truth. There was sure to be an alternate exit as Powell had originally claimed.

About halfway down the first corridor, a great crash echoed from back in the dungeon, followed shortly after by the *clanks* and *clunks* of iron bouncing off of stone. Was it Barret? Conrad gingerly looked back to see a dark figure lumbering toward him; its swirling, glowing, red eyes slowly shrinking down into two focused dots. It was the first time he had seen Mr. Willoughby move since being imprisoned.

Panic set in as Conrad turned and began dragging himself down the hallway at a faster pace. In his hurry, he had forgotten to take one of the lanterns from the dungeon, and the further he traveled, the darker it became. He would have to rely on his memory, now.

"A left, then four rights, which brought us to the same corridor… then, we took a left after that, followed by a right. So, the true path is two lefts and a right…" he mumbled.

His legs had lost feeling, and he was light-headed, but his instincts and the shrill breaths of Willoughby pushed him forward. After taking the first left down a new corridor, Conrad heard footsteps from behind. *Not Willoughby*, he thought. They were too quickly paced. Someone, or something, was following him. He stopped and looked back, but as had been the case when he walked the corridors with Powell earlier, nothing was there.

Conrad continued down the corridor, but at a slower pace. His injuries had caught up with him, and even the rush of his escape couldn't power him through the pain and loss of function. His right foot began to drag, as it was the right ankle that had been burned by Powell's touch. Both legs had been hurt by the mutated animals of Bosfueras, so even his left leg couldn't do much lifting.

Eventually, Conrad reached a new corridor by turning left. He heard the footsteps behind him once more. The breaths of Mr. Willoughby were also present, but they echoed from far off. Whatever transformation was occurring with Barret couldn't have ended. Otherwise, he would have caught up and confronted him. It had to be something else.

"Come out and face me," the strategist said. His voice bounced down the hall, but there was no response.

Despite his worries, it seemed that, for now, his best option was to push it out of his mind and continue on. After all, stopping too many times would allow the monstrosity lurking behind to catch up. After a painstaking walk, he made a right-hand turn down the last hallway before the dark essence chamber. It was the same as before: A glowing, purple hue clung to the walls and beckoned him.

The final stretch, Conrad thought while limping ahead. A smile grew on his face as he neared the glowing room. Finally, freedom. It didn't matter if he wasn't out of Bosfueras, yet. After escaping the rotten dungeon, he'd find a way. If for no other reason than to see Lucia and the others once again.

Distracted by his happy thoughts, Conrad's dragging foot caught something on the floor and he stumbled, crashing to the ground just shy of the dark essence room. Despite the excruciating pain that was jolting through his body, Conrad turned over and looked up to see the culprit: Before him stood a hunch-backed man with pointy ears, bucktoothed fangs, and solid red pupils that glowed. His skin was a washed-out white, but he was covered in grime and filth. His hair was comprised of a couple of thin strands of brown, and his clothes were torn up.

A pained breath escaped from Conrad's dry lips. "Who are you?"

"Ye don' know me? Heh… I'm one of the hooligans… heh… everyone always forgets about Daniel…" Despite a ghoulish appearance, his voice had felt very human: nasally yet shrill. Somehow, it only made him creepier.

"I thought there were only five of the hooligans: Brice, Gus, Gilbert, Powell, and Barret," Conrad said. He tried to prop himself up, but his arms proved too weak and he collapsed back to the floor.

"Hehe… everyone… heh… always thinkin' I ain't with 'em… hehe…" the creepy man said as he knelt and stroked the outsider's cheek with one of his long, sharp nails.

"I don't remember you on the Mt. Couture expedition…"

"I didn't go. Hehe," Daniel replied before an awkward silence overcame the duo. The creepy man started drooling. Conrad tried not to flinch when the disgusting mucus landed on his shirt. "Daniel had a fear of the dark back then, y'see… heh…"

"I see," Conrad said as he pushed with his arm to sit up. This time, he was successful. "When you took in the dark essence… you became a dungeon-dweller of sorts."

"Heh… that's right… no one ever comes ta visit Daniel down here… they say I play a lil' too rough… heh…" the creepy man said, his red dots for pupils never breaking eye contact.

"I'd prefer it if we chatted outside. What do you say?" Conrad asked.

"No… heh… Daniel don't like the light anymore…"

A nervous smirk came to Conrad's face. "I don't suppose you'd be willing to let me go?"

"No… Daniel would like to play… hehehehe!"

With one hand, the creepy man picked Conrad up by his shirt and then tossed him into the glowing room. He landed hard on the unforgiving floor before it turned to a roll, and the world spun around him as an odd mix of black, gray, and purple. He came to a sudden stop when his shoulder struck something hard enough to send a jolt of pain surging through his body. He looked up with half-open eyes to see that he'd rolled all the way to the stone stairs along the wall. *This was his best chance.*

The strategist scrambled and crawled around to reach the stairs. He started to climb up on all fours, but Daniel caught him by the left leg and dug his nasty nails into the calf, through his boot. Conrad cried out and yanked his leg away. Then, while turning, he cocked his arm back and swung his fist at Daniel's pale face, but the creepy man caught his arm by the wrist.

Wide-eyed, Conrad watched helplessly as Daniel squeezed and he heard the *crunch* of his bones. He wanted to scream louder than ever this time, but couldn't find the energy to unleash anything more than a whimper. All he could do now was look up at the freak of nature hovering over him, and pray that death would come quickly.

"Come on! Play!" Daniel shouted as he slapped Conrad off the side of the head. Even a casual swipe had dazed him. Yet, the daze didn't last long. Soon, he lost all sense of his surroundings and could no longer move. His vision went black, and he choked on his own breaths.

"Daniel don' like it when they don' play… heh…"

The creepy man dragged him off the stairs and back to the middle of the room.

"Please… let me go…" Conrad squeaked out.

"Daniel gets so lonely down here… hehe… you want Daniel to be lonely?"

"No, no, I-" Conrad got out before the creepy man slashed him across the cheek with his nails. The sting of the three slices throbbed, and he could feel the blood trickling down.

Something about the attack had brought out a second wind in Conrad. Perhaps the frustration of his failures had finally gotten to him, or it may have been that he was sick of being abused; but in that moment, the strategist remembered an important detail: the dagger stashed in his boot. It was his final chance to get away.

As Daniel stood over him, ready to take another swipe, Conrad reached into his boot with the opposite, undamaged hand. In one swift motion, he pulled the blade out and stabbed the creepy man in his stomach.

A stunned Daniel let out a gasp as Conrad twisted the dagger for maximum pain and then slashed further as he pulled it out. Now coughing a sea of red onto the wretched floor, the creepy man backed up slowly toward the well of concentrated dark essence. Between the fidgeting fingers that had grasped Daniel's midsection, Conrad spotted intestines and blood. Normally, his weakened state would have invited a follow-up attack, but the strategist was certain that something else would finish him off.

Daniel's left heel caught the curb of the well and he tripped backward, plunging into the darkness with a gasp. The goopy liquid swallowed him whole before he could thrash or make any further noise. It let out several bubbles as if digesting a bad meal.

Conrad gazed upon his dagger: It was dripping with dark red blood. He kept it in hand while turning to the stairs once more, and out of desperation, began crawling up. However, from the corridor behind and off in the distance, he heard a noise that had haunted him for far too long: *the breathing*.

CHAPTER 25
TRANSFORMATION

As the moon shone down on Bosfueras, Lucia and Dalton sprang into action. They snuck into town once again, this time hiding between the alleyways and carts or carriages in the road to avoid detection. Most of the townsfolk had gone indoors for the night. Only the guards lurked, and they tended to hover about the citadel and dungeon to the west.

"I believe there to be a pattern in the collective behaviors of these people," Dalton whispered as they took refuge in the humble backyard of a hut. "Did you notice it?"

Lucia cocked her head before looking down in apparent thought. "Aside from their resistance to damage and pain? Their *focus* is what caught my attention."

The warrior nodded and smiled at his student. "A little *too* focused, methinks. So? What is our plan?"

She opened her mouth, but no words came out; perhaps taken aback that he would push for her to take the lead. After a deep breath, she said, "I say we attempt setting fire to the buildings again."

"Oh? And why do you think that?"

"While earlier today, their response-time was impressive, it was also telling. On our way here, you may remember that we passed over a river," Lucia said, pointing across town, to the southwest. "Based on the trajectory of the river and where those townsfolk came from to put out the fire, I believe their water source to be somewhere over there."

TRANSFORMATION

"Agreed," Dalton replied.

Again, she pointed, but this time hard to the left. "Almost all of these homes have an outdoor lantern, hanging on a post. If we start fires on the eastern end of town, not only will they be slower to respond due to it being nighttime, but it will be a longer distance to the water, too."

"This plan assumes that they will ignore us while putting out the fires, though." Dalton tried his best to hide a smirk. He was very much playing the teacher checking on his student's work.

Lucia held up a finger and smiled. "That's the other half of what was telling about their response, earlier. The path up the cliff is so exposed that nearly anyone rushing to fight the fire should have seen us running up it, especially in our armor. While possible that they could have mistaken us for guards, I find it hard to believe that not a single person came up to inspect for themselves. It is as you said: They are a little too focused. Whatever devilry is going on in these lands has made them dangerously single-minded; so much that they can press on through mortal wounds or fight a fire faster than anyone else in the world not named Aldous."

Dalton let out a few muffled chuckles. "Well said. Now, let's assume that you are correct: We start the fires and they ignore us while putting them out. What's our play to find and rescue Conrad?"

"We must infiltrate either that peculiar stone building or the church… I just don't know which."

"My gold coins are on the stone building. I have seen dungeons that look similar in the past. It likely goes underground and doubles as a hidden fort. Some even house mazes to confuse potential invaders," Dalton said as they exited the backyard of the hut and began walking toward the east end of town.

"The only trouble is that any dungeon worth a damn will be locked up. How many more gold coins are you willing to bet that those armored guards are the ones who hold the key?" she asked.

"All of 'em," he replied with a knowing smile. "It seems there will be no avoiding it: You will soon have to put your skills to the test against difficult opponents. I think that you'll be surprised at the results."

Lucia scoffed. "I'll just try to stay out of your way."

There wasn't a single guard on the eastern side of Bosfueras, but there were plenty of lanterns hanging on posts. Lucia and Dalton gathered one after the other, lit them up, and threw them near wooden shacks and houses. They were careful not to hit their targets directly, as that would alert the unsuspecting townsfolk sooner. In short order, the pair had started over a dozen small fires, and it didn't take long for them to grow into true threats.

By the time they returned to the alleyways at the town's center, the duo could hear panicked shouts coming from behind. The eastern section of town glowed a dark orange and cinders floated through the air like fiery snow. As they exited the alleys and began braving the roads, the pair brushed past speedy townsfolk carrying buckets of water. None of them even glanced their way.

"They're even more efficient than I thought," Dalton said as they walked through the town's main road. "We won't have much time."

"So, let's start another fire," Lucia replied, pointing to a new lantern hanging from a post on their left.

The pair walked over, gathered the lantern, lit it up, and threw it at a wooden house next to them. They repeated the process for a few other homes in the area, each bigger than the last. Larger targets meant that larger blazes might catch on, and in little time at all, the buildings became imposing infernos. More townsfolk approached with buckets, but they ran past the duo and the fires they had set; instead opting to head east.

"As we thought, they are hyper-focused, but why have they ignored this newer fire we've set?" Lucia asked.

"It's simple," a voice echoed from further up the street. Dalton turned to face Brice, and by his side was one of the hooligans, though he did not know him by name. "They have chosen to focus on the fire that is more of a danger to spread. These flames 'round us can wait, because the closer to the citadel ye get, the more prevalent flame-resistant stone buildings become. What do ye think of our collective? I say they're the next step fer mankind."

"A step backward for sure," Dalton replied while drawing his sword.

Brice laughed. "I knew that ye'd show yer faces, eventually. And I just knew somehow that it would be Conrad's lil' friends... is this all that have come to rescue him? I thought he'd be more popular!"

"The Dark Wizard *did* predict that there would be more," the other hooligan said before narrowing his eyes briefly, and then widening them. "But he didn't say nothin' about havin' to fight Dalton Rayleigh..."

"Calm yerself, Powell," Brice said with a venomous grin. "Don't forget that we have surpassed him! He is only human. We'll make short work of these two before they ever get to lay eyes on Conrad."

"So, he is still alive…" Lucia muttered before letting out a relieved breath.

"Well, for now, mayhap. I left him with Barret, and I must be truthful: I think he wanted ta kill the ninny!" Brice replied before bursting out into maniacal laughter.

Before he could cackle any further, though, an arrow flew into his eye with a loud *splat,* as if a vegetable had just been squashed under a boot. Brice gasped before toppling over like a chopped-down tree.

"Next?" Lucia asked as she obtained another arrow from her quiver. Dalton smiled at his student. She hadn't missed a shot with the bow, yet. Soon, he thought, he'd give her that 'little push' that would rejuvenate her fighting spirit.

She next took aim at Powell, who showed neither shock nor concern for Brice's condition. He instead wore a confident smile.

"A fine shot," Brice said as he sat up and pulled the arrow from his eye socket. Although it had originally left a gaping, bloody hole, Dalton and Lucia looked on in horror as fleshy webbings began spreading about, and the eye reformed: First the white of his eye, then the pupil, then eyelids, followed by the lashes.

"But, how?" she asked in disbelief.

"I told ye, we're takin' the next steps for mankind," he replied as the house to their left fully came ablaze and the fire raged on. Dalton looked over his shoulder to see that the hellscape they'd created was slowly simmering and trails of smoke were starting to plume. The flames would be doused in less than an hour. *Change of plan*, he thought. The 'little push' could no longer happen under his supervision.

"I'd bet anything this has somethin' to do with black gold," Dalton said before eyeing his student. "We can't approach this like a normal fight."

Lucia unleashed another arrow, this time at Powell, who let it close in on his chest before reaching out and catching it. The warriors looked on in silent shock as the red man tossed it to the ground. The arrowhead steamed, sizzled, and bent against the dirt and rock, and the shaft had disintegrated into nothing but ash.

"Impossible…" she muttered.

"Nothing is impossible with this power we've obtained," Brice said as he walked toward the duo. Powell strode alongside him. "The Lord of Darkness cures what ails us, and turns our weaknesses into the greatest of strengths. Ye've already caused so much damage to this fine town, so I'm afraid we won't be takin' ye as prisoners."

"Something ain't right with his skin," Dalton whispered to Lucia while looking at Powell. "It's like he's made of lava."

"What can we do about that?" she replied quietly.

Dalton grasped at a small pack hanging from his hip. He retrieved four small white pellets. "These will create a smokescreen. Instead of wasting time on these fools, you go for the dungeon. I'll try to hold 'em off."

Lucia frowned. "But I can't-"

"No. You *can*," Dalton interrupted before smiling at her. "Remember how I told you that I could never defeat your father back when he trained me? It was because he continued to improve alongside me. When it comes to you and me, the situation is the same. I think you'll be surprised at how much you've improved, this past year. Whoever your next opponent may be, I do not envy them."

"Even so, I won't leave you to face these two monsters alone."

"Take these. They'll come in handy," Dalton said as he handed her a couple of the white pellets. "Now, go and get your man!"

"But-"

The warrior ignored her pleas and threw a white pellet to the ground at Brice's feet. It exploded into a great puff of smoke that covered the road and even obscured the nearby fires.

"Too late! I've already decided. Now, go! Meet me at the beach after you've rescued him," he said. To his surprise, she listened, and dashed into an alleyway, out of sight. He let out a chuckle. She had probably only obeyed because it involved saving Conrad.

As the smoke faded, Dalton brought out his shield and slid his arm through the straps until they were at his elbow. Then, he drew the long sword and pointed the blade upward, so it rested atop the shield. Such a stance was rare for him to take, but with the supernatural abilities that Brice and Powell had already demonstrated, he was feeling defensive-minded.

"What was the point of that smokescreen if ye weren't gonna run away, idiot?" Powell asked with a scowl.

"The girl! She's gone!" Brice shouted before a sudden calm came over him. "But no matter, we can dispatch of *him*, easily. She won't get far."

"That's right!" Powell added with a grin. "Mayhap you *are*

Faiwell's greatest swordsman, but it makes no difference. You're still only human!"

As Powell ran at Dalton, his eyes fell to the damaged boots that had melted away at the bottoms, and the ground steaming with each stride he made. His suspicions had been confirmed: He wouldn't be able to touch him directly.

The red man lunged out and attempted a jab, but instead of using his weapon or shield, Dalton sidestepped. Powell stumbled briefly from hitting nothing but air and transitioned into a backhanded swing with his left arm. Dalton once again managed a dodge by backpedaling, but out of the corner of his eye, he saw an odd black substance headed for him. It looked to him like a pack of snakes flying through the air. He threw up his shield to the left and was hit with a crushing impact that sent him crashing to the ground and rolling for a distance before finally stopping.

Dalton looked down at his shield while making it to a knee. His eyes widened at the sight of a great dent; though it had thankfully missed his arm. Just what had the big-nosed man launched at him?

"Do ye understand, now?" Brice asked as the black tentacles extending from his shoulder retracted and formed back into his arm. "It don't matter how skillful ye are. We are all-powerful."

"Power in unskilled hands is worthless," Dalton replied with a smile.

"Are you done with your stupid proverbs?" Powell asked. His face had grown redder, and he was steaming through his heavy clothing. Strands of hair fell from his head, little by little.

"Not quite," he said. As a matter of fact, he'd come up with a plan.

⁓

Lucia ran as fast as her armor would allow to the west side of Bosfueras. The citadel loomed as she passed various buildings that were becoming more and more stone. Her legs grew tired, but the orange glow behind her was a reminder that she was on borrowed time, and with that, she was able to push the burning calves out of mind.

Eventually, the wide, rectangular stone building came into view across the street, to her left. Within the archway of the entrance, there was one armored guard. It was a surprising decrease in security compared to before, and when she looked up at the citadel, she understood why: Over a dozen guards swarmed atop its high walls, and she imagined that even more were guarding the cathedral within.

With a pit growing in her stomach, Lucia approached the guard, eyeing the poleaxe in his hand. Already, she would be at a reach disadvantage, and unlike her, he was wearing a helm to go along with his armor. If he was fully trained, or anywhere near Dalton's skill level, then she was doomed from the start.

"Stand aside," she said, summoning all of the bluster she could. With a smile and nod toward the inferno at the east end of town, she continued, "I'd hate for you to end up like the others…"

The guard scoffed through the opening of his helm before turning and inserting a key into the door. Upon facing her once more, he let out a low-pitched chuckle and held his poleaxe extended outward.

"This is your last chance to surrender," Lucia said, her mind scrambling for the correct response to his polearm. *The shield*, she thought, reaching back for it. It would be unconventional to wield with the long sword, but it was her best option to negate the reach disadvantage.

She couldn't understand the foreign language that he responded in, but the tone had said it all: He wanted a fight, and based on the key he had just inserted into the door, he seemed to like his chances. With the shield strapped to her forearm, Lucia drew her blade and gripped it as tight as she could with a single hand. She had visualized her defensive strategy, but what about offense? With the force of only one hand behind her blows and against his full armor, no less, she would have to attack his relatively few weak points. The joints? The seam between his shoulder plate and helm? *No*, she thought as he neared her with staggered steps in his crouched stance. She needed to disarm him before aiming there.

As the guard leaped from his crouched position and charged her, Lucia let out a stuttered breath; not out of fear, but of surprise. *He's slow*, she thought as he attempted a stab with the spike atop the axe head. Lucia bashed it aside with her shield and followed up with an arced slash of her blade that landed on a couple of his gloved fingers with a *crack*.

The guard grunted and released one hand from his poleaxe, and with that, his next move was obvious. He attempted to wield the polearm with one hand and brought it back from her left with a horizontal swipe. This time, of course, the attack was even slower, and she casually blocked it with her shield.

As it bounced off with a noisy, metallic *clunk*, Lucia brought her other hand to the sword grip and caught the bottom of the axe beard before pulling the opposite way with all of her might. She watched with a smile as the poleaxe spun through the air before landing several paces away.

With his weapon too far away for him to give chase, the armored guard resorted to his sidearm: a long sword of his own. However, even if he was resistant to pain, a couple of his broken fingers refused to close around the grip, which was sure to weaken any strike or attempted block, she thought.

Lucia let the shield drop from her forearm and gripped her blade with both hands once more. She reached her long arms outward, extended a leg back, and baited her sword to lure the guard into a foolhardy attack. She approached the man, who took a basic stance of his own, and they tapped blades.

As soon as she heard the sound of metal clanging, Lucia sprang into action, reaching her blade and simultaneously pushing his to her left. As his sword flailed under a weak grip, she plunged her blade in between the guard's chest plate and helmet, scoring a direct hit on the lower portion of his neck. Lucia ripped the sword out and blood spurted briefly before the guard dropped his stance and covered the wound with one hand. While trying to stop the bleeding in vain, he adjusted to a one-handed style.

"Persistent..." she trailed off while assuming the same long guard stance as before. She could hear his strained breaths through the helm, and his armor had been decorated in red, courtesy of her earlier attack. Now, it was only a matter of picking which joint to attack next. The end was near.

Suddenly, the guard closed in and took a wild one-handed swing with his sword. Lucia blocked the weakened swing with a mere tilt of her blade, and thanks to the lack of recoil, she pushed his sword back and landed a heavy chop on the joint where his forearm and upper arm met.

The guard's arm bent like weak grass against the wind on contact, and he let out a confused grunt as the sword fell from his hand. Blood dripped from the black joint between his armor, and the guard sagged with heavy breaths as he stood between Lucia and the door unarmed: a last-ditch effort to stop her. Without hesitation, she charged in and laid a heavy horizontal slash on the other seam where his shoulder and helm met, and, since the tendons in his right arm had likely been severed, he was unable to stop her.

A fleshy *crunch* echoed in the archway of the stone building as the guard stumbled back and crashed into the great iron door. He slumped over and took his hand off of the neck wound, after which waterfalls of blood spilled out of both sides, pooling messily at the dirt below.

Confusion overcame her as she kept eyes on the motionless man. Had he merely been unskilled? Or was there truly something to what Dalton had been saying, earlier?

With little time to contemplate, Lucia retrieved her shield and shoved the felled guard leftward before kicking the door open. Inside, she could see grimy, stone stairs leading down into a pool of darkness. She grabbed the key from the door and closed it behind her. While descending, her eyes caught on to a light source: Some torches and lanterns were at the bottom, off to the left. With her vision adjusting to the dark, Lucia also noticed a couple of cells that featured several broken bars each, but most obvious to her was the man huddled over in the corner; he appeared to be vomiting.

Upon reaching the bottom of the steps, Lucia drew her sword and shield. "Where is Conrad? What have you done with him?"

The man stood, ceased vomiting, and then turned to face her. There was some sort of white substance pooled at his feet.

"Much better…" he mumbled with a relieved breath. "Who the hell are you supposed to be?" Bits of white liquid spewed from his mouth as he asked.

Lucia approached with caution, raising her shield and resting the long sword atop it, pointed in his direction. "I am here for Conrad."

The bug-eyed man gasped before looking to the cells.

"Damn it all!" he cried, then let out a monstrous hiss that petered out into an odd series of buzzes. Lucia tilted her head as the man calmed himself and smiled. "I'll give you whatever pieces are left of 'im!"

With inhuman speed, he made a run toward the hallway behind her. Aiming for his neck, she took a one-handed, horizontal swing with her sword, but the bug-eyed man ducked it by rolling on the ground. In a smooth motion, he hopped up and continued ahead. Lucia was taken aback at his impressive reflexes.

"Wait!" she cried as he dashed into the dank, dark corridor. Lucia took a step forward to give chase, but she stopped herself and turned her gaze to the lanterns. She would need one to navigate through the darkness.

TRANSFORMATION

~

IN THE CIRCULAR dark essence chamber, Conrad's slow, painful crawl came to an end when he reached the top of the stairs. With the door to his freedom but a mere meter away, all he would have to do was reach up from his downed position and pull the handle. To his right, he could hear the breaths of Mr. Willoughby, but he didn't dare look, for it would likely dishearten him, and he was on his last reserves of strength as it was. With a weak groan, he stretched his arm out and grabbed the handle.

Before Conrad could open the door, the chamber rumbled and an explosion went off behind him, shaking him enough that he lost his grip on the handle. However, the lack of heat and the constant glow of purple off the chamber walls told him that the explosion hadn't been of flame. Rather, it had almost sounded like a geyser of water spouting off. He looked back to see that Daniel had emerged from the well, and he had transformed into a hulking three-meter-tall monster. He remained pale with the same solid red pupils, but his body had become more beast-like. His grotesque hands now had long claws instead of nails, and his feet had become great, oppressive hooves that clicked with each heavy step. He was covered in the dark essence, and much of it had splattered out into the room, including the ceiling and walls.

"Daniel would like to play... hehehe..."

Conrad found himself at a loss. Thanks to the dark essence, Daniel was likely stronger and more monstrous than ever. Meanwhile, he had next to no energy left. As he began to give up all hope, something else caught the strategist's attention: Mr. Willoughby. The other monstrosity stood next to Daniel, looking up at him, then began growling through its long, vile teeth.

"Willoughby wants ta ruin Daniel's fun? Go away!" the creepy man shouted as he brought his claws together and stabbed it in the stomach.

However, Willoughby showed no signs of pain or distress from the blow. Daniel tried to pull his claws out of the beast's abdomen, but a dark red webbing sprouted out and latched on, immobilizing the arm completely.

"Let me go!" Daniel cried in a distorted voice as he brought his other claws back for a strike.

By then, it was already too late. Mr. Willoughby threw a booming backhanded swing at Daniel, connecting with his face so loudly that it stung Conrad's ears and made him dizzy. Like a heavy rock dropped on a pile of jam, red splattered everywhere, including onto the strategist. He gasped when one of Daniel's red eyeballs landed in front of him. Little bits of brain matter stuck to the ceiling, and much of the dark blood hit the wall behind Daniel's now-headless body.

Before the corpse could fall, Willoughby caught it in the nasty red webbing and pulled it closer. The monster opened its unnaturally large mouth and feasted upon the body. Conrad squirmed as he heard the crunch of the bones. Yet, with his disgust came a new opportunity. He turned back and tried to open the door once more. That was when the soul-crushing reality hit him: *it was locked.*

He couldn't help but laugh. It was the perfect metaphor to describe his horrid experiences in Bosfueras. Mr. Willoughby picked the remaining lower half of the corpse up, and to Conrad's horror, its jaw opened even longer and wider than before; reminding him of a year prior when Greed had feasted on Wolfgang as if he were a roasted chicken.

It then shoved the remainder of the body down its mouth, and rather than chew, it absorbed. Willoughby grew to nearly the height of the room's ceiling, and let out an unbearable hiss that paralyzed Conrad, causing him to sag down. He was no longer able to speak or even move his eyes. He had no choice but to watch the monster slowly approach.

Willoughby opened its mouth and from it shot the same dark red webbing that had trapped Daniel before him. He couldn't even squirm under the tight strain of the web and his lack of strength. Now completely helpless, the monster loomed over him, descending its grotesque index finger and thumb to his face and using them to pry his mouth open.

Conrad's mind was panicking, shouting, and thrashing; but his body, even his mouth, refused to obey. He looked up with wide eyes and a thumping heart to see Willoughby open its mouth unnaturally wide. After a moment of sheer terror, the monster let out a black liquid, which poured like hot tea into Conrad's mouth, and then down his throat. His brain told him to choke; to spit it out, but once again, the body refused. Instead, as a natural reflex, he swallowed it.

In a moment of what should have been sheer panic, he began to feel a strange sense of ease. It was similar to his experience with the Dark Wizard's black gold. An empty void, but a peaceful one; one without thought or consequence. His everyday stresses, pains, and sorrows disappeared as he closed his eyes and embraced the dark.

∽

Lucia's long strides through the dark corridor grew even longer and faster when she heard Barret's distorted voice from up ahead.

"Willoughby!" he said. It had come from a room at the end of the hallway, and it was glowing purple. "What in the hell…"

She burst into the chamber and skidded to a stop, her lantern swinging and squeaking in hand. There was much for her to take in: Barret stood ahead, his back turned to her. He faced a grotesque monster that reminded her very much of Greed from one year prior. And the beast, she noticed with a gasp, was standing near Conrad, who had been cocooned in some sort of red webbing on the stairs across.

"Conrad!" Lucia cried. He remained motionless and silent. "Are you alright? Say something!"

She waited with bated breath for a response. Had she arrived too late?

A long sigh of relief escaped her lips to see him squirming under the red webbing, and he turned his head to face her. It almost looked as if he'd just awakened from a nap.

"Be careful…" Conrad said sheepishly. "They are far stronger than humans."

"I suppose that makes it strategy versus brute force, then," she replied with a snort. He let out a weak chuckle.

Barret looked up at the monster before him and said, "Kill her. Now. I will take care of Conrad."

He began walking toward the strategist, but Willoughby sidestepped and got in his way.

"The hell're you doin'? I gave you an order! Stupid beast!"

Lucia watched on in shock as Willoughby wound up its backhand and swiped at Barret, nailing him in the jaw. An unbearable splattering noise bounced off the walls of the chamber, dark red blood and teeth took flight, and Barret stumbled rearward until his back hit the wall. The bug-eyed man's jaw hung by a thread, but it wasn't that which filled Lucia's heart with horror. As he stumbled back toward her, she noticed a dark organ dangling where his tongue *should have* been.

"Nuthleants..." Barret mumbled as he lumbered toward her. "Nuthleants..."

Lucia placed her lantern on the floor and drew the long sword. Barret continued, as if in trance, until he got within range, and she slashed diagonally down at his head. The sword cut deep into the dazed man's skull and black liquid mixed with red slushed out, but to her surprise, he didn't show pain or even react at first.

She pulled her sword out of Barret's head and raised an eyebrow to see her blade covered in a thick, black goo. Now shaking and hissing aloud, Barret collapsed to the floor, and his body began to visibly change. His hissing became deafening as he hunched over and his back convulsed. Yet, over those hisses, she could hear even louder *cracks* and *crunches*, as if all bones in his body were breaking. Then, out of Barret's back burst translucent wings that Lucia could only make out the outlines of in the room's purple glow.

Barret's face melted like mud sliding off a building in the rain. His bulging eyes were the first to fall from what remained of his face. His normally pale skin gave way to something much darker underneath, and when Lucia saw that the red flesh fell off of his face in favor of that hard, dark exterior, she finally understood what he was transforming into. However, the change was not yet complete and the monstrous man curled up into a ball, no longer focusing on anyone in the room.

"We've gotta get out of here..." Lucia said as she turned her attention to Willoughby. She pointed her blade at the beast and took a long guard stance.

"Wait! Use the lantern!" Conrad called out. She looked back to where she had placed it on the floor. "It is weak to fire!"

Lucia turned to pick up her lantern, but she felt a sticky substance grab hold of her wrist. She turned back to see the beast with its giant mouth open and a disgusting tongue extended out: The culprit for halting her.

With a battle cry fueled by nerves, she slashed at the tongue with her sword, causing it to give way and unravel like a sliced rope. The monster let out a mutated cry that brought to mind several animals at once, but instead of giving up, it opened its mouth once more and shot out the same red webbing that enveloped Conrad. Lucia dodged by rolling to her left, but that had only served to keep her further away from the lantern.

The monster seemed well aware of what dangers the lantern might pose to it, and so Lucia was certain that she would need a distraction.

That was when she remembered the white pellets given to her by Dalton before they had split up. She grabbed them from a pouch around her waist and threw both at Willoughby. They exploded into a cloud of smoke and it quickly filled the chamber.

Shrill hisses were let out as Willoughby fired the red webs into the smoke at random. One had managed to pin down Lucia's left leg, but she lunged out and extended her long reach all the way to retrieve the lantern.

The trick now, she thought, would be targeting the beast in the smoke. As the thought entered her mind, however, she noticed its most obvious giveaway: Its glowing, red-ringed eyes. They stood out like sore thumbs in the haze.

Without a second thought, Lucia threw her lantern at the red eyes poking through the smoke. She heard the glass shatter and the flame ignite, followed by the shrill cries of the monster. Willoughby thrashed about in the smoke, tilting back and forth as if teetering on the edge of falling over. Eventually, the fire grew so large that she could see its entire lumpy body through the smokescreen, and Lucia began to wonder if her tactics had been a mistake. The smoke had been trapped in the chamber for some time, now, and it was eliciting more and more coughs. Even worse, Conrad was vulnerable, and she wasn't sure if it was safe to cross the room yet, with that vile monster flailing about.

∽

CONRAD WATCHED through squinting eyes as Willoughby's towering, fiery form wandered through the smoke, flailing, until tripping over the edge of the dark essence well and falling in. The beast let out one last wail before making contact with the substance and igniting it. The result was a mighty explosion that shot up straight into the ceiling and cut through it like a knife through hot butter. Hues of red, yellow, orange, purple, and black blinded Conrad; while his ears strained against what sounded like a thousand shrieking souls bursting from the underworld all at once.

He shuddered when the sheen of armor reflected over his glazed eyes, but then he realized that it had been Lucia diving up the stairs and hovering over him. He focused on her crescent-shaped tattoo, twitching with each *thunk* of debris striking her back.

When the explosion ended and the rumbling settled, Lucia, still hovering, frowned down at him. "How did you manage to find so much trouble?"

Conrad chuckled and was surprised at the lack of accompanying coughing fit. "All I know is that I've never been happier to see you."

Lucia's mouth hung open for a moment, but then she smiled and plopped on top of him, embracing so hard that Conrad thought all of the breath had been pushed from his lungs.

"Could you cut me out of these webs?" he squeaked.

"Oh, right…" she trailed off, then stood over him. With the long sword in hand, she cut at the red webs. "We have much to catch up on."

"Indeed, we do. And I'm sorry to say, but I won't be of much use walking or fighting, from here on. I've sustained so much damage and infection that I can't even feel the pain anymore," Conrad replied with a laugh.

"Is that so? You look fine to me," Lucia said as she cut the last of the webs.

The strategist sat up and curiosity clouded his mind. Why was he able to move so easily again? Where was the pain? He looked down at his legs and his ankle no longer showed burns, and nothing was broken. He reached back and felt his shoulder, only to find small scrapes that had turned to scabs.

"I'm healed…" he muttered.

"Should I be worried?" Lucia asked as the sound of buzzing began to fill the room. Beyond the fading haze and the light of the moon poking through a great hole in the ceiling, Conrad spotted Barret. He seemed to have sprouted wings, and it was tough to get a good view, but something seemed horribly wrong with his face. It seemed *inhuman*. "We need to leave."

"This door should lead us to the surface," Conrad said as he stood with his dagger in hand. "Only one problem: It's locked. We need a key."

"You mean *this*?" she asked while holding up a key and smirking. Conrad smiled back at her as she inserted the key into the hole and unlocked the door. The hissing and buzzing intensified behind them.

They opened the door, entered, and immediately slammed it shut. Lucia was sure to lock it before they continued down the new corridor, where they could see slits of moonlight poking through at an angle. As they walked, a heavy crash against the iron door echoed behind them, but it refused to give way.

"I'm sorry, by the way," Lucia said.

"For what?"

"I read your letter two weeks early."

Conrad snorted at the ridiculous notion. "A forgivable offense. If you hadn't arrived tonight, then I'd have died for sure… or worse…"

"Although…" she trailed off, rubbing her chin and looking up. "It was actually my nosey fool of a teacher who read your note. So, you can blame him if you wish."

"Where *is* Dalton, anyhow?"

"To distract Brice and Powell, he stayed behind in town while I made a rush for the dungeon."

"Facing down those two will be a tall order," Conrad said with concern in his eyes. "Even for him."

"Somehow, I'm not worried," Lucia replied with a shrug. "There is a ship waiting for us at the crescent-shaped beach, to the west of town. He is to meet up with us there."

From Lucia's reassuring presence and Dalton's unbeatable battle prowess, Conrad felt at ease. It was as if nothing had changed, even if, through his harrowing experiences, everything had. For now, he could push the uncertainty of his healed wounds to the back of his mind and focus on catching up with his friends.

∽

MEANWHILE, on the other side of the great door, Barret stood, banging away uselessly at the reinforced iron. The metamorphosis had changed him to such an extent that he could no longer be considered a man. Instead, he had the head of a fly, proportional to his size; and wings that had grown out of his back. Rather than speak, he merely let out hisses and buzzing noises. His movements were twitchy, and his fly-mouth squirmed as if looking for the next meal.

Soon, he found that meal in the form of Daniel's guts, which he sucked dry while clinging to the stone wall and ceiling with his new fly legs. Next, he roamed the floor like a ravenous dog and feasted on the flesh that had formerly made up his own head. After sucking down the last of his nutrients, Barret's bulging red eyes focused on the hole in the ceiling, and he flew out of it and back into town.

CHAPTER 26
THE GREAT BOSFUERAS FIRE

At the center of Bosfueras, Dalton dodged a swipe from the steaming Powell and continued to backpedal as he unleashed a flurry of punches and kicks that narrowly missed.

"Quit movin' around!" cried the red man.

Dalton opened his mouth to retort, but his tongue was stilled when out of the corner of his left eye, he saw the black tentacles of Brice flying at him. He raised his shield a mere moment before impact and felt a heavy blow that pushed him back and brought him down to a knee. A glance down revealed another sizable dent in the shield. It was probably the last attack he could block, unscathed.

"We're all honorable gentlemen, aren't we?" Dalton asked as he slowly stood. "How about we fight one-on-one?"

"As if we're gonna fall fer that! They always said ye were the greatest swordsman in all of Faiwell, but ye don't seem like much to me…" Brice said.

"Oh, I see…" the warrior trailed off with a glint in his eye as he pointed at Powell. "You don't think he can take me on his own, do you?"

Powell's already red face began to resemble a beet, and the steam shooting out through his clothes melted at the fabric. He was now barefoot from his boots fading away. It had become clear that frustration and exertion led to a higher body temperature for the red man; so much that it was even taking a toll on his body. His eyebrows had gone missing, and so too had the hair atop his head.

Dalton looked over his shoulder to see that the townsfolk had not yet gotten to the nearby fires that he and Lucia set. He had a hunch; one that would require him to lure Powell close to, or even into, the inferno nearby.

"I can take him alone! He's nothing!"

Powell charged in and took a swing so powerful that the steam from beneath his fading clothes plumed out and slapped Dalton across the face. However, it had also provided a smokescreen, and the warrior used this cover to sidestep while leaving his left leg extended outward. His armor sizzled and nearly shattered on contact, but it proved a fruitful strategy, as Powell stumbled for a few steps before falling and then rolling into a fiery house.

Flames erupted from the impact as Powell let out a distorted cry and Dalton watched on in awe. The inferno grew until it doubled in size, and little trails of flame began dancing in a circle until drawing back in and mixing with ash and soot. Now, the soot was taking shape, and so too were the dancing flames around it: a human shape.

"Uh-oh…" Dalton muttered.

From the fires emerged a flaming Powell. His clothes had deteriorated, but so too had his human form. Underneath the blanket of fire was a dark figure with glowing, red eyes.

"Ye idiot! Ye've made him even stronger!" Brice said with a laugh.

Powell held a palm out, and a trail of flame gathered around him before settling into his grip in the shape of a ball. With a casual flick of his wrist, he tossed the fireball at Dalton, who jumped to the right and felt its nearby heat as he hit the ground. He looked back to see that another house had been set ablaze by the reckless attack, and it was spreading far quicker than anything he or Lucia had managed earlier.

"Not much regard for your own home, eh?" the warrior asked.

"Anythin' to shut your hedge-born mouth!" Powell shot back. He made a jerky pushing motion with his other hand, and a stream of fire shot out in his direction. Dalton gasped and dove for cover once more. He looked up from the ground to see that he'd struck yet another building, but this one was stone. The stream of fire had charred its edges, but the damage was minimal.

"Oi! Cut that out, Powell! Ye'll burn down the rest of Bosfueras!" Brice said.

"Shut the hell up!" The fire around Powell flared up in reaction to his outburst. "I'm the strongest of the hooligans, now. I don't take orders from you anymore."

Brice grimaced and extended his arm. Out came the dark tendrils at speeds nearly imperceptible to Dalton's human eyes. Powell dove to his right to avoid, but one of them pierced into his leg, and he let out an animal-like howl of pain. In reaction, the newfound flames around his body spread, and the tendril burned up and crumbled into cinders.

Powell responded with a sweeping hand motion that saw a flame stream spurting in Brice's direction, but by pulling at the ground with his tentacles, he swiftly evaded. In that time, the red man had closed in, and their battle of bizarre abilities quickly turned into a brawl. Dalton watched on with mouth agape as Brice flung himself forward with the extra strength of the tentacles and tackled his underling through a shack. A fiery explosion erupted, and the warrior had to duck for cover as the flaming debris flew his way.

By the time he looked back up, Powell was in the process of unleashing his greatest stream of fire yet, and Brice flew back under its pressure before striking another house that crumbled under the heat and force of the blast. In only a few seconds, the hooligans had destroyed several buildings and helped spread the fires, rather than put them out.

Brice emerged from the fiery heap with rage in his eyes. Most of his body had turned dark, and rather than take a human form, he was beginning to resemble a walking octopus with his many tentacles flailing about.

"Ye insubordinate knob!" Brice shouted as he pounded on the wreckage with his tentacles. Flaming debris shot everywhere, once again forcing Dalton to take refuge. This time, he hid around the edge of a nearby stone building.

The embers from the wreckage spread to yet more homes and they began to burn in little time. Dalton watched in stunned silence as Powell cried out and shot up a wall of flames that pushed Brice back. The red man walked out of the fire with a confident stride in his step.

"You have pushed me around fer too long!" Powell said with a clenched fist. "But now, you little cretin, *I'm* in charge!"

Powell pushed his hand outward and a torrent of flame flew in Brice's direction. The big-nosed man tried to maneuver by diving to his left, but part of the fire hit him and burned off a couple of his tentacles. They began regenerating, and in short order, they returned, wriggling and twisting with as much vigor as ever.

"There ain't no way yer puny fires can kill me," Brice said, crossing a couple of the tentacles as if they were arms.

"Then, I'll just have to burn that ugly mug of yours off!" Powell cried as he boosted himself high into the air with the flames at his feet.

The big-nosed man grinned and extended his tentacles like a snake striking its prey. However, the true attack came when, from each tentacle, several sharp tendrils branched out in dozens of different directions. The red man gasped as many pierced into him at once, halting his momentum and causing him to drop like a fly.

Powell struck the ground in a sad heap, and soon it smoldered around him as he let out a frustrated, pained cry. His right eye had been impaled, and so too had his chest. Brice cackled as he painstakingly brought the sharpened tendril stuck in the eye socket down to the chest, cutting through Powell's neck and collarbone in the process. The red man screamed in agony, but the worst was yet to come. Next, Brice lifted him with a single combined tentacle, like meat on a skewer.

"I already told ye to learn yer place, fool. But ye never were much good at listenin' were ye?" Brice asked with a sadistic smile. "If ye ain't gonna work toward our cause, it's time to put ye down!"

He pulled the tentacle back with Powell still skewered and flung him into a new shack. The building exploded into flames upon impact. After a few moments of admiring his handiwork, Brice turned to face Dalton, who found himself wishing that he'd run away sooner. Yet, with such an extraordinary battle unfolding, he'd completely forgotten his surroundings.

"Now, it's *yer turn*," Brice said as he pointed one of his tentacles in the warrior's direction. Dalton gripped the edge of the building he'd taken refuge behind. As the situation stood, escape seemed unlikely.

However, before either of the two could make a move, a great column of fire roared by to the left of Brice, leaving a long trail of embers and another fiery shack in its wake. The big-nosed man grunted and then fell to the ground. The tentacles at his left shoulder and his left leg had been burned off. With twitchy eyes, Brice rolled over and looked up to see Powell alive and well, standing by the shack he'd been flung into, earlier.

The fiery man held both hands out and howled with laughter as flames from the surrounding buildings gathered into a wall of fire no less than four meters tall, surrounding him.

"Farewell, ye little runt!" Powell shouted, but before he could utilize the towering inferno, a loud sizzle sounded off, and vapor clouded the road as he stumbled and fell; coughing as if drowning.

Dalton gasped to see several of the townsfolk with buckets in hand, throwing water at their own comrade. With each splash, the fire shrank and the smoke grew. Now on his knees and writhing, a jittery Powell looked up to see a fully recovered Brice standing over him.

As more men arrived with buckets of water, Dalton saw the opportunity to flee and meet up with Lucia at the beach. After sneaking around the stone building, he made a mad dash toward the northern inclined path across town. He didn't dare to look back.

"P-please... stop..." Powell begged as another bucket of water splashed onto him. His raging flames had turned to embers, and his new dark form sagged underneath.

Brice held up a hand and the townsfolk ceased all movement. He approached Powell with a grin and then crouched down so that he was at eye-level. "Dalton got away because of ye. Ye've disobeyed me for the last time."

With panic in his red eyes, Powell looked to the townsfolk. "Don't listen to him! I'm yer new leader! I'll lead you ta prosperity! To dominance over all others! Forget about Bri-"

A haunting cackle echoed between the fiery buildings as Brice raised his fist, and his loyal underlings obeyed. Powell writhed in agony on his knees as the townsfolk dumped dozens of buckets of water on him, all at once. In much the same way as a normal man bathing in flames, his soot-like skin slowly peeled away as he begged and pleaded for them to stop. Yet, he may as well have been talking to a wall; Brice was in complete control.

Too weak to summon the nearby fires and surrounded by steam and smoke that had come from his fading body, Powell's own personal hell had come to life. He struggled and whined like a pig realizing that it was about to be slaughtered by the butcher. Perhaps Brice was imagining it, but he could have sworn that a tear had even streamed down his simmering cheek.

After his flames were extinguished, Powell's dark form melted and broke down like a wax figure in the heat. His red eyes and mouth sagged down his now-lumpy body, muttering unintelligible words as he turned into a large puddle of black.

Brice looked down at his underling with contempt. "Ye shoulda known yer place... and yer place, my friend, is scum at the bottom of my boot!" He brought his boot down with a heavy *thump* and the black puddle splashed all about. The degraded remnants of Powell's eyes and mouth spread across the dirt like a ruined painting, never to be finished.

The big-nosed man turned with conviction to face the townsfolk. "We must kill the intruders who set fire to our land! Head for the beach! And bring all of your weapons!"

∽

Meanwhile, Conrad and Lucia had reached the end of the underground hallway, where an old, rusty door awaited them.

"Is anyone else here?" Conrad asked as they exited through the creaky door. The secret passage brought them outside, where the river flowed.

"No," she replied. "It's a long story... although there are some pirates who came along for the ride."

"Ah, that's good. I'm sure they're formidable."

"They are certainly *not*," Lucia said with a chuckle. "But more importantly, how do we get to the beach from here?"

"You said we have to get to a ship?" Conrad asked, to which she nodded. "This river dumps out into the ocean. I'd bet the bay is nearby."

"Is there any other way?" Lucia asked, looking down at her armor with concern written on her face.

"Well, the only other way I know of is the steep path up the cliff at the north end of town," he replied with a shrug. "But we'd have to go a longer distance, and it's quite a climb. Could be risky."

"Very well..." Lucia replied as she began to strip her armor down. As she tore the chest armor off and threw it into the water, her shirt rode up and Conrad could see the extreme red all over her torso.

"I feel bad for not asking earlier. How are your burns?" he asked.

"While they are bothersome, I've decided to look at them more as reminders so I don't make the same mistakes again," Lucia replied as she ripped off the leg armor. "But I must admit that I'm jealous. From all the horrible things you said they did to you, it seems they've given you something to heal your wounds."

"I don't think you want what I have..." Conrad said with a nervous chuckle. Deep down, he knew that the dark essence coursed through his veins, and was likely the only thing standing between him and death's embrace. But what if it had imparted something worse than death? What if his destiny was to become a mindless monster, like Willoughby?

After Lucia tore down the last of her armor, she reattached the quiver to her back and sword at her hip, while discarding her shield. Her getup was similar to what she had worn at Mt. Couture: a tight shirt and mid-length skirt combo, sans the shoulder armor. Perhaps the joy of his rescue was overcoming him, but under the light of the moon, she was more radiant than ever. The red crescent-shaped tattoo around her eye seemed to glow, and her dark ponytail danced in the wind to a rhythm that simply felt *right*. His eyes wandered down to her legs, which seemed to go on for days, and now a silly smile was plastered on his face.

"I hate to ruin your vacation," she said with a smirk. Conrad spiraled out of his dreamy state and back to reality. "But what do you say we leave this hellish place?"

He smiled back and nodded. "Agreed."

The pair jumped into the river and simultaneously looked back upon the rocky foundations of Bosfueras as they drifted. The night sky was alight with red and gray thanks to the flames and smoke respectively. Trees from the woods obscured their view of the fire, but from the glow alone, it looked as if half the town was burning down.

Conrad was sure to direct himself and Lucia down the left river branch, which dumped them into the ocean and near the southeast side of the beach. They could see the ship at the dock further west, but as they walked onto the sand, there was no sign of Dalton.

"Oi!"

The duo turned to see the warrior charging across the bridge near the shipyard. The Bosfueras townsfolk were hot on his heels, running down the hill from the northeast. All of them carried weapons and sharp farming tools. Leading them was Brice, whose arms had become many dark tentacles that he was using to drag himself forward faster than any man could run.

As an arrow flew by Dalton, he put his head down and sprinted across the beach.

"Conrad! Good to see you… alive and well!" Dalton said between heavy breaths. "But, erm… we need to get… the hell outta here!" He pointed over his shoulder with a thumb to the bridge, where a mob of at least 200 people charged forward.

Another arrow whizzed by the trio. The ravenous hoard grew closer as Dalton, Conrad, and Lucia made a mad dash for the ship.

"Kill them!" Brice shouted.

∽

ON THE SHIP, Captain Auber, Ebbie, and Franco awaited their passengers. Earlier on, they were nervous, but it had been long enough that boredom set in, and all of their worries washed away. Eventually, Auber and Franco had elected to play cards in the captain's quarters while Ebbie kept watch from the crow's nest outside.

"What do ye think of the sails?" Auber asked as he placed a nine of diamonds on the table.

"They are imperfect, but beggars can't be choosers. We may move slower than normal, though," Franco replied as he put down a six of spades. "That's 15 for two points."

The captain flashed a confident grin. "If we leave tonight, it'll be no problem, in other words." He placed a six of hearts down. "That's 21 fer two!"

"Sometimes, proceedings don't go according to plan, cap. We should plan for an attack before those two warriors return," the navigator said while placing a ten of hearts down. "That'll be 31 for two."

"Bah! How do ye always do that?" Auber asked with a grimace. He wanted to flip the table over.

"In this game, there are more cards worth 10 than any other number, so getting to 21 is a bad idea because there's a good chance that I'll have a 10, jack, queen, or king."

Auber scoffed. "I dunno why I bother. There ain't nothin' fun about mathematics!"

"So, you don't want to play another round?"

"I didn't say *that*." The captain huffed. "At any rate, I'm sure things'll turn out fine. Them crazies from the town have no idea we're here, and I'm sure our new friends will be sneaky."

"I think you are forgetting a few important details…" Franco trailed off with a frown.

"Captain!" Ebbie's hollowed-out voice struck the cabin like a strong gust of wind.

Both Auber and Franco rushed out of the quarters and onto the deck. Ebbie looked down at them from the crow's nest with concern on his round face.

"What is it?" the captain asked.

"The good news is that those two armor-clad folks are on their way back, and they seem to have found their friend."

"Excellen-"

"The bad news is that they're bein' chased by the whole damn town!" Ebbie finished.

"Wh-wha?" was all Auber could get out of his quivering lips. He ran over to the deck's railing and laid eyes on the beach to see Dalton, Lucia, and another man running alongside them. Behind them was a huge crowd wielding weapons and farming tools alike, and they were closing in. Dozens of arrows sliced across the moon in dark streaks. "Oh, come on! Why can't anything go according to plan?"

"What shall we do, captain?" Ebbie asked.

"Prepare to set sail!"

Franco raised an eyebrow. "We're going to leave them behind?"

"That'll depend on how fast they are," Auber replied with a nervous gulp.

～

On the beach, Lucia noticed movement from the ship as she ran and muttered between breaths, "Those… cowards better not… abandon us…"

"I'm sure… they're just trying… to get a head start…" Dalton replied.

The vessel began to move slowly but surely as the trio sprinted for the dock, their breaths short and dry. The beach practically rumbled at the heavy strides of the mob behind, and between their shouting and the sounds of arrowheads striking sand nearby, the trio did not dare to look back.

As they finally set foot on the dock, Brice's voice flared up from behind. "They're trying to escape! Man the catapults!"

"Pain in the arse…" Dalton muttered. The boat was about three-quarters of the way up the dock. "It will be close… our window is small…"

After one final push where they ran faster than ever before, the trio reached the ship, but there wasn't much dock for them left to run on; less than ten full strides remained.

"Get on, quickly!" Ebbie shouted down from the crow's nest.

Dalton was first to hop on, and then Conrad. Both of them held their hands out for Lucia, and she took them as her legs flailed off the edge of the dock. For a few moments, she dangled over the vessel's edge, but with the sure hands she had taken, there was no worry in her heart.

With a couple of grunts from on deck, Conrad and Dalton pulled Lucia up and over, and the trio collapsed to the floor, all breathless and laid out with child-like smiles on their faces.

"I can't believe... we made it!" she cried before rolling over and wrapping an arm over the strategist. With her hand on his chest, she could feel his heartbeat, and with each passing moment, it grew faster.

"We ain't out of the woods, yet," Dalton said. Lucia turned over to see that he was sitting up, and his expression was grave. "They've manned the catapults."

"I've got it covered, mate!" Captain Auber said as he ran over to his steering wheel.

With some distance from the dock, the captain spun the wheel to his right, sharply sending the ship in that direction.

"Brilliant move, captain!" Ebbie shouted from the crow's nest.

Dalton and Lucia looked on as rock and stone that surely would have made short work of their current vessel all missed, far to the left and eliciting great splashes. While the trap between the shipwrecks had worked well against them and any other approaching ship, a fleeing vessel was a different story. Once past the dock, a simple right-hand turn was all that was necessary. The unwieldy nature of the catapults meant that they had no hope of adjusting their aim in time to hit them.

After gaining some distance, the volleys of rock stopped splashing behind, and Lucia let out a sigh of relief, sagging against the railing and chuckling. Conrad approached and took her hand. She wanted to groan; not because of him, but because she caught Dalton grinning out of the corner of her eye. Why did he have to keep on meddling?

"I owe you a great debt," he said before turning to the others. "To all of you, really. If I'd been left in that rotten dungeon for any longer, I would have died, or perhaps even worse-"

His eyes widened, and Lucia's ears immediately picked up on why: From behind the ship and over the gentle breeze of the night, she heard a buzzing; one that grew louder and more invasive with each passing moment. She turned and looked over the railing, to the ship's back-left.

A large, dark figure approached them rapidly. Soon, his translucent wings became apparent against the reflection of the moon off the water, and that light showed his giant fly face and twitching fly legs.

"What in the blue hell *is* that abomination?" Dalton asked with disgust on his tongue.

"Barret…" Conrad muttered with worry on his face. "The Dark Wizard imbued a chosen few with enhancements, but all of them turned into grotesque monsters as a result. I'm sure you noticed the tentacles of Brice."

The warrior nodded. "I had the misfortune of dealing with both him and Powell at once. The only reason I managed to escape was because they began fighting amongst themselves."

"If you've seen what they can do, then you know we can't let Barret board us. We'll be torn to shreds."

"He ain't gettin' on board," Dalton replied as he reached to his back for an arrow. He grabbed one, then searched for the bow at his hip. His eyes widened upon patting his thigh a couple of times. "Uh-oh…"

"Where is your bow?" Lucia asked. The buzzing grew louder.

"Before reaching the beach, I was stripping down my armor to lighten up and go faster. I must have thrown it out accidentally."

Lucia sighed. "It's alright. I've still got mine. Take the shot and end this."

She held the bow out for her mentor to take, but he smiled, shook his head, and then pushed it back toward her.

"*You* take the shot."

"But you're the best marksman we have!"

"Your aim has been true all day. I've yet to see you miss a target," the mentor replied with a sly smile. "And I can tell just from your glow that you fought and easily defeated one of those armed guards… am I right?"

"It's true," Lucia said, eyeing Barret with worry. He was no more than 20 meters away, now. "But what does that matter?"

"On the contrary, it matters a great deal. Your fighting spirit has nearly returned. End this trip by wasting that approaching freak of nature, and you will finally prove to yourself that you are capable."

"I really think that you-"

"No. It should be you who fires the shot. Don't you agree, Conrad?"

THE GREAT BOSFUERAS FIRE

The strategist nodded without hesitation.

"And you, Auber?" Dalton asked.

"Cut the sentimental knobbery and fire the damned thing!" the captain said with a scowl.

Lucia took a deep breath and turned toward Barret, who'd gained considerable ground on them. If she were to miss, then he'd surely catch up and land on the ship. She drew the string of the bow back with as much force as she could muster and closed one eye. All sound and motion seemed to stop in that one moment when she let go.

Her eyes remained fixed on the arrow soaring through the night sky until it struck Barret in his chest, sending him spiraling down into the water, hissing along the way. As soon as they saw the great splash from Barret's impact, the ship erupted into cheers and Conrad ran up to Lucia and wrapped an arm around her shoulder. It had been an arduous victory, but one worth celebrating. Franco broke open a stash of booze in the cargo, and the singing, dancing, and relaxing began.

As they celebrated and the distance between Bosfueras and the ship grew, Lucia and Dalton couldn't help but stare off into the smoke and fire that littered the landscape. Somehow, both knew that this wouldn't be the end. There would be hell to pay for the great Bosfueras fire. Their mutual thoughts were interrupted, however, when Conrad brought drinks to them, and they merrily began a binge that would last throughout the night and into the next day.

Even if the celebrations and happiness would only be temporary, the trio of survivors from Mt. Couture had reunited and met some new friends along the way. They set sail for Endoshire, Sigraveld to soon meet up with the rest of their comrades.

CHAPTER 27
ROYAL DECREE

"By the Gods… how could I have forgotten?" Lord Roland asked as he watched an entourage of horses arrive in Thironas city center.

Most of the steeds were ridden by knights carrying both Sigrian and Mithikan flags, but they were all there to protect one carriage in the middle. A radiant brunette woman stepped out with several men flanking her as Lord Roland rushed outside to greet the royalty. She wore a red silk dress with white patterns along the collar and elongated sleeves. Her lengthy hair sported a sparkling silver tiara which housed several strings of silver traveling down to her shoulders. Her fair skin reminded Joel of silk, at least from afar.

"What's tha big deal?" Alistair asked in a bothered tone as he watched through the window. "We should be spendin' time figurin' out a way beyond the grand wall! Who cares about this lass?"

"That is Princess Ella," Pierce said as he approached the window to look for himself. "She is one of the Sigrian king's many daughters."

"I ain't impressed! She ain't even from around here! Why does Roland gotta drop everythin' fer her?"

"Because she will soon be the queen of Mithika," Greta chimed in as she too approached the window to see. She was chewing on a cooked piece of meat right in Alistair's ear, and Joel struggled not to laugh at the visible irritation on his round face.

"Ya know, fer a wee lass, ya sure do eat a lot!" the big man said.

"Try starvin' yer whole life. Then, you'll understand the value of readily available food," Greta replied before narrowing her eyes at him. "I'm sure that's a lost cause with you, though."

Joel and Pierce looked at each other and both of their cheeks flared out.

"Oh, that was rude! All I'm sayin' is that ya can chew yer food before swallowin'. Don' be a gowk!"

"A gowk? How dare you!" Greta said angrily, then turned to Pierce and mouthed, "What is that?"

The dagger-eyed man could only shrug. Joel didn't know what it meant either, but it was nice to have a light-hearted moment nevertheless.

"She's right, though," Pierce said, nodding his head at the window. "That woman is to be the next queen. Roland was caught unprepared for her arrival, and now the best he can do is grovel at her feet and pray that she is kind."

"I don' get it. Royalty set their children up ta marry other royalty all tha time. Life goes on!" Alistair replied, shaking his head.

"While you are correct, there is a rumor going around that, if true, would change the makeup of this entire country…" Pierce trailed off ominously while gripping the windowsill. "As you should all be well aware, the Sigrian Kingdom controls these lands. The Mithikan king is only called such to please the people. However, ruling from another country is difficult. Ever since the incident with the centaurs, Mithika has enjoyed relative freedom from the whims of Sigraveld. Some believe that once Princess Ella marries the Mithikan prince, she will become this country's true ruler. It's not a stretch to believe that she would do the direct bidding of Sigraveld, thus ending any hint of Mithikan sovereignty."

"Well, that's just rude! We Currens wouldn't allow such a travesty ta take place! We'd overthrow their rule!" Alistair boasted.

"Quit actin' so high and mighty!" Greta butted in. "You haven't even given Mithika a chance because it hasn't happened yet!"

Before the big man and little woman could get to arguing, Joel tugged at Alistair's sleeve. He had an idea; one that he needed him to translate for the others. The big redhead gasped as he sent the hand signals along.

"That's a mighty fine idea, lad!"

"What did he say?" Pierce asked, his nose twitching. "Perhaps I should take up sign language…"

"It ain't so bad after a few months of practicin'!" Alistair said while giving him a hard slap off the back. Pierce flinched at the playful gesture. It was obvious that he had a ways to go before fully recovering from his injuries. "Anyway, Joel says that we should get Roland ta ask tha Princess if she'll grant us permission to pass the grand wall."

Pierce gasped. "That *is* a great idea... although Roland doesn't appear to think she holds him in high regard."

"Better than nothin'," Greta said as she got to work on another plate of meat. She talked with her mouth full, much to Alistair's visible annoyance. "We've been sittin' around here for three days, now! We gotta do somethin'... I mean, couldn't that monolith have been destroyed by now?"

Joel signed to Alistair once more.

"He says we can't know fer sure. When tha Greed monolith broke, tha Guardian Beast pushed him back into tha Cold World. There was no real change ta our world after tha incident."

"Even though there are some aspects of it which weren't well thought out, I must say that the monolith here is well-guarded. The Lake Watcher is deadly, but even more so, Zamarim cannot be bypassed. He can take over your mind with a snap of his fingers," Pierce said.

Despite his friend's optimism, Joel had a bad feeling. If all were truly well, then why hadn't Aldous returned?

⁓

In the city center, a crowd gathered to watch as the Sigrian princess and Lord Roland approached one another. Roland bent the knee and bowed before her.

"It is an honor to have you in our great city, m'lady."

"Rise." Her voice sent ripples through him that stuttered his breaths. He had been stricken with such regality and command, all with one simple word.

The lord stood and their gazes met for the first time. She truly was pleasant to look at, as had been rumored; though she carried with her a certain aura that made him feel inadequate. As a lord, he had spent his fair share of time around princes and princesses, but it felt like Ella was at a higher echelon, somehow.

"Shall we dispense with the pleasantries, Lord Roland? I'm here to put you back on schedule; to ensure you put an end to this troublesome famine," the princess said as they began walking toward the clock tower.

"I must assure you, m'lady, that we're doing everything within our power to-"

"You must do better, then," she interrupted with a formal smile. "If my father has informed me of this city's troubles, it means that it's a big problem. Rarely does he see fit to mention Mithika. You see, he sent me here to marry because I'm his least favorite daughter."

Roland raised an eyebrow. "I don't know why the king would take notice of one particular famine... unless it were in Sigraveld."

"That is not for me to say. What I do know is that he grows tired of the constant challenges of this country. I see potential, but first, I must make sure the lords are performing their duties up to standard," Ella said.

"Your Highness, we cannot simply force a famine to end. It is entirely up to the land, and right now, it is not cooperating," he replied.

"I understand that, but there are a puzzling number of resources which, as I've been informed, go unused," the princess said as they reached the clock tower building. She continued walking as if expecting the door to open on its own. Funny as it might be if she walked into it face-first, Roland jumped ahead and held it open for her. "For example, to the south, there lies a lake that likely teems with fish, fresh water, and other resources."

Lord Roland could only sigh.

"Yet I am told that you choose to instead use the river, which is double the distance, therefore doubling the work, and thereby halving important resources at your disposal," Ella said as she sat at a table stacked with papers. She brushed them aside like annoying flies buzzing about her. A few knights stood on each side of her chair, and Roland sat across from her.

"There are reasons for such measures. The Lake Watcher is an ever-present threat. It is why we built that grand wall many years ago; and why the guards would shoot at anyone who try and gain passage to the lake."

Ella let out a vain chuckle. "That old legend? How long ago was that conceived? A thousand years ago? Two? Even if it were real, surely such a creature would have died by now."

"That is not what I've been told," Roland replied. The princess cocked her head. "Ometos has confirmed that the Lake Watcher remains."

"'Ometos'? That's another adjustment we must make around here. The outdated Mithikan Gods are uninspired and difficult to follow."

Roland smiled. "I don't mean the *God* Ometos. I refer to the man who has helped keep this city afloat. If you are interested, I could arrange a meeting with him, after you've settled in."

"A fine idea. I have many questions for the man who single-handedly fed your people a few days ago."

"Ah, so you heard?"

"Of course. Whenever handouts are given, the people will chatter and gather," she replied. "However, that raises the question of where the supplies are coming from. *Nothing* is free, in my experience. Even when you are royalty."

"Indeed… but before you meet him, how about I show you to your room?" Roland asked.

"Very well. Lead the way," Princess Ella said.

She and her entourage followed Roland past the busy men sifting through paperwork, and into a long hallway. At the end of the hallway, he led them into a luxurious room; spacious and well-decorated with paintings and fresh flowers; the latter of which was only possible thanks to his stalling tactics outside. They weren't the nicest flowers, but they added a good scent to a hastily-cleaned room. The bed was both tall and wide with extravagant sheets hanging from the high poles, and across from it was a window with an equally extravagant shade.

Roland bowed and left the princess and her guards to settle in. He made his way up the clock tower and back into his office, where Joel and the others awaited him.

"So? What was she like?" Greta asked between bites of bacon. "Is she as pretty as they say?"

"Yes, I would have to agree that she lives up to those expectations. But she is even more demanding than she is beautiful," Roland said.

"She ain't married to tha prince yet! She can't force ya ta do nothin'!" Alistair replied in defiance.

"True, but if I value my title as a lord, it would be wise to do as she commands."

"What does she want you to do?" Pierce asked.

"For one thing, she'd like to meet with you. She is suspicious of the fact that you supplied food to the people for free."

"What nonsense! Why would she complain about free food?" Greta asked.

"She has her reasons, of course, but what concerns me is that already it sounds like she is doing her father's bidding," Roland said with crossed arms. "So, it seems the rumors are true. This arranged marriage is only so Sigraveld will have more control over Mithika."

Joel nudged Alistair, then made hand signals to him. The big redhead looked back and his eyes widened. "Oh, right."

He cleared his throat and said, "Oi! Roland! Joel had a grand idea. If this lass has some authority, we should ask her ta call off the guards of the wall an' let us in!"

The lord raised an eyebrow. "That *is* a good idea. Especially since she wants us to start using Lake Teras as a resource."

"But usin' it as a resource truly is dangerous," Alistair said.

"True, but for the purposes of getting through *now*, it gets the job done. We can worry about the princess' misconceptions later. I'll propose the idea to her at lunch, today. Will the rest of you join us?" Lord Roland asked.

The group collectively nodded. It would be an odd meeting of minds to be sure, but Roland was now focused on how best to obtain Princess Ella's help. For that, he would need everyone present.

∽

WHEN LUNCH CAME AROUND, Joel found himself sitting at a grand table in the heart of the building that connected to the watchtower. He felt underdressed compared to Roland, and it became especially apparent when Princess Ella walked into the room. She had changed into a whole new gown, and it was crafted from the finest silk.

After she sat, the meal was brought in from the back. Ham, white bread, and wine were served: a meal saved only for royalty and lords, especially in the difficult times of the famine.

"I wager all of my gold that I can eat more than you." Joel's ears perked up. He looked to his left to see Greta snickering in Alistair's direction.

Alistair scoffed. "And *I* wager that you don't got no gold ta bet with."

"So, you admit that you cannot beat me?" She wore an arrogant smirk. *Now is not the time*, Joel thought with narrowed eyes.

"Of course I can! A keen warrior like me'self needs a lotta food ta keep his strength up!"

"My man hardly eats at all, and he bested you in combat, did he not? I say yer a lightweight."

The big man leaned in, and there was fire in his eyes. "I am now gonna eat more than anyone in this room combined, just ta prove ya wrong…" Joel was shocked. In the past, even when attempting to whisper, Alistair had always spoken loudly. Yet, this time, his words had come out eerily quiet. "Prepare yerself!"

All in the room flinched at the outburst, and the princess' guards raised their weapons. Both Roland and Ella held their hands up, and the men stood down. Joel buried his face in a palm. He couldn't believe it: They were going to have an eating contest in front of the princess.

Greta and Alistair were quick to grab full plates, while Joel and Pierce grabbed meager portions. Roland and the princess took average portions. All in the room got to eating, and it didn't take long before conversation picked up.

"So then, which of you is the one they call 'Ometos'?" Ella asked, leaning in. Roland nodded toward the dagger-eyed man.

"It's a pleasure to meet you, Majesty," Pierce said.

"And you as well. After all, you've been helping to feed the people…" the princess trailed off before taking a sip of wine. "Although, I wonder… how could you have gained the resources necessary to feed them for free?"

"I have my ways," the dagger-eyed man said with a smile.

"You won't tell me?"

"I made a deal. It was of no personal expense to me, so I have no problem with rationing the food off while the famine remains."

"No ulterior motives? You must excuse me. I find that hard to believe," Ella said.

"Well, I do have one 'ulterior motive'," Pierce replied before kissing Greta on the cheek. She seemed too busy devouring her food and comparing her progress with Alistair to notice.

"Ah… a peasant woman? How quaint."

Pierce raised an eyebrow and frowned.

"Your Highness, I would like to make a suggestion, if I may?" Roland jumped in.

"I'm listening," Ella said, then folded her hands and rested her chin on them.

"You mentioned earlier that Lake Teras would be a valuable resource to us. I agree, but I'm sure *you* can agree that the safety of Thironas should be our top priority…" the lord trailed off.

"Yes, and the sooner we open that lake up, the sooner this city can prosper. A prosperous city is a safer one," she replied.

"To be certain, I propose the following: Call off the guards atop the grand wall. Let us through today, and we'll check to see if the Lake Watcher is alive and a threat," Lord Roland said.

"That silly legend? Again?" Ella asked with a smirk.

"Please. Just to be sure. We wouldn't want to unleash a monster onto this beautiful land."

"If it will ease your mind, then I suppose that I could mention it to the king."

"I propose that we do this today. No kingdom nonsense to slow the process down."

Princess Ella paused and then narrowed her eyes. "You're keeping something from me. Tell me. Tell me now."

Alistair let out an obnoxious laugh while spewing crumbs of the white bread. "Ya wouldn't believe us even if we told ya!"

"Let me guess… big man, red hair, loud… you must be a Curren," Ella said. Alistair frowned and opened his mouth, but then he eyed Greta, who'd finished her plate and gone for more. In a rush, he got back to shoving food into his mouth. "I'm willing to listen, at least. I'm sure whatever you tell me couldn't be any more ridiculous than that Lake Watcher legend."

Pierce chuckled. "The Lake Watcher is *very* real. Why don't you cross the wall with us and we'll show you?"

"You're serious?" the princess asked, looking around the table. All remained stone-faced.

"I'm afraid so," Lord Roland said

"Fine. Let's say I believe these silly stories. I could send a whole platoon in there to kill the beast if I wanted to," Ella said as she pushed her plate forward.

"Why do you think we wish to cross the wall?" Pierce asked, leaning back in his chair.

"Are you telling me that *this group* aims to kill a legendary monster?" Ella replied with wide eyes.

"What's wrong with that?"

"Well, I can see Lord Roland holding his own, of course. But the rest of you… how should I put it? Don't appear cut out for battle?"

Pierce shot a knowing smile at Joel, but in truth, her assumptions didn't bother him in the slightest. Alistair, on the other hand, stood and slammed his fist into the table. The princess' guards turned their attention to the big man and pointed various weapons at him. Ella called the men off.

"Everyone's always underestimatin' me! But I can hold me own! Give me a chance ta prove it!" the big man shouted. This time, remnants of the ham flew from his mouth.

"I must say that having witnessed their skills in battle, they're a more capable lot than you may realize," Roland said.

"I see… well, if you feel comfortable fighting beside a rag-tag group like this, then I won't stop you," the princess said to some smiles across the table. "*However*, I will be sending five of my men to accompany you. I think there is something you aren't telling me. Perhaps they will dig it up. If you do find a monster in that lake, I'm sure they'll be of some use."

"Excellent," Lord Roland replied as he stood and pushed his chair in. "I'll be taking a trip to the armory in preparation. Any of you who need to stock up can come along."

"Come visit me in my room when you are ready to go. But I don't want to get your hopes up, either. Many Mithikan knights and guards recognize me as the future queen, but it is not official yet. My orders may fall on deaf ears," Princess Ella said as she stood and made her way for the exit. "Still, I'm interested to see where this all goes. So, I shall help you if I can."

After the princess and her entourage left, Alistair and Greta concluded their eating contest, where the big man emerged victorious thanks to snagging an unfinished piece of ham from Joel's plate. With that, the competing duo traveled with Roland to the armory. Joel and Pierce stayed behind, as they had all that they would need. The mute hobbled over to Pierce, who was sitting at a table, re-wrapping some bandages.

Joel found a pen and paper and then got to writing: Their only way to communicate. He slid the paper over to the dagger-eyed man.

How are you holding up?

"To tell you the truth, I don't think I've ever been hurt this badly," Pierce replied as he looked down at his bandaged hand. "But I'm not the only one who's hurting. Your shin still looks to be in rough shape."

When the time is right, we can push through the pain, as we were taught.

"As we were taught…" Pierce repeated with a snort. "Our time at the academy was brutal, looking back. But it was valuable time. We would be long dead if not for their teachings. You would do well to remember them." The mute cocked his head. "I got a front-row seat as you did battle with *the other*, and then when you faced Angus. Your form is sloppier than before, perhaps from a lack of practice... but there can be no doubt that even when you swung your sword, there was no threat to it."

I won't kill anyone again. Even picking up my sword fills me with disgust.

"Your vow of peace is admirable, but for now, you must put it aside. Our enemies don't care about your refusal to fight, Joel. They'll go right ahead and kill you anyway. Do you think the Dark Savior cares about non-violence? Do you think Angus would hesitate for even a moment if he had the opportunity to kill you?"

You're right. I've thought about that a lot over these past couple of years. If it leads to my death, then so be it. I deserve it.

"You did what you had to do all of those years ago. There was no right answer. That's why there are two halves of me, now," Pierce said with a chuckle. "But make no mistake: We are at war. A silent war against the Dark Savior, and the entire realm is at stake; not just your life. If you continue inserting yourself into this fight, you will eventually face a crisis. And in that crisis, you'll have to decide: You can stick to your principles and allow your friends to die; let all that you treasure to be crushed. Or you can fight back. No one will think less of you for it."

It has worked for me so far.

"How long? How long before it cripples you? How long before it gets one of your friends killed because you couldn't do what needed to be done? Your enemies give you no quarter, yet you give them infinite chances. The only possible result is that you will lose."

Never again.

Pierce laughed and then sat back in his chair. "Stubborn to the last. Same old Joel..."

Everything has changed for you, though. How did you meet Greta?

"She's great, isn't she?" Pierce replied with enthusiasm. "I first met her back on that mountain. The other me thought that she was trying to plunder the house, but she was simply exploring. She drew me out and taught me many important things about this land. As you may recall, we never had to worry about catching fish back in Stellinam or at the academy. Well, around here, with the famine, it's about all I can get to eat. She showed me the best way to catch them, and it worked.

She's known nothing but hardship and peasantry her whole life, but it has imparted on her valuable knowledge and skills."

Joel smiled. He knew that when Pierce couldn't shut up about something, he was fully committed to it. The two luxians caught up on many subjects while the others were gathering supplies. Eventually, Roland, Alistair, and Greta returned. They were sent to some private rooms to prepare themselves.

∼

As Pierce and Greta got changed in their room, he happily recalled all of the nice things he had said about her earlier. He smiled while glancing at her as she took her shirt off.

Pierce's eyes widened when he saw that something about her was different. "Hold on…"

Greta had finished putting on a new shirt, but he walked over and lifted it to check once again. "Hey! What're you-"

The dagger-eyed man gazed upon her pooched-out belly. It was a near-perfect half-sphere.

"Are you pregnant?"

"N-no… why do you ask?" Greta stepped back from him and pulled her shirt back down.

"You are…"

"Th-that's not true! I've just put on a lil' weight!"

"It explains everything. The belly, the clothes, and all of that food," Pierce said while chuckling and shaking his head. "I feel like a fool for not noticing sooner…"

Greta let out a defeated sigh. "It's true."

"Why didn't you tell me?" he asked.

"You are a protector of these lands. How could I ask you to be a father on top of that? An' now that you know about it, I suppose you'll force me to stay behind…" she said, looking down.

"That goes without saying. We must protect our child. And *of course* I'd want to father our child along with you," Pierce said.

"Really?"

"Yes." A smile came to his face. "A luxian and human hybrid, eh?"

"Will this be the first child of its kind?" Greta asked.

"I doubt that, but still, how unique! I can't wait to meet them."

"That means you should stay behind, too."

"You know I can't do that. I failed in my duty as Keeper of the Key.

It's time to make up for my mistakes," Pierce said as he grabbed his Ometos mask and looked upon it with sharp eyes. "This is the best I can do… hopefully I can hold on."

∼

AFTER EVERYONE GOT READY, the group departed among Princess Ella's fleet of knights. As they road toward the grand wall, Alistair looked around the coach, as if he'd dropped something on the floor or in between seats.

"Finally convinced the lil' one to stay back, eh?" he asked with a sly smile.

"I found out that she is pregnant," Pierce replied with excitement in his eyes.

"Oh, really? Who's tha father?"

Joel reached over and slapped him off the back of his head. The big man turned around angrily, only to do a double-take upon realizing that it had been his mute cohort. He gave a congratulatory nod to Pierce.

"Thank you, old friend. This means that I need to make it back alive. I want to meet my child, after all."

"Hold up," Roland jumped in. "Without Greta, how can we be sure that *the other* won't return and attack us?"

Pierce reached down and retrieved his Ometos mask. He put it on so that the sad face was right side up. He then pointed up to the more menacing, upside-down face of the mask. "If you see *this*, you'll know that it's him."

"Would he really flip tha mask around, though? That seems a wee bit daft!" Alistair said.

"It's simply the habit that we've established. It's as natural for us as dressing in the morning is for you… so, pay close attention. I'm going to try and hold him off, but if something happens, at least you'll know."

The group eventually reached the grand wall at the north end of the lake. There was a gate pushed inward with murder holes and archery slits carved out for an easy shot against any intruders. The guards atop the wall immediately pointed their bows toward the entourage as they approached, and in response, the knight up front brought his steed to a halt.

"Princess Ella, future queen of Mithika, will speak before you, now!

Hold your fire!"

The guards atop the wall looked at each other, and after a moment, lowered their bows as commanded.

The princess appeared out of the side of the carriage and walked to the front of the line. Some of the guards let out audible gasps, and quiet chatter picked up amongst their ranks.

"As future queen of this land, my first decree will be the destruction of this wall, which has denied the good people of Thironas their own resources for far too long. To ensure that Lake Teras is safe, I have gathered a group to enter beyond the walls here today," Princess Ella said before gesturing back to the coach.

Roland hopped out of the carriage and led the way, with the others following soon after. They stood behind the princess while trying to look as formidable as possible, despite their obvious injuries.

"In addition, I will be sending five knights from my personal guard in for their protection," she said. Five armored men approached from behind. "Will you comply with my request? Or will I have to travel all the way back to the capital and explain to the king why you wouldn't let me through?"

The guards atop the wall gathered and whispered to one another. After a short time of deliberation, the gate in the wall lifted.

"By the Gods, it worked…" Roland muttered.

Ella turned to him and smiled. "When this is all through, I'd daresay you owe me some favors."

"As you wish, Your Highness." He did his best to hide the uneasiness in his words.

"Worry not, Lord Roland. These favors will be for the betterment of Mithika, not myself. You may think that I am here only as a pawn of my father, but not all is as it seems. I have grander plans than acting as a puppet of Sigraveld, but I'll need help from lords like you." She walked past him with graceful strides, unbothered by the potentially treasonous words she had just spoken.

Though he'd turned somewhat pale out of nervousness, Roland looked back at her in genuine curiosity. Frightening and demanding as she may have been, he couldn't deny her alluring qualities. He would certainly grant her favors, especially if it would benefit his people.

Keeping that in the back of his mind, Lord Roland led his group beyond the wall, seeing Lake Teras up close for the first time. Its uninviting, murky waters did little to ease his nerves.

CHAPTER 28
END OF NIGHTMARE

Aldous groaned as the scenery around him changed into a blue void. He had lost track of time, but it felt like days since Zamarim had trapped him in the illusion of his own memories. In rapid succession, he had lived out many of his life's most significant moments, and most of them hadn't been pleasant.

"When will you end these games?" he called out into the void. There was no response. "Listen to reason! I am on your side!"

The blue landscape slowly morphed into an indoor location. Aldous immediately recognized his surroundings: There were freshly-made holes in the floor and walls, grand marble columns, and a golden throne that had been obliterated from battle. It was cold; ice and snow filled the room, and it smelled like burning metal and blood.

The Mountain King, clad in his tattered armor, toga, and crown, smiled back at him with wicked intent. Next to him was a wall of ice.

This was a recent memory; the conclusion to his battle with the Wizard King of Mt. Couture.

"You'll have to kill him…" the Mountain King said with a smirk as he nodded toward the ice walls. Aldous looked over to see that a newly-revived Henic was chipping away at the ice walls with his pick-axe. "The choice is yours! Will you betray your friend and kill him? Or will you join us?"

Aldous looked on as Henic continued to chip away at the ice with his pickaxe. He shuddered, knowing what would happen next, but there was nothing he could do. He was merely a passenger; an observer of events that had already come to pass.

The old Wizard pressed his walking stick into the ground and the remaining ice and snow of the prior battle gathered into an indoor blizzard. Aldous recalled that he had used a similar strategy before, and got a significant hit in on Olivier as a result, but things were different after the Wizard King had retrieved his artifact: the chalice. With his artifact in hand, the Mountain King wouldn't need to expend as much magic on spells cast.

"You won't be able to hide, this time!" Olivier cried. Through the thick veil of white, Aldous could see him gripping his luxmortite chalice in both hands and raising it overhead.

A wall of omnidirectional fire spread across the room as fast as any arrow could fly. Aldous, heart beating louder than thunder, held his walking stick out to absorb the flames at the last moment. Even still, he felt the sting of scalding vapor and Henic's harrowing cries haunted him until they finally dispersed, and all fell silent. The intense residual heat kept him from opening his eyes at first, but when he did, the old Wizard couldn't help but marvel at how much destruction had ensued: The throne had been fully annihilated, several columns had fallen, the murals were destroyed, the weapons along the walls had disappeared, and so too had the treasures. Some of the walls and floors had blackened, and he could see the reverse outline of where Henic had been vaporized; a veritable shadow of his former self.

Olivier grinned. "How long will you delay the inevitable?"

A green light shot out of his chalice and Henic took shape once more. The soul-enslaved miner flinched as if only just now reacting to the flames that had annihilated him earlier.

"Wh-what happened?" he asked.

"You failed the first time. Try again."

Henic began walking toward Aldous in an awkward fashion. His face reflected shock and confusion. The old Wizard held his walking stick up in a defensive position.

"I cannot stop myself!" Henic said.

"I know…" Aldous muttered.

Henic leaped forward and brought his pickaxe down, aiming for the head. Aldous hopped to the left and then smacked him over the skull with his walking stick in response. Henic crashed to the ground and remained motionless.

"Your efforts are in vain," the King Wizard said, holding a hand up.

Over his head formed a great column of marble. He threw the pillar in their direction, and Aldous had no choice but to dive out of the way.

An explosion of green light spilled from underneath the skidding column as Aldous looked up from the floor with a fire in his eyes. "That's twice now, you've killed him!"

"And that makes *three times*, now, that you have failed to save him!" Olivier replied as the green light flowed into the chalice. In mere moments, the energy shot out once more and Henic stood in the throne room.

"I've had enough of this!" the soul-enslaved miner cried. He wound up to throw his pickaxe at the Mountain King.

However, before he could complete any sort of throwing motion, all of his movements paused, as if time had stopped for him alone. Henic's whole body trembled, and blood trickled down from his nose.

"Now, now. Attacking your new master won't do you any favors," Olivier said.

"What is the point of this madness?" Aldous asked, clanking his walking stick off the floor in frustration. "You could kill me at any time and take me as your soul-slave. Why are you torturing him?"

"If I did that, your soul could only be materialized as an ordinary man. I cannot resurrect a Wizard properly; no one can! I resort to this so that you might see reason and join me."

That was when it dawned on Aldous that Olivier had simply wanted a fellow Wizard in his company. As he watched the memory unfold with a clearer mind, he had come to pity him in some ways. He had become bitter, lonely, and tainted by the black gold; something that the Council had expected him to accept with honor.

The old Wizard pointed his walking stick toward the hole in the ceiling and said, "I'll never join you. You'll have to kill me."

"I've got all the time in the world! I'm sure you will learn to think differently…" the Mountain King replied as a cloud of snow burst into the room. He held his chalice up and scoffed. "But I must once again say that you Elementals lack creativity!"

Another wall of fire spread about the throne room, but by then, Aldous had already been lifted by the heaviest portion of rising snow. He felt the scalding vapor sear his ankles, but burst from the hole in the ceiling just in time to escape; just in time to hear Henic's howls of agony echoing out along with him.

"I'm sorry…" he muttered while on a knee.

Aldous remembered how ashamed he was to run, but looking back, there was little choice. Olivier was only going to continue using Henic as torturous bait, and releasing him from his imprisonment meant that he would have to kill the Mountain King; a task that was simply beyond him at the time.

After standing, the compromised integrity of the roof became apparent when the old Wizard wobbled and he felt cracks in the stone. Still, he would have to risk making a run for it. He didn't have long before Olivier would catch on. While putting his head down and dashing through the heavy snow and slippery stone atop the castle, he heard a *thud* from behind.

"That won't do you any good!" the Mountain King cried.

The old Wizard looked over his shoulder to see several small bolts of lightning flying at him, and at such a close range, there was no time to react. The streaks struck his legs and sent ripples through his body, shocking him in every sense of the word. He had not truly been hit by lightning in over a hundred years.

Aldous stumbled as his legs ceased to work correctly and he rolled down the left side of the roof. While falling, he pointed his walking stick at the Wizard King, and a stream of fire shot out: flames he had stored from the earlier wall of fire. The Mountain King snickered and held his chalice out. In a split-second, a thick sheet of steel formed in front of him, and that was the last Aldous saw of his response before careening too far over the edge for his eyes to catch anything more than the orange glow of the explosion.

Spinning in midair to brace for the fall, Aldous gasped when he found himself face-to-face with a snow mound. The next thing he knew, the old Wizard was surrounded by white and cold, and he began burrowing through the depths of the snow as a mole would in the dirt. The trouble, however, was that he couldn't see where he was going. Instead, he had to wander aimlessly, hoping to reach an area suitable for escape. After working up a sweat for a while, he poked his head out of the snow and found himself back in the pine tree forest to the west.

At that point, there was a difficult decision that laid on his plate: He could choose to try sneaking back through the Mountain King's castle or to re-enter the mines and pass through the Nightcrawler's den. Aldous chose the former, though he'd always wondered what could have been, had he gone the other way. Through the snowy trees he snuck, hoping to evade detection, but soon he caught wind of one of Olivier's floating eyeballs spying on him, and near the end of the forest, one of the soul slaves approached: It was a mountain troll, big and green, huffing and puffing. He dragged a large club through the snow.

With a forceful gesture of the walking stick, an icy wind swarmed the troll, and when the snow settled, he was frozen solid; almost as if he'd been surrounding by a giant crystal.

Wind picked up as he pushed through the last stretch of forest, and it grew worse and worse until he reached the clearing before the castle. He looked up in terror to see the Mountain King hovering above, smiling down at him.

Aldous shielded his face as the frigid wind slapped him and Olivier chuckled. "Your command over the snow is admirable, but let's see you control *this*!"

With an authoritative point of his finger, a disturbance in the raging winds became apparent; like the tide drawing in before the largest wave yet. Snow swirled in front of Aldous until it nearly appeared solid, like a wall. Quickly, it transformed into a great funnel that towered up into the clouds. The old Wizard's eyes widened when icicles shot out and pierced into the nearby trees like arrows.

Pressing his walking stick into the ground, Aldous summoned as much might as he could and tried to disperse the snow, but the wind was too powerful. His only option was to run. As he turned to leave, however, many of the soul servants blocked his path: the provocatively-dressed women, the fur coat-adorned men, the slavers, a troll, the avian, and Henic stood before him.

"I'm sorry, Aldous… can't… control myself…" Henic muttered as he pointed his pickaxe at the Wizard. His soul-enslaved cohorts readied their weapons as the rumbles of the ice tornado closed in from behind.

"I must apologize, too…" Aldous replied, pointing a hand in the direction of the group. The snow at their feet rose and gobbled them up like an alligator snatching its prey on a watery surface.

He made a run for it and didn't dare look back as he heard the violent wind creeping up on him. However, before he could make it back into the forest, a hand reached out from the snow and grabbed his ankle. It was large and green; probably the troll, Aldous thought. He struggled to free himself, but to make matters worse, more hands popped up and grabbed him around the ankles and feet.

The violent wind grew closer than ever as Aldous turned to face the inevitable collision. In seconds, the tornado swept him and the soul slaves up and whirled them around. Aldous recalled all of his panicked thoughts as he felt the ice dig into his skin and cut him. Most of the soul-enslaved were spared a long punishment, bursting into green light in short order and exiting the deathly funnel of snow.

It wasn't long before the dizzying winds killed all inside except for Aldous, and that was when the ripped-up pieces of tree entered the tornado. There was nothing he could do as the first trunk hurdled into him, nearly causing a blackout. Looking back, Aldous was sure that it had only been the scratches of the darting pine needles and his desperation that had kept him awake at that point.

He closed his eyes and concentrated to the greatest extent of his abilities. He couldn't fully control the snow, but little by little, he could push himself along. Each time the snow pushed Aldous, he got closer to the edge of the tornado. Finally, after one big push, the old Wizard found himself flying out of the ice funnel.

In the few seconds it had taken him to get his bearings, Aldous had already flown over the Mountain King's castle. The edge of Mt. Couture neared, and if he didn't act soon, he'd go careening over the mountainside with only the rocks below to comfort him on his descent. With exhaustion setting in, Aldous closed his eyes to concentrate. A large, snowy hand shot up from the ground and caught him. It then closed up to make a fist and lowered back into a snow bank beyond the castle.

Shame washed over the old Wizard, as he recalled this part of the dreaded day best. Now bloodied, bruised, and deep in the snow, he could feel the Dark Savior's presence from Edith's success in destroying the monolith. In his cold cocoon, he rose to a knee. Joel and the others had needed him. The *whole world* had needed him. Why was it then, that in that moment, he could not find his second wind? Even to this day, it was a mystery to Aldous, who struggled to do anything that might change his vision; but the past was set in stone, and on that day, he decided to sit back down and lean against the ice at his back until he nodded off. As world-altering events unfolded in the Gold Pit below, he had been sleeping. Truly, he was no better than the do-nothing Wizard's Council.

The scenery faded until he was in the blue void once more. What else could Zamarim possibly have to show him? He had made his point, loud and clear. Perhaps Aldous *was* acting reckless due to his failures, but it still didn't change the fact that there was a plot to destroy the seven seals, and something needed to be done about it.

END OF NIGHTMARE

∼

Zamarim frowned at Angus in the blue, yet empty space. Though they had gone through some of the giant's memories, he had resisted to an unprecedented degree.

"How are you able to fight back?" he asked with hints of frustration on his tongue. "Only the most powerful of the Wizards should be able to resist me, but you are merely human…"

"That's where you're wrong," Angus said, wagging an index finger at him. "I have progressed beyond 'mere human', as you so eloquently put it."

The Wizard King scoffed. "What does that make you, then?"

"Who's to say? I have other questions on my mind. For example… if *this* is the best a Wizard King has to offer, does that mean I am beyond Wizards, even?"

"Don't be ridiculous. You have resisted me to an extent, true, but I am still in control."

"Why is it, then, that you've not taken your gaze off of me from the beginning?" the giant asked with a smirk. Zamarim could only groan. "You need not say. I know the answer: I could escape from this place without your utmost attention."

"You seem confident. Eager, even. How about we dive a little deeper into your memories, then?" he replied, holding out a hand and clawing at the giant's mind. "Show me why you are here."

Angus strained against the probing at first, but soon after, let out a long breath through his nose. "A fine idea…"

The blue space faded and a new scenery took shape around them: Zamarim stood in a wooded area, but the trees were withered and without leaves; all except one gigantic tree that cast such a shadow on him that it almost seemed like nighttime, despite the sun's yellow tint bending and poking through the branches. The tree before him was most certainly alive and well, towering at least a hundred meters high in his estimation, and filled with an uncountable number of green leaves up high.

After taking in his surroundings, the Wizard King realized where this memory was taking place: It was the northernmost end of the Dead Woods, which resided in the Faiwell settlement of Federland. As it had been told to him, most of the trees here withered and died due to the substantial nutrients absorbed by the grand tree standing before him.

He followed Angus into a small opening of the tree and raised an eyebrow to find that the inside was similar to a fully furnished home. There were several rooms and hallways made entirely from the trunk of the tree that they walked through. Paintings hung from the walls, and basic furniture like tables and chairs made it feel lived in. Eventually, Angus stopped in a room with a big bed.

Zamarim walked around the giant and gazed upon the blonde woman lying under some covers. She looked groggy and detached; like someone who had lost the will to live. She made no movements save for long, heavy breaths that seemed to disrupt the entire bed. Most odd, however, was that she was nearly as wide as the bedframe. He had never seen a living human so overweight before. He could also see that underneath the covers, there were several immobile tentacles where her legs should have been.

"I've brought some supplies, my dear," Angus said, obviously forcing cheerfulness into his tone. It still managed to come out stoic, somehow. The blonde woman let out a disinterested groan. "Now, now, don't be grumpy."

"I have nothing left to live for, Angy," she replied in a husky voice.

"That's not true."

"It is. I lost my chance at ultimate power, and my ability to move. And now? Look at me…" She seemed out of breath from the few words she had spoken. Zamarim couldn't help but take pity on her.

"That will all be fixed," Angus replied while placing the supplies on a table to his left. He sat on the bed next to the blonde woman, with what little room was available. "You have been invaluable to the Dark Wizard's plans. He has told me that once we truly unleash Greed, he will allow you to fuse with him, this time with *you* in control, and all of your ailments will be healed."

"My father thinks otherwise."

"You need not worry about him. I may not be as powerful as you are soon to be, but I have still progressed far beyond human abilities. I could kill him with ease if you so desired," Angus said.

"Oh, Angy!" the blonde woman said, clapping her hands together. "Kiss me."

Angus leaned over and placed both hands on her chubby cheeks. They shared a kiss for a while; long enough to make Zamarim uncomfortable.

The Wizard King cocked his head. "So, there *is* a Dark Wizard involved…"

After the kiss finally ended, Zamarim approached the blonde woman lying in a bed. She wore a warm smile that refused to fade. Her gaze, which seemed kind and full of cheer at first, began to feel malicious. Her chubby face turned a goopy black; like tar, and her eyes became yellow. Suddenly, everything faded to dark, and slowly but surely, a pair of giant yellow eyes revealed themselves. It was unlike any vision he'd witnessed before; as if it were happening *now* and not as a memory. The malice-filled eyes grew closer with each passing second, and more and more, Zamarim felt light-headed.

Then, in a split-second, the vision returned to how it was before. He was back inside the great tree of the Dead Woods. Angus stood and looked at him, breaking the flow of the memory and loosening Zamarim's control of the situation.

"*Of course* the Dark Wizard is real. Did you truly think a group of humans could bring down the Greed monolith alone?"

"Then, let us dig further into your memories. Reveal to me his identity!" Zamarim cried while holding a hand out and closing his eyes so tightly that they trembled. The scenery faded back to the blue void, but soon after, a new area faded in: This time, they were in a grand cathedral on a stormy night. Green flames danced upon candles held high, and an organ blared in the background to the tune of rumbling thunderclaps and pounding rain against the roof.

Zamarim sat at one of the benches and observed in silence as Angus was strapped to a swiveling table. A large, cloaked man loomed over him, and two more cloaked men came from a back room, each doing their part to carry a cauldron. If this truly *was* a Dark Wizard, Zamarim thought with a furrowed brow, then it was odd that he'd be using a cauldron. Normally, only Witches used them.

"Are you prepared to transcend your humanity?" the Dark Wizard asked. Zamarim was stricken by his deep voice. It filled the cathedral with power and dread.

"Yes."

"Very well…"

The Dark Wizard held a hand out and recited an incantation:

> *Slara teat feinum*
> *Pleite an chroide*
> *Resnu domin altigh*
> *Etus perios doam laitem*
> *Teig dorchae accadh tu*

SEVEN SEALS

Etus imverte isteam doam nearem
An duino as exuan

Twisted Tongue, Zamarim thought with a disgusted snort. He could vaguely make out the wording to know such a thing, but he knew not what spell it was for until he saw the dark liquid rise out of the cauldron. The Wizard King then noticed that Angus' arm was black and blue; and it had a long slice going down from shoulder to palm.

The dark liquid flowed through the air, dancing like a snake to a charmer, until it eventually poured into the wound on Angus' arm. After it all dumped in, the giant cried out in a sudden pain and began squirming.

"This is part of the process. Remain still, or you will die," the Dark Wizard warned.

A foreboding wind shot through the church and blew out all candles except the ones near Angus. Instead, those candles flared up and shone a brighter green. The howling wind became deafening, but only for a moment. Soon, Angus' struggle ceased, and all fell silent.

"You have been reborn. How do you feel?" the Dark Wizard asked as his helpers unstrapped him from the swiveled table.

"The greatest I've ever felt," he replied. The slice and bruising on his arm had disappeared.

"Excellent. I can feel that the dark essence has resonated well with you."

Angus didn't respond to his cloaked cohort, and instead looked back at Zamarim, breaking the memory once more. The candles of the chapel stopped their flickering and froze in place, and all sound ceased. The Wizard King gritted his teeth. How could an untrained man resist him to this extent? Was it this dark essence at work?

The giant smirked and then nodded his head toward the Dark Wizard. "Don't you wish to see who it is?"

Zamarim walked onto the stage, undeterred by Angus' boastful attitude or even the bizarre change in environment. He was still in control, after all. On approach of the Dark Wizard, it became apparent just how big he was: Nearly a full head taller than the King Wizard himself, and a bit larger than Angus, even. Still, Zamarim knew himself to be all-powerful in his domain and placed an authoritative hand around the hood. There was a moment of hesitation; an ominous feeling that gave him pause. He ignored those feelings, though, and ripped the hood back to see who it was.

The face of a snake covered in darkness popped out at Zamarim, its glowing red eyes eliciting a gasp. He stumbled back as the snake transformed into a dark substance, shooting into his mouth like a vile waterfall. Zamarim held his throat in vain as he felt the darkness spread about his body. The stresses and fears of what might come soon floated away, and so too did his mind. Though the dark was overtaking him, it was oddly relaxing, and he was quick to give in. Cracks began to take shape all around the cathedral, and though his glazed-over eyes did not pick up on it, his ears surely heard the shattering of all around him, and then there was nothing. Sweet, beautiful, *nothing*.

∼

MEANWHILE, Joel and the others walked the shoreline of Lake Teras. Pierce led them toward a shack to the east. As he had told them, it was where the Wizard Scout of the Famine seal, Thurick, resided. With his abilities, he could take them to the island at the lake's center.

After a long, uneventful walk, the group reached Thurick's shack. Further ahead, the aforementioned Wizard rested in a rocking chair with his straw hat tilted downward. The dagger-eyed man let out a sigh and approached him. He tapped Thurick's shoulder lightly.

"Wha-what? Please don' hurt me!" Thurick pleaded nonsensically as he fell out of his chair. He tipped his hat up and narrowed his eyes from the ground. "Oh, it's only you."

"Is that any way to speak to the Keeper of the Key? Your partner?" Pierce asked.

"I'd take you more seriously if you weren't always wearin' that ridiculous mask."

A muffled snort escaped the mask and he crossed his arms. "I don't suppose you've encountered any fellow Wizards of late, have you?"

"As it just so happens, a feller who could control the water passed by the other day," Thurick said. Pierce looked back to Joel, who nodded to signify that it had to have been Aldous. "An' then, a buncha humans came through and walked the path that the other Wizard created! That was a strange day... did they open up the wall ta humans or somethin'?"

"No. Those were bandits that you let in," Pierce replied before sighing.

"Ah, what's the big deal? I'm sure Zamarim could take care of 'em easily!" Thurick's tone was so laid back that Joel wondered if he had any cares in the world at all.

"Well, have ya heard anythin' back from 'im?" Alistair asked.

"No… I had assumed that he killed 'em."

"This is going nowhere…" Pierce muttered. "We need to reach the island at the lake's center. Will you take us?"

"Why should I?" Thurick asked as he sat back in his rocking chair.

"The fate of this city, and perhaps the world, depends on it," Roland jumped in.

Thurick laughed and then looked at Pierce. "Where do you find these people?"

"He's right, though. You must realize that the Famine monolith is in danger," Pierce said.

"Is it, now?" the Wizard scout said with a roll of his eyes. He attempted to tilt his straw hat back down, but Pierce held it up. "Do you mind? I'm tryin' to get some rest."

"Would you like me to report you to the Wizard's Council? I know that you've been enjoying the high life here, sitting around and doing nothing all day. But with my report, I could have you back on cleanup at headquarters," Pierce said.

"Ugh… I hate cleanup…"

"So, help us out, then. We can't make it beyond the Lake Watcher without you."

Thurick sighed. He stood and then cracked his knuckles. "I think yer overreactin', but fine. I'll take you across."

The knights sent by Princess Ella conversed in private. They appeared to be confused. One stepped forward to address Lord Roland.

"What is going on, here? What does any of this have to do with the Lake Watcher?" he asked.

"It sounds like you gentlemen have been fed lies," Thurick said with a derisive laugh.

"A *white lie*, mayhap," Lord Roland added. "The Lake Watcher is real and can kill us easily, but it is *not* the true threat of this lake."

"We didn't sign up for this. Your defiance of Princess Ella's wishes will not go unpunished."

"Oh? Are you lot going to punish us?" Lord Roland asked as he and the rest of the group drew their weapons.

"Erm… no… I'm gonna report back to her. You are on your own

from here." The knight turned and signaled to the men that they were leaving.

"Well, that didn't take long," Roland quipped.

"They woulda slowed us down, anyway!" Alistair said. "Now, bring us ta tha island, mista Wizard! I gots a new axe ta break in!"

The big man looked to see that Thurick faced the lake, already concentrating. Rocks from the lakebed crept up out of the water. A pathway was being built.

CHAPTER 29
TRIALS OF TERAS

Bartholomew Montgomery shook his head and rubbed his eyes. When all became clear to him, he flinched in surprise; Angus stood over him with an outstretched hand. He took the giant's help and was lifted as if he were a child.

"Fancy seeing you here, big fella," he said.

"You have done well to come this far," Angus replied.

"We have a treasure to find, after all."

"Indeed… and we are so close," the giant said, looking back to the cave entrance. "On that note, I have good news. There is one less person for us to split it between."

Bart rubbed his hands together. "This deal keeps gettin' better and better. So, what are we waitin' for?"

"How did you reach this island?"

"Why does it matter?"

"No human could have gotten past the Lake Watcher alone. Did the Wizard help you, as I predicted?" Angus asked.

"There was a Wizard, just as you said… he was able to part the water and made a path. Some of my men were still killed by that vile monster, but he saved us," said Bartholomew.

"I see." Angus turned his attention to further down the tunnel. Only a couple of flames provided light off in the distance. "Did you come in here with him?"

"He entered before we did. In fact, he told us to wait outside for him to return. Naturally, we're here for the treasure, so we didn't listen. After all of those nightmares, I must admit that his advice was sound," Bart said.

"You need not worry about that anymore. The one who put us all in that trance is incapacitated."

"That's a relief," the bandit leader said as his underlings approached. When they reached the pair, Angus addressed them.

"The treasure is in the depths of this cave. However, the Wizard who helped you earlier wishes to keep the treasure hidden in this place. We must be cautious of him, for he might use deadly force to his ends. He could be lurking anywhere…"

"But he didn't seem like the kinda fellow who was out to kill," Giles said.

"His motivations mean little," Bart jumped in. "It was kind of him to bring us here, but the only reason we journeyed to this forlorn island in the first place was to obtain that treasure. Something you must learn as a bandit, young one, is that we take what we can, when we can. Anyone in our way is an enemy."

"Yes, sir…" he replied sheepishly.

"I'm sure that the treasure won't be easily reached. There is little time to waste, so let's get moving," Angus said.

"Erm… one suggestion, if I may?" Norman asked. The giant gave him a nod. "I ain't sure how long it's been since we fell under that odd spell, but I'm thirsty as all hell."

"You raise a good point," Angus said, flicking his dry tongue. "Very well. Let's take a quick water break."

"What about food? I'm hungry!" one of the bandits complained.

"Don't you remember? The only fruit we found on this island dissolves in your mouth!" Bartholomew replied. Angus raised an eyebrow but said nothing.

～

Meanwhile, Joel and the group had hopped onto Thurick's rock platforms as they rose out of the water. The Wizard Scout had worked up a sweat and grunted through gritted teeth each time they shot out before the group, slowly but surely. Joel remembered Aldous mentioning that he was probably the strongest of all Scouts, but he was still surprised at how much effort and time it was taking for each platform to raise. Perhaps he'd been spoiled by his Wizard cohort's mastery of water and lightning, but Thurick's struggles did little to inspire confidence. What if the Lake Watcher were to attack? Would he be able to defend them?

"Are you sure this is safe?" Pierce asked, seemingly echoing the mute's concerns. "Couldn't you raise these a little higher?"

"That would drain too much magic. The less I have to do, the more likely it is that we reach that island…"

"Whoa, hold up!" Alistair called out from behind. "Yer tryin' ta tell me that ya haven't made it ta the island before?"

"There wasn't a need," Thurick said with an eye roll. "Zamarim always communicates with telepathy."

"Tele-what?" the big redhead asked with bewilderment written on his face. Joel nudged the big man and made hand signals. "Oh! Why didn't he just say 'he spoke ta me in mah mind'? Quit usin' fancy-speak fer nothin'!"

"Do you truly believe that these people will be of any help?" Thurick asked, looking back at Pierce with a smirk.

"There's more to us than meets the eye," Lord Roland butted in.

"If you say so…"

"We could always use your help," Pierce said. "We can handle the bandits, I'm sure, but there will be one among them who goes beyond human capabilities."

"Another Wizard, mayhap?"

"No, this one is… something else entirely. I don't know what to call him, but even my dagger was unable to kill him. But with *your* great powers…"

Pierce looked back at the group as if to signal that it was time to butter Thurick up.

"Yes, I've been told that you are among the most powerful Wizards," Roland added.

"Even though ya smell and seem lazy, I too can tell yer real strong, lad!" Alistair said. Joel shrugged because he couldn't say anything.

"We'll see if I feel like it," Thurick said.

"That's all I ask," Pierce assured him.

∽

ALDOUS AWOKE from his slumber with a start. After his dream world collapsed, he had been sent to a plane of eternal darkness. He'd floated there for some time and eventually figured out that something had gone wrong for Zamarim. With that in mind, he had been able to break the spell through his willpower. Any Wizard worth their salt had at least *some* subconscious training to combat Psychics, as a precaution. Snapping himself out of a vision was no problem for Aldous, so long as a Wizard of Zamarim's caliber was not in control.

He stood to the cracks, aches, and pains in his knees and back from a long-term lack of movement, and then looked around to see that the blue light streaks along the walls and ceiling had long since faded. His first instinct was to light it up once more and get a good view of the area, but chatter echoing from down the tunnel disturbed him.

Aldous thought that it could have been the bandits whom he had previously told to wait outside, but something didn't feel right to him. He sensed an unsettling presence. Instead of confronting the chatter, he chose a cautious approach: The old Wizard remembered that there were two sets of stairs on each side of the room. He took the set to the left, which brought him to an opening that led down a long corridor. It made for a good, if basic, place to hide for the time being.

∽

Angus and the Mithikan bandits made their way into the central room, noticing the two lit torches to the left and right.

"See that torch stand? Light it up," the giant commanded as he walked to the right and did so himself. Bart walked to the left and did the same.

The bandits gasped to see streaks of blue light travel along the walls and eventually clash at the ceiling to make one brilliant light that ended any semblance of darkness in the cave.

"Wh-what is this? I've never seen such a light source before," Bart said, his eyes as wide as gold coins.

Angus snorted. "This is the technology of the Ancient Ones. Even after all of these years, we have been unable to match such convenience. Just another reason that we must become more focused; less on the selfish desires of the individual, and more on the needs of the collective."

"Whatever gets us that treasure, big fella," Bartholomew said with a chuckle.

"So, what do we do now?" Giles asked.

Angus and the bandits scanned the area. There were sets of stairs on each side of the cave, and in the middle was a circular, dark blue platform that fit into a hole in the ground. Some of the blue streaks went down and through the hole. The platform had four chains attached to it, all hanging from the ceiling.

"This appears to be one of the Trials of Teras," Angus said.

"What's that all about?" Norman asked.

"Legend has it that the treasures are protected by a series of puzzles and booby-traps. I suppose this means we aren't in for an easy payday, gentlemen," the giant explained as he walked over to the circular platform and pushed a foot down on it. It wobbled under the pressure, but only slightly. "I believe that this will descend to the treasure if we can get it working."

Bartholomew looked up at the chains. They ran directly into each of their own holes in the ceiling. He then gazed at each set of stairs and the corridors that they led to.

"The mechanism to get them working must be there," he said, pointing to each set of stairs.

"I may be able to get us down there without the need for these silly games," Angus said as he flexed his right arm and a loud *crack* echoed off the cave walls. "But perhaps you should check around while I try my method. Just beware that Wizard. As I said, he is our enemy."

Bart's eyes widened when fragments of bone grew from the giant's arm and swirled around until it enveloped it entirely. At the end, where Angus' hand would be, an axe head formed. With each passing second, the layers of bone thickened all the more, until it became several-fold the size of an ordinary axe head.

"Erm... alright..." Bartholomew muttered with notable hesitation. He looked to one of his men. "We'll take the right side. Giles and Norman, you take the left."

The bandits split up to each side of the cave and walked up their respective stairs.

∼

Now atop the stairs, Giles felt a nervous pit form in his stomach as they entered the corridor. There were several slits flanking him in the long hall, and though it was somewhat lit up by the blue streak on the ceiling, it was still a muted shade of dark. After having relived his worst moments via Zamarim's mind prison, he was more on-edge than ever.

"Keep movin'," Norman said as he increased his pace, gradually leaving him behind. "We're bandits now, Giles. Don't be a coward."

Giles held in a snicker and rolled his eyes instead. Norman had a way with words that could make *anyone* angry, he thought. One of his top reasons for joining up with Bart had been strength in numbers. He desperately wished to avoid another night like the senseless slaughter of his family; to feel strong. Being around Norman instilled him with the opposite feeling, however. And to make matters worse, Bart had seemingly led them into a situation where they'd all be helpless. More and more, he was regretting his decision to join the bandits.

While trapped in his regretful thoughts, Giles felt his arm being tugged. Then, a great force suddenly pulled him into one of the slits in the corridor. He let out a brief gasp before a hand covered his mouth. He began hyperventilating and struggling until the hand at his mouth and one on his shoulder turned him around and revealed their owner. Giles let out a quiet sigh of relief to see Aldous pressing a finger up to his lips and slowly releasing the hand from his mouth.

"Are you lost already?" Norman's voice echoed from the corridor.

"No..." Giles trailed off as he looked to the old Wizard for clarification. Aldous nodded. "I'm just checking something out. Go on without me, I'll catch up."

"Fine by me."

After waiting a few moments, Giles raised an eyebrow at Aldous and whispered, "What are you doing here?"

"I could ask the same of you," Aldous replied under his breath. "You don't belong with these people. Not if they're working with the big fellow."

"Yeh, yer Wizard friend said the same thing. He forced me to live out my worst memories as punishment."

"He did the same to me."

"So, he's not yer friend?" Giles asked.

"It is a complicated situation. His loyalty lies more in protecting this island than any kind of friendship," Aldous said.

"Is there really a treasure on this island?"

"Oho... it ain't a treasure, I'll tell you that much," Aldous replied with an odd mixture of amusement and dread. "Underneath this place lies an unspeakably powerful monster. If it is successfully unleashed into this world, Thironas will be left in ashes, and it will signal the beginning of the end for mankind."

"A little dramatic, wouldn't you say?" Giles asked.

"Not at all. The lot of you, save the big fellow, know not what you are searching for. You should leave while you have the chance."

"So, Angus has been lying to us? He hired us to infiltrate the island."

"You are not starving citizens of Thironas?"

"I am, but not all of us are. It would be more accurate to call ourselves bandits," Giles whispered as the corridor rumbled under a smashing impact from back in the circular room. The duo braced themselves against the wall as more rumbles and noises erupted. They sounded much like a gong being struck. It had to be Angus and that makeshift bone axe of his, he thought.

After the commotion settled, Aldous chuckled. "You are no bandit, m'boy."

"How do you know?"

"You remind me of a friend of mine…" he muttered while looking outside the slit, smiling. "Besides, I am sure that by now, Angus has told you lot that I am your enemy. I doubt you'd be speakin' to me if you truly felt that way."

"I don't trust him," Giles said as a look of concern swept over his boyish face. "But if what you say is true, why would he wanna release such a monster?"

"It is not by his choice. He does the bidding of a Dark Wizard and a corrupt noble. Does that explain it?" the old Wizard asked with a chuckle.

"Indeed. I may not know of any Dark Wizards, but I am well-acquainted with corruption," Giles said as a great crashing noise filled the corridor and seemed to shake all of the cave. The impact was heavier than before, though the effects were briefer than Angus' previous strikes. From afar, his keen ear picked up on jingling chains.

"Everyone! Come back to the main room! I have found a way down!" Angus's husky, monotone voice echoed.

Giles looked back to Aldous, who gave him a nod. "Go. I won't be far behind. We must wait for the correct moment to strike."

He exited the slit and looked back to see Norman approaching. "Find anything interesting?"

"Nothing of consequence," Giles replied. The pair returned to the main area of the cave.

They were shocked to find a great hole in the floor where the platform once hung. The bandits gathered behind Angus and looked into the hole. The platform had fallen no more than a few meters down.

"Is the treasure down there?" Bartholomew asked.

"I believe it is," said Angus.

"And that was the so-called 'trial'?" Norman asked with a scoff. "It was hardly a challenge!"

"Not for me, it wasn't. But for normal men? It would have been near-impossible, I'm sure," Angus replied with crossed arms.

Giles looked up at the cut chains. Each was at least five inches thick and made of metal. No ordinary man could have cut through it.

"Then, what do you need us for?" Bartholomew asked. The giant glared back at him, and the bandit leader flinched. Giles brought a hand down to the hip, where his weapon lay. He wasn't so sure that it would do him any good, but it at least seemed that his distrust was somewhat shared.

"Never a good question to ask," Angus said as the bone axe retracted back into his arm. "But I'll be honest with you: You were meant to be a distraction."

Bart cocked his head and frowned. "For the Lake Watcher?"

"For the Wizards. The Lake Watcher could have killed the lot of you in seconds, but if you were to reach the island, the one who guards this place would need to put more effort into subduing a group."

"Those dark dreams we were having… you broke us out of them, didn't you?" Giles asked.

"In a way, yes. Part of that was because he had to trap a group of us, including a fellow Wizard. That was an added bonus… if he hadn't been caught in those dreams, it would have taken me far longer to break the spell. Even in stasis, you lot likely would have died from water deprivation," Angus explained.

"What you are saying is that you don't need us anymore, then," Bart said as he drew his sword. Giles and the other bandits brought out their weapons shortly thereafter.

"Calm yourselves. I intend to see our deal through to the end. You must realize by now that it's useless to attack me. If I wanted you dead, it would have already happened," Angus said as he approached the hole in the floor. "Now, follow me to the treasure."

The bandits looked at each other with unease as the giant hopped into the hole. Giles heard the *thud* of boots striking metal below. Bartholomew sheathed his blade and the others were at ease. He motioned them to follow.

Giles remained behind as the others hopped in, and he looked to the left corridor to see Aldous watching from the shadows. The old

Wizard nodded at him, and with that, he jumped down into the depths of uncertainty.

∼

With the island in view, Thurick breathed a sigh of relief as a new rocky piece of path rose from the water. "Perhaps the Lake Watcher doesn't mind my presence, after all."

"And just what is that supposed ta mean?" Alistair asked.

"So far as I know, only Zamarim can control the beast thanks to his command over the mind. Making it to the island unscathed was never a sure thing, but it would seem-"

The Wizard Scout interrupted himself, and it was apparent to all in the group behind him why. To their left, charging at them like an enraged bull, was a great, dark bulge in the water. Waves flared out in its wake and grew larger with each passing second, and the water hissed at them in warning.

"The Lake Watcher!" Pierce called out.

Thurick whimpered before raising his arms, and along with them came walls of thick rock; sprouting on each side of the group until they were boxed in. Under the straw hat, Joel could see sizable beads of sweat leaking onto his shirt, and his rapid breaths seemed to shake his entire body. He could hardly blame him. If this Guardian Beast was anything like the Nightcrawler, then all of them had ghastly deaths in their near-future.

"Well, now whatta we do?" Alistair asked.

"We wait," Thurick said as he wiped sweat from his brow. "An' then, I'm gettin' the hell outta here. Nothin' is worth the fate that awaits us if the Lake Watcher captures our group as prey."

All on the rocky path drew their weapons and stood on edge as the wavy waters outside slapped the walls. However, there was no impact from the charging monster. Had it turned away? Or did it have something else in store?

Alistair looked at Joel. "Oi! Do ya think yer sword can cut that monstah?"

The mute tilted his head and then shrugged. For some reason, he hadn't thought of the idea before.

"We may have to find out for ourselves, soon," Pierce said, approaching Thurick. "Is there nothing else we can do?"

The Wizard Scout didn't respond and continued to stare ahead into the wall in front of him. Pierce grabbed him by the shoulder and began shaking him.

"Hey! Are you listening to-"

Thurick's head folded back like an accordion, and everyone shuddered at the sight of the skull-like face staring back at them, upside-down. All color and life had been drained from him, and his eyes had imploded into little clots of blood. At his neck, a red tongue-like organ had pierced through, and the grotesque gulping noises in addition to its expanding and retracting made Joel sick to his stomach. The tongue was poking through the rock wall ahead, and if it had been that easy for it to get through for one mere organ, then the Lake Watcher was surely only playing with its food for now.

Pierce rushed over and swung his dagger at the Lake Watcher's tongue. It bounced off to the gasps of all in the enclosed space, but a black liquid spurted up and the beast let out a cry that reminded Joel of a distorted trumpet. The tongue let go of Thurick and shot back to the outside through the hole that it had created earlier. The corpse of the Wizard Scout collapsed to the rocky floor that he'd once created, and with that impact, everyone's collective shoulders shot up to their ears at the *cricks* and *cracks* of his remaining muscles tearing and bones breaking.

"We're close to the island…" Pierce trailed off as he held his palm out and sliced it. The blood spilled out onto his dagger and it pulsed a powerful blue.

"What are you doing?" Lord Roland asked.

"Getting us out of here… I hope," Pierce said as he pointed his dagger upward and held on with both hands by the hand guard. "Grab hold, just like this."

"W-we're going to fly?" the lord asked, wide-eyed.

"Yes," he replied with a nod. "I've only ever done it under my own body weight, but one more person should be fine."

Roland grasped his hands around Pierce's, and in short order, they began to ascend.

"Hang on tight. If either of us falls, we're as good as dead," the dagger-eyed man said before looking down at Joel and Alistair. "I'll be back for you two."

The pair lifted high into the air and floated toward the island. Joel and Alistair, meanwhile, stood back-to-back with their weapons drawn. The big redhead held his newly-acquired battle axe outward in a defensive position while the mute did the same with his luxmortite sword. Thurick's corpse lay next to them, a dreadful reminder of how easily they could be killed.

"Well lad, this could be tha end fer us…" Alistair muttered as the wretched trumpet-like bellows of the Lake Watcher bounced off the outsides of the rock walls. "I just wanted ta say that it's been an honor fightin' alongside ya. Most folks don't think I'm worthy ta fight with 'em, but I know ya think differently."

After a long pause, the big man snorted. "Well, aren't ya gonna say anythin' nice about me?"

Joel shrugged. He couldn't communicate with him since they were back-to-back. "Oh, right…"

Sooner than expected, Pierce descended back into the walled-off rock platform. "Who's next?"

Joel pushed Alistair forward to volunteer him.

"No, lad! You should go before-"

Suddenly, an eruption of rocks flew at the trio, bouncing off the other walls and peppering them with cuts and bruises. Joel was the first to un-shield his face, and before him, at the water's surface, floated the Lake Watcher. Its soulless craters-for-eyes stared with killing intent, and it lifted its long snout and let out that dreaded trumpet-like bellow once more, numbing all of his senses.

"Both of you! Grab on!" Pierce's muted words barely reached Joel's ears as the Guardian Beast approached.

Alistair dragged a dumbfounded Joel by the back of his shirt and then wrapped his arms around Pierce's waist. The mute, finally snapping out of his stupor, grabbed hold of the big man's legs as they lifted off into the air.

Joel squirmed as the whips and cracks of the Lake Watcher's tongue assaulted his ears from below. Pierce grunted from above, his blood dripping down and onto a slipping Alistair. He'd already tried to adjust his grip around Pierce's waist a couple of times, but it always threw the delicate balance of the flight off, causing them to wobble.

Wanting to take his mind off of what was going on above, the mute, against his better judgment, looked down to see the Lake Watcher shooting up at him like a playful dolphin, only several-fold larger. With all the strength that his core could muster, Joel pulled his legs up and felt the wind of the beast slap his boots. A light mist reached his face, and it was oddly refreshing despite the dire situation. It felt like a full day had gone by before they reached the island and the splashes below them ceased.

The trio crashed to the grassy ground upon landing, and all of them were slow to rise.

"I'm tempted to tell you how close that thing was to getting you," Roland said, helping Joel to his feet. The mute let out a long breath and then gave Pierce a light pat on the back.

"Ya really came through fer us. Thanks!" Alistair said as he playfully smacked him on the shoulder. Pierce flinched in response.

"There is no time to waste," Lord Roland said. "Where do we go from here?"

"The island's center," Pierce replied, walking past him. Blood continued to drip from his palm.

"Will you be able to continue? That slice looks bad," the lord said.

"This?" he asked before holding up his hand and chuckling. "*This* is nothing."

∽

BACK IN THE CAVE DEPTHS, Angus and the bandits approached a great stone door. Next to it was an open torture device with spikes inside of it. Its iron finish was heavily rusted, as if not touched for a long, long time.

"What is that thing?" Bartholomew asked.

Angus chuckled. "Another one of the trials."

"This doesn't look like somethin' to laugh about…"

"I suppose not. I've encountered this torture device before. They call it an 'iron maiden'. You throw someone in there and shut the door… then, the blood pools in the bottom. With enough blood, the door will open," said the giant. "Back at Mt. Couture, this same test was a requirement to escape from a maze. We found a way around it with the explosive mushrooms, but I'm sure there aren't any around this time."

Bart grimaced. "Which begs the question: Why laugh at something like this? If you plan on betraying us-"

"I will do no such thing," Angus interrupted. "Back when I first encountered this test, I was but a man. I no longer have to play the silly games of the Ancient Ones."

Angus made a fist and then flexed his arm with a pained grunt and a loud *crack* to go along with it. Within seconds, bone sprouted from his arm and formed a molding around it. Over his fist, a great, white hammer took shape; easily larger than his head.

The bandits flinched when, with one gargantuan swing, the bone hammer made an impact crater in the thick stone door. After a second swing, the cave rumbled and half of it was knocked down. With the third and final swing, the last of the door shattered and shot into a new passageway where the blue light came to an end and lit torches were the only sources of light. The bandits looked at each other with slacked jaws while the bones retracted back into Angus' arm.

"I like this fella," Norman remarked.

The bandits followed Angus into the darkness, unaware of his true intentions, but drawn in by his abilities and promises all the same.

CHAPTER 30
THE OTHER SIDE

Angus led the bandits on a dank, rocky pathway with lit torches flanking them down the stretch. Each of them had taken a firebrand for themselves, but in addition, the giant was purposely snuffing flames out as he traveled along.

"What is the purpose of putting these fires out?" Bartholomew asked.

"The Wizard who opposes us can control fire. I'm doing this to ensure our safety. He'd char each of us down to the bone without hesitation," Angus said. Giles cast a suspicious eye on him.

"Why are ye givin' him a look like that?" Norman asked aloud. Giles let out a stuttered breath and then shoved him, but it was too late to try quieting him down. The others had taken notice, and their faces demanded an explanation.

"Well…" Giles trailed off, his mind scrambling for excuses. He'd already sided with Aldous; it was just a matter of him showing up. At present, he couldn't hope to oppose the others, but with a Wizard by his side… "I've been thinkin': If the Wizard is as cold-hearted as you say, why would he save us from the Lake Watcher? He could have killed us at any time if he wanted to."

"That's a good point," another bandit added.

"Why would *our client* lie to us?" Norman asked.

"Indeed. I have been honest with you all up until this point, have I not?" Angus asked.

"We're losing focus of what's important here: the treasure," Bartholomew said with crossed arms. "We have yet to encounter this Wizard since awakening from the nightmare. Why would we now?"

"I am certain that he will eventually show up to oppose us. Down here, without the aid of water, lightning, or fire, he will not be able to stop me. The lot of you are another story," said the giant. "But we'll worry about that when it happens, I suppose."

The group continued until they reached a system of tunnels. Before them were eight different paths that appeared to go off in separate directions.

Bart's nose crinkled under the orange light of his torch. "Another trial?"

"Not what I expected, but most likely, yes," Angus replied, huffing. "I suspect this will be the final obstacle. One last attempt to slow us down. Perhaps they will be laced with traps."

"Shall we split up, then?"

"That would be for the best. All paths may lead to the treasure, but just in case, we should call out when we find it," the giant said.

With that, Angus and the bandits went their separate ways, choosing five different tunnels at random. Giles wasn't sure whether to feel safe to be away from Angus or horrified to be in the confines of a tunnel that may have housed deathly traps. All he knew for sure was that he had to survive until the end; to lend a helping hand to Aldous, on the off chance that he might need it.

∾

Aldous jumped into the depths of darkness, where Angus had cut down the circular luxmortite platform. He landed with grace, like a cat, and then stepped down to survey the new area.

His eyes widened upon seeing the rubble of the stone door. He'd been sure that the iron maiden torture device would at least slow them down, but it was yet another trial that they'd managed to bypass. It had to be Angus, he thought. He was sure that the disturbing presence he'd felt before was the giant. He no longer felt human.

Continuing along the path, Aldous noted the doused torches. Somehow, Angus, and by proxy Drake, knew of his abilities; another troubling thought. It began to feel more and more like he was walking into a trap, but what choice did he have? With everyone having been released from the blue void, he had to assume that Zamarim was somehow incapacitated. If that were the case, *he* was the Famine monolith's final defense.

After a short walk, the old Wizard reached a series of branching paths. He knew this to be the final trial of Teras. With a clank of his walking stick, he created a little ball of lightning that hovered just above to combat the darkness. Aldous looked down and closed his eyes. He searched his memories for the correct path, knowing full-well that the wrong choice could mean the release of Famine. He opened his eyes and pointed his walking stick toward the third tunnel from the left. At least the final trial would be significantly easier thanks to Zamarim's absence, he thought. Normally, throughout the tunnels, the Wizard King would probe an intruder's mind or subject them to unpleasant visions until they willingly turned back.

∽

Pierce led the way through the island forest at a brisk pace. His palm was still bleeding from when he had saved the others from the Lake Watcher. Heavy, muffled breaths bounced around beneath the mask. Joel could tell his friend was distraught, mostly because he had trouble keeping up. His shin had swollen to nearly double its original size from his battle with Angus, and each step taken was more painful than the last.

"What's tha deal with them fruits? I've never seen anythin' like 'em!" Alistair said as he looked at the trees. Dark violet fruits beckoned them from high up.

"Stay away from those," Pierce warned between breaths. "They are an imprint of Famine."

"What does that mean, exactly?" Lord Roland asked.

"Each spawn of the Dark Savior was locked away in a different world, as you know. Over time, however, each of the split identities has been able to push through and influence this world once more. In the case of Famine, that means the destruction of our crops, but also these strange fruits have been growing. I don't know exactly what they do, but it can't be good, considering the source."

"Ah, so it's like tha black gold from Greed?" Alistair said.

"Exactly. Back then, when we locked them away, we had no idea they could leave their imprints from *another world*. That's why everything is going wrong now…"

"We can stop it still, can't we?" Roland asked.

"No," he replied while shaking his head. "We can only delay the inevitable. Keep it on the other side for the time-being. Someday, Famine's influence will grow too powerful, and he will be free once more."

"As long as it's not today," the lord added with feigned cheer.

Eventually, the group reached the cave at the island's center. Pierce let out an exasperated sigh and came to a stop. Joel, Roland, and Alistair looked at each other in confusion. The mute approached his friend and gave him a tap on the shoulder. Pierce jerked his head back, as if shocked. Sweat ran down what little of his forehead wasn't covered by the mask, and it was dripping from his chin. Joel gestured to ask what was wrong.

"The situation looks bad," Pierce said as he turned back to the inside of the cave. "Zamarim should have established contact by now."

"I thought this Zamarim fellow was supposed to be one of the strongest Wizards in the world. How could Angus have beaten him?" Lord Roland asked.

"I don't know… but I had a bad feeling from the beginning. He was confident in his ability to get past him, even though Zamarim could easily put us all to sleep and starve us to death if he wanted to," said the dagger-eyed man.

"Well, there ain't no time ta waste, then!" Alistair said as he stepped ahead of the group and into the cave.

"You should follow my lead," Pierce said.

"Don't tell me yer *nice side* is underestimatin' me, too? We already know what we're up against! Meat-stain and some boggin bandits. So what? I'll chop 'em down with me new axe!" the big redhead bragged as he held the axe up in triumph.

"Let's not get ahead of ourselves," Lord Roland chimed in. "We don't know anything about the inside of that cave. Your time will come, my friend. But for now, I think that Ometos should take the lead." His gaze turned to Pierce, and Joel couldn't help but nod along. Like a true leader, Roland was keen to understand everyone's strengths and weaknesses.

"That's what I meant. If Angus and the bandits haven't gotten through them already, we'll need to complete the Trials of Teras to reach the monolith," Pierce said.

"Have ya ever made it through before?" Alistair asked.

"Only once, and it damn-near killed me," Pierce said while

wringing his hands. "But Angus is beyond any of us when it comes to strength and ability. He may have found ways around the trials."

Joel stepped to the front of the group and made hand signals to Alistair. "Ah, he's got a point. Aldous will be in thar. He can help us, too!"

That was, of course, if Aldous was alright. The fact that he hadn't been in contact for days was beginning to worry Joel. The old Wizard had always found ways out of sticky situations in the past, but this time, things felt different. It felt like Angus had planned out how to defeat them all. From stealing the key to preying on the mute's hesitation in bringing harm to others, all had gone the giant's way thus far.

As the group trudged down the tunnel, a glowing, blue room beckoned them from afar. At the new section of cave, Joel could see that it was well carved-out; a perfect circle. Stairs ascended each side into separate corridors, and at the center was a great hole where four broken chains dangled above.

Alistair smiled. "I recognize these lights! We had 'em at Mt. Couture, too."

"A specialty of our people," Pierce said with a nod back at Joel.

The mute, however, was distracted by the big hole in the floor. He walked ahead until he was at its edge. Below, under a weak veil of the blue light, he saw a circular platform, and based on its color, it was almost certainly made of luxmortite. He motioned the others over to join him at the ledge.

Pierce looked up at the shattered chains. "Just as I feared. Angus made short work of the first trial. I imagine the second won't be any different."

"And is there a third?" Lord Roland asked.

"Yes, but it can't be overcome with strength. It is a game of luck, determination, and time. There are several different tunnels, all leading to Zamarim's chamber. Some paths have traps, while others are long and winding. Only one of them is short and safe. In addition, Zamarim probes the intruder's mind and plagues them with horrifying visions that would melt even the strongest determination, but if something happened to him…"

Joel placed a hand on the dagger-eyed man's shoulder and gave him a reassuring nod. *No more time to waste*, he thought while leaping into the hole. However, in his rush, he had forgotten about the injury to his shin. He let out an inaudible gasp as the impact sent a jolt of painful lightning up his leg before he rolled forward to lessen the blow.

He returned to his feet with a hobble and then looked up to see the concerned faces of the others. He fought through the pain to force a smile and then waved them down.

Soon, they reached the second trial, where a stone door lay in pieces on the rocky floor.

Pierce sighed. "Not good…"

"But not surprising, either," Roland replied. "We already knew the big man could pack a punch. "Now, let us hope that he didn't know which path to take in the third trial."

"I don't think there's any way that he could know." A muffled laugh escaped from beneath Pierce's mask. "Even *I* don't know the correct path. Last time, I chose a tunnel that was filled with traps."

All in the group remained silent as they continued along the darkening tunnel. Eventually, they reached the branching paths. Of the eight tunnels, three emitted no light. Four of them were illuminated, while one was noticeably dimmed, but still held a slight glow.

"Perhaps the amount of light coming from a tunnel is a hint of which one to take," Roland suggested.

"Aldous can control fire. Maybe he made use of tha flames?" Alistair asked aloud.

"If that's the case, why would several of the tunnels hold no light?" Pierce asked. "Even still, I think it's a sign that they've been traversed. Perhaps one of the tunnels with light would be best to travel through."

"Shouldn't we split up? Ta cover more ground?" Alistair asked.

"I am not sure how dangerous the other tunnels are, but I would rather err on the side of caution," Pierce said, pointing to one of the dimmed paths. "All I am certain of is that *this one* is filled with deadly traps. I was lucky to escape with my life."

After some deliberation, the group decided to stick together and ended up taking the tunnel furthest to the left.

∼

As he walked, Aldous held a hand out and gathered flames from a torch until it was reduced to a mere ember, and then stored it for later use. Certain that he was on the shortest, safest path of the trials, the old Wizard was preparing for the very real possibility that he would soon be protecting the monolith.

Soon, a whole array of colors caught Aldous' eyes from off in the distance: From yellow to blue, to green. He recalled that Zamarim was an avid collector of Runes: Stones with ancient writing carved into them, each with their own ability to be used by those wielding them. Shortly after their death, a mage's soul was said to fly off to the great beyond as all others did, but their magic would not go with them. Instead, elsewhere in the world, it would be imprinted onto stone. Even ordinary humans could tap into the magic of Runes with the correct mindset, but being so rare and difficult to find, they typically found their way into the hands of Wizards, anyway.

Aldous' walk turned to a run, and in short order, he reached Zamarim's chamber. Before him stood a grand throne made of stone, up against a rock wall. Hanging from the wall in an arched pattern were a variety of Runes; the most he'd ever seen all at once. Golden torches lined the chamber on each side, and at the foot of the throne lay the Wizard King. The glow of the Runes bounced off of his bald head.

"No…" Aldous muttered as he rushed over and then knelt to check on him. He let out a sigh of relief to see that he was still breathing, at least.

His happiness was short-lived, however. If Zamarim was out cold, it meant that he truly *was* the final defense between Angus and the monolith. Unless he could somehow wake the Wizard King up. Aldous wasn't sure what had happened to him, but if there was anything he could do, he had to at least try.

Aldous grasped Zamarim's shoulder and shook him. There was no response. He shook him again, this time with more force, and then a blue wave of energy shot from out of his head, knocking the old Wizard back and to the ground.

A vision flashed before Aldous' eyes, similar to the replaying of his memories before. He found himself in an old hut, shaking hands with a young man with boyish, rosy cheeks.

"A pleasure to meet you. My name is Aldous. And you are?"

The boy held up a piece of paper that read:
JOEL

"Not much of a talker, eh? Nothin' ever happens 'round here, m'boy! We'll have to communicate somehow, to pass the time," Aldous said with a chuckle.

Joel began to make hand signals, to which the old Wizard cocked his head.

"Ah, sign language! Good idea. I learned USL so long ago; it'll take some time to remember, but I'm sure I can get the hang of it."

As if surfacing from the water, Aldous let out a loud exhale when he snapped out of the vision and back to reality. Zamarim was still out cold, but at least it was a sign of life. Did he dare disturb the Wizard King again?

∼

Confusion overtook Joel. He and the others had just been knocked back by a blue shockwave that filled the tunnel. Yet now, he found himself in the embrace of someone and was unable to move. Around him, through watery eyes, he could see treetops dancing in the wind, and it appeared he was at the base of a mountain.

"It is time," a grizzled voice called from behind him.

The mute turned to see an old man in a blue robe, but not Aldous. He seemed familiar, but-

Suddenly, he turned back involuntarily to the girl he'd been embracing. Her black, mid-length hair flowed too much in the wind to cover tears rolling down full cheeks, and one look at the dark gown she adorned told Joel exactly who he was looking at before their eyes even met. *Riza*, he thought with an attempted gasp, but nothing came out. His mouth hadn't even moved. Instead, he kissed her on the forehead before turning and walking away.

Now, Joel was beginning to understand. This was a memory; an especially vivid memory playing out before his very eyes. Could it have been the work of Zamarim?

"I'll miss you…" she mumbled. Her voice was stricken with grief, which he knew to be an exceptionally rare occurrence.

He stopped and turned to say goodbye, but nothing came from his mouth save empty air. Joel let out a defeated sigh and turned around. He threw a hand up and gave a quick wave as he walked away and all around him faded.

∼

Lord Roland sat in the quarters atop the clock tower in Thironas. Sitting across from him was a distraught old man sifting through papers. It was the previous lord of Thironas, Robert.

"I am sorry that you have to inherit this mess," the old man said.

Roland snorted. "It's funny. Most would be honored to receive such a title…"

"Mayhap luck will be on your side. For your sake, I hope so. It is the only way that you can succeed. The king, of course, doesn't understand how crops work. He thinks we have control over the famine, somehow," Robert said while shaking his head.

"There has to be something we can do," Roland said.

"It'd be best to start worrying about yourself. By this time tomorrow, I will have been executed. They need *someone* to take the fall."

"You could run away."

"At my age? Don't make me laugh! I'm too well-known, too old, and too hated. They'd catch me in no time."

"Is there anything I can do for you?" Roland asked.

"Yes… tell the cook to prepare dinner, would you? I plan on enjoying my last night alive," Robert said.

"As you command."

Before he could leave the room, however, Robert grabbed him by the shoulder and turned him around. There was a fiery frustration in his eyes.

"Let me tell you something, Roland. Having power over people ain't all it's made out to be. You take the blame for all that goes awry, and in Thironas, you don't even get to enjoy the high life!" Robert said with some chuckles that quickly tapered off. "When you take the title of lord, forget about honor. Forget about dignity. Do what you must to get by, understand?"

"You would have me rule with an iron fist, then? Somehow, I don't think that will go over well. I'd be executed in record time."

"I never said that," he replied, holding up a finger. "What I *am* saying is that my generosity, my caring, and my accomplishments mean nothing after tomorrow. You will share the same fate if you act as I did. Instead, you should do whatever it takes to get results. One day, that may require you to be the kindest, most giving lord this land has ever seen. On another, it might mean snuffing out dissidents. And sometimes, you'll have to be sneakier and more underhanded than those wretched thieves that live down below…"

"If only we could be granted access to the lake. That would quell some of the famine's effects," Roland said.

"That just reminded me. Tonight, I shall bypass the wall. I must know if the legends are true… or if we've been suffering for no reason."

"I'll come along-"

"No," Robert interrupted as he walked past Roland. "I will go alone."

"But the guards will shoot you down," he replied.

"Well then, cancel the dinner. I'm going out on my own terms!" Robert proclaimed as he left the office and all around Roland faded.

∽

ALISTAIR'S MIND raced as a training session with his older brother, Triston, played out before him. They fought with wooden batons in the vast fields of the MacRae farm. The big man was, for the first time in his life, pushing his brother back with a variety of swings that he'd learned from Dalton.

"Not bad, lil' brother!" Triston said as he smacked the redhead in the hand with his baton. Alistair flinched and dropped his wooden sword in response.

He put his hands up to show he had surrendered, but Triston smashed him in the face with the baton anyway. Alistair crashed to the ground and looked up with anger in his eyes. His brother let out an obnoxious laugh.

"Oi! What's tha big idea?" Alistair asked, feeling for splinters in his cheek.

"Do ya think the enemy is gonna care if ya surrender to 'em? They'll hit ya anyway!" Triston said as he held a hand out.

Alistair took it and his brother hoisted him up. "It's just practice…"

"I'm startin' ta wonder if all them stories ya told us about the minin' expedition were true, Ali. Ya sure did win a lotta battles fer a guy who can't fight."

"I can so fight!"

"Somethin' tells me yer friends saved ya more than you saved them," Triston said as he put hands to hips. "I suppose it don't matter much now, though. Yer back on the farm, where ya belong! Just because ya ain't much of a fighter, don't mean ya can't do good work out on the fields!"

The big redhead sighed as the memory faded and his insecurity grew.

∽

THE OTHER SIDE

Pierce's two selves watched on, helpless, as one of their worst memories played out before them. In the basement, on *that dreaded day*, he stood back with a big smile as his father Jed retrieved something from a chest. The smile turned sour, however, when he saw the sparkles of the black gold in his dad's hand.

"Beautiful, isn't it?" Jed asked. The dagger-eyed boy was speechless as his father held the black gold out in his palm for him. "Well? What are you waiting for? Take it."

"I can't…"

"What nonsense! It is the most precious thing I own! And I want you to have it. How could you turn down such generosity?"

"Do you understand what that is?" Pierce asked with a particular emptiness in his tone.

"But of course. It is a gift from our Dark Savior. The one who will ensure luxian tyranny comes to an end, bringing peace and harmony to all. Only the most sensible and caring of us all understand that…" Jed trailed off as he closed his fist around the black gold. "You *do* understand that, don't you?"

"No, father. It has corrupted your mind! You have to fight it!"

Jed sighed. "I was worried about this. It would seem you've gone down the wrong path."

"You're the one who's wrong. What will be accomplished by following the crusades of such a monster? One who seeks to 'help' others by destroying us? He isn't helping anyone! Can't you see that?"

"Those who do not follow the Savior's will must be stopped; they are *evil*," Jed said as he approached his boy and put a hand on his shoulder. "But you are my son…"

The two halves of Pierce stirred; one wishing to turn away, the other wishing to fight. Both, however, were helpless to change what was already set in stone. They were merely passengers on a hellish ride.

Like a frog snatching a fly, Jed grabbed him by the arm and dragged him over his shoulder with sudden force. Pierce flipped in midair and then landed face-first against the chest, numbing his nose and ringing his ears. He snapped out of his daze upon sensing the miasma of the black gold beckoning him.

The dagger-eyed boy stood and turned just in time to see a back-handed slap connect with his jaw. Pierce stumbled and looked back up at his enraged father; his eyes had turned a light tint of yellow. He felt blood trickle down the side of his lip.

"I suppose that I'll have to beat some sense into you," Jed said with utter disdain. "Even if you're rotten like the rest of them. I'm willing to try and show you the way."

The scenery faded out as Pierce watched his father's fist fly into his eye, and again, the two halves of Pierce stirred. One couldn't take anymore, and *the other* wanted more than anything to fight.

∼

JOEL RUBBED his eyes and sat up. He was back in the tunnel, and echoing off the walls were the gasps of the others. It sounded as if they'd awakened from nightmares, and for all he knew, they had.

Roland was the first to stand. "What the hell *was* that?"

Alistair rubbed his forehead and watched as Joel made hand signals to him. He translated, "Joel thinks it must'a been Zamarim."

"Isn't that a good thing? It means he's alive and well," said the lord.

"Aye…" Alistair said in an uncharacteristically quiet tone.

"You alright?" Lord Roland asked. "It is unlike you to speak with such finesse."

"Oh… right… that dream I had… reminded me of some bad things, is all," the big man replied.

"You too, eh?" Roland asked before his gaze turned to Joel. "And what about you? Everything good?"

The mute nodded and looked back to a groggy Pierce. He readjusted his mask and stood slowly.

"How about you, Ometos? All clear?" Roland asked. He did not receive a response.

Pierce walked toward the group at a lumbering pace that increased with each step. Joel narrowed his eyes, then took a step back. He looked into the eyes of the masked man, now jogging toward him. Something wasn't right.

"The mask!" Roland cried.

Pierce had flipped his Ometos mask back around to the more sinister expression. It was no longer their friend among them, but *the other*.

Joel drew his sword as Pierce charged with a full-on sprint. A moment later he was within range and leaped out at the mute while drawing his dagger. He attempted a horizontal slash, but Joel swiped his sword to the right, deflecting the luxmortite blade.

"Oi! Bring tha real Pierce back!" Alistair called out as he drew his battle axe and charged at him.

He came to a sudden halt, however, when Joel held a hand up. He glanced back and shooed them away.

"What're ya playin' at, lad? I ain't leavin' ya behind! We're stickin' together!"

"No, he's right…" Roland said as he placed a hand on the big man's shoulder. "Let them settle the score. *We* have a monolith to protect."

"But I can't-" Alistair was silenced by Joel, who kicked dirt back at him. The big redhead took a deep breath and turned to leave along with Roland. From further down the tunnel, Joel heard him call out, "You can beat that knob, Joel! Do whatcha gotta do!"

If only it were that simple, he thought.

"No Greta, no Angus, no Famine… no more distractions," Pierce said as he twirled the dark blue blade in his hand.

Pierce lunged out with a right-handed stab, which Joel sidestepped. The dagger-eyed man then swung in an arced motion to his right, which Joel blocked by holding his blade vertically upward. However, as the *clang* of their clash rang off the walls, Pierce delivered a speedy kick to Joel's injured shin. His mouth hung agape in a hopeless attempt to cry out in agony, but as usual, his suffering was in silence.

Joel fell to the ground, and though his first temptation was to hold his leg in anguish, he knew another attack was coming. He rolled to the left as the *thunk* of metal striking ground sounded off behind, and then used his hand to propel himself upward and onto his good leg. The mute hopped backward until he reached the wall, where he could support his full weight. He tried to put some pressure on the injured shin, but the pain was intense, and he jerked his foot back up as a natural reaction.

"Your foolish defense-only strategy is why I was able to land that kick," Pierce said while slowly approaching. "Returning to the state of mind that allowed you to kill my parents would increase your chances of winning. But you won't do that, will you? You're too busy trying to convince yourself that you have a pure heart."

Joel pushed himself off of the wall and put most of his weight on the good leg. He winced at the nerve-pinching pain in his swollen shin, but took a new stance with his sword: He stood sideways, with most of the pressure on his uninjured back leg. He held his sword with only his right hand, and it was pointed downward to his left.

Pierce scoffed. "What is that supposed to be? A human sword art?"

He approached quickly with the dagger held overhead. As he brought it down, Joel swung his blade upward and diagonal to meet it. While the blades clashed, the mute continued his sword's curved arc and brought the dagger along, upward and to his right. Amid their combined swing, Joel pivoted and grabbed Pierce's weapon-wielding hand with his left, then twisted it to disarm him.

As the dagger *clanged* off the ground, Joel started to point his blade toward Pierce's chest, but two things at once stilled him: The banshee shriek of Osanna rang in his ears and his leg flared up as he put weight on it to pivot. Wincing both in terror and in pain, that split-second was all that Pierce had needed. Joel regained focus just in time to see his left hand hooking across, mere inches from impact.

At the last second, Joel turned his cheek to make the booming hook a glancing blow to his jaw. He stumbled back as Pierce made a dive for his dagger. Both regained their footing in short order and then took new stances.

"Regardless of what the *nice guy* says, I think that even *he* realizes the truth about you." Pierce pointed his dagger with righteous judgment. "See, I take the stage when times get tough. I deal with rogues and thieves, and I kill when it is required. Meanwhile, *he* comes out for happier times; when Greta is around, or among friends. The fact that I am out here now says it all, don't you agree?"

The mute took a step back and held his stance.

"Because your peaceful ways will eventually get your allies killed, it would be in their best interest if you died here today..." the dagger-eyed man trailed off as he plodded ahead. "Or at least, that *would be* the case, if not for me. After I kill you, I'll fulfill my promise: First, I'll slaughter your big-mouthed friend, and then I'll leave these wretched lands to go and find Riza."

Joel crinkled his nose as he raised his sword overhead and shimmied forward. He'd have been growling if he was able to. Once within range, the mute made the first move by stepping forward and bringing his blade down. However, instead of a straight vertical slash, he tilted his sword to the left for an angled attack. Pierce picked up on the well-hidden move and blocked, two-handed, with his dagger.

In mid-clash, a blue shockwave suddenly plowed through the tunnel and hit them. Eyes wide and filled with blue, Joel felt himself being transported to a new vision; one that he recognized immediately when it took shape. He and some other young luxians in training stood in a row, out in a grassy field. Before each of them were gagged human men who were tied up to boards. They wriggled and squirmed like flies trying to escape a spider's web.

With tepid steps, Joel approached one of the tied-up men. Next to him stood an official of the luxian army, clad in light chainmail and a traditional tunic filled with blue patterns. Joel drew his blade and started to swing, but a mere inch from impact, he halted.

"What are you doing?" the official asked.

"He's defenseless," Joel replied.

"We are at *war*. The enemy is ruthless, and you must be equally so, or you will die a dog's death."

"I'll be in the heat of combat out at war."

"If you cannot do what must be done now, then you will falter later… and it'll get you killed," the official said. Joel lowered his head. "This isn't only about you, young one. Your allies, your friends, your family, and your lineage: They all hang in the balance. Not only do you shame them with your inaction, but you doom them to extinction, too. Why would you let that happen? To take pity on a vile creature who'd rape and pillage your people without hesitation?" Joel's breaths became heavy and his grip tightened on the sword. "No. You cannot let that happen. Kill him. Kill him now!"

Joel exhaled as if surfacing from the longest dive he'd ever been on, and thrust his blade into the man's heart. He gasped and squirmed as the blood pooled in his shirt and then stained the grass below. Joel and the official watched in silence until the man slumped over and ceased all movement.

"Good," the official said as his vision began fading away. "Now, let us take you to the next test. This next scoundrel will not be gagged. He will plead for his life. I expect you to show no hesitation. Understood?"

"Yes, sir."

∽

PIERCE FOUND himself on the shores of a cold beach where the tide was strong and waves violently crashed every few seconds. In his hand was a wooden baton, and across from him stood Joel. They were within a circle of fellow classmates, having a practice battle.

Both sides of Pierce remembered this exchange well. It was the final time they had faced each other before the incident with his parents and the black gold. Much like the current battle in the cave, Joel took a stance where he held the baton up and over his head with two hands.

Joel made the first move, bringing the baton down at an angle with great ferocity. The wooden sticks clashed, but as they did, Joel brought his left foot behind, and with great strength, he pushed Pierce, blade-first, backward. The dagger-eyed boy tripped over the foot and fell with a *thud* to the sand. Before he could react, he felt the sting of the baton slap him in the chest.

"Two points for Joel!" an instructor called. The crowd of students began clapping.

"Too slow, Pierce," Joel said with a smile as he held a hand out for him to take.

As the scenery washed away along with the tide, *the other* came to realize that Joel was about to attempt the exact same move, back in the cave. *Not this time*, he thought.

∼

When Joel came back to reality, he realized that not even a split-second had passed: Their blades were still clashing and he could finish his move as intended. The mute tried to shift his leg behind Pierce to begin tripping him up, but he responded with a foot maneuver of his own; bringing his leg back while pointing his toe to the ground to trip Joel, instead.

While Joel stumbled back, unable to put full weight on one of his legs, Pierce pushed his blade away, and in the follow-through, nailed Joel in the eye with an elbow. Blood spurted and then dripped from his eyebrow as he hobbled back and finally regained his footing. He instinctively closed his eye instead of wiping the blood away, for even a brief distraction might be enough for his foe to find an opening and exploit it.

A muffled chuckle came from beneath Pierce's mask, and Joel couldn't help but smile as blood dripped down his cheek, and then to his chin. While one luxian was laughing in triumph, the other put forth a smile that hid despair; for he realized that his options for a peaceful solution were desperately few.

CHAPTER 31
FAMILY

Aldous waited with bated breath as footsteps from one of the eight tunnels grew closer and closer. A dark presence reared its ugly head and had his stomach in knots. It had to be Angus and whatever devilry he carried with him, he thought.

Making his way into the dimmed light of torches and Runes, the giant stopped well ahead and cracked a smirk. "I suppose this means I didn't take the quickest path… do you remember me, old man?"

"Of course," Aldous replied with a nod. He noticed some arrows were sticking out of his back. The traps had hit him, yet he showed no sign of pain or slowing down. "You were one of the Gold Fever-infected miners from the Mt. Couture expedition. I believe Angus Grouchet was your name?"

"I was allied with the Gold Fever-infected, but I wasn't one of them," Angus corrected as Norman and one of the other bandits appeared behind him.

"You should have listened to me. Nothing aside from death will come to you down here," the old Wizard said, looking to the bandits behind the giant.

"We don' take orders from you!" Norman shot back.

"Yer tryin' to keep us from the treasure! We know everything, now," the other bandit added.

"Treasure? There are no treasure-majiggers down here. You've been lied to!"

"He'll say anything to protect the treasure," Angus assured them. "He will try to kill us if we go any further."

There was a deafening silence about the air. It was clear to Aldous that the bandits, aside from Giles, were firmly with Angus. Could he perhaps tell them the truth to quell their aggression? The thought swirled in his mind as they approached him. Yet, he knew that without direct evidence, they wouldn't believe him. In their minds, there was a fortune at stake.

Aldous swung his walking stick and a wall of fire formed in between him and the men. The bandits stumbled back with fright-filled gasps, but Angus was undeterred. He walked through as if passing a gentle stream and bathed in the flames. His cloak burned off, revealing a damaged plate armor and chainmail underneath, and the smell of burning flesh and molten metal clogged up the chamber. Upon exiting the fiery passage, Aldous noted that the skin on his arms had peeled down to lower layers, but before his very eyes, in mere moments, the skin layers regenerated and wrapped back around his heavily muscled arms like a blanket. With a grunt, the giant's shoulders flexed, and the arrows in his back popped out.

"H-how?" Norman asked. Aldous frowned; it was exactly as he had feared.

"With the Lord of Darkness on my side, there is little I cannot do."

"But are you not human?" Aldous asked. "Only a mage should be able to do what you've just done."

The giant scoffed. "I have progressed far beyond a mere man. A dark essence flows within me, now, and with it, I can perform feats that would take you decades or even centuries to learn, old man."

Aldous thought back to the Mountain King. He had explained to him that the black gold could be used for more than simply turning groups of men into crazed mobs. He had been able to keep himself alive by using it when his Anima was transitioning from light to dark. In the right — or wrong — hands, could it have been used to enhance humans?

"The black gold, then?" he asked.

"You catch on quickly... that's why I think it'd be best to take care of you now. I have my orders, after all," Angus said as he rolled his neck, eliciting a loud *crack* that sent shivers down Aldous' spine.

While normally, no man could physically overpower the old Wizard, Angus' considerable size and the mysterious properties of the dark essence gave him pause. He could not discount the fact that the

Dark Savior's power coursed through him. Had it given his strength enough of a boost to make him a true threat?

"Orders from Drake, right? He wishes to use me as a scapegoat, doesn't he?"

"Correct again. A dead scapegoat is better than one who can defend himself. You will die today, and the Wizard's Council shall blame you for the second broken seal," the giant said to a grimace from Aldous. "It's not your fault, really. I can sympathize with your situation. You wish for an overcrowded bureaucracy to take immediate action against fast-acting foes. Ultimately, for that reason, you will lose."

"Not if I stop you here and then present you before the Council."

The giant frowned and began lumbering toward him with raised fists. Aldous brought his walking stick up to a defensive position.

"Is that stick your artifact?" Angus asked. Aldous' eyes widened. "Heh… you Wizards sure do underestimate people. You didn't think I would know about that, did you?"

"It's not something we often talk about, but every now and then, I share it with humans that I like or see potential in," Aldous replied with a smile. "Before we come to blows, tell me this much: Were you enhanced through the works of a Dark Wizard?"

"Yes. In fact, I have no worries in telling you that everything you've likely suspected is true," Angus replied with a husky chuckle. "I hope that provides you with some modicum of peace before I kill you."

"I appreciate that," Aldous said as the flames from the torches at his side dimmed. "But you don't know what I'm capable of."

"On the contrary, we know *everything* you can do. By now, it must have occurred to you that Drake led you here on purpose," said Angus. A bead of sweat rolled down Aldous' cheek. "Aside from Mt. Couture, this is the best monolith location to isolate you. We're close enough to the island's middle and deep enough underground that it would take too long for you to summon water from the lake, and all you have to use are those pathetic flames, and mayhap some from the tunnel passage you took to get here… I hope you use them well."

Aldous snorted as the flames slowly transferred to his walking stick and enveloped it. "It was you who put out the torches on the earlier path, then?"

"That's right."

Angus walked forward with no attempt at a guard or defense. Aldous figured he must have had great confidence in his regenerative abilities. A plan started to take shape in his mind.

Before the first blow could be struck, however, another shockwave erupted from out of an unconscious Zamarim's head and all turned to blue in its wake. Aldous tried to fight it, but even his mind training could not stand up to a Psychic at the pinnacle of his power.

∼

IN THE TUNNEL, Pierce continued to back Joel into a corner with quick stab attempts. The mute eventually felt his back hit the rock wall, and in that split-second, he noticed the glint of the dagger headed for his neck. With no time to react, he could do nothing but gasp quietly and close his eyes. However, to his surprise, the killing blow never arrived. He opened his eyes to see that Pierce had stopped short.

"I suppose that makes us even," he said. Joel let out a sigh of relief. He had pulled up short before striking a critical blow in their previous fight. Pierce must have wanted to even the score, he thought.

Before he could readjust himself, the dagger-eyed man threw a left-handed jab that connected with his jaw. Spit flew from Joel's mouth as he stumbled back and slumped against the wall. With no time to recover, the mute watched as the black blur of Pierce's boot drove into his ribs. He hunched over and dry-heaved, but even that was interrupted when he was grabbed by the hair and thrown back into the wall.

With ringing ears and stars in his eyes, Joel found himself face-to-face with Pierce, who knelt over and took his mask off. Without a word, the dagger-eyed man spit in his eye. Joel stirred and attempted to bring his sword up with a free hand, but Pierce caught it by the hand guard and ripped it from his grip. The muted *clangs* of his sword across the tunnel signaled the end. What else could he do to defend himself?

Pierce followed up with a vicious left kick to Joel's face. This time, blood spewed from his mouth and he tumbled over. He landed face-down and his aching body refused to move thereafter, despite the ever-present danger. The dagger-eyed man grabbed his hair once more and propped him up against the rock wall. Joel's eyes were glazed over and his head was spinning.

"Wake up," Pierce said indifferently before slapping him across the face. It shocked Joel out of his stupor, but only enough to see and hear; his body refused to move. "I want you awake for the final blow."

With a deep breath, Pierce pulled his dagger back. Joel closed his

FAMILY

eyes and they trembled as the shrieks of Osanna and the bloody gurgles of Jed dominated his ears.

Yet, before the final stab could be made, Joel felt himself being blown over. His eyes sprung open to see the mysterious blue shockwave from before passing through both him and Pierce. In but a moment, the cold confines of the tunnel faded and a new scenery took shape.

Not only had his environment changed, but *he* had changed, too. Suddenly, he was a young boy, hiding in the darkness of a crawlspace below some stairs. Though he could not see, he could *hear* plenty, and the struggles outside of his hiding spot became more harrowing by the moment. Splintering wood, clashing blades, and bodies thudding off the floor dominated his ears until suddenly, there was silence.

Joel knew this to be one of his earliest memories; and one of his most repressed. He couldn't believe what Zamarim's magic had just unlocked.

"Spare her… please!" a man cried out in luxian. It was the voice of his *birth-father*. At that moment, he didn't care that this was only a vision. The mute strained his mind to bend the memory to his will; to bust out of the crawlspace and help him, but to no avail.

He heard flesh pounding on flesh, followed shortly by another thud. "Spare me your voice, luxian trash."

That had been in King's Tongue, Joel thought with a shudder. Now, he could be certain of the outcome. This was the invasion where-

A piercing, fleshy sound reached his ears, and Joel fought against the memory once more. He could hear the muted gurgles of his father from beneath the stairs, but his younger-self merely shivered in reaction and forced his eyes shut.

Next, he heard the pained cries of a woman, and then another struggle unfolded. More skin striking skin and some more splintering wood sounded off before a body thudded into the outside of the stairs, making Joel flinch.

"Damn you…" the woman muttered in luxian between breaths. That had to be his birth-mother. "J-just kill me… and leave…"

The men just outside began laughing before he heard more thuds against the stairs. He could picture them bashing her head against the wood.

"Hold still!" one of the men said.

Another struggle unfolded, and Joel fought against the memory for

a third time. No matter what he did, his younger-self remained still, staring into darkness and taking in the dreaded noises.

"No! Stay away!" She kicked, sometimes hitting the wood of the stairs, sometimes striking her attackers, but eventually, he could hear that she was pinned down.

The shrieks of Joel's birth-mother stirred his mind, and then he thought of the gurgles. *My God*, he thought. It wasn't only the gurgles of Jed and the banshee shrieks of Osanna that had been haunting him. In some cruel twist of fate, they had also been reminders of the senseless deaths of his parents.

"Ack!" one of the men cried as a loud slap echoed in Joel's ears. "Why, ye lil' bit-"

Next, the mute heard a mushy, stabbing sound, and the same man cried aloud in pain. It brought a tiny bit of peace to Joel's otherwise unsettled mind, but he knew the outcome of the exchange.

"Filthy luxian!" he shouted before another slap rang outside the staircase. His birth-mother's body thudded against the wood, but she had no time to cry out before a fleshy stab entered Joel's ears. And then another. And another. Her weak moans fell silent after the fourth and final stabbing.

The man outside snorted as the others laughed. "Burn this shithole to the ground!"

Those laughs quickly turned to cheers, and he heard the destruction of more furniture outside of the crawlspace.

Joel felt tears streaming down the wide-open eyes of his younger-self as the darkness slowly morphed into a new environment.

Now, he was crawling through the wreckage of a pillaged city. The putrid smell of decay and burning corpses filled the air. He knew this to be the aftermath of the invasion that had killed his birth parents.

With a crinkled scroll in hand, Joel let out a stuttered breath as he spotted a half-eaten piece of fruit in the grip of a charred corpse that was riddled with arrows. His weak limbs clawed up the smoldering wreckage until he reached the dead woman, and with considerable effort, he pried the fruit from her cold fingers and desperately shoved it in his mouth. True to his memory, it tasted awful, but it had been days since his last meal and desperation had taken hold. Off in the distance, he spotted a group of soldiers approaching. He recognized the uniforms as luxian and continued to gnaw at his poor meal instead of fleeing. At the forefront was a black-haired man in tattered armor.

"Hello there," he said, approaching with an outstretched hand. "My name is Jed. What is your name?"

"Joel…"

"Not much of a talker, eh Joel?" he asked with a laugh. "This is no place for a child. Where are your parents?"

He pointed to one of the houses down the street; or what once was a house. Like the others, it had been burned to the ground.

"I see," Jed replied before eyeing the scroll in his hand. "What's that you've got there?"

"A map."

"Interesting. Could I have a look?"

Joel handed it to him tepidly. Jed unrolled it and then tilted his head with wide eyes. "This is a map of town, isn't it?"

Joel only nodded.

"You drew this?"

Again, he nodded.

"What do these Xs mean?" he asked.

"Danger," said Joel before leaning in and pointing to some Os on the map. "And these are the places I've slept overnight."

"And the squares?"

"Food."

"Not many of those…" Jed smiled and then rolled the map back up. "This would be quite helpful for my men. Do you mind if I borrow it, just for now?"

After some hesitation, Joel replied, "That's fine…"

"You are quite resourceful to have lasted this long on your own. But still, you cannot last much longer. Why don't you come along with me? We'll get you some food and water, and I have a boy who's about your age. I'm sure the two of you would get along."

As he took Jed's hand, the environment morphed around him until he was back in Stellinam at the Thaeon residence. Unlike on *that dreaded day*, it was spotless as ever and irradiated a freshness that made him feel cozy. Joel was still a young boy, and this time, he was eating a meal cooked for him by Osanna. She turned from her counter and flashed a warm smile that still took him aback to this day. There was not a single hint of the malice or vitriol that she was to display years later while under the black gold's influence.

"Well? Aren't you going to eat? I hope you like ham."

"I do like it…" Joel muttered as he forked the food around. "But how long will this last?"

She cocked her head. "What do you mean?"

"You've been treating me like I'm a part of your family-"

"That's because you are, Joel dear," she interrupted.

"Are you sure you want to take me in? Won't it be more difficult with another mouth to feed?"

Osanna chuckled. "You are too young to be worrying about such things."

The luxian boy shrugged as she approached and sat next to him. She then kissed him on the forehead.

"You and especially your parents were dealt unfortunate fates, but I believe that everything happens for a reason. Perhaps a destiny of some kind. I couldn't say exactly why, but something tells me that you will do the Thaeon name proud."

That one had stung. Joel was now desperate to see the end of what had started as a happy memory.

Tears involuntarily filled his eyes, but unlike the despair that had overcome him now, he knew them to be of joy. "I-I will make you proud. I-it's a promise."

"Very good. It may not have been under pleasant circumstances, but I couldn't be happier that you found your way to us. From here on, no matter what, you will forever be my son."

The words echoed in Joel's mind as the vision faded away. He couldn't help but wonder if she would say the same thing today.

∼

PIERCE WALKED out of his home in the mountain to see a small Mithikan woman drinking from the stream in the clearing. Her dress and corset were disheveled to put it kindly, and there was so much dirt on her face that it made her teeth seem blindingly white.

"Do you have a death wish?" he asked through his Ometos mask with enough venom to down an elephant. "Leave this place and never return. I'll only say it once."

She looked up with a crinkled brow, and both in the vision and while watching the memory, even *the other* had to stave off laughter. Her cheeks were flared out with so much water that she now looked like a chipmunk. The Mithikan woman took a large gulp and then spit out the rest before scowling back at him.

"You don't own the water, ya glutous!"

Even though it was only a memory, both sides of Pierce were

shocked at how energetic and fiery she was. He had expected her to be a pathetic, babbling beggar like the rest of the lowly peasants back in the city.

"What are you doing here?" he asked while approaching.

"Lookin' fer food. What else would I be doin'?" she asked while drawing a dagger from a sheath hidden under her dress.

"Believe me, mine is better," Pierce replied as he brought out his dark blue blade. She grimaced at him, but under the mask, he felt a smile taking shape.

With that, *the other's* presence shrunk and shrunk, until he felt insignificant. A snorting laugh muffled off the mask.

"What's so funny?" the little woman asked while holding her weapon up.

The dagger-eyed man let out a sigh and closed his eyes. He took off his mask to flip it around but then paused. He remembered that back then, for some reason, he was not worried about preserving his anonymity around her. Perhaps it was her tiny stature or her obvious survival instincts, but she'd reminded him somewhat of the luxian women he'd grown up around. So, instead of putting the mask back on, Pierce shrugged and threw it over his shoulder. The woman cocked her head as his happy gaze turned toward her.

"If you are hungry, I have food stored up," Pierce said, his voice reflecting higher spirits. He gestured toward his home at the end of the field.

"Is it fish? Cuz I'm tired of eatin' fish," she replied.

"I'm not skilled at fishing, so I don't have any of that," the dagger-eyed man said with a chuckle.

"Why are ye suddenly bein' so nice to me?"

"I don't think you'd believe me even if I told you... but let's just say I'm enjoying my freedom. And I'd like to enjoy it with you."

Her nose crinkled and then she shook her head before turning to leave. "Yer an odd feller ta be sure."

"Can I at least get your name?" Pierce called back to her.

"Greta!"

"I'm Pierce. Come back anytime," he said as she entered the latch to leave the field.

"Maybe I'll show ye how ta fish!" she called from down the hatch.

The vision faded out and then the scenery morphed into the great marble bridge of eastern Thironas, where Pierce and Greta sat atop the railing with fishing rods overhanging. Once again, *the other's* presence shrunk. Any anger and hatred for Joel had become distant.

"Ain't ye tired of eatin' fish, yet?" she asked. "It feels like I see ye every day, now."

Pierce wanted to smile, but the memory demanded that he keep his eyes on the river below. On that day, he had a lot on his mind.

"I can stop showing up if you prefer."

"I never said *that*," Greta replied with a playful shove.

"Good. In that case, I have a request." Pierce could feel the lump in his throat. It was funny to re-experience these nervous feelings all over again. "Will you come up into the mountain and live with me?"

She raised an eyebrow, but that surprise soon gave way to apparent nerves of her own. Her cheeks quickly turned red, and she turned her gaze back down to the river. "Nah."

"Wh-why not?"

"Cuz yer treatin' me like a helpless lil' girl again," Greta said before snorting. "I've been survivin' on my own for a while, now. I don't need no help."

Without looking, he traced the remnants of a bruise under her right eye, eliciting a wince. "Are you sure?"

Greta groaned. "Yes."

"And what if *I* need *your* help?"

Even so early on in their friendship, he'd known that Greta's presence reduced *the other's* destructive influence. He had believed that she would be the key to bringing balance to his life and reuniting his two minds back into one.

"What do you-" Suddenly, Greta jerked forward, so much that she nearly fell off the railing. Her fishing line held on by a thread, and the same went for her balance. Pierce sprang into action and caught her by the waist. "Oof! It's a big'un!"

He pulled against the strain of the flopping fish below, and with such force that the pair tumbled backward, off the railing and onto the unforgiving marble. Greta turned over and landed on all fours, hovering over him, while Pierce felt the glow of his cheeks as he lay on his back, staring up at her. She lowered herself and just like that, they shared a kiss while embracing.

Greta pushed herself off and said, "Well, I suppose I could at least visit ye more often…"

With that, the scenery changed around him once more: this time to his bedroom. Pierce lifted Greta and placed her onto his bed while they kissed. Both stripped out of their clothes and threw them to the floor.

As Pierce took his shirt off, Greta said, "Hold on! Somethin's missing." The dagger-eyed man tilted his head as she pointed at his midsection. "Where da hell is yer belly button?"

He raised an eyebrow and looked down. There was no hole in his abdomen like human men had. Back then, he had completely forgotten about that difference between luxians and humans. An involuntary laugh escaped his lips.

"Remember how I said that you wouldn't believe me if I told you about myself?"

"Try me."

"I'm not human," Pierce said, crossing his arms.

Greta chuckled, but when he didn't laugh along, she stopped. "Yer serious, aren't you?"

"Completely. I don't suppose you've ever heard of the luxians, have you?" he asked.

"Loo-juns?" she asked, her head cocking and nose crinkling.

"How about 'the Ancient Ones'?"

"Oh yeh, I've heard of 'em, but ain't they just ancestors to humans?" Greta asked.

"No, we were a different species entirely. But easily confused with men and women. There are some differences, though. Like the lack of belly button."

"That's a bit odd, but right now, it ain't important..." she trailed off before narrowing her eyes and pointing at his pants. "Unless a belly button isn't the only thing yer missin'..."

"N-no! Nothing missing down there!" he choked out.

"Good. Will you come here an' kiss me, then?"

The vision faded away and a profound happiness swept over Pierce. He found himself back in the tunnel, and *the other* seemed a distant, unpleasant memory. At that moment, Pierce realized that he was in the midst of a stab with his dagger, and Joel was the target. He steadied his hand to stop the thrust and shuddered upon looking down at his bloodied and battered friend.

"We've got to stop meeting like this." Pierce withdrew his blade and then grabbed his Ometos mask. He flipped it over and then put it back on before reaching out to the mute. With a grunt, he hoisted him up and asked, "Were you going to let me kill you?"

Joel only nodded. The dagger-eyed man attempted to take him

under his shoulder, but Joel pushed him off and stumbled before gaining balance against the rock wall. He then pointed down the tunnel.

"I cannot leave you here. Not in your condition."

The mute shook his head and pointed emphatically to the path before them.

"Stubborn as always…" he muttered. "Very well."

Pierce held his palm out and reopened the wound with his dagger. Blood poured out onto the luxmortite blade, and it glowed a bright blue.

"I'll be back for you," Pierce said as he pointed the dagger forward, gripped with both hands, and flew away, straight as an arrow, and nearly as fast, to boot.

His heart thudded against his chest as the roar of the wind filled his ears through tight turns in the corridor, but now was no time to be afraid. He'd failed to protect the key, and now his monolith was in danger. He would defend the seal, or die trying.

※

BACK IN THE CHAMBER, as the visions of their memories faded, Aldous charged a surprised Angus. He swung his fiery walking stick at the giant, but he dodged with a long stride backward. Angus responded with a left jab so harsh that it punished the howling wind around his arm; but mid-punch, Aldous ducked while nailing him in the ribs with his flamed artifact.

The intense heat of the blow melted through his chest armor and pierced skin. At first, flesh melted off of his torso, but it was a short-lived victory. To Aldous' horror, the regeneration began: Blood and the lower layers of skin gave way to fresh, new skin that didn't have a single blemish on it.

"You see? It is useless," Angus said as he ripped a metal shard from his chest armor off and tossed it to the ground.

"If you're so sure of that, why did you try to avoid my first attack?" Aldous asked with a smile. "You are far from invincible."

The old Wizard charged once more, but this time, Angus didn't back down. The giant threw a thunderous punch that stilled Aldous' heart. He narrowly avoided it by shifting his body to the left.

Undeterred, Aldous aimed his fiery walking stick for Angus' head; thrusting it toward his temple, but the giant caught the stick before it could reach him. The Wizard watched in growing surprise as the flesh melted off of the giant's hands without any sign of him flinching. Soon, he could see the white of his bones. Yet, even with so much of his skin and muscle melted away, he held the artifact firm.

Angus pulled the walking stick from Aldous' grip and threw it toward the chamber entrance, by the bandits, who were just now recovering from their visions. After the exchange, Aldous detected a stinging sensation in his cheek. He felt it with his hand to find something sticking out. Blood streamed down and into his beard as he retrieved a hard, white object the size of a small rock.

"A bony-do?" he asked while dropping it to the ground.

"One of my knuckles," Angus said as he clenched his fist, which had become a stump with all of its knuckles missing. Slowly, the bumps in his hand reformed while loudly cracking. His other hand, meanwhile, was in the process of making itself new muscle and skin around the bone that had been previously exposed.

"Full of surprises, aren't you?" Aldous asked as Bartholomew appeared from his tunnel. He was panting heavily and there was soot all over his face.

"It appears I've missed much."

"Yer damn right, boss!" Norman said as he walked over and kicked Aldous' walking stick further back, near the tunnels. "Angus is tryin' to get us that treasure, but the Wizard's out for blood, just like he told us! Luckily, he has been disarmed."

"It sounds to me like we should help our client out," Bart said as he drew his sword. The other two bandits followed his lead.

"I'm the one who could use some help, here…" Aldous said as he looked back at Zamarim. He was still out cold.

∼

IN THE TUNNEL, Roland and Alistair's collective shoulders shot up to their ears as the roar of the wind sounded off behind. In an instant, a blue blur shot past them, to which both dove to the rocky ground in response. Alistair looked up just in time to see the boots of Pierce flying around the bend at breakneck speeds.

"Ometos…"

"Does that mean what I think it means?" Roland asked.

"Joel's fine! He may not wanna kill nobody, but his skills with tha sword are world-class!" Alistair waved him off and flashed a braggart's smile. "Yeah, I'm sure he's fine…"

"Do you want to go back and check on him?"

The big man looked down and then let out an annoyed grunt. "You go ahead of me!"

Both men went their separate ways, and Alistair couldn't help but think that despite the mute's insistence that he leave earlier, he could have made a difference if he'd been given a chance to fight alongside him. He only hoped that it hadn't cost Joel his life.

∽

ALDOUS SEARCHED his mind for a peaceful solution as the bandits drew near with their weapons at the ready. As a Wizard, it was expressly forbidden for him to bring them any harm. He'd made an exception for Angus due to his dangerous plans and equally dangerous capabilities.

"That won't be necessary," Angus said without looking back.

"We're only trying to help you," said Bartholomew.

"I appreciate that, but this opponent is beyond you three. Only *I* can beat him," the giant said as he walked forward. "Sit back and enjoy the show."

"Very well…"

The old Wizard backpedaled as Angus approached him, and he then closed his eyes to focus. A disturbance in the wind caught his attention. It came from one of the tunnels, and whatever it was, it was *fast*. He opened his eyes and held a hand out, palm-first.

"No use in bluffing. We both know you've got nothing left to use," Angus said as he pulled his arm back to strike a critical blow: A sharp bone protruded out of his forearm like a sword. Aldous remained still as the night and cool as could be.

As Angus' booming punch approached his face, Aldous could see over his shoulder that Bartholomew and his men had been bowled over by a bright blue light, headed straight for the giant. He was almost certain that his eyes were simply mistaking it due to the high speed, but beneath the blue glow and parting dust, it looked like a man hanging onto a flying dagger. In a split-second, the dagger plunged through Angus' spine and emerged from a hole in his chest armor before he could complete the punch.

The masked man had let go of the blade just before impact, and he rolled wildly to the left as blood spurted from Angus' chest wound.

FAMILY

The giant stumbled forward with a gasp, and that was the opportunity Aldous had been waiting for. He lunged out and pressed his palm into the chest armor, and the cave became alight with yellow and white; and loud *zaps* and *sizzles* overcame the senses until it was unbearable, even to the old Wizard.

When the dust settled, Aldous stepped back from a steaming Angus, whose skin was charred dark red. He fell to his knees and opened his mouth, but only a putrid smoke came out. His eyes, dull and gray, rolled back into his head before he finally toppled over to the ground, motionless.

Aldous let out a relieved breath as the masked man struggled to his feet and then approached Angus' body. He reached out for his dagger but stilled his hand as little bolts of lightning flared out with a loud crackle.

"Careful, now. I gathered the natural lightning from all of our bodies and then directed it through his armor to stop his heart. But the bolts are still coursing through his body, and touching anything would certainly bring you harm," Aldous said before snapping his fingers. Just like that, the tiny, dancing bolts dispersed. "Alright, now you can retrieve your dagger-majigger."

The masked man nodded in thanks before kneeling and then yanking his luxmortite dagger from the body. "His regenerative capabilities made him difficult to damage, but you bypassed that problem by attacking his insides. I'd heard about your mastery of lightning, but even still, I'm impressed, Aldous."

"Ah, if you know me by name, then that would make you Ometos, wouldn't it?"

"Yes, and I am also Key Keeper of the Famine seal… but you can just call me Pierce."

"I've heard that name before." The old Wizard raised an eyebrow. "A luxian named Pierce who wields a luxmortite dagger… could you be Joel's-"

"It's a long story, but yes, I am the very same Pierce that Joel has probably told you about," he interrupted with a chuckle. "He and the others are on their way, but right now, we have more pressing matters. For example…" Pierce pointed behind him. "What happened to Zamarim?"

Aldous looked back to see the Wizard King still lying on the rocky ground, unconscious.

"He tried to probe his memories," the old Wizard said as he nudged his head toward Angus. "I cannot be sure of what exactly happened, but methinks the rotten influence of the Dark Savior — a *dark essence* — poisoned Zamarim's mind. He is breathing, but not responsive."

"I see. Well, at least the threat is neutralized for now," Pierce said.

"I hate to ruin your celebration, but…" Angus trailed off.

"No…" Aldous muttered as he turned to see the giant sitting up. Underneath the steam, it appeared that his terribly burned skin and the hole in his torso had healed.

Past the giant, he could see the bandits finally stirring, and a heavy-breathed Giles had just joined up with them. If it came down to it, Giles and Pierce would need to oppose Bart and his men while he focused on Angus.

"I have to hand it to you both. You were crafty enough to stop my heart. Even *I* wasn't sure if I could come back from that," the giant said as he got to his feet and loomed over them. "But that's enough of these games. Where is the monolith?"

"I'll never tell you," Pierce shot back.

"Erm… what he said!" Aldous added.

"What about those glowing rocks around the throne? Is that the monolith?" Angus pressed.

"No." Zamarim's sturdy voice made Aldous' ears twitch, and in shock, he turned to see him standing up. Just like that, the tides had turned back in their favor. "Those are Runes."

"A bit unnecessary to tell him that, wouldn't you say?" Aldous asked with a raised eyebrow.

"Quiet, fool," the Wizard King snapped. "I don't take orders from non-believers."

"'Non-believers'?" Aldous repeated. He narrowed his eyes and noticed that Zamarim's pupils had flashed yellow, and then red. "It can't be…"

"Well, isn't this a pleasant surprise?" Angus said with crossed arms. "I suppose you've finally seen the light… or the dark, depending on how you look at it."

"What's going on?" Pierce asked. "Is this the Gold Fever that I've heard so much about?"

"I'm not sure. Normally, it requires exposure to the black gold," Aldous said before returning his gaze to Zamarim. "You have to fight it! If anyone has a strong enough mind, it's you!"

The Wizard King ignored Aldous' pleas and looked at Angus with a smile. "To hide it, my throne was built around the monolith."

"No! What are you-" Aldous let out a choking gasp as his throat closed.

Zamarim held a hand out and clenched it slowly. Soon, Aldous began to see stars, and his head felt light as a feather.

"Fight it!" he choked out.

Angus, in the meantime, walked toward the throne of stone. Pierce tried to stop him with his fading luxmortite dagger, but before he could make a full swing, the giant swatted him away like a fly. He soared to the other side of the chamber and cracked his head against the rock wall. Blood from the back of his head sagged down along with his limp body.

"Take care of him, would you?" Angus commanded without looking back. The bandits approached Pierce with their weapons drawn.

∼

Giles rushed to the masked man's aid. "Wait!"

"Step aside," Norman said.

"We had it all wrong! There ain't any treasure in here. That big fella is gonna unleash a terrible monster!"

"What nonsense!" Bart replied with a laugh. "Move, or you will be moved."

"You call us your 'brothers' and say that we are 'family'… if any of that means something to you, then you must listen to me!" Giles pleaded.

Bartholomew cocked his head and then lowered his weapon. Relief swept over Giles at first, but then his boss let out a maniacal cackle that sent shivers down his spine. Norman and the other bandit joined in on the laugh.

"Are you really going to oppose us?" he asked, his laughter tapering off.

Giles grimaced. The prospect of a three-on-one fight didn't bode well, but even if it were a duel, he wasn't so sure that he could defeat any of them. It would be easier to step aside and allow some stranger to die instead of himself. Yet, a fire burned in his chest; one that he couldn't ignore.

"Do you know why I joined up with you?" Giles asked, to which

Bartholomew shrugged. "Strength. Unity. Belonging. I was tired of bein' pushed around; of bein' helpless. Under your leadership, I was sure that I would learn to be strong and find success. Why is it, then, that with each passing hour, our group dwindles? I think it is because I was wrong about you. You afford your men little to no camaraderie, and for that, you are forever weak."

"In your final moments, I will be honest with you," Bart said as he raised his weapon once more. "A bandit only looks out for one person, and that's themselves. There is *always* an ulterior motive, even when someone is showing you kindness. Whether it be because they're your blood and it's their duty, or if they want something from you. Do you understand what I want from you? And all bandits that I lead? Subordination. You have questioned me and shown dubious loyalty throughout this mission. You are *useless* to me."

"Ye always were too much of a do-gooder, Giles. I tried ta help ye, but yer soft. Soft comrades will get us killed. Nothin' personal, but we'll do what we've gotta do," Norman added as the trio of bandits approached with weapons ready to strike.

"And *you* were always a lousy friend, Norman."

The bandit leader scoffed. "Go ahead and say whatever you must to be comfortable before the end. The conclusion will be the same: You and Ometos will die."

"You'll have to go through me, too," a well-built man said as he rushed past the bandits and to the side of Giles. The men stopped in their tracks.

"Aren't you Roland, lord of Thironas?" Norman asked. "What the hell are ye doin' here?"

"Ometos is the only reason we have been able to feed the masses, of late. You will not bring harm to him."

"You have no authority here," Bart replied. "We will do what we must."

"So much for being 'family'…" Giles trailed off as he readied his rickety weapon. He hoped that Lord Roland could do most of the heavy lifting.

CHAPTER 32
THE BEGINNING OF THE END

Angus approached the throne and held up a fist. With a pained grunt, bone sprouted from his arm and covered it in layers to make a giant hammer, much like the one he had used to destroy the stone door at the second trial.

With a malice-filled smile, the giant took a swing at the stone slab that was the throne's seat. Rocks and pebbles exploded outward in a dazzling display, striking Angus enough that he had to shield his eyes. As the dust settled, he could see that it had cratered on contact, but the structure remained standing. With a ferocious battle cry, he unleashed several booming swings in succession, not stopping to admire his handiwork until he could see a piece of the black monolith and its glowing, inscribed text.

"Ah, there it is..." Angus looked down at his arms to see dozens of cuts and scrapes from the wild debris, and he could feel blood dripping down his forehead, but it didn't matter. Like every other time, his skin regenerated from the damage, good as new. With the dark essence aiding him, he was practically *invincible*, he thought with a smirk.

More aggressive swings saw rock and stone alike shattering and flying all about the chamber; so much that the dust became like a thick fog that was slow to leave. Underneath the veil of the haze, the dark monolith and its glowing, inscribed text loomed over him. Glowing even brighter and in all sorts of hues were the Runes, which remained hanging on the wall behind in an arch shape. They had odd patterns and writing carved into them that reminded him somewhat of the ancient language.

"Are you sure that these Runes aren't part of the monolith?" he asked while looking back at Zamarim. The Wizard King still held a pinched hand out at Aldous, whose face had turned purple.

"No, those Runes are a part of my collection. I keep them here in case of…" Zamarim trailed off, now wide-eyed.

"In case of what?"

"Intruders…" the Wizard King released his grip and Aldous fell to the ground, wheezing and panting like a sick dog.

Zamarim buried his face in a palm and began straining.

"It appears there is no time to waste…" Angus muttered as he pulled a fist back. He paused for a moment and growled as several more bones grew out of his arm and wrapped around to make the bone hammer even larger.

The giant threw his whole body into the swing, and when his bone hammer collided with the monolith, it shattered apart so loudly that it sounded like thunder. All nearby shielded their faces as chunks of stone and pebbles rained down on them, and a horribly violent noise captured the chamber. Yet, it wasn't only the explosion of stone that had shaken the foundations of the cave, but the opening of a portal. A gateway of swirling dark took shape where the monolith had once stood, howling at any who dared stand near it like the inside of a seashell, magnified a thousand-fold.

As the portal to the Cold World opened, Zamarim fell to a knee and puked out a black liquid. After leaning over and seeming to contemplate his situation, the Wizard King looked up at Angus with a scowl that could kill with its look alone.

"I'm amazed that you were able to force the dark essence out of your body, even if you had only taken in a little," he said with crossed arms. "But you were too late. Famine will be walking amongst us soon. I don't know about you, but I'd like to see him up close."

"I'm afraid you won't have that opportunity," Zamarim replied as the giant raised an eyebrow. The Wizard King turned his gaze to Pierce, who seemed to have regained consciousness, but still lay up against the rocky wall where blood from the back of his head had streaked down along with him. "Pierce! The key!"

Zamarim held out a hand as if waiting for him to toss it over. Angus couldn't help but chuckle when Pierce shook his head slowly.

"I'm sorry… he stole it from me…"

"And believe me when I say that it is *long gone*. I suppose you could try reading my mind again to find out where it is, but we both know how that would turn out," said the giant with a snort.

With an icy glare, Zamarim threw his hand out in Angus' direction, and the giant felt a sudden, invisible force that sent him flying back and into the cave wall with a great *thud*. His eyes droopy and his back pounding from the impact, Angus looked down with a shudder to see that his feet were still off the ground, yet he was still pinned up against the wall. With gritting teeth, he tried to move his limbs, but struggle as he might, he could only manage to make them shake and strain. Somehow, the Wizard King had gained control over his body.

~

Across the chamber, Roland clashed blades with Bart. The bandit leader attempted several diagonal swings in a row, each faster and more aggressive than the last; but with experience on his side, the lord knew he was sure to wear out at such a prolonged intensity. With mere flicks of his wrist, Roland blocked each slash attempt, and every *clang* of the clashing swords saw Bart's breaths growing heavier.

Eventually, Bartholomew tired and stumbled with one of his swings when he stepped backward instead of blocking, as he'd trained him to expect. The lord then stepped forward and connected with a stab to his lower-left abdomen. A weak gasp escaped Bart's lips before he hopped back from the blade.

He covered the wound with one of his hands, but blood spilled out through the fingers. "Bah! Who would have thought that a spoiled noble would be so keen with his sword?"

"Even the rich are not spoiled in these parts," Roland said with a chuckle.

"How about we make a deal, then? We'll cut you in on the treasure profit if you stand aside," Bartholomew said. Each word seemed to leave him more and more breathless.

"Treasure? There *is* no treasure," Lord Roland replied with a grimace. He turned and then pointed at the dark void where the monolith once stood. "Your reward for helping the big fellow will be a monster that steps out of that portal to kill us all."

"You lie!" Bartholomew shouted as he rushed in with a one-handed lunge.

Roland attempted to sidestep, but the blade cut into his right arm while he dodged. However, it was a glancing blow and did little to hinder him from maneuvering his claymore under Bart's hand guard and catching the blade on it. With a sudden, forceful swing, Bart's weapon was ripped from his hand and flung away.

The bandit leader hopped back in defense as his sword bounced off the ground, far to his right. Roland held his sword outward and closed in to pressure a surrender, but Bartholomew was not finished resisting: He drew two daggers and held them at the ready while taking a crouched stance. The lord took note of the blood continuing to spill from Bart's stomach and with his weapon's reach advantage, he felt confident that an offensive flurry would end the duel.

Roland lunged out for a stab, but with his right dagger, Bartholomew parried by shifting the blade to his upper right and then attempted a stab with his left dagger. Lord Roland sidestepped the stab attempt, but took notice of the right dagger now chopping down for a follow-up attack. He brought his sword along with the right dagger to ward it off, and the pair clashed up high: two daggers against the claymore. The superior weight of the claymore, however, allowed Roland to push him back.

Bartholomew returned to position, holding his daggers upward and facing toward each other as his defense. Despite the previous resistance, Roland was confident that the blood loss was affecting him. *One more attack*, he thought, again.

The lord charged in with an overhead swing, which Bart blocked with both daggers up above. He then transitioned to warding off the claymore with his right dagger and closed in with his left outreached. Roland backpedaled in response, but the bandit leader continued to chase and eventually reached him. The dagger cut into the side of his right arm, but before any significant damage could be done, Roland threw a desperate kick that landed in Bartholomew's gut.

An exasperated gasp escaped Bart's lips as he stepped back and then began wheezing. Lord Roland glanced at his right arm. It was bleeding and painful, but not enough that it was useless. The problem, though, was that despite his injuries, momentum was shifting in favor of Bartholomew. He grunted in frustration, for however tempting it was to go for the finishing blow, his best option was to play defense until blood loss brought him down. With the portal open behind him and his opponent's surprising endurance, he was unsure if there was time for such a strategy.

THE BEGINNING OF THE END

~

Giles did his best to fend off both Norman and the other bandit, but since it was two-against-one, they quickly backed him into a corner. He darted his eyes to Pierce, who showed signs of life but was not on his feet, and then he looked back to his former comrades.

"Norman…" Giles trailed off with a nervous chuckle. "We grew up together. Surely, we can work somethin' out."

The bandit laughed derisively. "That's the problem with ye: Always thinkin' small. Is friendship gonna feed me? Will it make me rich?"

"As I said before…" Giles smirked as he attempted a horizontal slash. "You always were a lousy friend!"

Norman blocked the attack before closing in and grabbing his sword. Before he knew it, Giles' blade had been thrown to the ground, and both of the bandits loomed over him with devious smiles.

"And *you* were always weak!" Norman said with excitement as he pressed the blade up against his neck. "I'm doin' the world a favor by ending yer pathetic existence!"

Giles closed his eyes. *Damn it,* he thought with a frown. Norman, nasty as he was, had a point. His weakness would not only ensure his death but the end of Ometos, too. It was the story of his life, and now, it would be the story of his death. In a state of bitter despair, he awaited the final blow.

~

Joel hobbled into the chamber with the assistance of Alistair's lowered shoulder. His eye was welded shut from the prior battle with *the other*; in fact, his whole face had swollen, but it did not hinder him from taking in the disastrous spectacle. Lord Roland struggled to fend off a man fiercely wielding daggers, and behind him, a small man had a sword resting at his throat, at the mercy of two others who irradiated malevolence.

The swirling, howling portal in the background had not escaped the mute's notice, for the shrieks reminded him of Osanna and his birth-mother's wretched final moments. For some reason, though, he focused on the blade at the small man's throat. Jed gurgling up blood helplessly flashed before his eyes, and he recalled the human war prisoners whose pleading had fallen on his deaf ears back then. If he could go back now, he'd have stopped himself. With so many conflicting emotions swirling in his head, one emerged above the rest: urgency. For now he knew what needed to be done, and he needed to be quick about it.

Thanks to the visions back in the tunnel, Joel had come to understand his hesitation; his greatest weakness. He was not afraid of violence but of death. Not his own death, but the death of his friends, his loved ones, and even his enemies. All of his life, he'd been around senseless destruction, and he'd often been the one dealing it out. It had taken its toll, and the deaths of his adoptive parents, who'd given him nothing but love before that dreaded day, had been the final straw.

But since his vow of peace had begun, what had he done to *prevent* death? Not nearly enough, he thought while drawing his dark blue blade. He had often sat back and let disasters play out before him, but if he wanted to involve himself in the battle against the Dark Savior, then it was obvious that he could afford to do that no more.

Alistair gasped as Joel pushed off of him and made a dash for the young man with the sword at his throat. A striking pain shot up his injured leg, but it only increased his urgency. His eyes widened in panic as the man brought his sword up for the killing stroke.

Joel gripped his sword in both hands and leaped forward like a pouncing tiger, and in one smooth motion, he swung his blade up to meet the falling sword. After a loud *clang*, followed by a *crack*, all nearby fell silent as the top half of the shattered sword bounced off the rock floor of the chamber.

The other man growled and then pulled his blade back for a strike, but Joel had already planned for that. With all weight on his good leg, he held his luxmortite blade out and poked it into the man's gut with enough force to frighten him into dropping his weapon.

Looking around for any further sign of attack, the mute was surprised to see both men on their knees and with their hands up in surrender.

"Y-you saved me… thank you…"

Those words had taken Joel's breath away. He looked back to see the young man, now standing and with gratefulness plastered on his face. This was the way forward, he thought: Swift, non-lethal action to prevent death. With his luxmortite blade going up against weaker metals, he could pull it off.

"Oof!" Joel turned to see the dagger-wielding man fall flat on his face, with Alistair standing over him. It looked like he'd used the butt-end of his axe's shaft to strike him in the back of his head, and that got the mute smiling. Even without luxmortite, the big redhead had found a way to end the battle without killing.

"Good timing," Roland said as he lowered his sword and then sheathed it.

The big man remained uncharacteristically quiet and merely stared past the lord. A sizable sweat was building on his brow.

"That's it, right thar…" Alistair muttered as he pointed to the swirling darkness ahead. "Tha portal to tha Cold World."

"Is there anything we can do?" Roland asked.

"Not without the key. It's all up ta them Wizards, now."

∽

Near the portal and up against the rock wall, Angus continued his struggle to escape the Wizard King's telekinetic grip, but he couldn't move any part of his body more than an inch or two.

"It appears you are not invincible after all," Zamarim said while gesturing with a finger. One of Angus' legs stretched and stretched until the unbearable rip of his tearing muscles and skin made Aldous' shoulders shoot up to his ears. In only a few seconds, Angus' leg had been reduced to barely hanging off of his blood-drenched bone. Although the giant grimaced and winced, he did not cry out in pain. "I suppose we'll have to see what your limit is, then."

The Wizard King gestured a finger at his head as if pointing with righteous indignation. Then, with a light pop, like a bubble, Angus' left eye exploded into a bloody sprinkle of rain. He wheezed and then slumped over, but he couldn't fall; for Zamarim's telekinesis held him up.

"Where is the key?"

"I'm sure it's around here, somewhere…" the giant replied with a smirk.

"Mayhap we should pop your head, next," Zamarim said before closing his hand into a fist. There was panic written all over Angus' rapidly expanding face. His cheeks grew red and puffy, and his remaining eye became obscured by how fast his face was growing. Blood burst and then poured from his ears, and even his remaining eye, but as he ceased his struggles and seemed resigned to his fate, the Wizard King suddenly stopped.

Zamarim lowered his hand and fell to a knee. He held a hand over his heart and shivered. Aldous shuddered at the sudden weakness exuding from him. Could it have been the dark essence? He closed his eyes in concentration, to see if he could get a feel for it, but found something else entirely. His eyes burst open and became wide with fright.

"Your Anima…" he muttered. "It has diminished so much…"

"I shouldn't be surprised," Zamarim replied while sulking. "I have sat on my throne and done little while innocent people have suffered at the hands of a long-lasting famine. All in the name of protecting the seal… and now I have failed in that regard, too."

The telekinesis faded and Angus fell to the ground like a lump of meat. As he struggled to his feet, Aldous gritted his teeth. He was already regenerating. His face had returned to normal size and the white in his formerly-popped eye had returned. Even his dragging leg was recovering. Newly-made muscle wrapped around what had previously been only bone.

"You have grown weak, old man," Angus said with malice on his tongue. His strides became smoother and quicker as the last remnants of his damaged leg healed. "Allow me to put you out of your misery!"

With a snort, Zamarim reached his arm out toward one of the Runes on the back wall and it flew into his hands. Inscribed upon it were glowing, white, wavy symbols. Before he could activate it, however, the giant protruded a bone blade from his forearm and slashed at him, knocking the stone all the way to the other side of the chamber. The Wizard King's eyes twitched and he fell to both knees.

In a panic, Aldous gathered all lightning in the chamber that he could, and formed it into a ball between his hands. Its glare and crackling didn't seem to catch Angus' attention as he pulled his arm back and took aim at Zamarim's neck. Before he could strike a killing blow, Aldous pushed the lightning ball at the giant and it erupted into a lightshow, complete with sparks, blood, and loads of vapor.

Aldous watched on with bated breath as the cloud of smoke began clearing. There were no signs of movement from within, but he still couldn't shake a feeling of dread.

His intuition proved correct, as when the vapor finally cleared, Angus stared back at him with his usual stone face, none the worse for wear. His clothing and armor were in tatters, but he was not. *That cursed regeneration*, Aldous thought with a groan. How could he get around it without an abundance of the elements at his side?

"That trick won't work again," the giant said as he leaped forward and sideswiped with his bone blade.

THE BEGINNING OF THE END

Aldous jumped back and started planning out a response, but his eyes widened when at the last second, he realized bone bolts — Angus' fingers — had shot out at unavoidably high speeds. Two lodged themselves into his body: One in the shoulder, and the other in the right side of his chest. He let out a weak cry as he fell to the ground.

Zamarim, in the meantime, had grabbed another Rune with telekinesis. It had a dark, glowing swirl inscribed into it. As Angus turned to face him, the Wizard King gestured the Rune forward, and it glowed a little stronger before a great vortex appeared between them. The new portal sucked in nearby pebbles and rocks, and Angus' feet began sliding as it pulled him closer. Just at the edge of the swirling darkness, the giant dug his bone blade into the ground and stopped himself from moving.

"Unbelievable…" Zamarim muttered as Angus made a fist with his other hand and pointed it at him.

Before he could shoot out a piece of bone, the giant was hit with a roaring gust of wind that drowned out even the unbearably loud portals in the chamber. The impact was so strong that it snapped the bone holding Angus in place and sent him hurdling into the vortex.

With only a split-second to hear his last gasp, the portal swallowed him up and closed. Zamarim dropped the Rune stone and collapsed to the ground. He and Aldous looked across the chamber to see Alistair holding the Wind Rune. He wore an uncharacteristically exasperated expression on his round face.

"Not many humans could effectively use a Rune on their first try…"

"That's because Alistair has the heart of a lion when pushed hard enough," Aldous replied, his voice weak and scratchy. He nudged his head to where the portal had just closed. "Where did you send him, anyhow?"

"I dumped him into the ocean," Zamarim replied with a chuckle. "Hopefully, the marinians will find and drown him."

"We have bigger problems, now," Aldous said meekly as he rose to his feet. His eyes twitched and then widened as a foot stepped out of the portal from the Cold World. It was a dark, barren foot; yet despite its thin, solid form, it looked as if it were gelatinous.

Out of the howling gateway fully stepped one of the Dark Savior's split identities, Famine. He was humanoid in both shape and size, yet he was covered by a dark, sludge-like substance instead of human skin. He was dangerously thin, with ribs protruding from his toxic skin, and his head was large and perfectly round; twice the size of the average man's head. Famine's yellow eyes were large, but sulking, and his mouth wore a permanent frown, as if he'd known nothing but despair for his entire miserable existence.

The monster hunched over as he walked toward the pair of Wizards, slowly but surely. A dark aura irradiated from him like a foul stench that refused to disperse. Aldous' eyes fell to the ground Famine had been walking on. He left smoldering footprints in the rock and soil.

"Help…" Famine whimpered.

"What do we do?" Aldous whispered to the Wizard King.

"I am calling the Guardian," Zamarim replied with closed eyes.

"What's goin' on?" Aldous heard a voice ask from behind. He glanced over his shoulder to see that it was one of the bandits.

Famine turned his droopy, inhuman gaze to Norman and the other bandit. Their eyes flickered yellow in response.

"Will you help me?" His voice was impossibly deep, but it was also sad. It sounded as if he was about to cry.

"What do ye need help with?" Norman asked.

"I have not eaten in ages…"

"We're starvin', too," the other bandit said as he brushed past Giles.

"Will you help me?" Famine repeated. His yellow eyes temporarily lit up.

Aldous looked back at the men in horror. Their eyes had fully turned yellow.

"Yes, we will help you," Norman said, entranced.

"Take my hand," Famine said, holding it out for them.

"Norman, stay back!" Giles pleaded, but the bandit pushed him aside like a stranger in a crowd.

The bandits walked to the monster like lemmings as Roland, Alistair, and Joel looked at each other in confusion. Aldous tried to get between them, but stumbled and fell as he ran. He was almost completely depleted of magic and strength from his near-death experience at the hands of Zamarim and the bone bolts stuck in his body. His head felt as light as a feather.

Zamarim held a hand out and another Rune flew into his grip under the power of his telekinesis. A blue, wavy symbol was inscribed on it. He pointed the stone at Famine with a strong gesture, and a rushing stream of water flowed out, as if from a large waterfall. Upon contact, the raging current burst into steam and did not allow the water to break and fill the chamber around him.

"What do we have that he cannot wither away?" Zamarim asked aloud as the two bandits approached the beast. He turned to plead with them. "Stay away! You'll die!"

"For the Savior!" they cried in unison. Deluded grins filled their faces as they took Famine's hand.

Aldous shuddered as the men deteriorated rapidly before his very eyes: First, they shriveled up as if they'd been mummified, then their skin peeled off like old, crusty flakes, and finally, they exploded into clouds of ash, which flew into both Wizards' faces. Aldous coughed and thrashed about while trying to blow the remnants of the men away, but as the dust cleared, he could feel their ashes on his face and all over his clothes.

"No…" he muttered, his despair shining through the infinite dark of the situation.

Pierce finally got up to a knee. With heavy, muffled breaths bouncing off the inside of his Ometos mask, he held his hand out to make the cut for his charmed dagger.

However, before he could slice his palm open, an odd yet familiar noise echoed from one of the tunnels. It sounded like an ill-tuned or distorted trumpet. In crawled the Lake Watcher, faster than Aldous had seen it moving in the lake, even. It was headed for its natural enemy: Famine.

The dark beast lunged out at Famine, and with its cone-like snout, latched onto his body. Aldous' mouth fell agape. Not only had the Guardian's body held up on contact, unlike the bandits, but *it was absorbing him*. The demonic hisses of the monster kept the old Wizard on guard; yet slowly, Famine shrunk and the gelatinous, tar-like substance covering his body seemed to lose its structure and sag. It was a frightening yet fascinating sight to see a spawn of the Dark Savior devoured, but the Guardian Beast did so until there was nothing left.

The Lake Watcher began crawling and slithering toward the portal to fulfill its duty, but for the first time Aldous had ever seen, it stumbled and plopped onto his great underbelly, as if stricken by illness. The distorted, trumpeting bellows that it had become known for turned to low-pitched wheezing, and it clawed ahead painstakingly. Finally, it reached the swirling darkness, and it tilted its head back before lunging forward. Out of its long snout and into the portal it shot a dark, gooey liquid. After a steady stream of darkness emptied into the Cold World, the beast appeared rejuvenated and hopped up to its front legs before scrambling into the portal, letting out one last distorted cry before it disappeared.

"W-was that Famine that it spit out?" Aldous asked, eyes wide.

"Yes. It absorbed him, as it tends to do to its other victims, but not even the Guardian can handle Famine in its system for too long. It'll have to repeat this process until we can think of a solution," Zamarim replied before standing with some effort. "I have no choice but to summon the Council."

A nervous chuckle escaped Aldous' lips. "What will you tell them?"

"You broke nearly every rule imaginable on your way here, Aldous." The Wizard King's nose crinkled. "You visited a monolith location outside of your own without permission. You brought humans to this island for the first time in a very, very long time... you even attacked a man, which is far beyond the scope of what a Wizard Scout is allowed to do in defense of a seal, especially while on probation! Expulsion from the Council has been dealt out for far lesser transgressions, in the past."

"I cannot deny my actions, but you must understand why I was so despera-"

Zamarim held up a finger, silencing him. "While I do not condone your methods, I must admit that your claims turned out to be true. It would seem there is a conspiracy to destroy the seven seals." He tossed the portal Rune to Aldous, who bobbled it in surprise. "Take that and use it to reach Endoshire quickly, if you can. While reading Angus' mind, I saw that this mysterious Dark Wizard plans on striking the Degenerate monolith next. I will stay behind and say what I must to keep the Council off of your trail, but in return, you must be the one to stop this nefarious group."

"I don't think any further efforts will prove fruitful. Now that two of the seven seals have been broken, it is the beginning of the end. The others will eventually fall..."

"Obviously, our situation is bad, but to say that it's already over?" Pierce asked, approaching with weak, muffled breaths. The others joined him from the backend of the chamber. "It's too early to surrender."

"Two out of seven have fallen in less than *two years*. After millennia without issues. At this rate, I estimate that the Dark Savior will be revived within the next five years," the old Wizard replied with the bitter taste of defeat on his tongue.

"Stop Drake Danvers and his Dark Wizard cohort, and we slow that process down," said Zamarim. Both his words and his posture felt weak. "And in that time, the Council may reach a solution."

Aldous shook his head. "When the Council arrives, and you tell them who's behind this, do you think they will take action?"

The Wizard King remained silent.

"But I suppose you are right. *Someone* needs to press on and fight back against these fiends."

"That is all I can ask of you," Zamarim replied with a bow of his head. "Good luck."

"We'll need much more than luck..." Aldous trailed off as he turned to face the others.

"Now, what?" Alistair asked.

"You, Joel, and I will travel to Endoshire, Sigraveld. I fear that we won't be able to stop them if Angus was but one example of what they can do, but we must at least try."

"Let me come along with you, then," Pierce said.

"I'm afraid you'll need to stay here," Zamarim jumped in. "We must face the Council, and that likely means being put on probation for our failure to protect the monolith."

"If probation or expulsion are our only options, why not leave ahead of time and help them protect the Degenerate seal?" he asked.

"That will incur a fate worse than expulsion, actually. For abandoning our posts, the Wizard's Council would class me a Dark Wizard and treat you as one, too."

"And they spare no mercy or expense for hunting down Dark Wizards," Aldous said with a solemn nod.

"That is why you must be cautious," Zamarim said with grave eyes. "You've been walking a fine line up until now. Endoshire is teeming with people. If you harm any of them or cause too great of a ruckus, you will be hunted, and they *will* catch you. They always do. And you might find death to be preferable to whatever punishment they impart."

A lump came to Aldous' throat. He knew the Wizard King to be correct. With regards to the Council tracking him, luck had been on his side so far. Endoshire was certainly a place where that luck might just run out. Yet, having come this far already, he knew that there was no turning back. Two seals had already fallen, and sitting back while a third was destroyed would make him just as bad as the Council that had frustrated him to no end.

"What about me? What should I do?" Giles asked.

Aldous returned a half-hearted smile. "Go back to your life. You don't want any part of this, believe me."

"I don' have much of a life to get back to," he replied before looking down. "Besides, I owe some of you my life. If there's anything I can do to help, then I want to."

"I suppose you've been through a lot, haven't you? We *could* use the help…"

Alistair gazed down at him and smirked. "He's like a human doppelganger of Joel."

The mute cocked his head and then hobbled toward Giles. They stared each other down for a moment, and then Giles said, "I don't see much resemblance."

"That's because Joel got his face smashed in! Give 'im a couple'a weeks an' then you'll see it!" Alistair said as he burst into a laugh. Joel let out an inaudible groan.

"As much as I'd like to join in, I'll have to get back to my duty as a lord… I don't suppose any of you could tell me if this incident will end the famine?" Roland asked.

"I wouldn't count on it," Zamarim replied.

"Princess Ella will be displeased…" he muttered with a nervous smile. He then turned and pointed at Bartholomew, who remained laid out on the ground at the backend of the chamber. "What about *him*?"

"Mayhap I can scrub his memory of these events. It will be difficult, though; my Anima has fallen lower than I ever could have imagined," the Wizard King said as a portal opened before the group. Aldous had activated the Rune.

"This will take us back to the outskirts of Thironas," he said.

∽

AFTER ZAMARIM TOOK a short time to alter his memories, the group carried an unconscious Bartholomew to the portal and tossed him in. Giles followed close behind, and then Lord Roland. Before Alistair jumped in, he approached Zamarim.

"Oh, I almost fergot! Here's yer Rune back, mista Wizard!" the big man said as he held the stone out for him.

The Wizard King smiled and pushed it back into his chest. "You seem to wield it well. Why don't you hold onto it for now?"

A grand smile spread across Alistair's round face before he nodded and then walked into the portal with the Rune in hand. Joel and Pierce embraced for a moment, but then the dagger-eyed man separated himself and removed his Ometos mask, his face reflecting the same sorrow that it did.

"I'd like to tell you that there are brighter days ahead for us, my brother," Pierce said. Joel returned a weak smile and gave him a pat on the shoulder. "But in our predicament, there are no guarantees. One thing I *can* promise is that we will meet again. Until then, I hope you remember what I told you before. You don't have to run away from what happened all of those years ago. You did what you had to do. Don't let it hold you back."

Joel nodded in response, which seemed to surprise Pierce. Though it would be in his own stubborn way, the mute was now ready to fight; to take swift action while preventing death.

With only the Scouts and Keepers of their respective seals remaining in the chamber, the feeling of failure and despair filled the air. For no one knew better than they just how catastrophic the past year and a half had been to the world's security. The atmosphere quickly became unbearable, and the mute turned to leave.

A brief wave goodbye was all Joel had left to muster as he walked into the swirling vortex of darkness. Despite the magic of the portal Rune, the trip to Endoshire would still take some time; and it was time much needed; to rest his mind, body, and soul. For he knew that, with the shadows of the past still hanging over him, the coming battles promised to be more trying and intense than ever before.

EPILOGUE

In a distant jungle of southern Turnersia, a waterfall raged on at the foot of a mountain, and behind the falls, carved into the bedrock, was an entrance to the most exclusive of organizations: the Wizard's Council. Of course, this was only one of several locations where the world's most powerful and wise mages met up, but they all shared the traits of being well-concealed or downright impossible for man to access.

Zequim and Axar appeared out of a portal behind the raging waterfall within a damp indentation of the cliffside. Before them stood a large, steel door. The Council leader approached and knocked. A slit opened up, and after having a brief look, the guard let both of them in. The inside was a long hallway filled to the brim with decorations and food on tables that flanked them for as far as the eye could see. Despite being built into a cliffside and underneath a river, it felt like they were in the home of a rich nobleman in the countryside. Their soft, graceful steps practically bounced off of the long, blue carpet that stretched down the hallway. Zequim focused on the golden patterns stitched into the fabric at his feet, and they brought a genuine smile to a face that was all too used to forcing them.

"It appears they went all-out for Paneus' celebration this year, eh?" Axar asked, snapping him back to reality.

"Yes, well, it is quite an achievement to remain in his position for…

EPILOGUE

erm…" Zequim wanted to groan. He did not know or care how long it had been, and he suspected that most Wizards felt the same way. "Such a long time."

"Indeed…" Axar trailed off. He raised one of his thin eyebrows. "Is something bothering you, sir?"

The Council leader eyed his assistant with annoyance. He had a knack for noticing smaller, bothersome details; including his current disinterest, apparently.

"Do you ever get the feeling that we are on the cusp of something horrible?"

"Sir?"

"I haven't been able to get the idea out of my mind: How do a group of unwitting miners break the first seal *ever*, when Mt. Couture is at its most dangerous?" Zequim asked. Axar sighed in response. "You don't find it odd? I am beginning to wonder if Aldous was ri-"

"Aldous would say *anything* to get his position back," he interrupted. "With respect, sir, you favor him too much. He broke all of the rules, disregarded all of his training, and he has the gall to point his finger at *us*?"

"I am not suggesting that Aldous was in the right for breaking our rules. I'm simply pointing out how unlikely it was that a group of humans would unleash Greed without outside interference."

"The Dark Wizard theory again? Or are we still suggesting that Drake Danvers, hero to the men of Faiwell, would not only betray his people but somehow know of the black gold?"

"We cannot be sure unless we give the investigation our full attention," Zequim argued, shaking his head. "Our recent guidance on human interactions; that is to say, limiting them as much as possible, could be seen as a lack of due diligence from the perspective of some. And if that perspective were to, say, come from a nefarious source, then they could certainly exploit it, could they not?"

"An investigation *was* carried out, though. It found that the black gold's influence was greater than we thought, and had infected Olivier the Mountain King's mind. It also found that the Scout and Key Keeper failed to uphold their duties and broke our rules," Axar said while shrugging. "We have our answers for why the Mt. Couture disaster occurred and are making corrections as we speak. Anything further is a waste of precious time and resources."

The Council leader chuckled as a glimmer caught his eye. He looked to the ceiling to no longer see stone, but a long stretch of glass.

Above, the clear blue rapids flowed, and he picked up on its every intricacy: From the plentiful, waving flora to the rocks and pebbles budging and rolling, to the fish swimming upstream; they provided him with a reprieve from the oppressive confines of the hall and showered him with the beauty of nature.

"Look at where we are, Axar." He gestured to the uneaten food and uncorked wine bottle on the newest table in a series of many. "*This* is a waste of time."

"Aw, don't say that…" the assistant trailed off, placing a sure hand on his shoulder. "Just enjoy the celebration and relax. There isn't much we can do, anyway. The Council has already voted on the matter."

Zequim snorted as a familiar disappointment took hold. "I suppose you're right."

At the hall's end, the pair entered a door on their right. Inside, they were greeted by a grand hall of marble. Columns supported the vast space, and there were hundreds of tables with flowery displays for guests to sit at. At the front of the hall was a stage. Many Wizards had already gathered and were chatting amongst themselves; most held a half-filled wine glass in one hand and fancy finger foods in the other.

"Only the finest for Paneus, eh?" Zequim cracked a sarcastic smile.

"Try to enjoy yourself, sir."

The duo split up and went to speak with different groups. Zequim joined with a small crowd toward the center of the hall. He listened in mid-conversation to a high-ranking Wizard named Eron. He had long, shaggy, and gray hair with a clean-shaven face. He wore a blue robe, and there was a large two-handed sword strapped to his back.

"-and so, I told them: I'm a Wizard, not a miracle worker!"

The group howled with laughter, but Zequim could only spare a few token chuckles. He caught the attention of Eron, who flashed him such a great smile that it felt forced.

"Look who it is! Our esteemed leader!"

"Always a pleasure, Eron," Zequim replied.

"How have the last few meetings been?"

"You'd know, if you would only show up for some of them."

The group laughed, but Zequim knew they were laughs because of his status, not how funny the comment had been. He did his best not to groan at the pathetic display.

"True enough! If only our meetings ever amounted to anything. Then I'd show my face more often," Eron said with a chuckle.

EPILOGUE

"I could have used you in those meetings..." Zequim trailed off before taking a bitter sip of wine.

"You refer to the Mt. Couture disaster? Sorry to say, but yer ol' pal Aldous seems to have lost his mind. Never mind how unhinged his claims are, I must say that it is quite a bold strategy for him to blame us while simultaneously demanding our understanding and resources. I'd say he's knee-deep in his own dung, and the stink has scrambled his brains!" Eron replied as the group burst out with laughter. "I would have voted against you as well."

Zequim shook his head. "You truly believe that a bunch of humans made it to the center of Mt. Couture and destroyed the monolith on their own? This is the first time a seal has been broken, and no one is taking it seriously."

"It has been thousands of years. One seal was bound to break. We're handling it, are we not?"

"Not well enough."

"Cheer up! You're thinking too much about it. There's no way another monolith could be destroyed before we fix the one at Mt. Couture," Eron said.

"*If* we can fix it," Zequim said with narrow eyes. "Those monoliths were created by a magic lost to time, and many great mages died in the process."

"The Guardian will stop Greed, then."

"For how long?"

"As long as needed," Eron said, his tone reflecting an impatience that grew more obvious by the word. "We have greater problems to address."

Zequim raised an eyebrow and looked around the hall, as if to point out how unimportant their gathering was, but no one else seemed to pick up on it. He sighed and then bowed his head.

"There are some other Wizards that I must get to speaking with, if you'll excuse me. Enjoy the party, my friends," the Council leader said before striding off. After gaining some distance, he heard crass chuckles coming from behind and felt a deep pit in his stomach.

At the edge of the hall, Zequim spotted one of the few troll Wizards, Kergem, standing by himself. He approached the big, green-skinned fellow, who looked down upon him with a wide smile and wiggling ears. Despite his hunched back, he still stood well over three heads taller and propped himself up with an equally giant staff. His dark blue robe strained against a bulging gut and shoulders that looked fit to carry a building.

"Ah! 'Ello thar, Zequim! Enjoyin' the party?"

"About as much as you are, I suspect," he replied with a playful snort.

"Even though ascendin' to a Wizard is supposed ta mean I'm a different race, they still look at me like I'm a troll."

"In time, more trolls will become Wizards, and it won't be as rare. That is the only reason they treat you differently, my friend," Zequim said with a knowing smile. "When I was starting out as a Wizard, the Council was not used to seeing folk from my homeland, Dhulbed, among them. But eventually, more of my countrymen joined our ranks, and it became a normal occurrence."

"I dun' think it's the same fer you. The Dhulbans were a reclusive lot around the time you became a Wizard, were they not?" Kergem asked.

Zequim raised both eyebrows and smiled. "You know your history."

"Once the Dhulbans started to interact with the outside world more often, they were welcomed with open arms by the humans. Sure, they may have looked a wee bit different, but it merely came down to a slightly darker shade of skin from the men of the desert. Your countrymen were still human, at the end o' the day, and it cannot be denied that most Wizards were once of that species. But *green folk*, like me'self? I'm not sure we'll ever be accepted."

"Funny how that works, isn't it? When it comes to the trouble that trolls caused so many years ago, all sorts of folk have a great memory. But when it involves something that could truly impact or harm the world right now? No one seems to care…"

"What do you mean?" Kergem asked while tilting his head.

"I'm sure you've heard about the Mt. Couture incident by now?"

"Ah… a bad situation to be sure."

"Why is it, then, that no one seems to care? Where is the panic? Where is the concern? What if another monolith is broken?" Zequim asked.

"A valid concern…" the troll Wizard replied, to which Zequim let out a sigh of relief. At least someone in the Council was willing to listen to reason. "However, there are greater worries to have in this world."

"What could be more important than *the world itself*?"

EPILOGUE

"Well, I've had some thoughts fer some time, now… the trolls are disliked, so why don' we force the people to like 'em? Show that they aren't so bad?"

Zequim rubbed his eyes in frustration. "We *cannot* control how people think, Kergem."

"Quite to the contrary! You know that we can…"

"I meant in a moral sense," Zequim said, his eyes narrowing. He'd gotten his hopes up too high.

"Fer what it's worth, I agree with yer concern about the seven seals. If you'd be willin' to side with me in the effort of troll acceptance, I could throw my support behind yer cause."

For the third time in under an hour, Zequim found himself wanting to groan, but he suppressed it. He knew that chatting about issues wouldn't get him anywhere with his peers. Everyone had already formed their own opinions, and no matter what he said, things wouldn't change. He spoke with Kergem more casually until the Wizards were called to their tables.

Fried catfish stuffed with peppers and lined with dumplings were served along with Turnersia's finest wine. Wizards didn't need to eat as often as humans or other creatures, but they regularly chose to for pleasure.

Axar sat next to Zequim and placed a cloth on his lap. He began cutting up his catfish and raised his fork to take a bite, but abruptly stopped and looked to his leader. Zequim already knew what question was coming.

"Is everything alright, sir?"

Zequim flashed a ferocity he'd not shown for a long time. He could see the fear in his assistant's eyes, and in his frustration, almost reveled in it. He wished someone, especially those closest to him in the Council, would *just listen*. Quickly, however, the angry thoughts dissipated, and the Council leader returned to his calm and welcoming demeanor.

"It doesn't seem to matter what rational discussion is had; everyone around here has made up their mind and come to their own conclusions. There is either a general apathy, where the higher-ranked Wizards are content to sit back and watch; or worse: They want something in return for their agreement. Their thoughts and feelings can be bought! How? How did this happen?"

Axar leaned in to whisper, "Your temperament has changed of late, sir. Ever since Al-"

"Enough about Aldous. This has little to do with him anymore," Zequim interrupted.

"Is that so? Ever since we tracked him down in Port City and he peppered us with his unhinged rant, you've acted differently. I can tell that he got under your skin," the assistant said.

"Do you think that was his intention?"

"Yes. As I said: He'll do anything to retake his position," Axar replied with poise. "Why don't you sit back and enjoy yourself, for now? A disaster occurred, but it was only *one occurrence*. That doesn't mean that all of our worst fears will come to pass."

He couldn't help but chuckle. "Mayhap the world truly is ending when *you're* the one acting rational between us."

His assistant smiled back before returning to his food. Zequim decided to work on his plate as well. After some time to feast, drink, and converse among Wizards at the table, Tobias, a mage clad in purple and draped in tassels woven from a unicorn's mane, took to the stage and cleared his throat. The hall fell silent, and their collective gazes beamed up at him.

"Thank you all for joining us today in celebrating the anniversary of Paneus' election to one of the 12 seats," he said to a smattering of claps from the audience. We'll let you get back to food and drink in short order, but first, a few words from our esteemed leader, Zequim."

Applause erupted this time, and beneath the veil of thunderous claps, he leaned in next to Axar and said, "This is news to me."

"You have a way with words, sir. I'm sure you'll be alright," Axar whispered back with a cheeky smile.

Zequim stood from his chair and made his way toward the stage. He was cut off, however, by a Wizard who adorned a green, round cap. The Council leader did not recognize him, so some apprehension entered his mind when he got close; as if about to hug him. However, he quickly realized that the Wizard was instead attempting to be discreet: He moved to within an inch or two of his ear and lowered his voice to chilling levels.

"The Famine seal has been broken."

The words rang in his ears like a million bells chiming at once, and a tingle ran down his spine, eliciting wide eyes and a shiver.

"You're serious?" Zequim whispered in return.

"This report comes directly from the Psychic Zamarim," he replied.

A lump came to Zequim's throat and it became difficult to breathe. Axar and the others had been wrong. This was confirmation that his

EPILOGUE

worst fears were coming to pass, and when looking for solutions, his mind was curiously blank.

"Is everything alright?" Tobias' voice boomed over the fading claps, bringing him back to a dreadful reality.

Zequim stepped away from the green-capped Wizard while patting him on the back. He walked up on stage and shook Tobias' hand before turning to face the hall of Wizards, who looked up at him with smiles and cheer.

"I hope you are all enjoying yourselves, today. It is always wonderful to see and converse with my fellow Wizards…" Zequim trailed off, searching for the correct words. "Today was to be a time of celebration. Our very own Paneus has held his chair on the Council for an admirable duration. Congratulations!"

The crowd applauded its loudest yet, filling the hall with enough claps and cheers to be fit for a king.

"Of course, I'd like to have celebrated, but I have some difficult news…" he said. The crowd's mood quickly turned sour and some confused grumbling broke out from a few of the tables. "The second of the seven seals has been broken. This time, it was the Famine monolith."

Silence overcame the hall. It had become so quiet that Zequim could hear his own stuttered breaths, reflecting his nervousness. For he knew that two broken seals were not a coincidence, and what he said next would be crucial in determining the Council's response. After an uncomfortably long period of quiet, grumbling picked up from the tables, and then talking. Finally, heated arguments broke out all around the hall.

Zequim cleared his throat to get the audience's attention once more. "Ladies and gentlemen, it has become clear to me that our recent outbreak of broken monoliths is not the result of misfortune, but *coordinated attacks*. Therefore, I am calling for a re-vote on the topic of the seven seals and how we should respond to such attacks."

The crowd broke out into groans, and then more arguments unfolded at the tables. The Council leader grimaced at the chaos.

A second omen of the Dark Savior's return had been presented before the Wizard's Council in less than a couple of years. With that, a difficult choice lay on the horizon: They could continue the course and make adjustments to measures regarding the Famine monolith after an investigation, or they could reverse their policy of non-intervention regarding humans and begin a proactive campaign in preventing another broken seal. The latter thinking, however, was not without its dangers. It had, in fact, led to the most recent Wizard war. Even Zequim, sure as he was that a proactive approach was needed for the more immediate threat, worried that there was no correct answer, and that they were on an uncorrectable course for disaster.

THE END

If you enjoyed *Seven Seals*, join the newsletter and receive free side stories set in the Dark Savior Series world! You'll get all side stories released up to this point, including *Slaying the Beast, Ground Into Dust*, and *The Seer's Game*. As more are released, you will receive those for free as well!

https://www.jimclougherty.com/subscribe-fantasy

What bonds can shatter steel? Find out in A Gathering of Strangers!

For more information and updates on the Dark Savior Series, visit https://www.jimclougherty.com/

Amazon Author Page: https://www.amazon.com/Jim-Clougherty/e/B07TXCK9XZ/

Your opinion matters to me. Let me know if you enjoyed this story:

Amazon Review Page: https://www.amazon.com/review/create-review?asin=B0CPT6B19G

Goodreads Page: https://www.goodreads.com/review/new/203539660-seven-seals

ACKNOWLEDGMENTS

I would like to thank Jean Clougherty, who gave me so much helpful feedback throughout the writing process and pushed me to improve in many ways. I'd also like to thank Kevin McDermott for his feedback on earlier portions of the story.

Finally, a thank you to all of the friends and family who supported me along the way. It has been a long, long journey, especially to this second edition. Your interest and enthusiasm for my stories truly helped me at the most difficult times.

Milton Keynes UK
Ingram Content Group UK Ltd.
UKHW011015290124
436893UK00004B/23

9 798989 399314